The Great Outdoors

ALSO BY KAYLA OLSON

THE LODGE

THE REUNION

THIS SPLINTERED SILENCE

THE SANDCASTLE EMPIRE

The Great Outdoors

A NOVEL

KAYLA OLSON

ATRIA PAPERBACK
NEW YORK AMSTERDAM/ANTWERP LONDON
TORONTO SYDNEY/MELBOURNE NEW DELHI

An Imprint of Simon & Schuster, LLC
1230 Avenue of the Americas
New York, NY 10020

This Atria Paperback edition June 2026

Interior design by William Ruoto

Manufactured in the United States of America

1 3 5 7 9 10 8 6 4 2

Library of Congress Control Number: 2025947219

ISBN 978-1-6680-9070-1 (pbk)
ISBN 978-1-6680-9071-8 (ebook)

To all the overpackers out there: I see you, I feel you, I *am* you. Don't let anyone talk you out of packing your entire coffee setup for that trip you're about to take—and, honestly, you should probably throw in some dark chocolate while you're at it.

To anyone who's ever been made to feel like they're too much (or too little, somehow at the same time): I hope you find your people, and that they love you for exactly who you are.

And for anyone who:

- ✦ Relates to the *Troop Beverly Hills* girls, and feels strongly that you were made for The Great Indoors and not, like . . . the wilderness
- ✦ Would 100 percent go on *Survivor* if not for the whole sleeping-outdoors-on-a-tropical-beach-in-thunderstorms-amid-spiders-and-snakes situation—
  and for anyone who agrees that all of the above *might* be worth it just to meet Jeff Probst and hang out in Fiji
- ✦ Knows every word (and all the choreography) to "A Little Bit Alexis" from *Schitt's Creek*
- ✦ Takes daily inspiration from the way Elle Woods went to Harvard just to prove a point to someone who thought she could *never*

This one's for you.

Prologue

Whoever came up with the term *the great outdoors* must never have had the pleasure of staying at a five-star hotel: where mai tais by the pool are only an order away and the spa gives all the refreshing rainforest vibes without anything venomous trying to kill you.

That's about as outdoors as it gets for me.

Which is why I should have known better than to fall for Caden O'Connor.

I should've known by his polite, insincere laugh when I told him the legendary story of the one and only time my mom went camping as a kid: how she and her five siblings helped my grandparents set up the tent, how they gave it their all for two entire hours in the middle of nowhere—but then the bugs set in, and so did the humidity and the lack of electricity, and they collectively decided to go check in to the nearest hotel instead.

I should've known on our first date, when he took me for that picnic by the lake. He'd hardly noticed the ants and the mosquitos, didn't seem to mind the sweat beading on his skin as the temperature climbed. I, on the other hand, hardly noticed anything else.

And I should've known by all the comments he made along the way—little things here and there about how long it took for me to get ready, how I couldn't go anywhere without packing my entire house, how I should learn to "live a little" and "be more spontaneous."

I brushed his comments off because of *course* having a plan was better than being spontaneous—being a generally risk-averse person who takes comfort in routine meant I wouldn't just get to live a *little,* but live a lot. I had no problem with his problems with me. Didn't even truly define them *as* problems.

Maybe if I hadn't brushed them off, I wouldn't have been so blindsided by the breakup.

It was going to be a pivotal night for us—I could just *feel* it. I wore my brand-new dress from Kate Spade, a bubblegum-pink A-line with delicate white daisies embroidered on the collar, and my hair has never looked more like that of Catherine, Princess of Wales, than it did that evening.

Which all turned out to be a complete waste.

It was a pivotal night for us, all right, but not in the way I'd imagined. There was no proposal over chocolate soufflés, no sparkling diamonds *or* champagne—just Caden and his whiskey sour and the way he casually mentioned he'd be leaving for a huge chunk of June due to a backpacking adventure in California that he'd signed up for on a whim.

One I was, apparently, not invited to.

"But what about Italy?" I asked. I had our entire itinerary planned out, hotels and a food tour and even a day on a private yacht. We'd been talking about it for months, though it hadn't yet occurred to me that I was the only one to ever contribute to our shared Google spreadsheet.

"Italy's not really my thing, Sadie, you know that."

I did not, in fact, know that.

"And backpacking is?" I pressed. "What happened to going on adventures *together* this summer? You made these plans—even though we'd already been talking about Italy—and on top of that you didn't even *invite* me?"

"Come on, babe," he said, voice dripping with condescension. "You'd be miserable out there. You'd *die.*"

I scoffed. "I would so not die."

He was probably right about the misery, but I refused to acknowledge it because it was beside the point. The point was, he should have let me make the choice for myself—and he shouldn't have planned the trip without me in the first place, especially since he knew I had my heart set on Italy.

"Sadie, come on," he said, as if we were both in on the same joke. "You *know* backpacking just isn't your thing."

"My . . . thing?"

He took a long sip of his whiskey sour. "Well, yeah. You like to be pampered, you like five-star hotels."

Like the ones on our Italy spreadsheet, my thoughts filled in as he paused, probably thinking the same thing and choosing to ignore it.

"You could never sleep in a tent," he went on. "You melt anytime the air conditioning takes too long to kick in. You can't live without espresso. You're too—"

"Too *what*?" I cut him off, leveling him with my best glare (which, in retrospect, likely had the ferocity and general vibe of a kitten threatening a dinosaur).

"Too extra for a trip like this. Too high-maintenance, you know?"

My only regret in that moment was that I had already drained my wine and there wasn't even a drop left to toss in his face.

"You could have at least given me the chance to *try*," I argued. "You could have at least asked."

Sure, I'm particular about certain things, a creature of both comfort and routine. But I'm also a person who thrives on being underestimated: nothing motivates—or infuriates—me quite so much as someone saying they think I'm not capable.

"I didn't think you'd be interested," he said with an unapologetic shrug.

"Then why plan it at all?" I asked. "And why in *June*, when we already had Italy on the calendar?"

We hadn't put serious money down—just some refundable reservations here and there—and it was beginning to dawn on me that maybe, *maybe*, I'd been too blinded by my own enthusiasm to realize he wasn't quite as into the whole thing.

"Honestly, Sadie"—those two little words made the bottom drop out of my stomach—"I've been thinking for a while that we might just be too . . ."

I held my breath, as if that could stop the inevitable.

"Too incompatible," he finally finished.

I blinked. "For a backpacking trip?" I said, the full weight of his words slow to sink in.

"For *everything*," he said. "You and me . . . it's been fun, babe, but long-term? I just don't see it working out. We're too different. We should stop trying to pretend this works."

"You can't be serious—are you serious right now?"

Had he never heard of *opposites attract*? That was what made us perfect for each other! So perfect I thought he might *propose*, not rip the relationship out from under me altogether. I was the bubbly overplanner, he was chill and go with the flow, and that was why we worked. We had our little differences, sure, but in a "You complete me!" sort of way. We balanced each other out.

That was when I realized Caden hadn't embraced—or even brushed off—our little differences like I had: he'd stockpiled them like matches, all these tiny little splinters between us, and then he used them to light us on fire.

I was so stunned, at the time, that my only thought was: maybe it was possible for me to salvage us before we completely burned down to ashes.

"I could still go backpacking with you, though, right? It's not too late to sign up?"

But then he laughed. *Laughed.*

"I mean, feel free to sign up," he said. "People eat that shit up on the internet! Girls who are out of their element and in over their heads? *Please* do a travel vlog, Sadie—I'd love to see that." He grinned. "You'd make *great* entertainment."

The way he said it did *not* sound like a compliment.

It was at that precise moment I knew: even if I did manage to prove I was more compatible with Caden than he thought, I wasn't sure I even wanted him anymore—

But that didn't mean I was opposed to giving him a front-row seat to my metamorphosis. I could sign up for the trip, fight through the misery, and *thrive.* Sure, it might be more than a little awkward being on a backpacking trip with my ex, but that was part of what appealed to me about the idea! I could watch his regret start to sink in, that he chose to let me go . . . and it would feel so, so sweet for him to admit he totally underestimated me, and was wrong to do so.

I left the restaurant feeling determined but disoriented, dizzy from the emotional whiplash I'd just experienced. And despite my best efforts to forget, the words *too high-maintenance* have been tattooed on my brain ever since that night. I can't unsee them. Can't un*feel* them. I've always been proud of knowing exactly who I am: of knowing exactly what I want, and the meticulous planning it takes to make sure I have, or get, those things.

Caden—chill, laid-back Caden—is the first person I've met who not only didn't praise me for being the most prepared person in his life, but made it sound like a bad thing. Like I was deficient somehow, like I was overly fragile and might fall apart the instant something didn't go my way, the instant circumstances were outside of my own control.

Which I was certain wasn't true at all.

When I told my best friend, Abby, what had happened, she took my side immediately—but hesitated slightly before starting in on the reassurances.

"What?" I'd said at the first lull. "What is it?"

She didn't reply until I pushed.

Abby looked me straight in the eye. "Okay. So. You're my best friend, Sadie, and I love you just the way you are. But—as your best friend, I can't lie to you. Caden isn't *wrong*."

I was quiet for a long moment.

"To be clear, I don't think he was right for breaking up with you over it, or for not inviting you on the trip, or for planning it when you were supposed to go to Italy," Abby went on. "But—c'mon, Sade. I think even you would admit you're one of the least flexible people on the planet. You like things to go your way."

"Who *doesn't* like things to go their way?" I'd argued, but it was futile.

My ex-boyfriend and my best friend both believed I had a significant flaw in the way I approached life—like I could only be happy and fun to be around under certain circumstances.

Certain *carefully curated* circumstances.

Well, screw that—I could thrive under *any* circumstances.

And I was absolutely committed to proving it.

To: sadiewhitlock@firefly.com; zoebear113@lotusyoga.com; joshers@hillsidecapital.com; silas@cephalopodcoffee.com; hunter@cephalopodcoffee.com; trey@cephalopodcoffee.com; brittany0721383@pepperdine.com; emma0728394@pepperdine.com; parker0721573@pepperdine.com

From: august.thorn@summitwildernessexpeditions.com

CC: jess.tanner@summitwildernessexpeditions.com; danica.jackson@summitwildernessexpeditions.com

Subject: Mackenzie Lake Loop Expedition @ Valerie Forest National Park

Dear Trekkers,

We are thrilled to welcome you to the Mackenzie Lake Loop Expedition in just a few weeks! This trail is one of the best-kept secrets of the Sierras, with no shortage of scenery and adventure. We look forward to exploring it with you very soon! Attached is our twelve-night itinerary along with our suggested packing list. We've taken care of all necessary permits (thank you for being on top of your paperwork!) and reservations. Travel safe, and we'll see you soon!

Best,
August Thorn
Senior Wilderness Guide, Summit Wilderness Expeditions

To: caden@beemail.com

From: sadiewhitlock@firefly.com

Subject: FWD: Mackenzie Lake Loop Expedition @ Valerie Forest National Park

Hey Caden—

I know we haven't talked since March, but I just got this group email from the trek people, and they didn't have your email in the mix for whatever reason. Forwarded it so you can have the packing list/itinerary/etc.!

Sadie

To: sadiewhitlock@firefly.com
From: caden@beemail.com
Subject: RE: FWD: Mackenzie Lake Loop Expedition @ Valerie Forest National Park

they didn't have my email in the mix bc I never signed up (missed the deadline)

have fun and don't die

—c

1

SADIE

"You *really* don't have to do this, you know," Abby says as I try for the thirteenth time to zip my pack shut.

No matter how many times I've shifted things around, no matter who sits on it, it refuses to zip.

"Oh, but I do," I manage, slightly winded from the effort of all this packing.

We've been over this countless times, me insisting I'll be able to handle the wilderness and Abby not even bothering to pretend she thinks it's a good idea.

"There will be bugs, Sadie," she says again now. It's practically scripted at this point. "Maybe even snakes. You don't like the outdoors—you don't like adventure! You don't have to do this."

"I *want* to do this," I say.

We've gone back and forth for weeks, ever since I found out Caden flaked on the trip. The phrase "have fun and don't die" still makes me want to scream.

"You know you don't have to prove anything to *me*, right?" she says. "When you're out there and hating it, just remember I was fully in favor of us spending every day together lounging by the pool. I don't want you to resent me."

"I could never resent you," I say, and it's true. Not even her completely wrong opinion about how I'm too much of a control freak to thrive in the wilderness could ever come between us.

Abby sighs. "I'm just afraid you're still doing it to prove something to Caden."

This—this stops me.

In all the times we've had this conversation, she's never said anything like this. It's always been the bugs, the snakes, the heat, the sweat, the climbing, the camping, and on and on. This must be the *real* reason she thinks I shouldn't go.

"I'm not doing it to prove something to Caden," I say reflexively.

But we both know that's a lie, and we both know I'm not a liar. Also, my vlogging equipment betrays me.

Abby gives me a pointed look.

"Okay, so maybe I am, just a little," I admit. "But I'm also doing it because it sounds *fun*. I read that you can see a bajillion stars at night in the Sierras—and there are waterfalls! *Waterfalls*, Abby!"

She usually has a quick reply for everything, but she's quiet now, studying me with a look that can only be described as supportive concern.

"Twelve nights is a long time to go without a mattress," Abby eventually says with big, sad eyes. She appreciates the great indoors as much as I do.

I pull everything back out of my pack for an honest assessment.

"I'm going to have to lose some of this stuff."

Once it's all laid out on my bed, I'm not even sure where to begin.

"A curling iron, Sadie, really?" Abby says. "And a ceramic coffee mug? *And* a coffee scale and your entire pour-over setup?"

She has yet to comment on the pink fuzzy slippers and silk pajama sets, but I suspect that's only because she hasn't noticed them.

"You do know there's not going to be any electricity?" she asks, holding up my spare phone charger, my AirPods, and my Kindle. "And, um—these sandals?"

I take my strappy espadrilles from her and throw them into the pile of clothes I eliminated from the packing list before she came over.

"I thought they'd be cute for my videos," I say defensively. "And we won't be hiking the *whole* time, right?"

Abby bites back a laugh. "They really are cute. But considering the circumstances . . ."

She glances at my empty carcass of a backpack, its entrails spilled all over the bed.

"Fine. I admit you have a point."

We eliminate a few more items, pink fuzzy slippers included, but I get to keep my silk pajama sets since they're made of breathable cooling material that will be practical *and* cute in the warm weather. I also keep the lightweight hand-crank solar charger I ordered from REI so I can use my phone to film the vlog, but ditch my regular one that plugs into an outlet. Abby helps me portion out all my coffee grounds so I can leave the scale behind, too, then finds the perfect spot for my LifeStraw bottle so I can filter water as needed. Half an hour later, the zipper slides all the way up without me even breaking a sweat.

"I'm going to miss you so much," Abby says with a pretty pout. "I hope you're not too miserable."

I slip a tube of lip gloss back into the pack, inspired by Abby's full lower lip. When she's not looking, I slip a pair of cashmere socks back in, too.

"I hope *you're* not too miserable when I come back and shout 'I told you so!' after I end up loving this life-changing experience."

She laughs. "I *hope* you're shouting 'I told you so!' at the end of all this. Truly."

Despite my bravado, I admit I'm a touch anxious about the whole situation—I'm obviously not going to tell Abby that, though, after how persistent she's been at trying to talk me out of it. Nothing in me *wants* to be away from electricity or air conditioning or my cloudlike mattress and soft, soft sheets. Nothing in me wants to get up close and personal with any snakes or spiders or . . . whatever else might be lurking in the wilderness.

But the point is, I got unceremoniously dumped because Caden thought I wouldn't survive a single day out there, even with a tour guide, and I'm nothing if not stubborn. He may not be on the trip anymore, but that's what the vlog is for—and I *know* he'll be watching. He said it himself: I'll make *great* entertainment!

I can do anything for twelve nights. I've read four travel guides cover to cover, memorized a huge list of poisonous plants and insects and snakes, and even tried to go without coffee for a few days. That was a disaster, hence the fact that I've wedged my entire coffee setup into my backpack, but what I'm trying to say is: I'm prepared.

"One last pool day before I go?" I ask, because of course I'm done packing with seven hours to spare before I need to head to the airport. I have everything planned down to the minute, from my first-class flight, to the hotel where I'll be staying tonight, to the car service that will drive me out to Valerie Forest National Park tomorrow morning.

Abby, when I confessed the extent of my indulgent pre-wilderness plans, said it sounded like I was on death row, choosing a luxurious last meal before my untimely demise.

She drives us into downtown Austin, to the JW Marriott, where we've set up camp every day so far this summer. She teaches middle school science, so aside from a couple of weeks of science camp duty, she has the entire summer off to relax. Abby's coworker Jonathan—who teaches algebra in the next classroom over—picked up a summer job at the hotel's poolside bar; he told Abby we were welcome to come hang out anytime, and we've embraced that invitation to the fullest. (Relatedly: If Abby and Jonathan aren't together by the end of the summer, I'm shoving them both in the pool to manufacture their romance myself—their flirting isn't exactly subtle.)

While Abby gets to just kick back and relax all summer, I have technically been on the clock during most of our pool days. I do training presentations for an educational software company, which requires a bit of travel, but things slow down considerably in summertime. No one seems to mind my poolside office when I'm taking meetings from home—especially not my boss, who thinks I work too hard as it is. He's been urging me to use my vacation days and was delighted when I broke the news about my wilderness adventure.

I didn't tell him I'd originally planned to use them for Italy—

I'm trying not to think about that.

"No laptop today?" Jonathan comments, dimples popping, when we go up to order our drinks—rosé for me and a spicy margarita for Abby.

"She's going on that wilderness thing I told you about, remember?"

Abby's cleavage is on full display in her low-cut bikini. Hanging out at a hotel pool all the time has other perks to it—there's almost no chance any of her local students will be here, so she's taken the opportunity to flaunt herself in clothes she wouldn't normally risk wearing.

"Oh, right," Jonathan says. "In the Sierras? California?"

I get the distinct impression he remembers every single thing Abby's ever told him.

"She's going to camp and hike and learn how to rappel, and maybe even *kayak*!"

Jonathan raises his eyebrows, probably trying to reconcile the idea of me in a kayak when I've hardly even dipped a toenail into the hotel pool this summer. I prefer to sit *near* the water, not actually get in it.

"By, um—choice?" Jonathan asks, and Abby smacks his muscular arm playfully with a stack of paper napkins.

"I've tried my best to convince her to stay here with me," she tells him. "But she's committed to living on the edge."

"Well, I can't wait to hear about it," he says. "Drinks on the house today!"

"Aren't drinks always on the house?" I say, momentarily confused, but then Abby elbows me in the ribs—I forgot Jonathan isn't technically supposed to let us have his daily employee beverages. "I mean, *thank you* for *these* on-the-house drinks, unlike every other day, when we most definitely pay for them!"

Abby and I settle into our favorite loungers (the ones that give us a good view of the pool *and* the pool bartender), sipping our beverages side by side. I savor this crisp rosé like it really is my last meal on death row.

"Feeling ready?" Abby says, setting her spicy margarita down on the table between us.

I take in the sparkling aquamarine pool; the Austin skyline; the abundant greenery, both real and faux; the satisfying rows of pool loungers, not a single one even an inch out of line. I can't believe I'll be trading all of this for the rugged wilderness of the Sierras.

"As ready as I can be," I say, sighing. "I'm going to miss you, too."

I'm also going to miss electricity. And air conditioning. And ice-cold beverages.

And, and, and.

"I know I've pushed back on the idea a lot," Abby says, "but it's only because I know it's going to be hard on you. It would be hard on *me*, too—I would die. Like, literally die, call the helicopter and airlift what's left of me out on a stretcher."

"Thanks for that image," I say, suddenly thinking of all the ways I could overheat or plunge to my death or be the unwitting victim of some poisonous insect. *Have fun and don't die.*

"What I was getting at," she goes on, "is that I think it's really brave of you to go for it, and I hope it's everything you want it to be. Even if it does sound horrible."

I laugh. "Thank you. That means a lot."

And it does. I honestly didn't know how badly I needed to hear it—how badly I needed to hear it from Abby specifically.

"I got you a present," she says, pulling a pocket-sized book from her bag. "It's not much—"

"It's *perfect*," I say, running my hand over the pale green cover, which reads: *A Hiker Girl's Guide to Bugs & Berries*. "I love it—thank you."

"I think it should fit in your bag," she says, smirking as she takes a sip of her margarita. "Barely."

My phone vibrates on the table between us, an area code from FRESNO, CA flashing.

I pick up.

"Hello?" I say tentatively, praying it isn't just some supersmart telemarketer.

"Sadie Whitlock? This is August Thorn from Summit Wilderness Expeditions," a deep voice says on the other end of the call, confident but laid-back in a way that immediately puts me at ease.

"I'll be one of your wilderness guides," he goes on. "Just wanted to let you know of an itinerary change for tomorrow—we're going to need to shift our start time later by two hours. Does that still work for you?"

A two-hour delay? I'll either have to rearrange plans with my driver or hang out at the drop-off point, I guess. And what will I eat? Are there bathrooms on-site? Are they *clean* bathrooms or, like, porta-potties? Is there a shady spot to sit while I wait? And why are we delaying the start time—is it something I should be worried about?

"Sure," I say as breezily as possible, trying to match his calm vibe. "That's totally fine! But"—I can't help myself, I have to ask—"everything's okay, though, right?"

"It will be," he says. "My coleader's flying in from Hawaii and her flight got delayed."

"Great!" I say, a little too enthusiastically. "I mean, great that it isn't worse. For the trek, I mean. I'm sure it's not great for her."

I was expecting something more like *We have a surprise infestation of rattlesnakes that will take exactly two hours to clear up!*, so a coleader stuck in Hawaii truly sounds like the better alternative.

"Yeah, it could be worse," he agrees. "I'll let you know if anything else changes—and I'm here if you have any other questions in the meantime, Sadie. Looking forward to tomorrow."

When I hang up, Abby raises her eyebrows at me suggestively.

"Well, *he* sounds hot," she says.

She's not wrong.

I sip my rosé, downplaying my interest. "You think?"

"Ummmm, did you not hear him? I wasn't even the one on the phone and his voice made me melt a little—so deep! So confident. I'd be sneaking into his tent for *sure.*" She licks a few crystals of salt from the rim of her margarita. "If I were you, anyway."

It's been three months since Caden broke up with me, long enough for the shock to wear off. I haven't dated since—haven't felt compelled to start anything with anyone else, knowing I'll be across the country for half of June. It hadn't even crossed my mind that I might meet someone *on* the expedition.

"There are probably rules about that," I reply.

She smirks. "Wouldn't that just make it more exciting?"

"Maybe for someone who enjoys breaking rules . . ."

Abby throws her head back, laughing. "Sadie. Just for two weeks, I think you should let go a little and not worry about doing everything perfectly. As long as it doesn't get anyone fired—or start a *literal* fire—I'm officially challenging you to not overthink things."

The look on my face must look particularly insulted because she laughs again.

"How about this," she says. "When you get back, we'll have the most luxurious girls' weekend ever here at the hotel—on me."

"With massages?"

"We'll get *two-hour* massages," she promises.

"And champagne? And chocolate?"

She sets her margarita down on the table. "Make it through the next two weeks, Sadie, and I'll buy you all the champagne and chocolate you can handle."

2

SADIE

For the first time in the history of mankind, I experience an eerily perfect travel day: we hit all green lights en route to the airport; not only do I fly first class, but there's an empty seat next to me; my hotel reservation gets upgraded to a luxury corner suite with a fantastic view—and later, when I order room service, they bring me complimentary crème brûlée.

The bed is a heavenly cloud: I sleep like the dead, relishing its comfort for as long as I can before my alarm goes off. Fortunately, I have a good cushion before my driver arrives, and it will take a lot less time to get ready since I only have a few outfits and limited beauty products to choose from.

Abby tried to talk me out of bringing my makeup—and as far as she knows, she succeeded—but I was able to sneak some foundation, eyeshadow, and mascara in with the lip gloss at the last second thanks to a Sephora vending machine in my terminal. I also might have bought a poncho (practical!), some hand sanitizer (diseases don't go away just because you're in the woods), a paperback rom-com (both thrillers that sounded good were set in the wilderness, so they were a hard pass), some fancy trail mix (never hurts to have extra snacks, especially when you're picky), and two old-school disposable Kodak cameras (see: the aforementioned waterfalls).

When I finish getting ready, I look downright rugged in comparison to how I look after my usual routine—but at least my minimal makeup makes me feel a little more prepared to take on this day. I give my naturally wavy hair one last blowout, leaving it long and loose underneath a simple black ball cap.

My driver pulls up precisely on time. We have a long drive ahead until we get to our meeting point, a museum at the edge of Valerie Forest National Park. I lose myself in the rom-com I picked up at the airport; the trip is so quiet and peaceful that I don't realize how far we've gone until I've finished the whole book and we're turning onto a rugged dirt road.

We wind down the road, making our way deeper into the forest, until a scene straight out of a painting appears amid the trees. A small building—more than a cabin, but practically miniature compared to the gigantic trees stretching out all around it—sits in a clearing, dappled sunlight turning green to gold.

My driver idles as I unload my pack from the trunk; his shiny black Mercedes feels entirely out of place here, its smooth lines at odds with the unpolished, natural beauty of everything around us. I tip him well, he heads back out the way we came, and now *I* am the only thing at odds with this place.

It's immediately clear that I'm overdressed, even though I really did try to succeed at the whole practical-but-cute wilderness aesthetic. In retrospect, perhaps my bright white Adidas Ultraboosts were not the best choice—the dirt path has already found its way into the fabric. Also, while my cropped lavender tank and black lululemon tennis skirt feel like they were made for keeping cool during a workout, the rough grass farther out in the trees tells me I should probably change into a pair of pants.

Not to mention I'm already struggling with my pack, and I haven't even made it to the museum's front door—it's possible I should have given less consideration to the question of how much would *fit* and more to how much I could comfortably *carry*.

I'm readjusting it for the third time when I notice him: a guy who looks roughly my age—thirty at the *most*—standing just outside the museum's entrance, arms crossed as he leans casually against the door, lips pressed tightly together in what's clearly an attempt to suppress his laughter.

I'd be furious if he weren't so alarmingly attractive.

Still, I feel a spike of indignation.

"You could offer to help instead of watching me die this slow death," I say.

"I didn't say a word." He grins, holding his hands up in innocence. "But since you asked for my help—ditch a third of what you've packed before we head out. You'll thank me later."

I recognize his deep voice immediately: this has to be August Thorn, the same guy who called yesterday while I was with Abby.

I'm not sure what I expected in a wilderness guide, but it wasn't *this*. Maybe I expected someone mid-forties and weathered? Not a guy with lean forearms who looks perfectly adept at—well, everything—and a mop of dark, disheveled curls; not a guy with teeth so white and straight that he looks like he could be an actor posing as a wilderness guide and not someone *actually* in charge of an expedition like this. He's wearing a black button-down that makes me think of Jeff Probst, and his blue eyes—

Are one hundred percent aware that I'm checking him out right now.

I adjust my pack again, hoping to distract from the wave of heat that fills my cheeks.

"Thanks for the advice," I say as he opens the door for me. "You must be August?"

He follows me inside. It's dark and cool compared to the sunny outdoors, only natural light streaming in through the windows.

"Everyone calls me Thorn, but yeah."

Thorn. It's so dramatic I almost laugh.

"Because you're prickly by nature?"

This makes *him* laugh. "No one has ever called me prickly before."

"With a name like Thorn? Come on."

The weight of my pack is suddenly nonexistent on my shoulders; he's finally decided to help me out a little.

"What do you *have* in here?" he asks incredulously, setting it on the floor with a thud. "Did you not get the packing prep FAQ page I sent over?"

I take it back: it's not cool in here at all. The heat clings to me, suffocating me, especially under the blanket of hair hanging loose against my neck.

"Yes, I got it," I reply, not quite able to dull the defensive edge to my voice. "I brought all that stuff."

"But . . . ?"

"I might have also brought a few more things."

He grins, shaking his head, and yeah—I think I might melt.

"I'm a creature of comfort, what can I say? I like to be prepared."

"I'm sorry to tell you this, but that pack? Is *not* going to be comfortable."

The knots that are already forming in my back say he might have a point.

"We leave in just under two hours," he goes on. "Which means you have just under two hours to choose your comforts—anything you decide not to bring, you're free to store in my office. I'll lock it up while we're gone." His expression softens. "We'll be covering a lot of ground each day. Best to bring only the essentials so you don't, like . . ."

"Crumple up in a pile of exhaustion and pain, grinding our progress to a halt?" I supply.

Thorn grins. "Something like that, yeah."

He picks my pack up again, then leads me down the hall and into a glorified mop closet. There's a laptop open on a tray table in the corner.

"*This* is your office?"

He shrugs. "Don't need much space when I spend most of my time outside. Let me know if you want any help?"

I don't want Thorn knowing the extent of every single not-strictly-practical thing I've brought, so I opt to sort things out on my own. There are a few employee lockers in here, so I pick an empty one and start narrowing down the contents of my bag yet again. Abby would be proud: I manage to eliminate a few of the things she questioned yesterday—a neck pillow, my backup jar of peanut butter, and my full-sized bottle of Viktor & Rolf Flowerbomb since I somehow also managed to bring a travel-sized one—along with the book I just finished and one of the disposable cameras.

I toss one pair of silk pajamas in, too—I'm trying to decide if I really need all three sets that I packed—when I hear a buzzing sound coming from over near Thorn's laptop. The sound intensifies, then culminates in a loud crash before continuing to buzz.

On the floor, facedown, is a smartphone. Fortunately, it's protected by a heavy-duty yellow case that looks like it could withstand demolition of any sort, maybe even a war zone.

I pick it up and poke my head out of the mop closet.

"Thorn?" I call out when I don't see him.

I make my way back to the main room, where I hear a muffled sound coming from the gigantic faux sequoia display built into the back wall; there's an opening where people can actually go inside to explore. I peek into the shadows—and see a very shirtless Thorn. There's just enough light to highlight every cut and curve of his perfect stomach.

"Um—hi," I say eloquently, and he whips around.

I wish the light were better in here so I could say for sure that he's blushing; I'm almost positive that he is.

He holds up two shirts, one in each hand.

"Had to change," he says, as if that explains why he's shirtless inside a fake tree.

"You make a habit out of changing . . . in here?"

He laughs. "Usually I change in the mop closet, but it was just a little bit occupied."

"So your next thought was this," I tease. "Not the restroom?"

"Didn't expect anyone to come in during the thirty seconds I was half naked, but apparently I can check that off my bingo card for this summer."

The words *half naked* hang between us, especially since he still hasn't put his shirt on. He seems to realize this at the exact moment I do, and tugs on another Jeff Probst shirt that looks identical to the last—just navy blue instead of black.

"You missed a call," I say, holding out his phone.

He takes it, his jaw tensing as he glances at the screen. Intense, brooding Thorn is somehow even more attractive than laid-back Thorn.

"Everything okay?" I ask.

"It's my boss," he says. "I should probably call her back."

"I'm done in the mop closet if you want more privacy than this fake tree," I reply.

He smirks, despite his tension.

Thorn leaves me alone in the dark enclave, and I swear it already feels a few degrees cooler now that he's gone.

This is going to be fun.

3

THORN

It's always something.

Just once before an expedition, I'd love for it to go as planned. If it's not bad weather, it's a wildfire. If it's not a wildfire, it's one of our trekkers forgetting something important—medication, sunscreen, hiking boots, underwear. The list goes on.

Today's interruption to the schedule is a new one, even for me.

"I'm sorry, she *what*?" I ask Danica, my boss, who's usually pretty good about letting me take care of any last-minute issues on my own.

Usually, the last-minute issues don't involve me being left without a coleader an hour before we're supposed to head out.

"Jess is still stuck in Hawaii," Danica repeats. "She had a delayed reaction to a jellyfish sting and missed her rescheduled flight."

I curse under my breath. "I *told* her it wasn't a good idea to commit to a hike the day after vacation."

At the time, all I was thinking of was the jet lag—*not* the possibility that she might still be far across the Pacific when we're scheduled to head out.

"You know Jess," Danica says.

I do know Jess. Stubborn and optimistic, gives her whole heart to whatever she tries, writes absolutely nothing down and usually gets away with it.

"So what now?" I ask. "Delay again until she gets a flight home?"

"Unfortunately, her entire right foot is swollen up past her ankle. I don't think she'll be ready to walk on it anytime soon, let alone do the hike."

"I'm on my own, then?"

"Well . . . not exactly."

Danica pauses for long enough that I actually start to worry. I'm not the worrying type—Jess and I are the same in that way, though I can't say I relate to her chaotic approach to . . . well, everything.

"What?" I ask. "What is it?"

"It's not that we don't trust you on your own, Thorn—if there's anyone who could handle a group alone, it's definitely you. You know the rules are there for a reason, though, right?"

Every hike must have a *pair* of certified coleaders, just in case, so that inexperienced trekkers won't get stranded in the wilderness on their own.

It's a good policy. Less pressure on me, and always good to have someone else around who knows what they're doing.

That said: I'm wary of how Danica's tiptoeing around whatever it is she's reluctant to tell me.

"Who's taking Jess's place?" I ask since she's still quiet on the other end.

"I'm sorry, Thorn—I tried everyone else first."

I can practically hear her biting her tongue.

"Who?" I repeat.

Danica sighs. "Matteo."

The silence between us is thick, even over the phone.

"I'm sorry," she goes on. "I know it's not the ideal dynamic."

"*That's* putting it lightly."

It comes out more like a growl than I mean it to. The last person I'd choose to spend an afternoon with—let alone *twelve nights in the wilderness*, where an entire group is relying on us to have good teamwork—is Matteo Sabatelli. After how he called me two years ago from Peru to tell me he'd felt the need for a change and had spontaneously moved there *with my girlfriend*, Blair, who had conveniently neglected to mention any plans about trading our eight-month-long relationship for a new one with Matteo in South America . . .

Yeah. It's safe to say Matteo Sabatelli is the last person on the planet I want as my coleader. It's hard to believe we were ever friends, let alone best friends. We haven't spoken since that phone call.

"Everyone else is either committed to other treks, out of state on vacation, or sick," Danica explains. "It was either bring in Matteo or cancel the whole thing."

She doesn't have to elaborate on why canceling wasn't an option—people have flown in for this. It's almost *two weeks* of their summer, not to mention one of the most expensive itineraries we offer. We can't afford to give refunds to an entire group. We can't afford to give refunds to anyone at all.

"And *he's* okay with it?" I ask. "Coleading with me?"

It's been long enough now that I'm over Blair. But Matteo and I—we were like brothers. His betrayal cut deep.

I didn't even know he'd moved back to California.

"Matteo will keep it professional," Danica replies. "I trust you'll do the same."

"Yeah, no, of course," I say. "The trek comes first. I can do it."

I don't *want* to do it. Not with him.

But I can. I will.

"You're sure he's reliable, though?" I ask. "You trust him?"

I'm not the only person Matteo ditched when he took off for South America—he left Danica and the tour company in a bind, too. I've had to pick up the slack ever since; it was a huge blow to the business to lose Matteo and Blair at the same time, and it's been difficult to find competent and committed replacements who stick around longer than a few months.

"I spoke with Matteo's boss from the tour group down in the Andes," Danica replies. "He had nothing but good things to say and told me he was sorry to see him go."

I sigh. It says a lot that Danica has decided to give him a second chance. At the end of the day, being a responsible and reliable leader is all that really matters—and Matteo always fit that description before he took off like he did. I'll just have to put my personal feelings aside and hope for the best.

"Not my first choice," I finally say. "But I'll make it work."

"Thanks for understanding, Thorn. I'll mark off some extra paid vacation days for you after this one, okay? I know this situation isn't ideal."

I close my eyes, trying to ward off the headache that's taken up residence in my skull. Paid vacation days sound great on paper, but in reality? There's never really a great time for me to actually step away. The last time I took off longer than a weekend was six months ago, when I spent the holidays with my dad out in San Francisco.

"Sounds good," I tell her.

Good isn't exactly the right word, but whatever.

"You still have Matteo's number?" Danica asks.

"I deleted it a long time ago. Send it my way?"

"Done. Okay."

"Okay."

The dead air hangs between us.

Another beat passes, and then Danica says, "You're the best, Thorn. And I'm so sorry for what he and Blair did to you—you didn't deserve that."

That means a lot coming from Danica; she's been nothing but professional in the wake of what happened, even though she would have been justified to complain.

As soon as we're off the call, I let out the string of curse words I've been holding back.

"Um—"

The voice in the doorway is a jumpscare like I haven't had in years, and the next thing I know, my phone is facedown inside an old mop bucket.

"*So* sorry," she says, tucking a strand of long dark hair behind her ear. "I changed my mind about one of the things I took out of my pack earlier—I swear I wasn't eavesdropping."

It's the girl from before, the one who caught me changing inside the museum's gigantic tree display. Everything about her is stunning: her light green eyes, the color almost unearthly; her tan, toned legs, which stretch on for days; her smile, with that one cute dimple.

It's too bad she's about to have the most traumatic two weeks of her life. Which, in turn, means *my* next two weeks are about to be miserable, too.

I've seen it so often I could write a book about it: city girl signs up for one of our excursions, determined to prove something to herself, then spends every single day regretting the life choices that brought her there. Women like this—in my own personal experience, anyway—always wear the wrong shoes and bring too much stuff, then complain about how heavy their pack is and how much their feet hurt, or they twist an ankle. They want Instagram-worthy snapshots without putting the work in to get to those places.

"Be my guest," I say, fishing my phone out of the mop bucket, which—thankfully—has only the barest trace of water left in it from the last time it was used.

"I'm Sadie, by the way," she says as she plucks a set of silk pajamas out of the employee locker where she left them.

Silk pajamas for a wilderness hike: now that's a first. The idea of her—the idea of *those* legs in those shorts—it's an image that sneaks up without permission, one I'm quick to try and shove down.

I've always made it a point to remain professional while at work, because I've seen it go wrong too many times when people don't. Leader/trekker flings never end well: someone always ends up with a broken bone, a broken heart, or both. Sometimes they end up out of a job. That's why we have rules now—we're not to get involved.

I've never had an issue with the rules. I prefer to keep the people in my care—and myself, and my professional reputation—wholly intact.

Silk shorts like those, though, could test even my own strong sense of self-control. Maybe I should tell her to leave them here in the mop closet.

Sadie leans against the employee lockers, eyeing me as I wipe the water off my phone's heavy-duty case.

"Everything okay?" she asks.

"Could be better."

Probably not the best idea to bad-mouth my coleader.

"Anything I can do to help?" she asks.

"Everything's all packed up and ready, but thanks for offering," I reply. "Now we're just waiting on the others."

Over the next half hour, the rest of the group arrives.

First are Joshua and Zoe, the engaged couple. She's got a diamond the size of the moon on her left hand, and I've already seen them kiss four times since they walked through the door. His hand is in her back pocket, her fingers are hooked through one of his belt loops—it makes me wish we had rules about PDA for the trekkers.

Next are the three collegiate athletes, Brittany, Emma, and Parker. They play tennis for Pepperdine and look extremely fit, like they'll have no problem hiking. Unlike Sadie—and Zoe, for that matter—these girls have the right-sized packs and are dressed in clothes that will work well on the trails.

The last group to arrive includes three guys in their early thirties who can best be described as coffee bros: they take their coffee *very* seriously, traveling the globe to source beans from all sorts of places, and own a handful of cafés up in the Pacific Northwest. From what I understand, this trip is meant to be a sort of leadership retreat for them. They have matching tattoos of their octopus logo on their forearms, which . . . says . . . a lot.

Sadie's already here, of course, the only one traveling on her own. She's changed into a pair of black leggings—a relief, since the last way I want to spend today is with my nose in the first-aid kit every five minutes, searching for Band-Aids. Bare legs are just asking for trouble.

And then there's Matteo.

He strides in, chill as ever, his dark hair longer than when I saw him last but just as unruly. You'd never guess someone like Matteo could leave such a trail of destruction in his wake—he looks like someone with a heart. Friendly. Laid-back. Puts everyone he meets at ease.

Seeing him now, I have to work to unclench my jaw.

The meet-and-greet is awkward.

Matteo suspiciously avoids eye contact with me as he makes his way around the room. With everyone else, he's very chatty: asking the coffee bros about their matching tattoos and the tennis girls' predictions for who will win Wimbledon. He's always been such a chameleon, reflecting back what seems to be genuine interest in whatever a person is most invested in—I've seen it so many times before, always thought it was one of his most admirable qualities.

Now all I see is a guy who pretends to care until you're standing in the way of something he wants.

I've tried twice now to get his attention so we can talk about the trek. It's always a good idea to make sure you're on the same page as your coleader, but it looks like we might just have to carve out some time tonight after we get to the first campsite. We're already getting too late of a start as it is, and the last thing I want to do is rush a group of inexperienced hikers through the first day.

"All right, people!" I call out in my loudest voice.

The chatter dies. Everyone but Matteo turns to look at me.

"My name is Thorn, and I'll be leading your expedition over the next couple of weeks," I say. "You all signed up for the expert-level wilderness trek, right?"

My attempt at a joke is met almost entirely with blank stares.

Sadie, at least, laughs. "Oh, for sure. Expert level, right here!"

Her comedic tone hits much better than mine did—the others at least look mildly amused now.

"*Excellent*," I reply. "But in all seriousness, while jokes might not be my strong suit, wilderness treks actually are—and between myself and my coleader, Matteo, you're in good hands."

Matteo gives a little wave, finally meeting my eye for a split second before looking away again.

"If you ever have any questions or concerns," I go on, "please reach out to either of us and we'll do our best to address them. We can't promise everything will be comfortable along the way—"

"If it's comfortable, you're probably doing it wrong," Matteo interjects.

"Exactly," I say, nodding in acknowledgment. "So, yeah: get comfortable with being uncomfortable—and get ready for a trek that might just change your whole life."

I always cringe at the wording, straight out of the leadership script we're supposed to quote in every intro speech, but no one ever seems particularly put off by it.

Matteo and I distribute backpacking bundles for everyone, which include pop-up tents and sleeping bags—standard procedure for every expedition. Some nights we sleep out under the stars, but most nights require setting up camp. All the more reason we need to get going, if we want to have any daylight left for that.

It takes another half hour of last-minute bathroom trips and shoe changes before we officially head out.

Matteo still hasn't said a word to me other than his comment during my welcome speech. It's not like I'm looking *forward* to speaking to him, but all the silence and history between us makes me feel on edge. I take up a spot at the front of the group, leading the way, while he settles in at the rear.

It's quiet on the trail, at first—only the birds and the breeze and the crunch of our boots on the path as everyone takes in the overwhelming majesty of the trees that stretch so high all around us. It must feel like such a contrast for many of them, no city skylines or tennis courts or cafés for miles.

For me, it just feels like home.

"I'm beginning to think I made some terrible choices," Sadie says quietly behind me, biting back a laugh.

I turn and follow her gaze down to the ground—she's wearing bright white Adidas running shoes, already tinged brown with dirt and mud.

How did I not notice before? I assumed she'd switched shoes when everyone else did.

"I hate to ask," I say, "but why didn't you change into your hiking boots before we left?"

I've got a sinking feeling I know the answer already.

"Well . . ." she says, and it's as good as spelling it out.

She didn't bring any hiking boots.

DAY ONE

Mackenzie Lake Loop Trailhead to Campsite at Valerie Forest

When hiking through the forest, always be aware of your surroundings: stay on the marked path, keep an eye out for uneven ground, and never hike alone. For your comfort and safety, proper clothing and footwear are recommended.

—Henry Herrington, *Backpacking the Sierras: A Beginner's Handbook* (Fourth Edition)

VIDEOS > FAVORITES > VLOG FOOTAGE

Sunlight pierces through the tree canopy above before the camera pans down to eye level. Four hikers, backs to the camera, trudge along a worn path in the forest.

> **SADIE (offscreen): Say hi, everyone!**

At the front of the pack, the guide keeps his eyes on the trail—but the three girls behind him glance over their shoulders and wave. The world blurs as the camera pans around to face the rest of the hikers, some of them quite far behind. Some smile and wave, others are too wrapped up in conversation to even notice.

The camera flips viewpoints, and Sadie's face fills the screen, narrating as she walks.

> **SADIE: It's Day One of my big adventure—I'm on a hiking expedition in California! I've never done anything like this before, but I love a challenge. Certain people back home think I'll *die* out here after one day—**

> **THORN (offscreen): Can you put that thing away, please? Certain people *here* think you might die after one day, too, if you don't watch where you're going.**

Sadie rolls her eyes.

> **SADIE: That's Thorn, our hiking guide. He's been a little uptight ever since we got out here on the trail—but in the interest of proving everyone wrong and *not* dying on the very first day, I guess I'll be following his advice now. Check my stories and reels for daily updates—as long as I have a decent signal—and be sure to turn on notifications so you don't miss the full vlog recap once I'm back home again!**

Sadie blows a kiss to the camera, and the video ends.

4

SADIE

I tuck my phone away.

The laid-back guy I caught half naked inside the fake tree is *not* the same Thorn who's been leading the way all afternoon: *uptight* was too kind, honestly. *Stick up his ass* might have been more accurate, but, well. I was trying to be nice.

He's been in a mood ever since that phone call with his boss.

"He really is uptight," someone murmurs from behind me, for my ears only.

I glance back and see the one girl I might have something in common with out here—the one with an engagement ring so large its weight is probably throwing her willowy frame out of alignment as we speak.

"You noticed, too?" I ask, slowing my pace so we can walk side by side. Her fiancé has been glommed on to her ever since they arrived, but he's lagging behind at the moment, making small talk with the guys from Portland.

"How could I not?" she says, rolling her eyes. "He keeps giving us this *look* whenever Joshua kisses me, like he hates seeing two people in love."

Thorn probably just hates seeing two people with their tongues constantly down each other's throats in such performative fashion—it's a lot even for me, and I'm a romantic!—but I don't say so. I'm possibly also just a *little* jaded: seeing two people so absorbed in each other only drives home the fact that I'm extremely single, extremely alone on this trip, and was supposed to be kissing my own fiancé in Italy right now.

"I'm Zoe, by the way," she goes on.

"Sadie," I reply, carefully stepping over an uneven patch on the path. My feet are screaming already and it hasn't even been two hours. At least the view is worth it: the winding path we're on is surrounded by the most massive trees I've ever seen.

"Nice to meet you," she says. "You're here on your own, or . . . ?"

How soon is too soon to share my entire life story and the circumstances that brought me—a city girl who loves soft sheets and sheet masks—to this rugged trail all by myself?

I think it's too soon.

"Yeah," I say with a shrug, as if there's no backstory to it at all. I nod to the giant rock on her finger. "And you're here with your fiancé?"

I already know they're engaged—not married—because they both made a point to mention it when we did the briefest of group introductions before heading out.

"*I* suggested we spend the entire summer renting out a castle in the French countryside, but did I get my way?" Zoe makes a face, plays it off as a joke, but I sense tension beneath her words.

Maybe I'm just projecting, though, since this trip stood in the way of my own European vacation.

"Let me guess, he surprised you?"

"Yes and no," she says. "We decided to do two trips this summer—he said I could plan France for July if he planned something epic for us in June. I *literally* found out *two days ago* we were doing this hike.

Here I was thinking California would just be a stopover on our way to Hawaii, or maybe Fiji."

I have *so* many questions.

"I've got a yoga studio, so I make my own schedule," she supplies before I get the chance to ask. "Joshua's in finance—he *says* he's not going to work while we're out here, but I'll believe that when I see it."

"My boss threatened to fire me if I tried to work out here," I say, and she laughs.

The trail narrows as it curves around a sizable rock, so we go single file for a bit. When it widens again, Zoe says, "So, first impressions of everyone: kiss, marry, kill?"

I've just taken a sip from my water bottle and nearly choke on my own laughter. "What?"

"You know! The game?" she says, laughing—at me or with me, I'm not sure. "You pick someone to kiss, someone to marry, someone to kill."

"Going on first impressions only?" I ask, and she nods. "I think I'd kiss the coleader—Matteo, right?" He's as attractive as Thorn, but also has an Italian accent. That said, there's something about him that kind of shouts *phobia of commitment*. "One of the Portland guys might make good marriage material?" I offer, because they seem nice and stable—not to mention they're into fancy coffee, like me, as I learned from the group intros.

"Let me guess," she says, eating my answers up. "You'd kill the uptight hiking guide?"

"I'd rather not kill anyone," I say. "We'd be lost out here without Thorn—*but*—if something did happen to him, at least I could wander the woods in peace without him telling me to put my phone away!"

She laughs. "Both very good points."

A bird flits across the path before settling onto a high branch.

"What about you?" I ask.

"Oh, for me? I'd go with Joshua on all three," she says with an eye roll.

I'm not quite sure what to make of that answer—they seem like the perfect couple on the surface, but she kind of wants to kill him? Maybe the undercurrent of tension I sensed earlier wasn't just projection after all.

Around the next bend, the world brightens as the woods open to clear blue sky. When I get closer, I see the sky isn't the main attraction at all: it's a rest stop with a postcard-perfect view of a trio of mountains off in the distance.

Thorn leads the way, the sporty girls just behind him, and then comes to a stop next to a plaque that reads HELEN THERESA PEAK SCENIC OVERLOOK. The whole clearing is paved in flat gray stones, and there are enough benches—or smooth rock ledges—for the eleven of us to sit and take a break.

"Good job so far, everyone," Thorn says once we're all gathered in the clearing. "We've been trekking through Valerie Forest today—it's the namesake for this national park and spans a sizable acreage of the northwestern part of this loop. What you see off to the southeast is Helen Theresa Peak, along with two lesser peaks known as the Two Sisters. The Mackenzie Lake Loop circles these mountains, so you'll be seeing them again throughout the trek. Beyond them is Mount Valerie—that's the mountain we'll be climbing on our last big hike. Now would be a good time for pictures and snacks before we continue on to our campsite."

Zoe raises her hand. "Exactly how much longer do we have to go?" she asks. "And when you say 'campsite,' you mean '*glamp*site,' right?"

Thorn's face clouds over. "Approximately two more hours. But I'm sorry—I don't understand the last question?"

"Glampsite," she repeats, looking to her fiancé for support, then to *me*. "Glamping?"

"Glamping, like 'glamorous camping,'" I add, and now Thorn's stormy face is trained on mine. "It's a thing. Like luxurious little semi-permanent tents where you sleep on real beds, with high-end pillows and bedding and string lights, but maybe also with a view of the stars through a translucent roof?"

It's possible this definition is on the tip of my tongue because I did my own research the night of the breakup, naïvely hoping it was the sort of trip Caden had signed up for.

If only.

"Um . . . no," Thorn says, clearly perplexed, running a hand over his stubbled jaw. "That is not at all what this is. What did you think the tent bundles were for?"

"The . . . tent bundles?"

She glances around; as soon as she spots the unfamiliar bundle affixed to Joshua's backpack, her confusion turns to panic.

"*Babe!*" Zoe shrieks as she swats her fiancé on the shoulder. "You told me it would be like *glamping*!"

"Emphasis on the *like*," Joshua says with a shrug. "Except more like just . . . regular camping?"

Yikes.

Everyone splits off into the groups they arrived with for the break, leaving me on my own. I would stick with Zoe, but she and Joshua are already off to the side, fighting and trying to hide it.

I pull out my phone again—Thorn *did* say this would be a good place for pictures, so I shouldn't get my head bitten off this time—and head over to take a quick video of just the mountains, then one more with myself in frame. To my relief, I'm not the only one trying to capture the moment: one of the coffee bros has an actual paparazzi-caliber camera with him.

I'm in the middle of posting the selfie to my Instagram—I have a single flickering bar of service—when the shadows beside me shift and someone clears his throat.

I look up and see Thorn, arms crossed, leaning back against the scenic overlook railing like he has all the faith in the world that it won't give out and send him hurtling over the edge.

His gaze catches briefly on my attempt to show the world how very brave I am by being here—but rather than commenting on that, he nods toward my shoes.

"Feet hurting yet?" he asks.

I tuck my phone away; I'll finish the post later.

"Oh, I'm fine," I say breezily. I like to think of this as a truth that's yet to happen, rather than an outright lie. "They're the most comfortable shoes I own!"

And infinitely cuter than hiking boots, I don't add.

It's not that I was unaware of the hiking boots suggested in the packing brochure—it's that I doubted their relevance to me, specifically. My beloved Ultraboosts have never failed me, and I worried an unfamiliar pair of hiking boots would be too bulky and heavy and a nightmare to break in.

Thorn might be a bit uptight, but he's really hot when he's at a loss for words.

"What?" I prod. "Just say it."

He gives me a sidelong glance.

"If I pull out my phone, will you say that again—about how comfortable they are—so I can record it?" His voice really is so deep, as Abby astutely pointed out. "I'd love to be able to play that back when you twist your ankle or slip while crossing a stream."

I can play this game, too.

"Oh, sure, of course," I reply. "Now I kind of want to twist my ankle so that everyone here will see that the *first* thing our fearless leader does when someone gets injured is—let's check the notes—pull out a voice memo to say 'I told you so.'"

He grins, point taken.

I take his point, too. "I guess I sort of thought hiking boots were more of a . . . general concept. Not, like, a specific requirement."

"A general concept?"

"You know," I say. "Like . . . something you could walk forever in and not get blisters? I once walked twenty-eight thousand steps in a single day at Disney World in these shoes."

Thorn shakes his head and laughs. "Where do I even start?"

"Do your worst," I say. "I can take it."

"Okay, so, first of all, this sort of expedition is the furthest thing from Disney World. Second, you walked twenty-eight thousand steps—at Disney World—in *those* shoes? Those exact spotless white shoes."

"They're not spotless or white anymore," I say, purposefully missing his point.

He gives me another look, one that comes off just a little flirty—which I'm certain, given all other clues, is entirely unintentional.

"Okay, so they weren't this *exact* pair," I admit. "I bought these new for the hike."

This really makes him laugh, blue eyes sparkling in the sunlight.

"What?" I say, and now I'm laughing, too. "I figured new ones would be better on my feet than beat-up ones. I swear I did put *some* logic into this decision—though in hindsight, I am willing to acknowledge that hiking boots might have been the better choice."

"For a hike," he adds, smirking.

"Look," I say, nudging him with my elbow.

He gives me a once-over from head to toe. "At what?"

Flat tone, one eyebrow raised: he's the poster child for the word *unimpressed*.

I point one toe as if Adidas has hired me to model a new line of hiking-chic Ultraboosts.

"Nothing broken," I reply. "Nothing twisted. Pretty sure I don't even have a blister yet!"

"*Yet* being the operative word," he says drily.

"We should make a bet—I bet I can make it an entire week of hiking without getting a single blister."

"And what will I get when I win that bet?" he challenges. "You'll have blisters by tomorrow."

"When *I* win," I counter, "you will simply have to admit my shoes are fine."

"Okay, well, that's never gonna happen. So when I win, *you* will have to give up one item from your pack."

"And leave it behind—here in the woods? Doesn't that, like, interfere with the whole leave-nature-as-you-found-it thing?"

"I'll put it in *my* pack," he replies. "Where you won't have access to it until the end of the trip."

I'm starting to think maybe this bet was a bad idea—I already left behind everything I couldn't live without. Maybe I should've committed to *three* blister-less days, not an entire week.

But I'm nothing if not stubborn.

"You're on."

"I look forward to carrying your espresso machine," he says, and he means it as a joke, but—

"Wait," he goes on, eyes wide as he takes in the look on my face. "You didn't *actually* bring an espresso machine, I hope?"

"Of course not."

"But?"

I roll my eyes with more drama than is strictly necessary.

"Fine," I say. "I *might* have brought a different sort of coffee situation so I wouldn't have to go without it the whole time."

"We rough it in a lot of ways out here, Sadie, but we're not monsters. We've got coffee built into our breakfast plans."

"*Real* coffee?"

"Real instant coffee, yes."

I scoff. "Say that a little louder—I want to see if the coffee bros riot."

"You'd really rather carry extra weight in your pack for two weeks just so you don't have to go without your *preferred* coffee?"

"You really expect people to be satisfied with instant sludge that whole time?" I reply. "I suspect the coffee bros will take my side when presented with the option to have some of mine."

This, unexpectedly, is the thing that cracks him.

"Let me get this straight," he says, laughing. "You not only brought your own special coffee, and something special to make it in, but you brought enough to share with *three* other guys."

I can't help it, I laugh, too. It does sound ridiculous when he puts it that way.

Not that I'll ever admit it.

I shrug, attempting nonchalance. "I had a whole box of beans ground before I came." I had two boxes ground, but details. "Better to have more than you need than to run out halfway through the trip."

His eyes light up. "Ah—see, *that* is where we're different."

I suspect we are different, very different, in more ways than just that one, but of course I don't feel the need to point that out.

"One reason I like my job is that you can never really prepare for every single circumstance," he goes on. "It makes you have to trust your gut, think on your feet. You kind of have to learn to adapt when things get uncomfortable. It's the best kind of rush, not knowing how things will play out and having to figure it all out on the fly."

"See, yeah, that sounds like my worst nightmare, Thorn."

He takes a long sip from his water bottle, looking at me in a way that makes me feel more seen than I have in quite some time.

I shouldn't have let my guard down like that—shouldn't have given him this much of a peek into just how extra I really am. I had every chance to start fresh here, for this group and its grumpy leader to see me as Go-with-the-Flow Sadie. Maybe even (oh, the horror) Instant Coffee Sadie.

To Thorn, I am currently Wrong-Shoes/Coffee-Snob/Put-That-Phone-Away Sadie.

"I sincerely hope you win the bet, then," Thorn says, twisting the lid of his water bottle back in place.

"Oh yeah? Why's that?"

He smirks. "Because if you lose, your coffee setup is going into my pack for the rest of the trip. On the bright side, hey, maybe it'll be a chance to try something new. Something outside your comfort zone: the wonderful world of instant coffee."

"Because being here in the first place *isn't* outside my comfort zone?"

He tips his head as if to say *good point*. "All I'm saying is, I hope you win—for the sake of your feet and your coffee."

"*When* I win," I reply, "I'm making you a cup of my coffee, and you'll totally admit I was right about that, too. That it was worth it to bring it."

He holds out his hand. "You've got yourself a deal."

I give it a firm shake—his hand is strong and warm and fits mine perfectly.

"Okay, everyone," he calls out a moment later. "We'd better get moving if we're going to set up camp before nightfall."

The sounds of zippers and chatter fill the clearing. I slip a little on the uneven rocky pavement, as if the universe is also trying to prove Thorn's point.

He notices, of course.

"Already rethinking that bet?" he says, loading his pack onto his back.

Preemptively mourning the loss of my beloved coffee is more like it, but it's fun to pretend I have even the smallest chance at winning.

"Just trying to wrap my mind around how long it'll take to get to camp," I say coolly.

And how long it'll be before I get my first blister. And my tenth blister. And how this is just the first day of . . . many, many days.

"Everyone good to go?" Thorn calls out once we all look more or less ready. "We'll take another quick break later, but we're going to cover as much ground as we can before that."

No one objects. Not out loud, anyway.

Today's first hike would've been enough for me—it's more time outdoors than I've had all summer unless you count the hotel pool.

I have a feeling Thorn would not count the hotel pool.

Now that I'm here, and the excitement is wearing off, it's finally dawning on me that I'm going to be out in the wilderness for *twelve days*.

As if on cue, a mosquito lands on my forearm. I shoo it away, then shoo its little mosquito friend, too, before they both settle in for a feast.

Thorn leads the way like he was born king of the woods.

I follow like a lululemon influencer who stumbled out of a photo shoot and found herself uncomfortably sweaty and surrounded by bugs.

How could I ever have thought this was a good idea?

5

THORN

Hours later, the voices have fallen silent behind me.

It's my favorite part of the day: robin's-egg blue skies fading to an endless expanse of lavender, the sounds of jays and chickadees and Western Tanagers settling in for the night amid the hum of insects. Off in the distance, a bubbling stream carves through the rugged terrain. It's nature as it's meant to be.

But then Matteo's yelling something from far behind me, his voice piercing through the calm dusk.

So much for serenity.

"What?" I call out. "What happened?"

"Can we hold up for a sec?" he shouts. "Hunter's getting a photo!"

A photo? A *photo*? The way Matteo shouted made it sound like someone had passed out.

Sure enough, one of the coffee bros has stepped off the path (into some tall grass, which Matteo should have warned him to stay clear of) and is aiming his telephoto lens at the trees.

I rub a hand over my face. I get wanting to have photos of nature—

there's a lot of beauty out here, obviously—but photography gear can be *heavy*. Sadie's not the only one who could've packed lighter.

"Good to go!" Hunter calls out a minute later, raising his camera as if to toast the occasion. "Thanks, y'all! There was this bird I just *had* to get a shot of!"

Suddenly I understand why the back of the pack has been so far behind us all afternoon. There will be five hundred more birds, and if we stop for him to photograph every one of them, we will never stay on track. It's the same reason I take issue with people who are constantly on their phones: it slows everything down, not to mention it's hazardous when they're not paying attention to where they're stepping. Too many people watch the world through their camera lenses instead of letting themselves just *be* in the moment.

But I keep my thoughts to myself, and we press on.

I could travel this trail a thousand times and it would never look the same. I *have* traveled it a thousand times. My dad took me all over the national parks as a kid, but this one was always his favorite. Taking a job as a hiking guide was a natural fit when I eventually needed work—I know every bend in the trail, every river, every lake. I know how the air shifts when a storm is brewing and how the landscape changes with the seasons; I could navigate Valerie Forest National Park without a compass while half asleep at this point.

Not only do I know these trails, though, I love them.

And I love helping *other* people fall in love with this place.

All of my very best memories happened out here—

Fishing lessons with my dad at Mackenzie Lake: I've always been the unluckiest fisherman on the planet, but that never seemed to bother him.

Stargazing with my dad: how he taught me to spot Orion and Cassiopeia and the Pleiades, and how it was our tradition to wish on shooting stars whenever either one of us had a birthday.

My dad and I getting caught in a rainstorm—my mom was there for that one, too.

Even before my parents divorced during my sophomore year of college, my mom rarely came hiking with us . . . and my dad's trail days are long behind him. Now it's up to me to keep our traditions alive, noting in my journal all the things I know my dad will appreciate, like subtle differences in the landscape and birds I spot along the way.

I haven't told him this yet—haven't told *anyone*, especially not Danica—but my days out here might also be numbered.

It was two months ago when a man named Sky Ranger (his real name; I checked) came on one of my hikes. He owns a number of backpacking tour operations across the States—Virginia, Hawaii, Texas, Arizona—and was on a mission to hike every national park in the country. He didn't come looking for a new employee, but at the end of our two weeks together, he pulled me aside and told me how impressed he was with my outdoorsmanship and leadership instincts. Said I could name my location—my price, too—and that I had a standing job offer to come work for him anytime. *Just think it over*, he told me, tucking a business card in the palm of my hand.

Well, I'm still thinking it over. Figured he'd go home and forget about me like everyone else does when they get back to the real world. They always say they'll keep in touch, but never do.

I assumed I'd never hear from him again. But then the email hit my inbox, today, just before we set off on this hike. *Told my business partner about you*, Sky wrote. *Offer's still on the table if you want it—let me know.*

This was right on the heels of Danica's effusive praise, a text she sent after our phone call thanking me for being the most reliable guide she's ever had.

I've never left her in a bind due to being stranded on vacation.

I've *definitely* never ditched my responsibilities to relocate to Peru on a whim.

It would be so much easier to say yes to Sky if I didn't love it so much out here, if I didn't have deep personal ties to the land itself—and if I didn't care so much about Danica and the tour company. Our ratings recently took a hit due to some not-so-reliable (since fired) tour guides, which means Danica's income has also taken a hit.

If I were to leave, it might be the company's kiss of death.

If this trek goes off perfectly, though—if everyone leaves a good review—we'll be well on our way back up to four stars or more.

But I'm trying not to worry about that. All I can do at the moment is my job. Stay focused, keep everyone safe, open their eyes to all the reasons I love this place—really help them have the experience of a lifetime—and save my own big decisions for later.

Our campsite is dusky blue when we finally arrive. The sun hasn't set yet, but it might as well have—it's hidden behind all the trees and rocks and craggy cliffs. Won't be long before we break out the flashlights.

Matteo and I slip easily into our old roles as soon as we get to the clearing. He loves making fire—and he's good at it—so I don't argue when he takes campfire duty. For once, we're not on a wildfire ban, thanks to some healthy rains over the last few months.

Which means I'm on tent duty.

I don't usually mind tent duty. If someone were to say, *Hey Thorn, I'll give you ten million dollars if you can set up a tent in under a minute,* I'd be swimming in cash (but probably still camping out in the woods, just with nicer gear).

Today, though? Tent duty is a headache.

We stopped earlier than I'd planned due to the waning light, so this clearing isn't the one I had in mind—and it's not quite big enough for the eleven of us. We can fit seven tents easily, but everywhere else is too muddy or too rocky or too close to the stream. We'll have to consolidate to make it work.

Not helping my headache: Joshua and Zoe are back to punctuating their every conversation with a kiss, despite their tense afternoon. Did he seriously tell her we'd be *glamping*?

"The three of us can share," Brittany offers, and her tennis teammates—Parker and Emma—agree. "We're used to rooming together on the road."

I don't want to point out that they'll practically be sleeping on top of each other tonight, since it's the only configuration that makes sense without shifting one of them to a stranger's tent (or putting Matteo and me together).

It's more complicated with the coffee bros.

There are three of them, but we only have space for two more tents. Hunter is six foot five, the human equivalent of a giant sequoia. He needs his own tent, for obvious reasons. Trey and Silas aren't exactly *compact*, though—they're both over six feet, so sharing would be tight at best.

"It's just for one night?" Silas asks.

Trey peeks inside, probably wondering how on earth they're both going to fit.

I let out a long exhale. "Our next stop has a lot more space, yeah," I say. "But we'll have to make up some ground tomorrow in order to get there."

"I don't know, man," Trey says. "I think I'd rather set up in the mud."

"You might have issues with stabilizing the pegs," I say as his face falls in disappointment. "But, uh, you could try it?"

He brightens and sets off into the muddier part of the clearing.

"It doesn't go like *that*, Zoe," Joshua says—right before their entire tent collapses in a heap.

I very much regret the fact that I told them to set up right next to me. Sadie will be on my other side, which should be mostly okay . . . unless she spends the whole night complaining like the last Instagram influencer who came out here.

"Wow," I say, heading over to check out her progress. "This looks pretty good."

Sadie beams, clearly proud of herself. "Did I do it right? I watched a lot of YouTube tutorials."

I laugh. "Your preparation paid off."

"Want the full tour?" she says, peeling back the flap.

"The full . . . Sadie, what on earth?"

I peek inside and it's like she's set up a miniature version of her own home. There's a small green book in the corner beside an LED touch lamp, along with a translucent bear canister holding lip gloss and hand sanitizer and bug spray and a small package of wet wipes—lavender-scented and eco-friendly, according to the label. Her pale pink silk pajamas are folded neatly on top of a small pillow (complete with what appears to be a satin pillowcase), with a matching eye mask on top and some cashmere socks tucked underneath. And there, in the far corner, is her makeshift coffee bar.

"You know you'll just have to tear all of this down in the morning, right?" I've never seen such an elaborate setup.

She shrugs. "Guess I'll have to become an expert at packing it all up again."

"Your back hurting yet from carrying all of that?"

It has to be. First-timers usually have an adjustment period even if they pack light—and Sadie did *not* pack light.

"It won't be after I sleep on *this*," she says, proudly peeling back her sleeping bag to reveal the inflatable plastic cushion just underneath, barely thicker than a yoga mat.

"Hate to break it to you, princess, but that's no luxury mattress."

"*Princess*?" she exclaims, eyebrows shooting up, drawing glances from Brittany and Emma, who have joined Matteo over by the fire.

"Well, when you say it like that, it doesn't sound the same as it did in my head."

She crosses her arms. "Which is how, exactly?"

"Like I was referencing *The Princess and the Pea*?" Heat creeps up my neck. "You'll still feel every rock, they'll just be a bit less jagged. That thing's no cloud."

"Well, then, I guess it's a good thing I also brought *this*."

She unzips her sleeping bag to reveal a rechargeable heating pad insert—not the worst idea, actually. In fact, it's kind of brilliant.

"Do you also have the rest of an entire REI store hiding in your tent?"

I can't help but give her a hard time about how much she's brought.

"As they say," she says, zipping her sleeping bag up and making the whole setup pristine again, "you can't spell *overprepared* without the word *prepared*."

I have to laugh. "Who says that?"

"You know. *They*." She keeps a straight face, stubborn as all get-out to win whatever this conversation has turned into. "And no, for the record—I only packed *half* of an REI."

We're interrupted by a cheer from across the clearing: Joshua and Zoe have *finally* stopped making out long enough that their tent is upright and, from the looks of it, functional. She's beaming as he lifts her high above his head, then spins her around like they're dancing—

But they're just a little too close to the tent, and her foot catches on the corner, and it all comes crashing down.

CAPTAIN'S LOG // AUGUST THORN

Day 1 • 10:35 p.m. • 75°F • Sunshine all day

TREK NOTES

Not the worst day, not the best. New group of trekkers seems reasonably solid—

- Tennis girls: Emma (not Emily), Parker, Brittany. Athletic, kept pace well, no drama.
- Coffee bros: Hunter, Silas, Trey. A little high on their own hype, but eager for adventure. Hunter's camera might be a problem if it keeps slowing our pace.
- Engaged couple: Joshua, Zoe. Ask Danica about PDA rules for future treks . . .
- Sadie: A bit of a mystery—not sure why she's here, this doesn't seem like her thing. That said, she did better than expected today. Look for ways to help her (if she needs it) without implying that she can't do it on her own. Her shoes are going to be an issue, and maybe her overstuffed pack, too.
- Matteo: We haven't spoken all day. It's getting awkward.

FOR DAD

- Spotted a Western Tanager in Valerie Forest
- He would have loved the view at the scenic overlook—one of those clear days where you could see for miles

DAY TWO

Valerie Forest • L'Heureux Falls Crossing • Cloverleaf Creek

Take extra caution when crossing streams, especially after a recent rain. Check for depth (below thigh-deep on the shortest person), speed (water no faster than a walking pace), and color (avoid turbulent, frothy whitewater) before entering. Remember the old adage: if in doubt, stay out.

—Henry Herrington, *Backpacking the Sierras: A Beginner's Handbook* (Fourth Edition)

VIDEOS > FAVORITES > VLOG FOOTAGE

SADIE: Hey, everyone—I made it through the night!

Sadie squints into the camera, then sweeps a hand through her hair before wiping some sleep from her eyes. The first rays of sunlight pierce through the nylon fabric of her tent walls.

SADIE: Sorry I look rough. But y'all—I did it! Was it comfortable? No. Was it fun? Also no. Does my entire body feel like death? You bet it does. I'm going to be very, very real right now: My legs hurt. My butt hurts. My feet *really* hurt. My back—actually, my back isn't too bad. The heating pad I brought worked pretty well, so I'll link to that when I get a chance. But, yeah. This is already the hardest thing I've ever put myself through on purpose, and it hasn't even been a full twenty-four hours yet. My reward for surviving? I get to do it all over again today! And tomorrow. And the next day. And a lot of days after that.

Sadie's smile falters, almost imperceptibly, for a split second.

SADIE: But you know what? I'm here. I'm fighting—I'm *doing* it. So to everyone out there who has a Caden O'Connor in their life telling them they'll *die* after one day of trying something outside of their comfort zone, I'm living proof that you can do it. You can do anything for a day, right?

6

SADIE

The full force of the pain doesn't hit until I've unfolded myself from my tent and taken my first steps.

If I had to guess, my body is approximately 85 percent fire right now, 10 percent determination, and 5 percent Advil. I don't spot any blisters—yet—but it's only a matter of time. I'm already dreading my inevitable loss to Thorn, the bet we both knew he'd win. Maybe I should make a cup of coffee for him this morning: He won't want to take my setup away if he gets hooked, right?

It's my best (and only) idea right now.

In the meantime, I'm determined to push through with a smile. No complaints—not out loud—because even if Caden's not here to witness this misery, I feel like he'd still sense it somehow. Thorn feels almost like a Caden proxy, anyway: I can read it all over his face, how he took one look at me and thought, *Seriously?* This *girl? She won't make it a day.*

I kind of need to prove something to him, too—especially after how he called me *princess*.

So, no. I will not be admitting, to Thorn or to anyone, that I felt every single jagged rock underneath me last night, even through my cushion and my sleeping bag and my heating pad.

The kettle is already in use when I reach the fire. I didn't bring my own—believe me, I considered it—since Abby pointed out that a kettle was on the list of supplies the tour group would be providing.

What I didn't count on were three other guys who were as into coffee as me. I wait patiently as Trey, Silas, and Hunter prep their AeroPresses. All the water is gone by the time they're through with it, so I have to wait even longer for my own to come to a boil.

I've just finished setting up everything I need—my favorite ceramic mug, a foldable filter that functions the same way my V60 does at home, and my premeasured coffee grounds—when I hear a throat clear behind me. I turn and see Trey, his hat with the Mark Rober logo turned backward.

"Onyx Coffee Lab!" he says, delighted, pointing at the box I set down with my gear. "You've got good taste."

I laugh. "I'm just glad I'm not the only one who brought fancy coffee on a wilderness hike."

"They said to pack only the essentials, right?"

This guy is buzzing so hard he probably had three fully caffeinated cups before seven a.m.

"Anyway," he goes on, talking just a little too fast, "I was just gonna offer some of ours if you want it? Unless you'd rather make your own, which I'd totally get. But if you want some, we've got enough. If you like Onyx, you'll like ours."

"Oh, right—you all own a coffee shop together, right?" I overheard snippets on our hike yesterday.

He points to an octopus tattoo on his forearm, its sucker-laden limbs curled and winding around to the other side. "Cephalopod Coffee out of Portland," he says. "That's our logo."

Anyone committed enough to get their brand's logo tattooed on their forearm is probably also committed to making sure said brand is of good quality—that it won't go out of business within two years, rendering said tattoo pointless and regrettable. Then again, he has a lot of tattoos, so maybe he just liked the way it looked.

"I'm good for today," I say, gesturing to my filter full of grounds, "but thanks—I'll totally take you up on that tomorrow."

Between waiting forever on the kettle and the time required to actually prepare my coffee, it'll be another ten minutes before I'm able to drink it. Back home, the slowness of this routine is one of the best parts: the smell of the coffee, the heat of the swirling steam, the soothing sounds as it drips into the mug—it's calming, and helps me start the day off right before I ever take a single sip.

Now, though, I'm increasingly aware of how long the process is. Instead of relieving stress, it's adding to it—everyone else has finished breakfast already, and I'm the only one still trying to wrap up. Matteo put the fire out the instant my water finished boiling, and the coffee bros headed back to their tents to pack up a little while ago. The others around camp are already doing the same. Zoe is the exception: she's off on her own, working her way through a complicated yoga routine while Joshua takes care of their tent.

Suffice it to say, I'm a little self-conscious.

My coffee is *finally* almost ready to drink when I hear footsteps behind me. I glance over my shoulder and see Thorn, eyebrows knitted together as he surveys my . . . situation.

"We'll be heading out in fifteen," he says. "Think you'll have your palace ready to go by then?"

First *princess*, now *palace*—

I don't give him the satisfaction of a reaction.

"Oh, yeah." I take my first glorious sip of coffee, the picture of nonchalance. "You should see my trophy case back home, I've won a few for speed-packing. Palaces included."

The corner of his mouth turns upward, the barest hint of a grin.

"Great," he says smoothly, not missing a beat. "Sounds like you've got it under control."

"*Completely* under control," I reply. "Blink and you'll miss it!"

But I absolutely do not have it under control.

I am the opposite of a speed-packer: it is a mystery beyond all mysteries how everything I took out of my backpack ever fit inside in the first place. Even when I consult the photo I snapped in the REI backpack aisle—a diagram of how everything should fit inside to make the most of the limited space—I can't make it work.

And everyone's waiting.

Waiting and *watching*.

The longer I struggle, the harder it gets. How do zippers work? Have I ever used one in my entire life? I'm sweating from the effort and it's barely nine in the morning.

Without a word, Thorn swoops in at my side and—after the briefest *Is this okay?* glance, which I definitely don't refute—starts slipping everything into my pack. He has to try three configurations before it works.

"You can have one of my speed-packing trophies after this is all over," I say quietly, for his ears only, too mortified to look at him. "Thank you."

He gives my backpack a little pat before moving on to take care of my tent.

"Hope you took notes," he says. "There'll be an exam tomorrow."

Heat floods into my cheeks—his tone is stern but his eyes are playful—and the whole scenario makes me want to crawl into a hole. Preferably a hole stocked with a nice clawfoot bathtub and eucalyptus bath salts and a chilled glass of rosé, but beggars can't exactly be choosers out here.

We're on the trail in no time after that. Thorn tells us we'll be spending most of today in Valerie Forest again, but that the campsite we're working toward is just outside it, about six miles from here.

I'm near the back of the pack today, just ahead of the tennis girls and Matteo. I hadn't realized he was so chatty—he's barely spoken to Thorn the whole time we've been out here, despite the fact that they're supposedly leading together. With the girls, though, you'd think there was a million-dollar prize at stake for who can ask the most questions.

Matteo is easily the front-runner in that contest right now.

Two miles in, the trees start to blend together, and I wonder how anyone ever made it all the way through this forest in the first place without getting hopelessly lost.

Thorn navigates effortlessly, pointing out the various birds that flit across our paths (I've already forgotten their names) and the sound of water in the distance. I have to strain to hear it at first, but the longer we walk, the louder it is—until suddenly, the woods open up and the water is right in front of us, a frothy, bubbling river that cuts across the landscape.

We come to a stop, waiting until everyone has caught up.

"Behind me is the L'Heureux River," he practically yells, fighting to be heard over the water. "The next segment of our hike will follow alongside it until we reach the main event: L'Heureux Falls. Please be extremely careful on this portion of the trail—the steps are rocky and can get slippery from all the mist coming off the waterfall."

His gaze lands on me, and my cheeks heat up: I can read everything he's trying not to say—between my heavy pack and my lack of hiking boots, I'm a disaster waiting to happen.

Have fun and don't die, Caden's voice tumbles through my head.

Emphasis on the *don't die*.

Matteo leads the way this time as we set off down the riverside path, which—at the moment—is still flat and dry and not that different from walking on the trail. Joshua and Zoe are directly ahead of me now, and seeing them together makes me wonder: What would it have been like if Caden had actually come on this trip?

In theory, it would have been nice to do this with someone I already knew instead of completely on my own. But at the same time, Caden and I wouldn't really have been *with* each other so much as awkwardly keeping our distance the whole time—in a group this size, it would have been lost on exactly no one that we have History™ together, and probably way more uncomfortable than I imagined. I'm really glad he wasn't here to see me holding up the whole trek this morning, or how Thorn had to repack my whole bag for me.

I'm also glad Caden isn't here to see me treading carefully up this rocky path. It's definitely getting steeper—the aforementioned steps Thorn warned us about—but they're still dry for now.

As soon as we round the bend, L'Heureux Falls comes into full view: the waterfall isn't quite *Jurassic Park* levels of majestic, but that's mostly because it's crashing over a solid rock wall and not the green jungles of Kauai. Still, it's gorgeous.

It's also very, very wet.

A fine spray of mist fills the air and covers every surface, rocky steps included. It only gets worse the closer we get to the scenic bridge overlook.

I slow to a snail's pace, terrified I'm going to slip right past the guardrails and into the river below, a cruel and early end to this wilderness adventure. What on earth was I *thinking*? Why didn't I realize hiking boots were on the list for more than just reasons of comfort—but for traction, too? I'm so green at this I don't even know what I don't know, despite all my research.

I take a few tentative steps, then a few more.

It's slow progress, and all is good—

Until the dark part of the next rock turns out to be moss, slick and slippery, and the toe of my right sneaker glides right out from under me.

My entire life flashes before my eyes.

I'm not thriving right now, not one bit. I'm flailing, trying to steady myself before I twist my ankle or fall to my death—

But just as I'm about to go flying into the rocky, raging river, a strong arm wraps around my waist, pulling me back from the brink.

My heart pounds, still very much in *I'm going to die* mode, but the rest of me is steady. The rest of me is safe.

"It's okay," I hear Thorn say, his calm, deep voice cutting through the crash of the waterfall. "You're okay."

His hand is at my hip, fingertips digging deep to hold me in place. He doesn't move a muscle, probably because I'm still giving *wild animal in fight-or-flight* vibes . . . or maybe because he's afraid I'll start to slip again the instant he lets go.

I blink, stunned and a bit shaky.

"You're okay, Sadie," he repeats. "I've got you."

"Thank you for helping me . . . again." I'm irritated that he had to, but grateful.

"It's what I'm here for."

He glances down at my shoes but, mercifully, doesn't give me a hard time about them.

Finally, he moves his hand off my hip. It's a thousand degrees cooler already. He keeps a close, vigilant distance behind me, ready to step in again if needed.

We slowly make our way up to the L'Heureux Falls Crossing bridge. I had hoped to do an epic vlog recording here, but all I can manage is a quick panoramic sweep of the scenery before my phone case is slick with mist. The stone steps are just as treacherous on the opposite side for our descent; I put one foot in front of the other until—finally—we're back on dry ground.

Thorn stays behind me the whole way, the two of us at the back of the pack even once we're caught up with the rest of the group and en route to whatever else might try to kill me out here.

He doesn't say a word.

7

THORN

It's a relief when we're off those damn steps.

That's the closest I've ever come to someone actually having an incident there, and it's more than a little terrifying to think about what could have happened if I hadn't been able to save her. Sadie's going to be the reason for a number of edits to the tour company's packing guidelines, but HIKING BOOTS MANDATORY will surely be the most significant.

This path is more uneven than the one we left behind in Valerie Forest, covered in little white rocks that don't exactly provide stability underfoot, but I'll take it. There's little chance Sadie—or anyone else, for that matter—will have another life-threatening incident on what's left of today's hike. Not due to footwear, anyway.

"It's really pretty out here," Sadie says quietly, pulling me out of my head after we've been walking for a while in silence. She's found her way to my side; the rest of the group is a good bit ahead of us, with Matteo leading the way.

"It is," I agree. From this vantage point, you can see Helen Theresa Peak and the Two Sisters off to the distant south, and a sprawling landscape of rocks and treetops filling everything in between.

A huge reason I do what I do is to get people to pay attention to this sort of beauty: what the world has to offer that isn't just shown on a screen, in air conditioning, with all the comforts a person might crave at their fingertips—distractions, everywhere.

All of this, though, requires me to bring clueless people out of their comfort zones. It's not my favorite thing at the beginning of a trek, but by the end—

That is what keeps me coming back to lead again and again.

I glance down at Sadie's dirty white shoes, then up her long, toned legs. She strikes me as a treadmill person.

"So what made you want to sign up for something like this?" I ask.

I'm genuinely perplexed. I thought I knew her type from the moment I laid eyes on her—a lot of which has played out exactly as I expected so far. That said, people like Sadie don't often sign up for these things on their own; they're usually dragged by a boyfriend or a best friend or a boss.

Or, like Zoe, outright lied to.

"The treacherous rocks, clearly," she says, and I laugh. "And also the bugs."

As if on cue, a mosquito lands on her arm; she slaps it away.

I size her up, determine she needs just a *little* roasting. She's making a joke like that, this soon after she almost fell from said treacherous rocks? She can take it.

"So which was it?" I ask. "*Eat Pray Love* or *Wild*?"

I'd put money on it that at least one of those books is hiding at the bottom of that overstuffed pack right this minute.

"I have no idea what you're talking about," she says—but the way she tries to hide her smile tells me everything.

I knew it.

"So you *didn't* wake up one morning after reading some sort of woman-needs-emotional-cleanse-after-hitting-rock-bottom book and decide you needed to do the same thing?"

She glances down at the uneven trail, concentrating hard so she doesn't trip.

"Okay, fine," she admits, her single dimple popping as she grins. "Emotional cleanse, yes. But no to rock bottom."

I want to ask more about that—why she felt the need for an emotional cleanse at all—because I can relate to that, unfortunately, even if I personally believe books like *Eat Pray Love* have sent more women home on crutches than with a healed heart.

Probably best to keep a professional distance, though.

"Are you some sort of influencer?" I ask instead. "Is that why you're always on your phone?"

She scoffs. "I am not '*always on my phone*,'" she protests, air quotes and all. "I've hardly looked at it all day!"

"Sure," I say, giving her a hard time even though she's right—she hasn't had it out as much as yesterday. I can't resist digging in a little, though. "Is that why I was woken up this morning by the sweet sounds of you talking to yourself inside your tent?"

She stops in her tracks, and the look on her face is priceless.

"Whoever Caden O'Connor is," I go on, because I really can't help it—Sadie was *not* expecting this, and seeing her flustered is a nice change from the way she's been trying to hold herself together out here, "he sounds like an asshole. *Screw* that guy."

I'm not sure if she wants to high-five me or slap me—for a split second, it looks like she's torn between both options.

No, yeah, she definitely wants to slap me.

"You *eavesdropped* on me?!" she says, eyebrows raised to their limits.

"Believe me, it wasn't on purpose."

"Caden O'Connor *is* an asshole," she mutters, but leaves it at that.

We've finally managed to close the gap between us and the rest of the group, just in time to hear Zoe ask, "Are we there yet?"

Joshua glances over his shoulder with an apologetic look. "Sorry, man," he says. "Zoe isn't used to this much walking."

Zoe swats his chest. "*Babe.* No. I'm just starving, that's all."

Why do people think a trek in the Sierras will be an easy walk in the park? We're out here for days on end. It's really not something you should casually decide to do unless you're willing to put in the work.

Then again, it sounds like Zoe didn't get to make that choice for herself.

"We're about an hour's walk from our campsite for the night," I offer, "but if you need to rest—"

"I just need a *snack*," Zoe interrupts, cutting a glare at Joshua. "I'm fine! Fine."

One of the tennis team girls—Brittany, the one with the long blonde ponytail braid and a paint-splattered visor—pulls a protein bar from her pack and hands it over.

"Oh . . ." Zoe says as she waves it away. "Thanks, but I'm allergic to peanuts."

"She's not allergic," Joshua adds flatly. "She just doesn't like them. You've got to stop saying that, babe, it's insensitive to people with *real* allergies."

"*I'm* sensitive," she protests. "They make me break out."

"But they won't, like, make you *die*," he says, losing patience. "I really think you should eat something—"

"I have roasted pumpkin seeds if you'd like some?" Sadie cuts in, pulling a snack-sized Ziploc bag from one of the zippered pockets of her backpack.

Zoe's face melts in relief. "Yes, please! You're a lifesaver."

I glance around the group and catch the tail end of an eye roll from Brittany as she stuffs the rejected protein bar back in her pack.

"So we're good, then?" I ask. "One more hour?"

No one speaks up—so I take that as an all-clear.

The sun dips lower over the horizon, and we make steady progress. It's still late afternoon, but we'll need to have a smooth crossing at Cloverleaf Creek if we don't want to set up camp in the dark. We're finally at the portion of the path that follows the curve of the creek, a quarter-mile stretch that eventually forks off in two directions: the left fork leads to another set of cliffs and small lakes, and the right—when water levels allow—leads straight to our campsite.

We should have no problem crossing the creek tonight. There've only been two times I've ever seen it impassable, and while it's rained more than usual over the last few months, we aren't freshly off any torrential downpours. At its highest, the water is shin deep.

"Aww, *sick*—we get to wade through that?" Trey says when we're all gathered at the edge, his eyes sparking excitedly.

"We have to *wade* through that?!" Zoe exclaims, horrified. "Where's the bridge?"

"You can wade through if you want," I say, more to Trey than to Zoe. "This water's calm enough—but I wouldn't recommend it unless you want your shoes to be soaking wet. For everyone who'd like to stay as dry as possible, there's a natural rock bridge."

A few of the rocks are jagged and angular, and one is a bit of a stretch to reach, but otherwise they're flat and smooth—it's a challenge of balance more than anything else, stepping carefully from one rock to the next.

"Pray for me," Sadie says with a grimace, glancing down at her shoes. "Can I just go barefoot?"

"Even riskier that way, unfortunately," I tell her.

Matteo demonstrates the most efficient way to cross, hopping from stone to stone like he's on *American Ninja Warrior*.

Not everyone is so light on their feet. Hunter struggles—his height comes in handy for making long strides over the water, but his balance isn't the best. Silas manages just fine; Trey doesn't even bother with the rocks and trudges straight through the water. He offers a hand to Zoe—Joshua made it across with no issues, leaving her behind to fend for herself—while Brittany, Emma, and Parker look like pros.

Sadie, at the back of the pack, is reluctant to step out.

I don't blame her, after what happened this morning—but we're the last two waiting to cross, and we're losing daylight quickly.

"What do you need from me?" I ask.

It takes effort to sound patient. I'm not sure I *do* sound patient.

She bites her lip, eyeing the rocks warily. "Sorry, sorry. I can do this."

"You can," I agree, trying my best not to scare off her sudden surge of bravery. "I'll be right behind you. It's not deep—all that's at risk here are wet shoes."

That's not *exactly* true—she could slip and hurt herself, in theory, if she were out here on her own—but I'm more than capable of preventing a dangerous fall. I'll steady her before anything like that comes close to happening.

She swallows, nods. "Okay. Okay, I'm going."

I don't believe it until the toe of her sneaker makes contact with the first rock—but it does, and she's solid, confidence already higher than before. She glances over her shoulder to smile at me, but wobbles just a little.

"Eyes ahead, not on me!" I instruct, a little more drill sergeant than I intend.

She listens, though, and makes her way to the next rock with ease.

I follow, one step behind.

"You can do it, Sadie!" Trey calls, ever the hype guy. "You've got this!"

It's smooth going until we get to the first jagged rock, its surface jutting out of the water at a thirty-degree angle.

"The trick with this one is to go quickly," I coach her. "Don't plan to stop on it—just put one foot on, then push off to the flat one right after it, okay?"

She nods, her entire focus on the rocks. We're *so* close. Three more rocks after the trickiest one and we'll join the rest of the group.

"Don't think too much about it," Parker calls out, to everyone's surprise; she's been the quietest of the three tennis girls so far. "Don't think about what could go wrong—just picture it going right."

It's great advice, and it works.

Sadie takes a deep breath, pushes off from one rock to another, then powers straight through the rest. Parker and Trey bury her in a hug when she's safely across; Emma and Brittany join in, too.

When Sadie finally pulls away, she turns to me, beaming.

No one has looked at me like that in a long, long time. It's a smile so open, so sincere, so unguarded—so *personal*, reminding me I'm a person, too, and not just the leader on the outside whose sole purpose is to get everyone from place to place.

Sometimes I forget that.

Sadie's smile stirs something in me, and it scares me: my first instinct is to push it away. The last person to look at me like that was Blair, and she ran off with Matteo to Peru . . . so . . . yeah. There've been other nice people along the way, of course, but they always leave and never look back. It's become a habit of mine to not get close in the first place.

I swallow, keeping my face neutral as I give her my most professional nod of approval. Falling for one of my trekkers is the *last* thing I need out here—it's against the rules, for one. I also simply can't afford to be distracted. What would have happened to Sadie today on those slippery steps if I hadn't been alert enough to spring into action?

Nothing good, that's for sure.

For her best interest and mine, I should probably keep my distance.

"Ready to head out?" Matteo says, addressing the rest of the group—but not me. Never me, not the entire time we've been out here.

One by one, they fall in line behind him. Sadie lets the others go first, hanging back to wait for me, and gives me another smile even brighter than the first.

"Thanks for today, Thorn," she says, that cute dimple popping once again.

That's when I know I'm in trouble.

8

SADIE

I'm so proud of myself I could cry.

Today was hard. Like *really* hard. There hasn't been a moment all day without pain of some sort—my shoulders, my back, my hips, my feet. A headache that started blooming somewhere around mile four. Add in my treacherous experience back at the waterfall, crying would make sense.

The creek shouldn't have scared me. It was, objectively, not scary—the water was so clear I could see fish swimming.

I'm proud of myself for not listening to the voice in my head that kept whispering *rocks are slippery, rocks are deadly, maybe rocks and rivers are not your thing.* I listened to Thorn instead—and Trey, and Parker—and their voices drowned out the anxiety.

I've survived another day.

I really want to upload some stuff to Instagram—but after finding out Thorn overheard me recording today's vlog footage, I'm a little self-conscious.

"Need any help?" he asks, glancing over at my efforts to secure a tent peg in the ground.

"Not sure why you'd think that," I reply. If I make a joke out of it, the truth will sting less: I, Sadie Whitlock—competent in *many* areas of my real life back home—have been an utter disaster out here. "Not like I've needed your help with anything else so far."

He bites down on a laugh. "Right."

I'm struggling with this particular peg, but too stubborn to admit it. He *knows*, too—about the struggle and the stubbornness, I can tell—but he gives me space, pretends he believes I've got it under control.

I do not have it under control.

It's partly secure, but I must have hit a root or something because the peg won't go in any farther. Thorn hovers behind me, silent but *there*, making it even more difficult to concentrate. I pull the peg out altogether, readjust the placement of the tent flap, and try again. It's better this time, but still gets stuck three-quarters of the way into the ground.

An abrupt and resonant clanging suddenly echoes through the clearing, startling me—I flinch so hard Thorn and I collide, the back of my shoulder making solid contact with his chest.

Matteo, apparently, has a cowbell. "Dinner in ten!" he calls out.

"*So* sorry," I say, laughing. "YouTube did not say there would be cowbells."

"Guess you must have watched the wrong videos. Are you okay?"

"Oh, I'm good—but are *you*?" YouTube also did not advise on what to do when you accidentally bodycheck your wilderness guide.

"You pack the punch of a hummingbird," he replies. "I'm fine."

"I don't know whether to be flattered or offended," I tell him, grinning. "So what's for dinner? Sushi? Steak? Ice cream?"

He laughs, playing along. "There's that research coming through for you again. If you're lucky, there'll also be chocolate lava cake fresh out of the oven."

"Please tell the chef I'd like raspberry sauce on mine." *Ugh*, I miss raspberries.

"Want to know a secret?" he says, leaning in conspiratorially. It's a nice change: a rare glimpse of the Thorn I met when I first arrived, before he became Super Serious Hiking Guide Thorn. "I have a bar of dark chocolate with raspberries in my pack right now."

I pull away and swat his arm. "Who's the overpacker now?"

He laughs. "If you're nice, I might share."

"Noted," I say, playing right back.

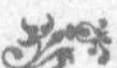

At dinner, we gather around the campfire, devouring grilled corn and a variety of prepackaged nuts and jerky and dried mango, all courtesy of Matteo.

This is the best corn I've ever had—and that's coming from someone whose best friend is absolutely obsessed with corn. Abby has dragged me across the country to not one but *three* corn festivals throughout our friendship together.

I've had every kind of corn imaginable. I've even had *this* kind of corn—the kind that's been grilled directly over the fire while the husks were still on—but maybe Matteo's just perfected his technique somehow?

Suffice it to say, it's pretty incredible.

"Don't get used to it," Matteo says as I reach for seconds. "There's only enough for tonight."

"Can we convince you to come be our chef up at the coffee shop?" Trey says, licking his fingers. "You're super talented, bro."

"Thanks, man. Reminds me of Peru—one of the guys I knew down there made it all the time." He grabs a second helping for himself. "I've thought about going to culinary school, actually."

Matteo's more talkative than I expected, especially after seeing how silent he's been with Thorn. While the rest of us are exhausted and ravenous after all the hours of hiking, Matteo has seemingly endless energy to burn. This is the fourth time he's brought up Peru.

It's also the fourth time Thorn has tensed up at the mere *mention* of Peru. He rips off his corn husk in rather violent fashion.

Whatever's going on between them, it most definitely has to do with Peru.

Sparks and embers flicker from the campfire as a trail of smoke winds its way toward the starry night sky. I haven't experienced darkness like this—aside from the warm glow of the fire—since I was a little kid out on my grandparents' ranch, hunting for constellations from the comfort of their enormous backyard hammock.

"You don't happen to have any s'mores stuff, do you?" Parker, the quiet tennis player with flawless brown skin and long black locs, sounds hopeful.

"Thought you'd never ask!" Matteo says with a wide smile, his teeth movie-star perfect even in near darkness. A few seconds later, he produces a bag of thick marshmallows from his pack.

Everyone springs into action, collecting twigs and loading them up with marshmallows.

Everyone, that is, but Thorn.

"You don't like s'mores?" I ask.

He shrugs. "Just letting everyone else go first. What's your excuse?"

"Oh, you know, just letting everyone else go first," I reply, matching his inflection tone for tone, an experiment to see if I can make him laugh again.

He does, and the sound of it catches me off guard—there's just something so attractive about the way he laughs, that deep voice and how surprised he always sounds to be laughing at all. It's like he's out of practice at it, like he's coming up for air after being underwater just a little too long.

We scrounge around for a stick to use and find the perfect one right behind my tent: it forks at the end, a double prong that will allow us to roast two marshmallows at once.

Thorn follows me back over to the fire, where a lively debate is happening about proper marshmallow-roasting technique—the coffee bros are all in favor of letting them catch fire and char until the entire outside is crispy and molten black, while the tennis girls are Team Ooey-Gooey-But-Still-Recognizably-Marshmallow. Joshua and Zoe are on opposite sides of the debate; the more I see how they interact with each other, bickering one minute then kissing the next, the more I wonder if their incessant PDA is the only interest they actually have in common.

Matteo, predictably, enjoys everything.

"How do you like yours?" Thorn asks me. He holds his hand out for my—*our*—stick. "May I?"

I snort. "Please, be my guest. And no strong opinions, really . . . I like them edible?"

I'm guessing Thorn has infinitely more practice at this than I do, as my experience with s'mores can best be summed up in precisely two categories: the kind I've made in the microwave at home, and the deconstructed s'mores-inspired desserts I've had at fancy restaurants.

Seeing as we're lacking in both the microwave and five-star-chef departments, I'm happy to let him take this.

He roasts our marshmallows until they're on the verge of catching fire, then pulls them out. I'm ready with a paper plate full of graham crackers and chocolate, and together, we assemble them.

Everyone settles into their own groups—tennis girls, coffee bros, Joshua and Zoe and their drama. I catch Matteo glancing our way when Thorn isn't looking, watch a decision play out on his face: there's no way he's coming over here. Sure enough, he heads over to the tennis girls, and they make room for him to join them, laughing at something he's said.

This, Thorn notices too.

I tilt my head toward Matteo. "So what's up with you guys?"

He coughs, narrowly avoiding death by graham cracker. "What do you mean?"

I study him. "The fact that you're supposed to be 'coleaders'"—I add air quotes for emphasis—"but haven't spoken a single word to each other since we've been out here?"

"That's not technically true," he says. "He's been talking all night, and I was within listening distance the whole time."

I smirk. "Okay, yes, that *totally* counts."

Thorn lowers his eyes, focusing intently on *not* choking as he takes a long sip from his water bottle to clear out his problematic bite of s'more. The longer it takes for him to meet my eyes again, the more I feel like maybe I should have thought twice before bringing it up.

"You know what?" I say. "I shouldn't have asked—"

"It's fine."

It's not. The silence stretches between us as he takes another bite. A tiny bit of gooey marshmallow catches on his lower lip, and he licks it away with a flick of his tongue.

I take another bite of my own s'more, not sure what to say now that I've made things awkward.

"You're pretty brave, coming out here all by yourself," he says, an abrupt subject change, not at all what I was expecting.

"You think?" I ask after another bite, as if it hadn't even occurred to me. In all honesty, I've been thinking it myself—but it's validating to hear it from him.

He gives a deep nod. "I do."

I take it in, waiting for another joke about *Eat Pray Love* or *Wild*—*both* of which are in my pack as we speak, by the way, but I will not be admitting that anytime soon.

The joke never comes. Instead, there's a thoughtful look on his face as he studies me. Like he's looking for the real answers to the question he asked earlier on the trail: What made me want to sign up for something like this?

I got broken up with for being too high-maintenance! a voice shrieks through my head, so loud I fear I've actually bared my soul to this entire campsite full of strangers. *I signed up out of spite to prove something to my ex, but he flaked, and now I'm here on this miserable adventure alone!*

"All of this is new to me," I tell him instead, something vulnerable and honest that doesn't feel like too much. Caden always closed up whenever I started sharing the depths of my feelings, said I should save that stuff for my conversations with Abby. "Obviously. But that was my goal, I guess—to put myself in a situation where I can only prepare so much for whatever's going to happen." And then, because even that much feels a little *too* raw for the moment, I twist it into a joke: "I packed my whole house for this trip, though, so I think we'll be good if an apocalypse hits while we're out here."

He laughs, throaty and deep. "Yes, I can see how a sleep mask and a satin pillowcase would come in handy for that," he quips.

"Being well rested during an apocalypse does sound optimal," I reply, and now we're both laughing.

"And the coffee?"

"That's for being *alert* during the apocalypse."

"And your lip gloss?"

"If our apocalyptic oppressors are easily distracted by the idea of kissing shiny lips that taste like vanilla, well—that could also be useful."

His gaze flicks down to my lips, just for a split second, then back up to my eyes. Instinctively, I look down at his lips, too. They look soft: it's a very good thing I'm not a distractible apocalyptic oppressor, honestly.

"I'm guessing you could justify every single thing you brought," he says, grinning.

"*And* every single thing my best friend made me leave at home."

"You do know an apocalypse is unlikely, yes?"

"We're out in the woods for almost two weeks," I say, only a little overdramatic. "No electricity. No refrigeration. No reliable internet signal. No mattresses or plush duvets. It's *basically* the same thing."

He shakes his head, then finally finishes the last of his s'more in one huge bite. I finish mine, too, the marshmallow now pleasantly warm instead of blisteringly hot.

"Let me ask you this," Thorn says after a moment. "Did you happen to bring a journal with you?"

"It was either a journal or *Eat Pray Love*," I can't help but admit. "I'll let you guess which one I chose."

He cracks the widest, brightest smile. "I knew it! You actually brought it with you?"

"No comment," I say, but of course I don't have to confirm it. "Why do you ask about the journal?"

"I recommend it every now and then when someone's brand-new at this—you'd be surprised to go back and read how your thoughts change from the first day to the last. People like you tend to get a lot out of it."

"People like me," I repeat. "People who aren't quite at rock bottom but need an emotional cleanse?"

If I say it first, it won't sting as much as it would to hear it from him.

But he just furrows his brows, gaze unfocused and fixed on the fire—until he turns and looks me straight in the eye.

"People like you," he says again. "Brave people who try something new, all alone, even though they know it will make them uncomfortable. People like me are used to this, but you—it's still *new* for you. You should write down what you notice, the good and the bad and the beautiful, and the things that scare you, and the things you miss from home. If you do it first thing in the morning and right before bed every night, I think you'd be surprised to read back over it after the trip ends."

I expected a lot of things out of this trip, but "wilderness guide who is in touch with his emotions and recommends daily journaling so I can process mine" was not on my radar—especially since my first impression after we got out on the trail was that he had a stick up his ass.

I have to say, I'm pleasantly surprised.

"That sounds great and all," I reply. "But perhaps you missed the part where I said I left my journal at home."

His eyes flash in the glow of the campfire. "Good thing I packed an extra for myself, then."

Before I know it, he's disappeared into his tent. When he comes out again, he's holding a slim cahier notebook.

"*You* keep a journal?" I ask, though perhaps I shouldn't be surprised.

"Every day for the last nine years," he says. "Some entries are long, others are just a single line."

"You must have shelves full of them by now."

"More like a box under the bed," he says. "And I burned a couple of them one time. On purpose," he adds when he sees the look on my face. "Some things you want to remember. And some things . . . you don't."

His words hang between us. He looks up to the night sky, at the impossibly gorgeous display of stars.

"Anyway," he says after the silence starts to stretch on too long, "if you need a writing prompt, you can start with 'Why I Should Have Invested in Hiking Boots.'"

I laugh and give him a light swat on the arm.

"Thank you," I reply, taking the journal and a blue ballpoint pen I didn't notice upon first glance. "I'll start it tonight."

He's quiet again, and only now do I realize we're the only ones still outside of our tents.

"Well," Thorn says suddenly, sounding more like his serious hiking guide persona and less like the guy who got momentarily distracted by my shiny vanilla lip gloss earlier, "I'd better let you get started, then. We've got another long day tomorrow and you'll want to get some good sleep."

The thought of hiking all day tomorrow is too much right now—everything is still aching from today from my head to my toes. My Advil barely made a dent.

"And Sadie?" he says just as I'm about to climb into my tent.

I look up. "Yeah?"

"Enjoy your sleep mask." He smirks like a guy who's never even *considered* using a sleep mask, let alone tried one.

"Oh, I plan to," I play along. "You're going to wish you had one at the crack of dawn."

He lets me have the last word, then heads over to the campfire, which has dwindled considerably since Matteo last fed it.

"You're not going to bed?" I ask.

"Just putting out the fire so it won't go unattended all night," he says.

"Need any help?"

He shakes his head. "Done it a million times. Thanks, though."

Inside my tent, I fumble around until I find the small touch lamp in the corner. Light blooms under my fingertips, bright enough to see the entirety of my tiny space and everything in it. I sit cross-legged with the highest part of the tent directly over my head, and open up my brand-new journal.

To my surprise, it's already been written in.

At first I think Thorn's made a mistake and given me *his* journal—his own personal one with his own personal thoughts—but I'm too curious to look away, and as it turns out, my name is the first word.

Sadie, he's written in a neat italic slant, *You can do this. —Thorn*

CAPTAIN'S LOG // AUGUST THORN

Day 2 • 9:42 p.m. • 73°F • Partly cloudy

TREK NOTES

Things that went smoothly today:

- Late start, but got everyone from place to place in decent time
- Minimal complaints from the group—bodes well for good ratings
- Great weather, good food—also good for ratings

Things that weren't so great:

- Matteo and I still aren't speaking. It's awkward, at best, but could be a real problem if we don't deal soon.
- Sadie—She's trying, which I appreciate. Her shoes are definitely an issue. This morning's late start was due to her elaborate setup.
- My own focus. Between Matteo and Sadie, I'm more distracted than usual—be careful to maintain focus tomorrow for the sake of the group.

FOR DAD

- Cloverleaf Creek looked healthy—not too high, not too low
- Saw two types of hummingbirds near the creek bed—Anna's Hummingbird and Calliope Hummingbird

9

THORN

I wake up from a dead sleep in the middle of the night.

It's windy—but I've slept through worse.

I sit very still, listen to the sounds of the nocturnal landscape: I hear a faint rustling, growing louder.

My first instinct says *bears*, even though I've never had an encounter in this part of the Sierras—there's a first time for everything, though. I've heard rumors of them raiding campsites in neighboring parks, in Kings Canyon and Sequoia and Yosemite.

All at once, the rustling stops.

The wind picks up again. Maybe I'm still half asleep, but it almost sounds like it's saying my name.

"*Thorn*," I hear again, more urgently this time—and also more distinctly human.

I unzip my tent and find myself face-to-face with Sadie.

The sight of her makes me forget everything, and for a split second the world is nothing but her silk pajamas and that mane of untamed hair and her eye mask haphazardly pushed up like a headband and her long, long legs—

But then she says my name again and it all comes into focus.

"What are you doing?" I whisper.

It's got to be three or four in the morning, and the last thing I want to do is wake up the entire camp.

"My tent, uh—it's kind of annihilated at the moment?" She grimaces, glancing over to look at it. "Can you come help me?"

"'Kind of annihilated'?" I ask, rubbing a hand over my face as my eyes adjust to being awake.

"Just come see?"

I climb out of my tent, and—oh—

There's a dark blob of fabric crumpled on the ground, limned in moonlight.

I can't help it, I laugh. "Did this, like . . . *fall* on you?"

She swats my arm playfully like she did earlier, when we were talking. I like it more than I should.

"*Yes* it fell on me, Thorn! Don't laugh!" Despite her best efforts, my laughter is contagious, and now we're both trying to stifle it. "I woke up thinking I was drowning—but it was just the tent on my face. I think the wind tore one of the pegs out of the ground, maybe?"

I bite back a smile. "Well, my first instinct was bears—"

"*Bears*?!" she practically shrieks, ripping through the silent night.

I hold up a finger to her lips.

Please, please, let the rest of the camp not wake up in a panic over the nonexistent bears.

"*Bears*?" Sadie repeats in a whisper-hiss. "I was under the impression that bears weren't a *thing* here. The website explicitly said 'lowest risk of bear encounters in all of the Sierras.'"

"There's always a risk of bears," I whisper back, shrugging. "Low risk isn't *no* risk. But I haven't seen one personally—and the people who have say they're mostly interested in food, not people-as-food."

"That is only mildly comforting, Thorn."

"Try to forget about the bears," I say. "Really, it *should* be comforting since I've spent more nights out here than in my own bed at home over the last six years. If anyone would have seen one out here, it's me. And I haven't."

This, I think, finally works.

I move over to inspect the fallen tent. She's right about the peg being torn from the ground—it's the one she was having trouble with before dinner. I should have checked it later, made sure it was secure. Given the high winds, it's no wonder it ripped right out.

Unfortunately, that's not all that ripped: the tent itself is torn clean through, a long gash in the fabric.

"What's the damage?" Sadie asks.

"Definitely not salvageable tonight," I reply. Possibly not at all.

I'll have to remember to ask Danica to bring a new tent along with the fresh batch of food when we meet up for a restock later this week—but until then, one of us will have to go without.

I make a snap decision. "You should sleep in my tent tonight."

She smirks. "Thanks for the invitation, but I'm not sure we know each other well enough yet for *that*."

"Wha— *Oh*." I see, now, what I implied. "I was thinking you could take my tent and I could sleep out here."

"With the bears?"

I laugh. "I thought I told you to forget about the bears."

She sighs dramatically. "I tried. But yeah, no, that didn't work."

I bend down to examine the carcass of her tent. "Your stuff will be good in here until morning—just grab your pillow and sleeping bag and I'll move mine out to make room."

"You're sure you don't mind sleeping out in the open?"

I grin. "I've done it countless times before. It'll be okay."

"What about tomorrow night?"

I take a deep inhale. I'm quickly learning that Sadie loves a plan and hates not having all the answers at once.

"That's for our tomorrow selves to worry about," I reply with calm confidence. "Let's get through tonight and go from there."

She looks like she's debating asking another question, but in the end, her trust in my answer wins out over her desire to know every single detail.

"Here," she says. In one fluid motion, she pulls her eye mask off and offers it to me. "You're going to need this more than I will when the sun comes up."

When I don't immediately take it—anyone who knows me would laugh at the idea of me willfully wearing an eye mask at all, let alone one made of pink silk—Sadie reaches out and guides my hand up to meet her outstretched one. She settles the eye mask into my palm and closes my fingertips over it before I can protest.

"You'll thank me in the morning," she says, grinning.

When we're all tucked in for what's left of the night, Sadie in my tent and me under the stars, I slip it on.

It's even softer than I expected, and more comfortable, too—and it smells like rosemary and mint, which I can only guess is the scent of her shampoo.

How am I supposed to sleep now?

It's not the rocky ground directly underneath my sleeping bag keeping me awake, or the unlikely threat of bears, or the way the sleep mask feels like a luxury I never knew I might possibly want, let alone *enjoy*—

No. It's that, after just two days out here, Sadie Whitlock has effortlessly unraveled the professionalism I'm usually so committed to maintaining . . . and the fact that, despite the voice in my head trying to tell me that trekker/guide relationships are off-limits, a louder voice is unhelpfully pointing out that I haven't been this intrigued by a woman since I met Blair nearly three years ago.

I'll just have to do better tomorrow. Head down, one foot in front of the other, resist the pull of getting close. At best, Sadie will leave at the end of the trek anyway, like everyone else always does. At worst, I could lose focus on my job—or lose my job altogether.

The thought scares me.

Even though Sky Ranger's offer is still on the table, I just don't know if I'll ever be able to leave the tour company—I don't know if I could ever leave this *place*. This place is part of my soul.

Maybe *that's* what scares me: I've built my whole life around these trails, this job. This park has been part of me for as long as I can remember—

So who would I be without it?

"What are you doing out here? And what the hell is that on your face?"

It's bright and early when I peel back Sadie's (surprisingly effective) sleep mask, the sun blinding even with Matteo's head eclipsing it.

"Good morning to you, too," I grumble.

I most definitely did not get enough sleep.

"Wind?" Matteo asks, gesturing to Sadie's fallen tent behind me.

"Yeah. I gave her my tent, and she gave me . . . this." I peel the sleep mask off, disappointed to find I already miss the comfortable fabric against my skin. The last thing I need is to become a sleep mask guy.

I glance around camp. No one else is up yet, though I'm sure that won't last long.

Usually, I love being the only one awake. I love moments of

solitude—the way the colors of the sky shift with the rising sun amid sounds of birdsong and babbling streams and leaves in the breeze.

Being the only one awake *with Matteo*? It kind of ruins the dynamic.

I groan inwardly, knowing what I have to do.

"Can we talk for a minute?" My voice sounds hard and uninviting even to me. "Before everyone else gets up, I mean. So we can, uh . . . get on the same page about . . . all of this."

Matteo, until everything went down between us, used to be the most happy-go-lucky person in my world. The most loyal friend, always offering to help before I even realized I needed it—especially since I've always had a hard time *asking* for it. His chill-but-energetic vibe was a magnetic force that drew everyone to him whether they realized it was happening or not.

I like to think that's how Blair fell for him. That it was an accident, something that happened without either of them realizing.

But then again, they both *accidentally* ended up moving to Peru together for the last two years. And conveniently neglected to tell me about it until it was too late.

This morning, Matteo is a dim version of his usual self: his demeanor is not quite heavy enough to show the gravity of how far our friendship has fallen—but still edgy enough to reassure me that I'm not the only one who feels it.

"Sure, man," he replies.

We walk in silence over to the bank of the stream. There's a boulder at the edge of the water, small enough to climb but wide enough for both of us to sit.

I settle myself onto it and Matteo follows my lead.

A trout swims past, oblivious to everything but the current carrying him toward his next meal.

That's how I need to be now, I decide: *Just be a trout, Thorn*, I tell myself. I need to focus on the mission, the hike, our next meal, our next stop—how to get the group from here to there. Not what Matteo did, or didn't do, in the past. That's irrelevant to the mission.

"Okay, so for today," I say, putting on a voice that's all business, "you can take the lead again. We need to cover a lot of ground in order to get to the lake by tomorrow night, so I'll need your help to keep us moving while I make sure the back of the group keeps up at a decent pace, and—"

"Thorn," he interrupts, the exhausted edge to his voice so sharp it cuts me right off. "Just say what you really want to say, man."

It's so unlike him—so direct, so assertive, so *un*chill—that every thought about the trek flies right out of my head.

Just say what you really want to say, man.

I'm not sure he's ready for what I really want to say.

Everything I can think of feels like it would just be salt in old wounds—and not just his. Salt in *my* wounds, too.

"Look, if you're still hung up on Blair, I get it. She's incredible. I tried not to fall in love with her, I really did."

My mouth goes dry. Where to even begin with all of that?

"It's not about Blair," I say evenly. "Blair can make her own choices, and clearly I'm not what she wanted."

It's actually more freeing to say this out loud than I expected: it doesn't feel like salt *in* a wound so much as salt on an old scar. I think there was some part of me, deep down, that feared it *was* Blair I was still hung up on.

"And honestly," I go on, "it didn't completely surprise me when Blair left."

Blair reminded me of a bird from the moment I met her, too much energy to stay in one place for long. I think I always knew she'd take off with some other guy one day, but I talked myself into thinking maybe I was the one who'd be worth staying for.

I take a deep breath. He told me to say what I really wanted to say, and this is it.

"But you—*you* surprised me. It wasn't just some other guy she left with. You were my best friend, Matty. You were supposed to be here to help me get through our eventual breakup, not be the reason it happened."

Matteo's face goes completely blank.

I was right. He wasn't ready.

And truthfully, neither was I. This feels like an entire *vat* of salt in a very raw wound.

"Are you still with her, at least?" I ask after a long minute.

He clearly regrets bringing it up. I bet he wishes he'd just let me keep talking about our itinerary for the next two days.

Finally, he clears his throat. "Yeah," he says, picking at a thumbnail, not meeting my eye. "I moved back to get a place for us to settle down."

The idea of Blair settling down anywhere just doesn't sit as it should—what I said was true, I never could imagine her staying with me forever, and I still can't imagine her staying with anyone else. Not even Matteo.

But I'm not about to say so.

"I didn't even know you were back until Danica told me," I say instead.

There was a time when we saw each other daily, when we knew each other's plans as well as we knew our own. He was my closest friend.

"Yeah, I realized last week that I was just kinda done with Peru," he replies. "We both were, but she stayed a bit longer to help with one more hike—they're sort of scrambling to fill our spots. I flew home over the weekend and reached out to Danica as soon as I got back since our savings won't carry us for long. I forgot how expensive shit is here."

Again: Where to even start? Am I hearing this correctly—that they just decided on a whim, *last week*, to ditch their jobs and move back to California together without doing any real prep work to secure jobs or housing or—

I can't think about it too much. It's a headache waiting to happen.

Was Matteo always this flighty, or has Blair just rubbed off on him? His sudden move to Peru was a blindside when it happened and seemed totally out of character.

Well, if this is the real him now, maybe he and Blair *will* work out: maybe they'll flit around the world together, tied to each other and not necessarily a specific place. Birds of a feather and all that.

"For the record," Matteo says, pulling me out of my thoughts, "I never meant for things to go like they did with Blair—it all just kind of happened."

How can he not see that this excuse doesn't actually make anything less painful? When he says *it all just kind of happened*, all I hear is *I liked what was happening too much to stop it.*

I'm not like Matteo: how people gravitate to him, how he makes friends everywhere he goes. It's much harder for me to let people in.

When he left, my world went silent for a long time. It's harder to make lasting friends when you're out in the woods with strangers all the time, in a leadership position that prevents you from getting as close as everyone else gets to each other . . . and then they all inevitably fly home, and the next group takes their place.

I'm still at a loss for words when the sound of footsteps—the crunch of hiking boots in gravel—saves me.

There's Hunter, his six-foot-five shadow long under the morning sun. He's got a speckled metal camp cup in each hand.

"Either of you want some coffee?" he asks.

Matteo and I spring up simultaneously. Neither of us says so, but I know without a doubt he's saying a silent thank-you to Hunter for getting us out of this conversation, just like I am.

We follow him back to camp.

The coffee, I admit, is very good.

DAY THREE

Cloverleaf Creek Campsite to Mackenzie Lake

Fed by glacial meltwater and snowpack, the rivers and lakes in the Sierras are renowned for their glittering, crystal-clear waters. Popular activities in these areas of the parks include fishing, kayaking, and swimming, with many such lakes set against a majestic mountain backdrop. Be sure to pack a camera (and your swimsuit)!

—Henry Herrington, *Backpacking the Sierras: A Beginner's Handbook* (Fourth Edition)

6:32 A.M. • DAY 3 • SADIE'S JOURNAL

Well: here I am out in the woods, and I have successfully made it through *two* entire nights without a) a pillow-top mattress, and b) air conditioning. And we only had *one* tent disaster, so I guess overall, that's a win.

Thorn thinks it would be helpful for me to write out my thoughts & fears & feelings so I can look back on them after all of this is over to see how much I've grown . . . and I guess there isn't a lot I love more than making lists, and I've always been an overachiever when it comes to assignments, so here goes:

Hard Things

- Heavy backpack
- SO MUCH WALKING
- Whyyyy did I bring these shoes
- Slick rocks
- Mosquitos suck (literally)
- Sweat everywhere
- Feels like I'm slowing the group down sometimes
- Uncomfortable sleeping conditions*

Scary Things

- BEARS
- Tent catastrophe nearly gave me a heart attack
- What if I have an emotional breakdown and can't call Abby?
- What if I get really bad blisters and can't walk?
- What if I get really bad blisters and lose my bet with Thorn (and lose my coffee due to said bet)?
- Drowning/falling off a cliff/twisting my ankle/pain & anguish of other types that I haven't yet considered
- BEARS (oh wait, just realized I already wrote that)

Good Things

- Nice people

- **Zero regrets about bringing my own coffee**
- **Caden isn't here to see me struggling**
- **Thorn—he's kind of hard to read sometimes, but has been patient with me (mostly)**

***It smelled surprisingly good in Thorn's tent—my guess is laundry detergent & lingering smell of soap on his clothes (pine?)(I will never mock that cliché again)(at least it's not sandalwood)**

10

SADIE

I'm going to need all the coffee in the world to get through this day.

Between my rude awakening in the middle of the night and the slab of rock underneath Thorn's tent, I'm surprised I got any sleep at all.

Not to mention the *dream*.

It involved a certain wilderness guide, the two of us sharing a single sleeping bag, his skin like fire against mine and his breath hot in my ear as he whispered all manner of unmentionable things that make me blush even now—and in my dream, I was as loud as he was quiet, so loud I woke myself up in real life. Darkness instantly turned to dawn, and I was alone in this tent with my eyes wide open and my heart racing and the deep, deep fear that I'd made those noises *out loud*, loud enough to wake up the entire camp.

The dream was so steamy I didn't dare write about it in my new journal: some secrets are just too risky to put down on paper.

I'm in no danger of forgetting, though. I still see him—*us*—every time I close my eyes. I can practically feel Thorn's hands on my body, his lips against mine, his . . . everything else.

The most surprising part? I wanted all of it back as soon as it was over.

To say it caught me off guard is an understatement.

Yeah, I've enjoyed chatting with Thorn and making him laugh. At the end of the day, though, the two of us couldn't be any more different. Caden broke things off because we were "incompatible"—but I feel like any potential connection with Thorn would be testing the limits of *opposites attract*.

He loves nature. I love how nature looks through panoramic windows, from giant plush armchairs in impeccably air-conditioned rooms.

He loves adventure. The most adventurous thing I've done before now is a ski trip up in Vermont—which taught me I'm terrible on the snow, but great at sipping cocoa beside a roaring fire.

He carries his entire world in a pack half the size of mine, while my gigantic one barely holds the essentials of my usual routine . . . if that.

Thorn and I are about as opposite as you get. There's no *way* we'd work.

I admit he's attractive. His hair, his smile, his voice—his *laugh*. Anyone with common sense would be drawn to him!

But, again: there's no way we'd work.

Right?

Even if, hypothetically, I found myself interested—and apparently I *am*, at least on some subconscious dream-world level—I can't imagine *he* would be interested in *me*. He probably wants an outdoorsy type, someone who's up for living minimally. Someone who doesn't film vlog footage while wearing silk pajamas and then make the whole group late because she absolutely *must* make fancy coffee *or else*. For example.

But what do I care what his type is? I couldn't care less, honestly.

Back to the coffee: everything I need to make it is in my pack, which is still over in my crumpled pile of tent unless a bear made off with it in the middle of the night. My clothes for today are still in my pack, too.

I unzip Thorn's tent, poke my head out.

Someone revived the campfire at some point, and the smell of it mixes with the pleasant aroma of coffee. Hunter, Silas, and Trey are up, along with Parker and Emma, circled around their coffee setup, while Zoe looks on from afar, snacking on dried fruit.

On instinct, I scan for Thorn. I don't immediately spot him—

But then my eyes lock on his light blue T-shirt: he's down by the stream, having what appears to be an intense one-on-one with Matteo. *Interesting.* His shoulders look good in that shirt, but not nearly as good as in my dream, when he had *no* shirt.

I tear my gaze away before someone catches me staring.

My mess of a tent looks even worse than I remember. I examine the fabric, run my fingers down the gaping gash. Thorn was right: it's pretty much unsalvageable.

I rummage around in my pack. It's much easier to get to my coffee gear with half of my stuff still in the tent, waiting to be repacked.

"Sadie!" Trey calls out from across the clearing. "Made a cup for you, as promised!"

Oh, right. I had forgotten he'd offered to share some of their company's coffee with me this morning—this is good, actually. Not having to make my own will buy me extra time to pack up my stuff. I refuse to make everyone wait on me again today.

He heads my way, carrying a steaming metal camp cup that boasts the same octopus logo as the tattoo on his forearm.

"Thank you *so* much," I say. I take a sip when he hands it over, careful not to burn my tongue, and it's definitely some of the best coffee I've ever had. "Wow, Trey—this is incredible!"

A cool breeze ripples through the air, leaving my own tattoo-less arms covered in goosebumps.

Trey's eyes drift down to my chest—

Which is when I have the unfortunate realization that I'm not wearing a bra, and these silk pajamas leave absolutely nothing to the imagination.

I cross my arms over my chest just as he realizes he's staring.

His cheeks go pink as he averts his eyes. "Glad you like it! I, uh, gotta go pack up—you can keep the cup for now."

He heads over to his tent, and not a second too soon.

"How'd you sleep?" a familiar voice says a moment later when I'm elbow-deep in my pack, hunting for a sports bra.

When I glance over my shoulder, there's Thorn, sipping on his own cup of coffee.

I'm still very much in my pajamas, and the chill in the breeze is most definitely still . . . hard to miss.

I grab the first thing I see (my toiletry bag) and hug it to my chest, but it's not quite wide enough to cover everything.

Not that I'm *embarrassed* of my oh-so-obvious nipple situation—they're nice nipples, thank you very much—but just the thought of Thorn noticing them is enough to send me straight back to my dream, and everything he did to them.

"How'd I sleep?" I repeat, buying myself time to figure out something true that doesn't make me sound like a princess out of her element. "It was . . . more comfortable than I expected."

Not a lie. It was. I just expected worse.

"How about you?" I ask.

"Decent," he replies. "Oh, here"—he reaches in his pocket with his free hand, pulls out my sleep mask—"thanks for this. It did help with the sun."

I take it and bite back a grin, fighting the urge to say *I told you so*.

"Couldn't resist some fancy coffee?" I say instead, nodding to his camp cup. "I can't help but notice I'm not the only one who brought enough to share."

"Wouldn't want it to go to waste, right?"

I grin. "Admit it—you *like* it!"

He takes another long, deliberate sip. His eye contact feels like a challenge. "It's passable."

His voice carries, loud enough that Trey overhears. "*Passable*?" he says, and I don't think it's just mock offense in his voice. "That's a single origin sourced directly from El Salvador! Gesha wash and everything. It's top-tier, bro!"

Thorn smiles sheepishly. "It's really good," he admits. "I was just downplaying it because, uh . . ."

There's no end to that sentence, probably because *I was just trying to get a rise out of Sadie*—while accurate—is even harder for him to admit than the fact that he really does like the fancy coffee.

Trey looks from Thorn to me, then back to Thorn. A slow smile spreads over his face.

"*I* see," Trey says with a very bro-like sparkle in his eye. "I get it. Okay. I'm gonna just—"

He points his thumb over his shoulder, then heads to the campfire where Hunter and Silas are packing up their gear.

"We should—" Thorn and I blurt out at the exact same time when it's just us again.

"Probably get ready for the day," I finish, and he nods, like that's exactly what he was thinking.

"Let me know when you've got everything out of your tent and I'll help you fold it up," he adds, suddenly all business.

"Thanks," I call after him—

But he's already on his way to check on someone else.

An hour later, when everyone's packed and ready to go, Matteo gathers us into a circle.

"Okay, people, listen up!" he says with special attention toward the tennis girls, who are whispering with each other, totally oblivious.

Matteo clears his throat.

Emma elbows Brittany in the ribs, and they all fall silent.

"For today," Matteo goes on, "I want you to pick one person you didn't know before you got here, and spend all of this morning's hike getting to know them."

"Like some cheesy icebreaker?" Hunter calls out as Emma asks, "Will there be a test?"

"Yes to cheesy, no to a test," Matteo replies, pointing at each of them as he answers. "Embrace the cheese, people! If you don't, we'll do even *more* icebreakers!"

A couple of people groan, but Matteo just grins.

"All jokes and threats aside, you came here to get outside your comfort zones, right? So let's take that first step."

Secretly, I *adore* a good icebreaker.

Give me all the scavenger hunts and forced-proximity get-to-know-you prompts: people tend to stay in their own lanes these days unless they're shoved out of them, so as someone who actually enjoys making new friends, I'm all in favor of it; I find icebreakers *fun*, not torturous.

It should be noted that I am not, and have never been mistaken for, an introvert.

I'm scanning the group, torn between approaching Trey—he's nice, and as a fellow coffee snob, I'd actually enjoy hearing all about their company—and one of the tennis girls.

But then I notice Zoe, looking around for her fiancé on instinct; I follow her gaze and see him chatting with Thorn and Trey. Parker and Emma have already paired up with Hunter and Silas, and Brittany is looking at Matteo like she would happily spend *every* day chatting with him.

"Looks like it's me and you," I say to Zoe. "Want to team up?"

Matteo joins us at the front of the group, Brittany at his side, while Thorn takes up the rear again. I'm hit with a surprising wave of disappointment at the realization that I won't get to talk to him—or even *see* him, really—until we stop for a break at some point.

On the bright side, maybe I'll be able to film some vlog footage in peace today. Zoe certainly won't care.

"Everybody ready?" Matteo calls out.

Ready as I can be, I think. My muscles are less sore today, but I've got a blister forming on my left heel, cushioned with more Band-Aids than are strictly necessary. I tighten the straps of my pack, adjust my sunglasses, pull the brim of my black baseball cap just a bit lower—

And then we're off.

11

THORN

Pull yourself together, man, I chide myself for the fifth time in three hours.

It's a good thing Trey and Joshua hit it off, because I am so not in the mood for an icebreaker. What's the point of forcing conversation with a stranger who's just going to leave your life as quickly as they came into it? I don't make a habit out of asking invasive questions even with people I *do* know well—same with answering them.

And Matteo knows it.

This trek has been an anomaly for me so far. I don't know if I'm just irritable because he's here again after being off the grid for so long, or if I feel off because I'm usually more on the same page with my coleader.

I certainly don't usually make a habit out of flirting with the trekkers—not to mention getting *caught* flirting with the trekkers—but there's just something about Sadie.

She's so out of sorts here, and already bug-bitten to hell . . . it's kind of adorable the way she's trying to pretend everything is fine. I didn't mean to be so casual with her on yesterday's hike, or last night over s'mores—her energy is magnetic, though. She's *easy* to talk to, no icebreaker-level forcing required.

Which is why I'm secretly glad Matteo told everyone to pair off, despite the fact that I hate it on principle: it gives me a reason to keep my distance in every sense of the word. A chance to cool off, to remember that this is my *job* and I am a *professional.*

A professional who might as well have been wearing a neon sign this morning advertising that my weakness is, apparently, brunettes in silk pajamas.

Fortunately, Sadie is now fully clothed in an outfit that at least resembles hike-appropriate clothing, and she's far ahead of me, almost everyone else in between us.

Joshua and Trey are a few steps in front of me, chatting like they've known each other for years. I've heard about the coffee bros' matching tattoos, Joshua's wedding plans with Zoe, and they've now moved on to an unexpected connection between them: diving with sharks.

"Zoe says I'm not allowed to go anymore once we have kids," Joshua says morosely. "Which I get, in theory, but—you know how it is—it's not like the sharks *want* to eat anyone. I stay out of their way, they stay out of mine."

Trey nods along. "Totally. Doesn't she know they hate the taste of neoprene?"

"That's what *I'm* saying!"

"What's the best place you've ever gone on a dive?" Trey asks.

Joshua considers it. "Gotta be between Oahu and Belize. You?"

"Galápagos, bro. Incredible."

I tune out again because—while I do love a good extreme sport that will get your adrenaline pumping—we've just arrived at our rest stop.

Will Matteo remember to give everyone a break? It's a miracle we've made it this far without him leading us in circles; every time I've caught a glimpse of him over the last three hours, he's been talking and laughing with Brittany like he's just one of the other trekkers and not the guy in charge.

I decide to give it a few more minutes. Stepping on his toes would only undermine his authority and piss him off—but at the same time, our pace has slowed considerably.

I'm just about to speak up when Matteo comes to an abrupt halt, looking around like he's finally realized where we are.

"Good news, everyone!" he calls out. "Time for a break. Take thirty and make sure you rehydrate!"

Everyone splits off into their familiar groups—everyone, that is, except for Joshua and Zoe. Joshua joins Trey and the other coffee bros, while Zoe gloms on to Sadie like a barnacle.

A wave of feeling—disappointment? Jealousy?—crashes into me.

I try to resist it. I don't *need* to talk to Sadie, should feel relieved that Zoe's standing in the way of another one-on-one conversation that would only spin me further out of sorts. This is a chance to get my head on straight, talk to some of the others.

A chance to try to convince myself that Sadie's just like the rest of them.

I head over to check in on Brittany, Emma, and Parker. They're all bright-eyed and laughing but fall silent as soon as they notice I've joined them.

"Never mind, I can leave!" I playfully hold my hands up in surrender. "A guy knows when he's interrupting!"

Emma tugs at my elbow, smiling conspiratorially as she pulls me in closer. It's a little more familiar than I'm comfortable with, but I don't resist.

"You can totally stay, it's fine. We were just talking about Brittany and Matteo—"

Brittany swats Emma's shoulder. "There's nothing to talk about," she says, but her eyes say otherwise. "He's just easy to talk to, that's all."

"He has a girlfriend," I say flatly, and her face falls.

It's abrupt, and maybe a little too rain-on-her-parade. If I'd thought for just *half* a second before speaking, I probably wouldn't have said it—

But Brittany seems nice, and Matteo really shouldn't have spent the last *three hours* chatting her up without telling her about Blair.

"He did mention a girl," she says, shrugging. "But maybe I misunderstood—he said she was in Peru."

"They're still together," I say. "I'm sure he didn't mean to give you the wrong impression."

Who am I, *defending* Matteo? And defending Matteo's loyalty to Blair?

Old habits die hard, I guess.

But if there's one thing Matteo isn't, it's a cheater—he'd never purposefully lead anyone on, or do anything to compromise Blair's trust. Then again, I also thought he'd never betray me like he did.

The rest of today's hike is a blur.

Exhaustion sets in for most everyone around midafternoon. Matteo and I are acclimated to this level of activity, but we work in an extra break to accommodate the group. Quiet sets in, too, the icebreaker pairings reaching their conversational limits.

It's a good thing we only have a little over a mile to go. We'll be staying at Mackenzie Lake for two nights, where everyone can have a good, long recovery from our first few days on the trails. We'll fish and kayak and have ample time for rest before continuing on to our next stop.

Mackenzie Lake is one of the places out here that's burrowed its way into my soul. The bad memories are outshined by the good ones—but even those are bittersweet.

The first time I can remember coming out here with my dad, I was around six years old. We went fly fishing and caught more rainbow trout than I've ever caught since; he has an uncanny talent for fishing that I didn't inherit. Most of the trout we released back into the wild, but we feasted on the rest: I remember watching in awe at the skill with which my dad cleaned and prepared them, his movements swift and precise. When I told him I felt sad for the fish, what he said stuck with me: *Everything has its purpose, son. Flowers don't live forever, and neither do fish. Neither do we. Out here, you can see the circle of life in action—nature as it was meant to be.*

At the time, I didn't really grasp what he meant by *neither do we.*

Now, though, I know. The fact that he hasn't been able to see Mackenzie Lake, or any part of the park, with his own eyes for the last few years speaks for itself.

I have these little traditions all over, things I do in his honor that only I know about—things he can no longer do for himself now that his breathing's gone downhill.

I take note of his favorite birds in Valerie Forest.

I carve out a moment of silence at the scenic overlook of Helen Theresa and the Two Sisters.

I quietly count the steps at L'Heureux Falls.

And at Mackenzie Lake, I always look for the perfect stone—something smooth and heavy and relatively flat that fits neatly into the palm of my hand—then send it skipping out over the crystal-clear water.

There are more things along the way, little rituals that make him feel close. I don't get to see him often these days—he moved out to San Francisco to be closer to his lung doctor, and my work schedule means my trips to the city are few and far between. He's in a relationship now, at least, so I'm pretty sure I notice his absence more than he notices mine.

It got a little lonely out here, if I'm honest, when Dad and Matteo and Blair all left within months of each other. I've been around people, sure, my job being what it is—but lonely's not the same as being alone.

By some miracle, we make up a little time in our last hour, even with Hunter stopping to photograph mushrooms, moss, and another bird perched up in a tree. It's been a long day, but I have to admit: the coffee this morning made a difference. Even I've had more energy out on the trail, and I'm positive it's helped the others push through.

It was good, too. *Really* good.

Another thing I'm finally—reluctantly—admitting to myself: I miss Sadie.

Joshua and Trey are nice guys, sure. But if I hear one more story about shark diving (*how* did they talk about it for three hours straight without repeating anything?) . . . I cannot be held responsible for my actions.

I miss roasting Sadie, and the way she's not afraid to roast me right back.

I want to talk to her again. And I hate that I want that, because it's a very bad idea: I'm on the job, I need to stay alert—trek flings are against the rules for a reason. All of these people are depending on me.

But it's only human nature to crave connection.

Fish and flowers can't fight the natural order of things, so what makes me think I'm any different?

12

SADIE

If Caden could see me now, trampling through the wilderness with this planet-sized backpack strapped to my shoulders, I think he'd fall over from shock. He truly didn't think I had it in me to break out of my comfort zone, didn't think I'd ever put myself in a position where I might not excel at something right off the bat.

This is anything but comfortable.

My body hurts; my feet, my legs, my butt, my back, my shoulders. I've also had another headache today, despite popping an Advil and trying my best to stay hydrated. I'm itchy, and sweaty, and despite my trifecta of weapons meant to combat the natural elements—dry shampoo, deodorant, Viktor & Rolf Flowerbomb—I am in desperate need of a shower (or, in lieu of that, a dip in a lake).

I feel the sudden urge to text Abby, reassure her that I'm still alive. My phone probably still has a sliver of battery power—I gave it a little charge this morning—but I doubt I'd get a signal out here. I'll have to dig it out of my bag later, once we're settled.

I imagine Abby back at the JW Marriott pool, flirting with Jonathan while she waits for her spicy margarita. Have they kissed yet? My gut says no, but I'd love to be wrong. If I had to guess what she's doing right this minute, I'd say she's probably stretched out on her lounger, reading a magazine or a novel as the sun beams down, the spa just a few steps away.

I do miss the spa.

And, obviously, Abby herself.

And the drinks.

I'm still dreaming of ice-cold everything when we crest the hill we've been climbing for hours and, suddenly, my breath catches—

The view down below is *stunning.*

When Thorn said we'd be staying at a lake for the next two nights, my mind filled in the lakes I'm used to in the Texas Hill Country: murky and muddy and surrounded by tall grass, maybe some cattle, a huge blue sky as far as you can see.

This lake is nothing like that.

This lake is glittering and gorgeous, nestled in the valley of a pair of rocky mountains that cut into the horizon. Overhead, the sky is still blue, there's just less of it—but it somehow feels like *more* with how it's reflecting on the water. Wildflowers bloom in chaotic patches that have grown up between craggy rocks; the trees, too, feel similar, tall evergreens that rim the jagged lakeline in scattered thickets. A row of brightly colored kayaks sits near the edge of the lake, their yellows and reds and ceruleans at striking odds with the natural landscape.

"*Wow,*" I breathe.

Only when Thorn responds—a low, quiet hum of agreement—do I realize the back of the pack has closed the gap between us. Our entire group gathers at the top of the hill to take in the view.

"Congratulations, everyone!" Thorn says. "That was *not* an easy climb. But the good news is, we've got a couple of days to rest and recover. We'll be spending the next two nights here, so let's go over some ground rules."

We can make campfires at our base camp, but not at any higher altitudes due to park rules.

Our tents should be set up in groups of two or three in the designated spots, and—for our own safety—reasonably close together.

Don't go exploring alone, don't go exploring too *far*, never leave base camp without telling Thorn or Matteo exactly what the plans are.

We'll do a few group activities each day, including kayaking for anyone who wants to participate. We'll have meals together at noon and in the evenings; we're on our own for breakfast. In just a little while, after we set up camp, we'll have a group activity: fishing, followed by a cookout.

"Thorn?" Zoe interjects, startling all of us.

He raises his eyebrows as if to say *go on.*

She glances nervously around the group, her gaze skipping quickly past Joshua's. "If anyone wants to do sunrise yoga, I'm a certified instructor. Meet me down by the lake tomorrow morning if you want to try it."

"Oh!" Thorn says, pleasantly surprised—and probably relieved—that she sounds enthusiastic about something. "Sure, yes. Great idea. Thank you, Zoe."

We head down into the valley to set up camp.

The descent is pure relief—the climb was subtle, but now that we're on our way down again, my pack feels lighter and less cumbersome.

"So, what's the sleeping plan for tonight?" I ask.

Thorn and I walk side by side, the first time since this morning we've been close enough to talk.

"This one's for you," he says, tilting his head backward toward the tent strapped to his pack.

The *extra* tent strapped to his pack, I now realize.

"Did that just magically fall out of the sky when I wasn't looking?" I ask incredulously. "Did I miss an REI somewhere back there?"

Thorn laughs. "It's Emma's. She's going to share with Brittany."

"She doesn't mind?" I ask. "You're sure?" At five foot eleven, Emma's the tallest of their trio—she's Japanese Hawaiian and played beach volleyball before switching over to tennis.

He shrugs. "Said they've been up chatting until two in the morning anyway, and that it might actually be easier this way so they can just crash where they are."

"Well . . . okay, then. That's nice." I cut a glance at him. "Thanks for carrying it for me."

"If this one rips apart in the middle of the night, you're on your own," he says.

I *think* he's joking—but my cheeks flood with heat.

It could have happened to anyone, I remind myself. If they wanted the tents to hold up under high winds, they should've made them out of, like, thick canvas or something.

Unlike our first two campsites, the landscape isn't conducive to all of us staking our tents in a circle—there are a lot of rocks around here, and a lot of trees, so most of the clearings are only spacious enough to handle two tents, *maybe* three. Brittany, Emma, and Parker call dibs on the clearing closest to the kayaks; Trey, Hunter, and Silas take the clearing that's big enough to fit three tents; Matteo sets up next to Joshua and Zoe without even asking Thorn for his preference.

Which leaves Thorn with me on the far end, in the smallest clearing.

My heartbeat picks up.

What if I have another dream? What if I have another dream with him *right there*, separated by only a little bit of nylon fabric? It's such a tight space that our tents will probably be touching. Will he feel it if I shift in my sleeping bag? Will he hear me if I talk—or worse—in my sleep?

"Looks like it's you and me," he says now, his deep voice pulling me out of my head.

I look up from my pack, where I've been digging around for my disposable camera and my phone. So far, I've only found the camera.

"Yeah," I say, standing so he's not towering over me. "Looks like it."

I can't quite tell how he feels—is he okay with this arrangement? Or does he wish Matteo hadn't made the choice for him when he staked his claim near Joshua and Zoe? He seems weighed down, and not just by the extra tent he's been carrying.

"Everything okay?" I ask, feeling him out. "I promise not to wake you up in the morning. I'll *whisper* if I record a vlog!"

He glances up at me, the corner of his mouth lifting just a little. "No, yeah. I'm good. Just a lot on my mind today."

Good seems like a stretch.

He turns to look out at the lake. "Don't tell the others," he says quietly, "but we scored the best clearing. This is my favorite view by *far*."

"I can't imagine any view here being bad," I say.

His fingers land lightly on my shoulder, the slightest tug urging me to shift over so I can see past the gigantic tree at the edge of our clearing. "See how the mountains frame the lake?"

I move closer, so close the dark hair on his arms tickles my skin. It's the barest hint of contact, but it feels electric.

Once the tree isn't blocking my view anymore, I see exactly what he means. "It's amazing," I say, taking it all in.

Even as I say it, I'm not sure whether I'm talking about the mountains and the light sparkling on the water and the wildflowers and the *majesty* of it all, pure and breathtaking . . . or him.

I raise my little Kodak camera up and snap a photo. It won't capture everything about this moment, but when I look back on it, I'll remember how Thorn was beside me, just out of frame.

"Want me to take one with you in it?" he offers.

I laugh. "Not sure I want to ruin the natural beauty with . . . all of this." I gesture down the length of my sweaty, tired body. "I'm sure I look awful."

"You don't."

His two simple words stop me right in my self-deprecating tracks.

My gaze finds his. A bird sings from somewhere off in the distance like we're in some kind of rugged, adventurous fairy tale.

"You don't look awful," he says, as if he's afraid I might have misunderstood the first time around.

I bite back a smile, feel my cheeks heating up.

He holds out his hand for my camera and I give it over.

An hour later, we're all set up down at the lake. There are just enough fishing poles for everyone—they stay here year-round, like the kayaks—and Thorn is about to give a much-needed demonstration. He clears his throat, waiting for Brittany and Emma to stop whispering with each other.

"Has anyone here been fishing before?" he calls out once they're quiet.

Every single guy in the group raises their hands, and so do Parker and Emma. Technically, I could raise mine, too—I went fishing on my grandparents' ranch a number of times—but not since I was in single digits. I'm not confident those skills have stuck around to adulthood.

Matteo passes out poles. Everyone who already knows what to do scatters around the lake, while Zoe and Brittany and I gather at Thorn's side.

"You're going to want to load the bait like this," he says, reaching into the small Styrofoam cup he brought with him.

I don't know what we're all expecting—some brightly colored lure, maybe?—but it definitely *isn't* the squirming worm he produces.

"*What* is *that*?!" Brittany shrieks, at the same time Zoe turns her head away, saying, "Nope, nope. I'm good. I don't need to touch that."

Its wriggling, slimy body is also the last thing I need to touch—but is this not *exactly* the sort of challenge I came out here for? I can feel Thorn's eyes on me, wondering if I'll back down in disgust too.

Absolutely not.

He holds out the cup, and I see now that it's full of dirt and worms. My confident smile falters, and I'm sure he can see straight through it. I swallow down the feeling of revulsion that climbs up my throat and pluck a worm out as fast as I can.

"Ew, Sadie, I can't even *look*!" Brittany wails.

Thorn holds the hook steady as I take a deep breath, knowing what I have to do.

I imagine I'm on *Survivor*, that Thorn is Jeff Probst presenting me with a covered dinner tray that turns out to be fish eyes instead of a delectable vanilla milkshake—that I'll be on track to win the million if only I manage to turn off everything in my body screaming *no!*

"I can do it for you, if you want?" Thorn offers, sensing my hesitation.

I shake my head, determined. "I can."

This is so we can eat dinner tonight, I coach myself. My stomach growls, as if on cue—protein bars and pumpkin seeds only get you so far out here. My body needs calories after all the hiking this week. *You don't need a guy to do it for you. You can take care of yourself.*

I hate every second—but a minute later, it's done.

Thorn loads worms for Brittany and Zoe, who reluctantly agree to participate after my show of bravery, then demonstrates how to cast the reel.

Zoe attempts to cast hers three times, each try worse than the one before—Thorn eventually asks if she just wants to take over his fishing pole, and she takes him up on it immediately. Brittany tries twice, then nearly sends the pole itself out into the lake on her third attempt.

Muscle memory kicks in for me, and I somehow get it right on the first try.

Thorn gives a low whistle. "Impressive, Sadie! Looking good!"

My cheeks go hot. I know he's talking about my surprisingly solid fishing technique, which apparently *did* carry over into adulthood, and not how great my lower half looks in these pants—but the way he's phrased it takes a moment to properly register.

I don't know what sort of magic happens next, but within thirty seconds—a minute at the most—something's tugging my line *hard*.

"Ahhhh, Sadie!" Brittany says, clapping excitedly, forgetting about the fishing pole in her hands. It falls to the ground, but she's far more invested in what's going on with me. "Reel it in!"

Even Hunter and Trey are watching from a bit down the bank as I reel in a good-sized trout. My face hurts from smiling—I did it! I caught a fish all on my own!

"Talk about beginner's luck!" Zoe says, still hanging on to Thorn's line, which hasn't moved even a millimeter.

It turns out to be so much more than beginner's luck—it's more like beginner's *miracle*. Over the next half hour, I pull in six sizable trout. Brittany catches one, while Thorn and Zoe don't have any luck at all. Combined with what the guys catch, we'll have more than enough to feed us all tonight.

I'm so proud I could *burst*. After days of feeling entirely out of my element and like I'm slowing the group down, I'm actually contributing something.

"Need anything else before I go help the guys prep the fish for dinner?" Thorn asks, glancing from Brittany to Zoe to me.

"A vat of hand sanitizer?" Brittany says, and Thorn grins.

"I've got extra up in my pack," he replies. "Happy to share."

Brittany follows with a spring in her step like she's on her way to the spa.

Which, for the record, I would also be doing—but Zoe's sitting on a nearby rock, elbows on her knees and chin in her hands, looking like she might just turn into a statue and stay there forever. Now that it's just the two of us, I can sense a storm brewing from the tension radiating off her.

"Everything all right?" I ask. "It's okay that you didn't catch anything—Thorn didn't, either."

"It's not that."

Zoe toys with her engagement ring, the diamonds glittering in the lingering rays of the setting sun. She spins it around on her finger, then slides it off altogether.

"I'm thinking about breaking things off with Joshua," she says, voice quiet and eyes low.

They present themselves as the perfect couple . . . but there are cracks. Clearly.

"And this is because Joshua wasn't up-front with you about the trip?" I venture. "How you thought you'd be going to Hawaii or Fiji instead?"

She nods, biting her lip as she absently turns the ring over in her hands.

"That," she says, her gaze hard, "and also a comment he made last night. He said he wants to keep diving with sharks even after we have a baby."

Wait. Is she pregnant? Surely I would have remembered if she'd mentioned that.

"Our *eventual* baby," she clarifies, seeing the look on my face. "He knows how worried I get when he goes out on his dives. I just don't think I can be with someone who's willing to risk his life like that—it's one thing when you're single, but when you have a family depending on you, it's just . . . *ugh*. He doesn't get it. And those trips are *expensive*, you know? Why would we dig further and further into debt for something that could end up killing him?"

She makes a lot of valid points, and I say so.

"Thanks," she says with a rueful half laugh. "Honestly, I think he takes his entire life for granted. He thinks he can run off and blow money we don't have to dive with freaking *monster* sharks just because he loves the adrenaline rush, with no regard for what I think about it. He thinks he can spring a trip like this on me—on *me*, knowing I absolutely hate this sort of thing—and assumes I'll go along with it without pushing back." Her expression darkens as she stares at the placid water before us, still toying with her ring. "Are you seeing anyone?"

It's an abrupt subject change, especially considering she hasn't asked a thing about my life since our first hour on the trail together.

A heated rant about Caden forms on the tip of my tongue—

But I swallow it down. I don't think it would make Zoe feel any better to know we broke up because he *didn't* invite me out here. There are parallels, some shared common ground—both Caden and Joshua made some wild assumptions about us—but at the end of the day, I'm out here because I chose to be.

Zoe can't say the same.

"I was," I eventually say. "We broke up a few months ago."

"Ugh," Zoe says. "I'm sorry." She swats at a mosquito. "Well, I told you all of my drama—you can tell me yours, too, if you want."

I swat another mosquito away.

"Thanks," I tell her. "I might take you up on that sometime."

The mosquito near her ear is stubborn—it doesn't get the message, and relocates down to the back of her arm. On instinct, she starts to slap it away—

But while the mosquito doesn't move, her engagement ring does.

"Oh *shit*," she says under her breath, both of us watching in horror as it flies from her hand out into the open lake, a good six feet from the rocks where we're sitting, maybe more. It's shallow and crystal clear here at the edge—but the ring practically swan-dived into the worst place possible, a deeper section of water that neither of us can access without jumping in fully clothed.

My pulse picks up. "No need to panic," I say, but it's futile.

The sun has dipped almost fully below the mountains, leaving everything bathed in dim dusky blue. Honestly, I doubt we'd be able to find it even if it had landed right here next to us in full daylight.

"That was his *grandmother's* ring," Zoe whispers, her face pale. "He's going to freak out, Sadie. What do I do?"

My mind races. There's no getting that ring back—not tonight, for sure. Probably not ever.

We could at least, maybe, put off the inevitable fallout.

"I've got a first-aid kit back in my tent," I say, thinking as fast as I can. "What if I doctor up your ring finger? You could tell Joshua you had an accident—fishing hook, if he asks—and that's what the bandages are for?"

It won't work forever, but it'll at least work for tonight.

Zoe melts in relief. "Yeah," she says. "Yeah, okay."

13

THORN

By the time we cook all the trout, everyone's too tired to do much of anything other than scarf their food so they can get to bed. Sadie and I end up on opposite sides of the campfire during dinner, and my eyes keep finding hers.

I quickly avert them the first time. The next time, too.

But by the third time, I can't look away.

She's beautiful: Her eyes are bright, lit up by the glow of the flickering flames. Her long brown hair—which was very straight when she first arrived—now has a significant wave to it, and I'm pretty sure she's not wearing makeup. When I first met her, I couldn't imagine her looking like a natural out here . . . and yet.

She grins when she catches me staring.

After dinner, we head back to the clearing where we set up earlier. I'm all too aware of her presence as she rummages around in her pack; I busy myself with triple-checking our tent stakes. I already know they're solid, but at least it's a distraction from the fact that it's just the two of us right now, alone in the place where we'll be sleeping together.

I choke on my own thoughts, suddenly having a coughing fit.

Sleeping near *each other*, I silently correct myself. *Not sleeping together.*

"You okay?" Sadie says, peering around from the other side of her tent.

I'm still hacking up a lung.

I wave at her, trying to communicate that I'm fine, but the message gets lost in translation. She's at my side in a heartbeat.

"Oh my gosh, Thorn—are you choking? Do you need the Heimlich?"

I shake my head, but the fact that I'm still wheezing isn't terribly convincing.

"*Water*," I finally manage.

She scrambles to find my water bottle, brings it over.

I guzzle it down. Sweet relief.

"Abdominal thrust maneuver," I say once I have my breath again. "That's what it's called now."

Sadie's face scrunches up in confusion. "What *what* is called? Your coughing fit?"

"The Heimlich," I reply. "They changed the name."

She doesn't ask why, and it's a good thing, because I don't remember the specifics.

"I'm glad you're okay," she finally says, watching as my breathing returns to normal. "Should I be worried? Do you have some sort of condition?"

Oh, just the Spontaneously Picturing Us in Bed Together condition, my brain unhelpfully fills in.

"No condition," I reply. "Just a fluke coughing fit. Maybe I kicked up a lot of dust while I was checking the tent?"

Sadie glances around the clearing, which isn't overly dusty at all. Now that I'm not on the verge of asphyxiation, I notice she has her iPhone in hand.

I nod to it. "Were you actually able to get a signal down here?"

She sighs. "Not even a little. I was hoping to text my best friend, Abby, and let her know I haven't died." After a brief pause, she adds, "Yet."

I laugh, which turns into yet another cough. I take another sip of water, clear my throat. "You might be able to get a single bar if you go up a little higher. It's too late to try tonight, but I can show you a good place tomorrow, if you want."

The last thing I need is to be making plans with Sadie.

But her face lights up—probably because it's the first time I've *encouraged* her phone addiction instead of telling her to put it away—and I know I'll be making good on that offer.

"Maybe after sunrise yoga?" she says hopefully.

Nothing excites me less than the idea of sunrise yoga.

That must be obvious, too, because she laughs. "Not a yoga guy?"

"I'm the least flexible person on the planet."

"That's impossible," she says, shaking her head, "because *I* am the least flexible person on the planet."

"Nope. You haven't *seen* inflexible yet, Sadie. I promise I'm the worst."

"Guess you'll just have to prove it," she says, eyes flashing playfully. "Tomorrow. At sunrise."

I see what she's done.

"I regret this already." I try to sound extra grumpy about it, but I can tell she's not buying it.

This is going to be a disaster—

But I'll do it for her.

"Knock, knock," a voice says flatly, interrupting the moment.

I turn, and there's Matteo, arms crossed and leaning against a pine tree.

"Any chance you've got a spare tarp?" he asks.

"I've only got the one."

"Can I use it tonight?"

"What for?" I ask, my curiosity getting the better of me.

Back when Matteo and I were friends, we could talk for hours out on the trails—none of this short, terse, trading one-liners crap. We had real conversations. Deep ones.

You'd never know we used to be close.

"Joshua and Zoe left their tent behind at the last site." I've never seen Matteo look quite this pissed on a hike before. "You'd think *one* of them would have noticed before now."

"You'd think," I agree. "Let me guess, they both thought the other had it?"

"Bingo."

"So, what—you're rigging up a tent out of my tarp?"

"Thought I'd sleep on it. Let them take mine since they're not used to sleeping outside."

Only I know how much of a sacrifice this is for Matteo. While I've never minded sleeping outside—and even prefer it in certain circumstances—he loathes sleeping out in the open. He's chill and easygoing in so many ways, but there's just something about letting his guard down with nothing to protect him that makes him too paranoid to sleep at all.

"Good for you, man," I say, and I mean it. Maybe he got over that particular fear while he was down in Peru.

When Matteo heads out, tarp in hand, I get back to where I left off, making sure our tents are extra secure. No wind disasters tonight—not if I can help it.

It's quick work, but I feel Sadie watching me the whole time.

"Should be good to go," I tell her when I finish.

"Thanks, Thorn," she says quietly, dimple popping as she grins.

She's so damn attractive. The silence between us starts to stretch—until a loud sound from somewhere deep in the woods echoes through the crisp night air.

Sadie startles, losing her balance for just long enough that everything in her arms falls to the ground; at a glance, it appears to be all the same comfort items she's put in her tent every night so far.

"What was *that*?!" she says, clearly unnerved.

I bend down to help her gather her things. "An owl, probably," I say. And because I can't resist, I add, "Maybe a bear."

She gives me a look, and I crack up.

"That's not funny," she says, but she's laughing. "Owls are terrifying, too."

"Can I ask which animals you *don't* find terrifying?"

"They're *all* terrifying," she says.

I can't quite tell if she's joking.

"Cats?" I prompt.

"Their claws are too sharp," she replies, holding out her left arm, where a long scar marks the crook of her elbow.

"Dogs?"

"Oh, definitely a hard pass on dogs, especially the huge ones—an Akita nearly pushed me off a bridge one time while I was on a run!"

"Goldfish? Ferrets? Rabbits?"

"Creepy, creepy, and creepy."

"How are *rabbits* creepy?" I say, laughing.

"My aunt gave me this book when I was a kid about zombie rabbits and they've terrified me ever since. Something about their eyes, I think? That and how quickly they multiply." She shudders. "The stuff of nightmares, honestly."

"Well, you'll be relieved to hear there are definitely no zombie rabbits out here—or anywhere else, for that matter. Your dreams are safe."

Sadie grins. She's clearly enjoying this as much as I am.

Something catches my eye on the ground beside her: it's the journal I gave her, lying open in the dirt. There's a lot more writing in it than just the note I left on the first page.

I reach for it—but she apparently had the same idea at the exact same time—and we narrowly avoid a head-on collision.

She's so close I could kiss her.

And maybe I would, under different circumstances.

But when am I *not* under these circumstances lately? My entire life for the last few years can be measured in miles out here on the trails—and in travelers wandering into my world, then right back out of it. Hellos and goodbyes in equal measure. Always professional, never too deep.

I clear my throat, widen the distance between us before I do something I can't take back.

I pick up the journal and brush off the dirt, deliberately looking at her face as I close it so she'll know I haven't read anything she's written.

"Here," I say, settling it at the top of the pile in her arms.

"Thanks," she says quietly. "For everything."

She disappears inside the tent, and I head to mine.

An hour later, I can't help but wonder how Matteo's faring out in the open. Should I have offered to sleep outside instead? Will he sleep at all? And why, after years of feeling bitter over what he did, do I actually *care*?

I'm too wired to sleep, and not just because of Matteo.

Sadie's light is still on. It casts a dim blue-green glow through the thin nylon fabric between us—her tent and mine are about as close together as they can get in this small clearing.

Is she reading? Writing in the journal I gave her? Maybe she fell asleep with the light on.

"Sadie?" I say after a while.

For a minute, I wonder if she's heard me over the low hum of distant cicadas.

"Thorn?" she replies quietly. "You're still awake?"

"Yeah, I can't sleep."

"Oh my gosh, I'm so sorry—is my light keeping you up?"

In a way, I think, but it's not the light itself.

It's the constant reminder that Sadie is right there with it.

"No, it's fine," I say. "Just a lot on my mind."

There's a pause, and then some rustling. Her light turns off and the whole world goes black; it'll take a minute for my eyes to adjust.

"Want to talk about it?" she says. "I just finished a chapter."

I turn over on my side, toward her voice. We could be face-to-face right now if not for our tents and the pitch darkness.

"Or we could just gossip about the others if you're not ready to go into it," she adds.

I grin. As the leader of this trek, as a *professional*, I really shouldn't encourage this train of conversation—but one night of pretending I'm just like everyone else out here couldn't hurt, right?

And it sounds a hell of a lot better than dwelling on Matteo.

"Not sure about gossiping," I say, "but maybe it would be good to talk about other stuff. Want to go sit outside?"

It's not against the rules to talk. It might be tempting to do *more*, sure—I'm only human—but willpower has always been one of my strengths.

I'm hyperaware of our tent zippers, the sound of them amplified by the relative stillness of everything around us. The moon is less than half full, on its way to becoming a new moon in time for the night we'll *all* spend sleeping out under the stars in a few days. It's just enough light to see Sadie and her silk pajamas—a green so pale it's almost white—her smile bright even in the darkness.

"How about over here?" I suggest.

We make our way over to a big, rocky ledge down by the lake. With everyone else silent or asleep, it's easy to forget we're not alone.

Sadie settles down close to me, hugging her knees to her chest. Her shorts are *very* short, especially with how she's sitting.

I force myself to look away.

"It's so beautiful out here," she says. "The travel guidebooks don't do it justice."

I've been out here before, but not like this—not in the middle of the night, and not with someone like Sadie. Not with anyone else at all.

I imagine what it's like for her, seeing this view for the first time. I never thought I was one to take nature for granted, but after seeing it day in and day out for so many years, the *newness* of it is something I haven't felt for a while. It's been a long time since I just sat in wonder.

We take in the night sky, and how the lake is a mirror reflecting the multitude of twinkling stars back up at it. The mountains pierce skyward from the far side of the water, blotting out everything behind them.

"So, Sadie Whitlock," I say after a moment, "how'd you learn to fish like that?"

She smiles, surprised. "My grandparents have a ranch in Texas," she says, tucking a piece of hair behind her ear. "We always fished at this little lake on their property—my granddad built a cabin there and everything."

"Never would have guessed you'd spent time on a ranch," I say.

"To be fair, once I figured out I could stay inside the cabin with a book while everyone else fished, I never looked back."

I laugh. "That tracks."

If I'd had a cabin to retreat into when it was clear fishing wasn't my strong suit, I'm not sure I would have used it—I loved watching my dad pull in fish after fish. His unwavering confidence that I would improve made me want to keep trying. Even Matteo had better luck than I did when my dad eventually taught him; he caught on quickly and provided dinner for the three of us more times than I can remember.

My dad never gave me a hard time about that, which I appreciate.

The memory lingers like a dense fog. When it finally clears, I catch Sadie in my peripheral vision, staring out over the starlit water.

"I had a talk with Matteo this morning," I say, breaking the silence.

I'm not even sure what compelled me to tell her. I hadn't really intended to bring it up—but Sadie is so easy to talk to it feels like I could tell her anything.

"More than just two words at a time?" she asks, the corner of her mouth turning up in a grin.

"You noticed, huh?"

She throws her head back and laughs. "Please. The way he stopped by to ask for your tarp? You've got territorial lion energy when you're together. Every hyena within a hundred miles would notice."

I shake my head. She's something else.

"I'm glad you brought it up, though," she goes on. "I saw you guys talking before we headed out this morning, and I *so* wanted to ask about it, but I knew it was a sensitive subject. Aren't you proud of my restraint, Thorn?"

Her eyes sparkle in the moonlight, and I can't help but smile. Leave it to Sadie to make the thing that's felt so heavy for the last two years feel absolutely weightless.

"I am, actually."

"Well?" she asks.

"Well, what?"

"How did it go? Did it help?"

"We're at least more on the same page about the hike now," I tell her. "I said more than I meant to about some other things, though, and he wasn't ready for it."

It's vague and I know it. I can tell she wants to ask more—what started such a rift between us?—but is trying her best to respect my boundaries.

Maybe it wouldn't be so bad to talk about it.

Maybe it wouldn't be so bad to talk about it *with her*.

"I first met Matteo in eleventh grade," I say before I can talk myself out of it. "He was an exchange student from Italy, and his family sent him to live with us for an entire year. I'd never had a brother—we hit it off right off the bat. At the end of the year, he asked his parents if he could finish out high school with us, and then he just . . . never went back. He was the closest friend I ever had."

"I'm sensing a *but*," Sadie says.

"But," I go on, and she gives a small smile. "There was this girl, a few years later, after college."

She shakes her head. "It's *always* a girl."

"He could have had anybody he wanted," I say. "But he wanted the one I was dating." I swallow, watch as a large heron swoops low over the water and lands on a distant rock. "Called me from Peru one day saying he'd decided to move there—and that my girlfriend had gone with him."

"So *that's* why you always make that face whenever he talks about Peru."

This surprises me. "I make a face?"

"Well, yeah. And it sounds totally justified—I would hate Peru after that, too. How *could* he?"

"I've been asking myself the same thing for years."

"Is he still with her, at least?"

"He is." And then, because something about her legs and her pajamas and her eyes in the moonlight compels me to, I feel the need to clarify: "I'm not still hung up on *her*, though. We were happy, and she was great, but I always had this feeling she'd move on eventually. The hard part was that she moved on *to Matteo*. That he not only didn't resist her—he uprooted his whole *life* for her."

Sadie studies me. "You lost your girlfriend and your best friend at the same time," she says sadly. "I get what you mean. Girlfriends come and go—but your best friend is supposed to be there for you no matter what, not part of the problem. And now you're stuck out here with him for nearly two weeks?" She shakes her head, brows furrowed. "I'm so sorry, Thorn."

She really does get it.

"If it makes you feel any better," she says after a long, silent moment, "I got blindsided by a breakup, too."

The wave of emotion that crashes over me catches me off guard, especially because of the thought attached to it: *How could any man let her go?*

"Don't look so shocked," she says with a rueful grin. "You'll laugh when you hear why—he said I was 'too high-maintenance.' He was always telling me I should 'live a little' and 'be more spontaneous' and rolled his eyes whenever I packed too much stuff or did too much research or made too many plans for our weekend trips."

But I don't laugh. There's nothing funny about that.

"He said those things?"

I'm not normally an *I-want-to-punch-him* sort of guy, but . . . I kind of want to punch him.

"He did."

Clearly, his words left a lasting impression. I've only known Sadie for a few days, and I already know enough to know there's some truth to them—she's definitely an overpacker who's afraid to be caught in a situation she's not prepared for—but he made those things into deal-breakers, and it sounds like he made it sting.

"He's the reason I signed up," she goes on. "We were supposed to be in Italy right now, but he said he wanted to come here instead—right before he said I wasn't invited, because he thought I'd 'die after one day.'" Her gaze flickers down to her hands. "Turns out he flaked on signing up altogether, though, so . . . it's just me."

I want to take back everything I said to give her a hard time about how much she stuffed into her pack. She had every chance to back out—to not come at all—but she still chose to be here.

"Listen," I say, and she meets my eyes. "The fact that you're out here at all, that you're pushing yourself to try new things that scare you and make you uncomfortable . . . it's a *huge* deal, Sadie. There's nothing 'high-maintenance' about a trip like this. You're doing the work, and you're doing a good job."

She blinks a few times in rapid succession, hugs her knees tighter to her chest.

"Even though I brought my whole house and my fancy coffee?"

"You're *prepared*," I fire back.

"And my shoes?"

I have to laugh. "Okay, your shoes are not ideal. But you haven't complained once about your feet hurting—or anything else, now that I think about it. And I *know* they've got to be hurting."

"They're absolutely *killing* me," she admits with a groan. "I'm miserable! I'm itchy, I'm sore. I'm a total mess—and my shoes are so *brown* now." Her hair falls like a curtain between us, and she tucks it behind her ear as she turns toward me. "Thank you, though. Really. All of that, coming from you?" She swallows. "It means a lot."

Her eyes lock on mine.

I can't look away.

I want to kiss her. *Should* I kiss her? We're close enough that it wouldn't take much. The slightest tilt of my head would put me halfway there, and if I'm reading things right, I think she'd meet me the rest of the way.

It's been so long since I've kissed anyone. And I've definitely never kissed a trekker—never wanted to, never got this close to begin with.

But the rules! my mind unhelpfully reminds me.

Sadie makes me want to break every rule.

I bite my lip until it stings, think of taking a cold dip into the lake: the restraint of it all tests the limits of my willpower, and I'm barely holding it together. The temptation is absolutely still there—there's a sizable part of me that wants to go for it, despite it being a *very* bad idea.

I'm on the verge of losing the battle when a loud splash shatters the moment. It's a relief in some ways, but in the end, only makes things harder: Sadie grabs my arm on instinct, so startled she practically lands in my lap.

"*What* was *that*?" she says breathlessly.

I scan the water and point at the culprit when I spot him: the great blue heron from before is now standing in the lake only ten feet away from us, still as a statue, as if he couldn't possibly have caused such a disruption.

"Lake monster," I deadpan.

She rests her head on my shoulder, playing along. "Keep me safe?"

"Yeah," I say as I wrap my arm around her, pulling her in tight. "That's my job."

We sit like this for a little while longer, neither of us daring to move. The heron doesn't move, either. If not for the shifting stars overhead, I'd believe it if someone told me time had just . . . stopped.

"Thorn?" she says sleepily.

"Hmm?"

"You're good at your job."

Her words are quiet, barely more than a whisper, but they echo in my head.

Even once we're back in our tents for the night, I can't stop hearing her voice: what she said, how she said it. How I'm not sure I believe her—I'm not sure what we did tonight is *good leader behavior*—but I desperately want to.

I am so far in over my head. I'll keep her safe, like I said.

But who will do the same for me?

CAPTAIN'S LOG // AUGUST THORN

Day 3 • So late I don't even want to look at my watch • Waning Crescent Moon

---

Can't sleep, can't focus, can't hardly see because I'm writing this without a flashlight, so this will be short. Forgot to skip a rock for Dad today, for the first time ever—not sure what to make of that except there's been a lot going on. Caught zero fish, to no one's surprise. Things are so tense with Matteo he didn't even give me a hard time about it. Sadie somehow caught half a dozen . . . pretty impressive. Best day I've had at Mackenzie Lake in a long time. Hoping I fall asleep sometime before the sunrise yoga session I stupidly agreed to.

DAY FOUR

Day at Mackenzie Lake

There's nothing quite so serene as watching the sun rise over the glittering alpine lakes of the Sierras—make a point to get up early at least once on your trip.

—Henry Herrington, *Backpacking the Sierras: A Beginner's Handbook* (Fourth Edition)

VIDEOS > FAVORITES > VLOG FOOTAGE

SADIE: It's Day Four of backpacking the Mackenzie Lake Loop in Valerie Forest National Park—and look where we are, everyone! The *actual* Mackenzie Lake!

The camera pans from one side of the lake to the other, its water sparkling and clear, before landing on the nonplussed face of a blonde in yoga gear.

SADIE: This is my new friend Zoe, everyone—say hi, Zoe!

Zoe waves, impatient and unsmiling. Her left hand has been doctored up with a smattering of bandages at the base of her ring and pinky fingers.

[Male voice, off-camera]: Your hand okay, Zoe? Should we take a rain check on yoga?

SADIE: What, Thorn? You're not trying to get *out* of this, are you?

THORN: Just making sure Zoe's not too hurt to teach class, that's all.

ZOE: Let's go, people! I'll be good, Thorn, but thanks. Sadie, can you get that thing to record me as I teach? This would make *great* content for my studio. But make it quick, okay? And make sure you get the lake and the mountains, too! And—

SADIE: I've got it, Zo, don't worry. "Great content" is my middle name!

Sadie's fingers pass in front of the lens as she settles the phone into place, then adjusts its position to frame Zoe and the lake and the mountains. Sadie looks straight into the camera.

SADIE [sotto voce]: Wish me luck, y'all. I'll report back later.

14

SADIE

Sunrise yoga is *brutal.*

For starters, I'm terrible at yoga on a good day. My definition of a *good day,* at the moment, is one in which a) I've had more than four hours of sleep, and b) my muscles aren't already sore from an intense amount of hiking. I feel like I have the hangover from hell.

I dragged myself out of bed mostly because I gave Thorn such a hard time yesterday about going—and also because I'm eager to *see* Thorn, especially after last night.

Last night . . . yeah. It was so worth it.

I'm also here because of Zoe. She was so enthusiastic about sharing yoga with us, and I know what it feels like when people don't match your enthusiasm, so I wanted to show up for her. But, um—if she wants people to come back again? Let's just say I could make use of a suggestion box.

"I thought yoga was supposed to be *peaceful,*" Thorn whispers when Zoe's out of earshot, adjusting Brittany's form, all of us inverted in downward dog.

"I never applied for the military for a reason," I agree. "Well, for many reasons. But mostly because I don't like the idea of people barking orders at me before I've had my coffee."

Thorn snorts. "As opposed to people barking orders at you *after* you've had your coffee?"

"Time for a plank, people!" Zoe calls out. "Keep that back flat or I'll come and *make* it flat!"

"So *threatening*," I murmur as I straighten out into my plank. "Better do what she says or she might come climb on top of us."

I glance over at Thorn, and oh—what a mistake—

His dark green T-shirt strains over his arm muscles, and I can see every sculpted curve of his shoulders, biceps, and triceps as he holds himself perfectly in the pose.

"I thought you said you were bad at this?" I whisper.

"Bad at yoga," he whispers back. "Not bad at this part. I do push-ups every day."

Of course he does.

"No talking!" Zoe yells, finally aware that we've been chatting during her class. "Take in the serenity of the moment, people!"

Out of the corner of my eye, I see Thorn shaking with silent laughter.

Stop it, I mouth at him, trying hard not to burst into a fit of giggles myself—but this only makes him laugh harder, and it's totally contagious.

Zoe gives us a look, but she's in the middle of correcting Trey, who can't keep his back flat to save his life.

Only a handful of us showed up this morning—Trey, Brittany, Emma, Thorn, and me. We're spread out in a single line on a flat, wide rock down by the water, close to the kayaks and where the tennis girls set up camp last night. The session hasn't been entirely bad: the view is amazing, and it feels better than I thought to stretch my body. Zoe knows what she's doing, yoga-wise, so the class would actually be pretty good if she weren't in such a bad mood.

She leads us through some sun salutations and on into some poses requiring a bit more balance. I absolutely nail tree pose, if I do say so myself.

Thorn, alas, struggles.

"You don't have to get your foot all the way up to your inner thigh," Zoe tells him, her hands on his shoulders to reinforce his balance. "You can just rest it lightly against your calf if that's better. Imagine you're a tree, and that your roots go deep into this rock."

Thorn's eyes light up, and I know he wants to crack the same joke I do—that trees don't make a habit of growing their roots into rocks—but we somehow both manage to keep our composure.

When we finally get to Savasana, also known as corpse pose, I'm surprised at how much better I feel. The things that ached before we started are feeling warm and loose, and best of all, Zoe seemed to mellow out a bit toward the end of class.

"The challenge of this pose is to get every single part of your body to relax," she says. "Close your eyes, listen to the sounds of nature. Let yourselves just be present in the moment."

It goes well enough until the smell of coffee finds its way over to me—Silas and Hunter and their usual morning routine, no doubt.

"How much longer are we supposed to lie here?" I say under my breath, opening my eyes just long enough to make sure Zoe's not close enough to notice.

"Until we're dead," Thorn replies, and that's it—I can't—

I burst out laughing, so loudly I've probably woken up any birds that, like me, had a late night.

On my other side, Trey starts to laugh, too, and it's all over from there.

"Thanks for showing up, everyone," Zoe says, sounding more irritated than grateful. "Same place, same time tomorrow."

It sounds more like an expectation than an invitation, but I know better than to point that out.

"Coffee time," Trey says, leaping up. "Let's *gooooo*. Thanks, Zoe! That was awesome."

Did he have coffee *before* class, too? Or has he just had so much coffee in his lifetime that it flows through his veins now, making him perpetually energetic?

Brittany and Emma hang back to ask Zoe some questions, while Thorn and I follow Trey up to the campfire. Hunter and Silas are seated on one log; Matteo and Joshua are on another. The only person unaccounted for, at the moment, is Parker—she must have slept in. (If this can even be called *sleeping in*, since it's still pretty early.)

"You weren't wrong," I say to Thorn as we walk. "You *are* the most inflexible person on the planet."

"Oh, you noticed?"

"It was hard to miss."

"That's an interesting way to admit you couldn't take your eyes off me," he says with a smirk.

"And that's a confident thing to say for someone who had, like, *maybe-we're-in-an-earthquake* balance issues—I couldn't help but be distracted every time you almost fell over!"

"Well, I can't help it if my hips are tight," he says, not even bothering to defend himself on the subject of his balance.

"Actually, you probably could if you stretched more."

"And what's your excuse?" he says with a wicked grin. "You couldn't touch your toes, either."

Touché.

"I should probably stretch more," I reply, and we both laugh.

A few minutes later, we're both sipping coffee from camp cups—the guys made extra again—the two of us pressed right up against each other due to limited space on the log.

"How was yoga?" Silas asks as he rinses off his coffee gear.

"Gonna be sore for *days*," Trey says, at the exact same time Thorn says, "Memorable."

"Zoe was in a mood," I add. "I'd never done *angry* yoga before."

Thorn gives me a subtle nudge in the ribs, and only then do I remember Joshua is sitting right there.

Fortunately, he doesn't seem to register my comment about his fiancée. He doesn't seem to be paying attention to anything we're saying, actually—he's distracted by Zoe herself, an uneasy look on his face as he watches her demonstrate a complicated pose to Brittany and Emma, who look on in awe.

"I haven't forgotten your promise from yesterday," I say to Thorn once the others have started to split off.

His face goes slack. "The . . . promise . . . that *I* made? To you?"

"Okay, so maybe it wasn't a promise. But you did tell me you could show me where I might be able to get a cell signal."

"Oh! Yes. It's a little bit of a hike, but if you're good for it . . . ?"

The very last thing I want to do after the last couple days of hiking is *more* hiking. But between the endorphins that have settled in after angry yoga and the artificial energy courtesy of the coffee, I'm feeling optimistic.

We head back to our tents first so I can grab my phone and he can grab his journal. I grab my journal, too, and then we head out.

The hike isn't long—but it *is* steep.

"It'll be so worth it," Thorn reassures me when we're halfway up and my legs are screaming.

"Because I'll be able to text Abby one last time to let her know I'll be stuck at the top of this overlook for the rest of my life?"

He laughs. "Because the view up here is incredible."

It's all wildflowers and rocks so far, but I give him the benefit of the doubt. We aren't going all the way up the mountain, but there's apparently a little enclave just off the path that overlooks Mackenzie Lake.

It feels like we've been climbing for at least an hour when we finally get there.

One look at my watch says it's only been twenty-three minutes. Thorn's right, though: it *is* an incredible view.

The enclave is little more than a rocky cliff, but it's not so narrow I'm afraid we'll fall. We sit cross-legged on the stony ground and take in the water below, along with our campsites just beyond its banks.

I pull out my phone, turn it on.

There's hardly any battery left—taking that video of Zoe during yoga drained it all the way down to 8 percent—but at least it isn't entirely dead. I wait and watch and hope, and then: a miraculous two bars of signal!

I beam at Thorn. "It worked!"

"Told you it would," he says with a lopsided grin. "Better text Abby while you can."

He pulls out his journal and starts writing, as if to say *here's as much privacy as I can give you.*

I snap the world's quickest selfie and send it to Abby.

Proof of life, I type out in a rush.

Only when I hit send do I notice an unfamiliar message in our text thread—she must have sent it sometime after I left, when I was already out here and didn't have a signal.

Missing you so much already! I know you probably won't see this until you're back, but just wanted to tell you how proud I am of you. You DID it, Sadie! You are the bravest person I know. (Also, Jonathan FIIIIINALLY asked me out to dinner! Torn between fancy French or something romantic but low-key . . .)

My battery percentage dips down to 6 percent.

I tap and hold on her text until my favorite pink heart emoji appears.

I miss you too and this message is so perfect I could cry, I write back, not even joking about the crying. **I'm so happy for you! I'm also so so so so so sore, and there are a lot of things I hate about being out here, but there are also a lot of things I like . . . one of them is named Thorn (and I can't wait to tell you all about him)**

It takes every ounce of restraint I have to not snap a discreet photo of Thorn, too—what is it about guys writing in journals on mountainside cliffs that is just so attractive?—and, instead, use what's left of my dwindling battery to check Instagram so I can finally upload a video or two from our first few days, and also to see if Abby's posted any pictures from her date.

As soon as the app opens, I know I've made a colossal mistake.

At the top of my feed, there's a carousel of photos posted by Gabriella Lawson, a friend of mine and Abby's that we met at a book signing one time and have stayed loosely acquainted with ever since.

She's posing on the back of a yacht in the first photo, wearing a fiery orange bikini that leaves absolutely nothing to the imagination—the location tag reads *Capri Isle, Sorrento, Italy*, and it looks incredibly glamorous. But it's not the towering rock wall behind her, or the glittering sea, or even Gabriella and her runway-worthy bikini that makes my heart stutter—

It's Caden.

Caden, with his arm around her, one finger hooked underneath the spaghetti-thin tie at her hip. Caden, who never wanted to spring for any dinner dates that were remotely fancy. Caden, whose idea of a weekend getaway included spontaneous road trips to ugly Texas beaches and motels that smelled like mildew.

Caden is on our vacation without me, in Italy, living like a prince, treating her like a princess.

And the cherry on top? I'm the one who introduced them.

I scroll through the photos, unable to stop myself.

My stomach drops when I realize: I recognize every single one of these places. I picked them out—I picked them out *for us*. The restaurants, the hotel. Every single detail has been plucked straight out of the shared Google Doc I created, except for the most crucial detail—

I was supposed to be there, too.

Olives and cheese and white wine in one picture, cacio e pepe in another. A hotel room that is the very definition of luxe, complete with a lush-looking bed covered in a rumpled white duvet. Expansive views out of open-air windows.

Breakfast in bed.

Espresso cups.

Her perfect crimson manicure.

Stilettos that even I wouldn't risk walking in, despite how incredible they look. They look especially incredible on her.

And then—at the end—the way he's kissing her, frozen in time for all perpetuity, preserved in her social media feed for the whole world to see.

I'm still staring at that last one when my phone dies. The image is burned into my brain: my ex-boyfriend—who dumped me for being too high-maintenance—on a glitzy trip to Italy that *I* planned—with someone I introduced him to—and not just *any* someone, but *Gabriella Lawson*.

Gabriella Lawson makes me look like an amateur when it comes to being high-maintenance.

Caden O'Connor is an absolute hypocrite.

He said he wanted to spend his time backpacking here in California, that Italy wasn't his thing. So why am I the one who's here, alone, while he's on my dream vacation with someone else?

My tears fall fast and hot. I try to blink them away, swiping surreptitiously at my cheeks to dry them before Thorn looks over and asks me what's wrong.

I need Abby, need to process this.

My portable charger is all the way back down at the tent, though, so I'm totally cut off from her until I can recharge it and get a signal again. At the same time, as much as I want to talk to Abby—hear her rant about how I'm better off without Caden and maybe she and I can just go on a girls' trip to Italy sometime instead—I kind of just want to throw my phone over the edge of this cliff and let it sink down to the bottom of the lake where I won't have to look at it ever again.

I glance at Thorn. He's still writing in his journal, oblivious to my crisis.

The journal is a good idea. I may not be able to talk to Abby, but I can write everything out like I'm writing to her, pretend it's a series of texts. I know her well enough to predict her response—she'd send me a string of emojis, various iterations of shock and dismay and anger.

I start writing, my pen fast and furious on the page.

Everything I've pushed away for the past few months comes roaring back in messy blue ink: the anger I felt when Caden blindsided me with our breakup, how he treated my tendency to thoughtfully overprepare as a personality flaw.

So what if I have preferences? So what if I'm particular? We only live *one life*—forgive me if I don't want to spend it in a run-down hotel looking at a pipe spewing something brown out into the waters of Galveston! Why would someone *want* to eat gas station hot dogs that have been getting wrinkly for hours (or—*shudder*—*days*) when there's a farm-to-table brunch spot two more miles away? Why would I buy a ten-pack of something cheap when I could buy *one* that will last longer for the same price? Why did he act like it was a bad thing that I like to have a plan—like I was some sort of control freak? I mean, yeah, I like to know what's going to happen. And I don't like being caught off guard or unprepared. Does that make me insufferable? Does that disqualify me from being girlfriend material?

The worst part is, he treated me this way only to start dating someone who is even *more* particular than I am. All the things that supposedly rubbed him the wrong way about me, all the things that made us *incompatible*—he's going to get ten times more of them with Gabriella.

And I cannot for the life of me reconcile the fact that he's in Italy.

The life Gabriella is living right now is such a stark contrast to where I am, roughing it out here in the middle of nowhere—

Those were supposed to be *my* olives and cheese.

My bed. My breakfast *in* that bed.

I desperately want that chilled glass of white wine, that view of the sea, that yacht.

I write and write and write, letting my most honest feelings pour out onto the page. And at the end of it, when there's nothing left, I have an epiphany.

The thing I'm left with is this: as much as I wish I had Italy and all the things I'd planned, I no longer want any of those things with *him*. Our breakup stung when it happened, everything he said—and his shameless audacity, now, brings that pain acutely back to the surface—

But it isn't *Caden* I want.

It's air conditioning. It's gourmet food. It's a manicure, and not the makeshift kind I plan to do in my tent later. It's everything I've been stripped of on this hike, all of the comforts that can blur the sharp edges of life when things get too painful or hard.

Without those little luxuries—when it's just me and my blisters and the bugs—the painful and hard things have nowhere to hide.

I look up, take in the way the sunlight catches on the lake.

Thorn's quiet beside me, but his journal is closed. He's giving me space, I realize, even though he finished his own entry.

A lump forms in my throat, and I bite the inside of my cheek. My tears have finally dried, and I'm determined to keep it that way.

As challenging as this trip has been, and as drastically different as it is from the Italian vacation of my dreams, I'm not sorry I'm here. Maybe I initially signed up out of spite to prove to Caden I'm stronger than he thinks—but if I'm honest, I think I needed to prove it to myself, too.

I couldn't care less about impressing Caden now. I have zero interest in being compatible with a hypocrite like him.

I feel a strange sense of peace settle over me. Clarity, contentment—

Closure.

Italy will still be there, waiting, at the end of all this.

As for today, I'm exactly where I need to be. And now I can move on.

15

THORN

"Everything okay in there?" I ask Sadie, who's been inside her tent for more than twenty minutes now.

We're supposed to meet the others for kayaking in five, but at this rate, maybe I should go on down without her. She was going through something up on the cliff earlier—but I knew better than to ask about it, or to even look like I noticed.

I noticed. It was impossible not to.

"Just a second," she calls out. "Sorry!"

When Sadie finally emerges from her tent, I do a double take.

She's wearing a white string bikini and some sort of sheer, sand-colored skirt that covers absolutely *nothing* up even though it goes all the way to her ankles. Between all that and the gold palm leaf earrings and her floppy sun hat, she's clearly mistaken *day at the lake* for *day at the pool.*

Not that I'm complaining. She looks good—*very* good.

"What?" she says, checking to make sure the essentials are covered by the small bits of fabric. "I thought we were going to the lake next?"

"No, you're right. We are," I say, resisting the urge to roast her a little. Has she ever *been* to a lake before? "It's just, uh—there's going to be a bit of mud. And sticks that might tear your skirt. But you look really nice," I rush to add, because I'm overcome with a strong urge to make sure she knows she should feel confident about how she looks.

Her eyes flash up to meet mine, a sudden blush turning her cheeks pink. "I look nice?"

"You do." I swallow. I'm having a hard time looking away.

"Thank you."

"We should probably—" I start, at the same time she says, "Should we go meet the others?"

She leads the way, and oh *shit* is that a mistake: her bikini bottoms are cut to show off her curves and a whole lot of skin.

I may not make it to the lake.

I force my eyes down even lower, and that's when I notice she has something stuck to her leg.

"Sadie?" I say. "You have something . . . uh . . . there."

She twists around to check out the back of her thigh, just above her knee, but the mesh skirt is in the way of her fixing it.

I thought she was blushing before—but that was nothing compared to now.

"*Yes* I brought wax strips to a wilderness excursion," she blurts out suddenly, misreading my confusion for judgment. "I'm very particular about my legs, and they drive me nuts when they're even a little stubbly."

I hold my hands up. "I didn't say a word."

"I heard you in my head, though."

I laugh. "What, exactly, did I say?"

"You were like, '*Sadie, you* know *you could've saved some space if you'd left those at home, right?*' And I was like, '*But it's just so much more* comfortable *this way*,' and you just shook your head and sighed."

"Wow—I said a lot in your head." I grin. "But that does sound pretty accurate."

Again, not that I'm complaining.

"Well, bringing all of that stuff was worth it to me," she says with a smirk.

She totally caught me staring, and probably (accurately) read my every thought.

"I didn't say a word," I repeat.

When we get down to the lake, the others fall silent, as if they're witnessing a rare bird. Especially the guys—but all of the girls, too.

"See, babe?" Zoe says, swatting Joshua on the arm before adjusting the asymmetrical strap on her navy-blue one-piece. "I totally could have brought my bikini. You look amazing, Sadie—I'm going to pretend we're on the Amalfi Coast right now!"

Sadie's face turns stormy at the mention of Italy.

"Thank you," she says. "I've always wanted to go there."

Matteo takes the lead on getting everyone set up with the kayaks, demonstrating how to get in and what to do if you tip over. Mackenzie Lake is large but not overly deep, so we'll have ample space to paddle around without being too cramped.

"Want to go together?" Sadie asks me.

I really should say no, make up some bogus icebreaking exercise just to put some space between us; we've gotten close so quickly, more than I meant to. And after how she looked like she desperately needed a friend, or a hug, or *more* up on the cliff earlier—and now that white-hot bikini and everything it doesn't cover—

It's just dangerous, is all.

It's a distraction.

I'm not on this hike for my own benefit, as much as I love being out here. My job is to make sure everyone stays safe and has a good time learning more about themselves while immersing themselves in nature.

That said, we'll be camping out at this location for another night:

I won't have to have hawklike focus every second of the day like I do when we're hiking. I'm human. I need rest—and *fun*—too.

I can be a diligent leader *and* I can spend time getting to know Sadie. As long as it doesn't get physical between us, I'm not technically breaking any rules.

"Sure," I say before I can take it back.

She chooses a yellow kayak and I pick out a blue one. We paddle across the serene water, the mountains looming larger with every stroke as we move farther from the shore and our campgrounds.

"This is fun!" Sadie calls out from behind me.

I glance over my shoulder and have to stifle a laugh at the incongruous sight before me: Sadie looks like a runway model who tripped off the catwalk and landed in a kayak, completely at odds with her surroundings. She's still wearing the floppy hat and the earrings, but left her mesh skirt in a heap by the water. It all just drives home what a stretch this entire trip was for her—and something about that makes me want to jump out of my kayak and into hers, physics be damned.

"You're really getting the hang of it!" I reply.

Her paddling was pretty uneven at first—I had to keep slowing down to make sure I didn't leave her too far behind, but she's picking it up quickly. I should have known she'd be a fast learner.

The water is tranquil and smooth, perfect for beginners. We follow the curve of the shoreline as we explore, even though we're not terribly close to it. It's easy navigating—until I see the rounded top of a large boulder peeking out just above the water up ahead. There are several dotting the lake, but I thought I'd steered us clear of them.

"We're going to have to make a turn now, okay?" I call out over my shoulder. "You'll need to shift your weight a little"—I demonstrate, leaning slightly to the left—"and then do a long stroke of the paddle on the right side."

"Like this?" she replies.

My kayak pivots just in time to see Sadie's valiant attempt at replicating the turn. She dips her paddle in like I've told her to—and she shifts her weight, too—but she shifts it to the *same* side instead of the opposite one, and the movement is just too much all at once. Before I can warn her, Sadie flips, shrieking, and goes under.

I'm out of my kayak to help before she even resurfaces. The water is shoulder-deep out here—not too deep for me, but Sadie's not as tall as I am. Her sun hat floats next to her upside-down kayak as her paddle drifts farther out.

She comes up gasping, laughing, her dark hair slick against her shoulders. Smudges of mascara rim her eyes, because of course she wore makeup for this.

"Did I do it right?" she says, clearly not taking herself too seriously. She bobs on her tiptoes, the water up to her chin.

I make my way closer and wrap my arm around her waist, lifting her up to give her a little more breathing room. The bare skin of her stomach feels slick and smooth under my fingers, and suddenly she has my entire attention.

"Never seen anyone do it better," I reply. "You're a fast learner."

She clings as I support her, her light grasp on my shoulder doing things to me that make me wish we were truly alone out here.

"Here," I say, taking slow, heavy steps through the water toward her kayak. "I'll help you back in."

We're almost there when her grip on me suddenly constricts, so tight at first that it takes my breath away.

It takes a split second to register the fact that it's not only her arms wrapped around me so tightly—it's her entire body. She's jumped up so that we're pressed close, zero space between the tiny fabric of her bikini bottoms and my swim trunks, her legs wound around me and crossed behind my back. Somehow her backside is now firmly in my hands, and her terrified face is a mere inch from mine.

"*What* was *that*?! Something brushed against my leg!"

I know better than to tell her *all* the possibilities.

"Probably just a fish," I say.

"There aren't snakes in here, are there? It felt like a snake, Thorn!"

She buries her face in my neck, her breath hot on my skin.

"Don't make me lie to you," I reply, one of my hands going instinctively up to her back, the knot of her bikini tie thick under my palm. "Ask me something else."

"Are the snakes going to eat us?"

I have to laugh. *This* I can honestly answer without freaking her out.

"I've been swimming in this lake hundreds of times, Sadie. I haven't been eaten yet, if that makes you feel any better."

The tension in her body eases, but she doesn't make any moves to let go—which is fine by me, as long as I tell myself I'm just being a good guide, that it's okay for us to be this close right now since I'm helping her through the water.

It's a stretch and I know it.

"Let's get you back in that kayak, okay?"

Once we're beside it again, she shifts off me so I can flip it right side up.

Getting Sadie *in* is another ordeal altogether.

It's too unstable, even with me holding it, for her to get in on her own without having solid footing underneath her. She tries a few times, laughing with every failed attempt.

"How about this?" I say, repositioning myself in the water so my knee is a makeshift stepstool. "Climb up and I'll help you in."

The water makes everything more difficult—slick skin and a kayak that doesn't want to stay put—but we get it together, and she's finally almost there. I've got one hand on each of her thighs, bracing her as she climbs in, biting the inside of my cheek to balance out all the other things I'm feeling with her bikini bottoms *right* in front of me.

"Bet you're glad I used the waxing strips now," she says, and I laugh.

I couldn't care less about the waxing strips—her legs under my hands would feel good no matter what.

She settles into the kayak, looking so proud of herself for finally conquering it.

"How are you going to get back into yours?" she asks. "And . . . what about my paddle?"

I follow her gaze out to the middle of the lake, where the yellow blades of her paddle are bright, blazing beacons on the green-blue water.

At least it's the kind that floats.

After an invigorating swim there and back to retrieve it, I hoist myself up into my own kayak and we're back in business.

Gotta be honest, though: I liked it better when we were in the water.

Matteo's been in a foul mood all evening. After our afternoon at the lake, he headed off alone, breaking our own rule. He's seemed on edge ever since.

We eat around the campfire, the various cliques mixing more than they have until now. Brittany's comparing sunburns with Hunter and Silas—Hunter wins that competition by a mile, having forgotten to sunscreen his entire back—while Joshua and Zoe continue to bicker with each other (as they've been doing all day). Sadie's sitting next to me but is chatting with Parker and Emma.

Which leaves Matteo and me. We're sitting opposite each other, the flickering flames a healthy barrier between us. No one else seems to be paying attention to the way he's keeping to himself tonight, scowling and silent. It's unlike him—he's an extrovert to the max. He was fine at the lake.

So what happened?

After dinner, I see him darting back toward the clearing he shared with Joshua and Zoe last night.

"Hey, man," I call after him.

He doesn't slow down.

"*Matty*," I say more insistently, but he continues to ignore me.

I would leave him alone if he were any of our campers. I *want* to leave him alone for personal reasons. But I feel an obligation to make sure he's okay—not just for myself, but for everyone who's looking to the two of us to keep them safe out here.

"Everything okay?" I try, a last-ditch effort.

This, finally, is the thing that makes him stop.

"'Everything okay?'" he repeats in a mocking tone that makes my blood simmer. "Everything's a nightmare, man. I don't need shit from you on top of all of it."

He's spiraling, hard. His Italian accent only comes out these days when he's upset, and it's very much with us right now.

My own pulse picks up. "What do you mean? Matty. Come on. Why would I give you shit?"

His face is hard, but he's clearly in a lot of pain. He fishes his phone out of his pocket and taps around on the screen, which casts an unnaturally bright glow in the dim twilight.

He passes the phone to me.

"Which part?" I ask, glancing down at the series of texts he's pulled up.

"All of it."

"These are from Blair?" I ask, and he nods.

He has her saved as BB with a bunny emoji between the initials; she probably saved it in his phone herself.

Heyyyyyyyy babe, hope you're having the adventure of a lifetime back in Cali! I miss you so so so so so so much

But

I have news

Please don't hate me, but I got this opportunity to do a contract with a tour company in Thailand for six months

I will regret it FOREVER if I don't take it, you know? And when they reached out, everything clicked, like, THIS is the next right move for me. I know we talked about settling down and growing roots together, but when I think about being tied to one place forever (and, sorry, one person) (not to hurt your feelings!!!) (I would feel this way about literally anyone) it makes me feel like I can't breathe

(I rlly hope you haven't put a down payment on a place for us yet, I would feel extra awful bc it's hard enough to tell you all of this as it is)

So sorry, babe, please please don't hate me

I'm flying to Bangkok tonight

And ugh I guess I should probably mention before you see it on insta that Stephen is coming with me

Thx for all the fun, I will never forget you and I hope you forgive me

I look up, stunned.

All the emotion has seeped out of his face and, apparently, leached into mine instead.

I shouldn't be speechless, but I am.

"Just say it," Matteo says. "I know you want to."

I take it all in, wait for whatever might be buried in me to surface.

Is there a part of me that's glad he's hurting in the same way he made me hurt?

It definitely feels like something has just balanced out in the universe—but I wouldn't say I'm *glad* about it. I've never been the vindictive sort, and underneath all we've been through, he's still like my brother. I don't want him to suffer any more than I'd want myself to suffer.

"I'm sorry, man," I say—and I mean it. "That really sucks."

Matteo scoffs. "You're not going to say I deserve it?"

If he keeps pushing me, I might.

His eyes are intense: a challenge. I breathe deeply and count to five before I say something I'll regret.

"Go for a night swim, sleep it off," I say. "This is just what Blair does—it's not about you."

Just like it was never about me.

I've had years to work through that, years to let it sink in. Seeing it happen to Matteo, though, is the thing that drives it home and makes it feel real.

Blair's in it for the fun, for the adventure. She doesn't want forever—not with Matteo, not with me, not with whoever Stephen is.

"*Did* you make a down payment?" I ask when he doesn't reply.

"I was about to," he finally says. "But I was waiting for Blair to say she liked the place, and then Danica called and I came out here instead."

"Bullet dodged, then."

"Yeah," he agrees. "Bullet dodged."

I shove my hands in my pockets, listening to the sounds of laughter back by the campfire as Matteo's world falls apart. He's in his own head, though: he doesn't notice the mosquito that lands on his arm, or the distant rumble of thunder, or Trey as he joins us on the path.

"All good over here?" Trey asks. "We were about to make s'mores and thought we'd see if y'all want any."

"I'd love one," I say. "Matty?"

Matteo finally looks up when I say his name, the nickname my mom gave him all those years ago when he first moved in with us. Only our family is allowed to call him that.

"Huh—oh, hey," he replies, the blank look on his face shifting into a bright smile that only barely reaches his eyes.

That smile is second nature to him, a fake-it-till-you-make-it defense mechanism I've seen a number of times over the years.

"No s'mores for me, but thanks," Matteo goes on. "Gonna go for a night swim."

"Oh, *sweet*, bro!" Trey says. "The guys and I might join you if you're up for some company."

Matteo forces a grin, tells him maybe he'll see them later, but I hear what he really wants to say: he's craving alone time—time away from everyone, where it can be just him and his heartbreak, no fake-it-till-you-make-it façade required.

"I'll be right there," I tell Trey, who takes the hint and heads back to the others.

Matteo's face falls as soon as it's just us again.

"Don't go off alone like you did earlier, okay?" I say, for his own good as much as mine; it's not a great look for a leader to disregard the rules we put on everyone else. It wasn't okay earlier, and it's *definitely* not okay now that I know what's happened with Blair. Back when we were in high school—and early on in our college days—he got reckless whenever he was upset. I'd assumed he'd grown out of those tendencies years ago, but the look in his eye is all too familiar.

He cuts a sharp glance at me.

"Who the hell cares if I do?" he says, another challenge.

I know better than to argue with him when he's in a mood like this. He heads down the path toward the water without another word.

10:00 P.M. • DAY 4 • SADIE'S JOURNAL

My phone is dead, so I have no clue what time it *actually* is, but it's dark and I'm in my tent for the night.

Today was . . . a lot.

It was one of those days where the good and the bad just really pressed up against each other. I'm too tired to write about everything in detail, but so I don't forget:

- Angry yoga: Zoe was in a terrible mood (bad) but Thorn made me laugh the entire time (good).
- Kayaking: I successfully paddled across the lake!! (GOOD!) But ended up *in* the lake when I tried to turn (so bad). Almost got eaten alive by a snake (ALSO VERY BAD). Thorn helped me back into the kayak, and even though he was side-eyeing my outfit I could tell he liked it . . . and he liked how close we were (A+ would fall into a lake again just to have more moments like that one).
- Cliff climb with Thorn: I should never have looked at my phone today (VERY BAD) *but* the way Thorn gave me space while I was crying . . . he's an incredible guy (good, obviously). Total and complete closure re: Caden (a long time coming!!). I definitely still miss air conditioning (ugh).

16

SADIE

Had I known how difficult it would be to paint my nails inside my tent—dim lighting, bottles threatening to tip over every time I shift even slightly, the *fumes*—I would have saved my manicure session for tomorrow morning down by the lake.

If I were back home, I would be treating myself to a spa day to finish off the emotional cleanse I had back on the cliffside. Instead, I'm doing what I can to pamper myself here—especially since tomorrow's another hiking day.

I started with journaling, then moved on to dry shampoo. The entire tent smells like a mix of Flowerbomb perfume and lavender pillow spray (and the aforementioned fumes), and I'm feeling fresh in my last pair of clean pajamas.

I brought a five-pack of sheet masks with me (Abby did not get a chance to veto those, as I snuck them in when she was in the other room) and decided on a "nourishing honey" one, which is currently working its magic on my face. And then, an even harder decision: it took forever to choose a shade of polish—Strawberry Scone, Lava, or Lavender Stems—but the fiery orange-red of Lava paired perfectly with my mood, so I started with that one.

My left hand is shakily painting my right fingernails when I hear yelling so loud it makes me jump, knocking into the bottle of nail polish that was balanced precariously on top of my journal.

Lava polish spills *everywhere.*

I rush to contain the damage, but it's too late: my sleeping bag now has a fiery orange splash right where my face will be later tonight, leaving only a little left in the bottle.

The yelling gets louder.

I poke my head outside my tent, looking around frantically for Thorn.

Only when we find each other, and he looks like he's seen a ghost, do I realize I'm still wearing the sheet mask.

"Sounds like Joshua, doesn't it?" he asks as I rip my mask off.

We listen together, trying to make out the words.

As soon as the second voice enters the picture, we have our answer.

"Definitely Joshua and Zoe," I say.

He scowls. Something about it feels intimate: like a peek behind the curtain of his trail guide persona, a flash of how he really feels about the other hikers and their drama.

I follow him over to their clearing, partly because I don't want to be alone back at ours, but mostly because I'm nosy.

Zoe disappears into their tent before she sees us, and half a second later starts heaving things out of it.

A sleeping bag.

A pillow.

A pair of boxer briefs.

A mass-market paperback of *Jurassic Park* that nearly hits Joshua in the head.

"Find somewhere else to sleep tonight," she says tartly, then zips herself in without another word.

Joshua stands there, stunned.

I'd be stunned, too, if *Jurassic Park* had just nailed me in the temple in the process of getting unceremoniously kicked out by the person I was engaged to.

"Hi, hello," Thorn ventures. "How can I help?"

Joshua squints, trying to make out where Thorn's voice came from. We're in relative darkness—Joshua and Zoe have an LED lantern illuminating their corner of the clearing, but we're just outside its glow.

We step forward so he can see us.

"I need *space*," Zoe says with an exasperated exhale as she emerges from the tent. "I'm suffocating."

Her hand is still plastered with the bandages I put on last night—this is probably *not* about the ring, then.

I hope I'm far, far away whenever he finds out she lost it.

"You can have my tent," Thorn offers after a moment.

"Your tent?" Joshua repeats, like the English language isn't quite computing with all the other noise in his head.

Thorn shrugs. "I like sleeping outside, especially in places like this. It's yours if you want it."

Joshua just sort of blinks at him.

Thorn claps his hands together. "Right. Okay. I'll go get it and be right back, yeah? Sadie—want to help me?"

He doesn't have to ask me twice.

I follow him back down the trail to our clearing.

"I'm glad we're sleeping way over here," I say under my breath.

Thorn gives a little half laugh. "Seriously. I don't envy Matteo having to spend the night near them."

We each take a corner and start pulling tent pegs out of the ground.

Attempting to pull them out, anyway, in my case.

"Did you secure these with cement?" I ask, breathless between efforts. "They—aren't—budging—at *all*."

He comes around to meet me, then slides the stubborn tent peg out with ease. "Just needed the magic touch, I guess," he says, his flirtatious smile making an appearance once again.

"I must have loosened it up for you."

He smirks. "We'll go with that."

"You must really like sleeping out under the stars," I say as he kneels to fold his tent into a small bundle. "And here I thought I was special when you gave me yours on the first night."

He glances up at me, eyes sparkling in the moonlight.

If this were a romance novel, he would say something like, "You *are* special, Sadie."

And for a split second? I honestly think he might.

But he just grins and finishes packing the tent, leaving me to wonder.

I'm on a yacht, sunbathing and eating grapes straight from the vine against the backdrop of coastal Italy, when a boom of thunder rips me right back to reality.

I sit straight up, panting.

A few fat raindrops land on my tent, and it isn't long before the patter becomes a full-on downpour.

Thorn.

Thorn was in my dream, I realize—he was the one feeding me grapes.

And now he's probably soaked to the bone.

I turn on my LED touch lamp and unzip my tent just enough to peek out. Wind and rain whip against my face; I spot him immediately, huddled under his sleeping bag, a poor excuse for an umbrella. I can just make out the scratchy sounds of a weather report coming from a radio somewhere.

"*Hey,*" I say, loudly enough so that he can hear me over the storm and the forecast. "You should come in here!"

"Sounds like this will probably be the worst of it," he says. "This heavy part shouldn't last much long—"

A flash of lightning cuts him off, casting everything in a split-second shock of brilliant white.

"*Thorn!*" I squeal.

"Okay, yeah," he agrees, rushing over to climb in with me, lime-green emergency radio in hand. "Sorry, but I'm about to get everything really wet."

He's not kidding—he's dripping on *everything*.

"I'd offer you some of my silk pajamas," I joke, "but they're all on the laundry line right now." Definitely *not* any less wet than they were when I hung them out to dry. "It's a little late for my poncho, but I do have an oversized hoodie—want to try that?"

He glances down at the puddle beneath him. There's no way either of us will sleep if he gets the rest of the sleeping bag that wet.

"I'll try it," he says. "Thanks."

He peels off his drenched shirt, revealing a torso straight out of my dreams—it's nothing I haven't seen before, as he was gloriously shirtless all afternoon at the lake, but it feels different somehow being this close, at night, in my tent. His athletic shorts are every bit as wet as his shirt; after a moment of hesitation, he takes those off, too.

Don't stare, Sadie.

Do. Not. Stare.

I tear my eyes away and dig around for my hoodie instead. I'm not at all confident it will be big enough for him, but it's worth a try.

He tugs it on, and we both laugh.

"Oh, *this* is a good look for you," I say. "The black boxer briefs really make it work."

"And here I was thinking it was the sleeves that made it work." He stretches out his arms—the ribbed cuffs pull almost all the way up to his elbows, showing off his strong forearms.

"Are you warmer now, at least?"

"Definitely," he says, though it's hard not to notice the goosebumps all over his arms. I reach out to rub them away on instinct, and we both look down, registering the contact between my skin and his at the exact same time.

I start to pull my hand away, but it snags his in the process and he holds on.

Stay, his hand says.

So I do.

His fingertips are rougher than mine, but not as rough as I would have expected for someone who lives most of his life outdoors. I look up and find him grinning, watching me.

"What's the story there?" he asks, nodding to my absolute wreck of a manicure. I never got around to painting the ring and pinky fingers of my right hand.

"A miserable attempt at pampering myself," I admit. "It sort of turned into a disaster."

I shift the touch lamp over so he can see the full damage on my sleeping bag.

"Is *that* what that smell is?" he says, laughing. "I thought maybe you were dissecting something in here."

"First of all, my best friend will think it's hilarious that your first thought was that *I* was dissecting something—she teaches middle school science." She's never made it through a full story about lab experiments without me getting squeamish. "Secondly . . . yes. That is, unfortunately, the smell. I knocked into it earlier when Joshua started yelling, and . . . well. You see what happened."

He shifts his focus back to my hand, lifts it up to inspect it. His touch sends both shivers and warmth coursing through me.

"And that's why you didn't finish painting them? It all spilled out?"

I shrug. "Mostly it's because I got distracted and fell asleep."

He runs his thumb over my ring finger, considering it. "Want me to finish it for you?"

It takes me a minute to realize what he means.

"Finish . . . painting my nails?" I guess. "You?"

He grins. "Why not?"

Maybe he's thinking what I am: it's a good excuse to touch me just a little more.

And who am I to say no to that?

I grab the Lava polish only to discover it actually did all spill out. "Well, there went that idea," I say, turning the empty bottle over in my hands.

"I know we only met recently," he says, "but would it be wrong of me to assume that wasn't the only bottle of nail polish you packed?"

Heat fills my cheeks, but I can't help but smile.

"I've got two more," I admit, holding up the bottles of Strawberry Scone and Lavender Stems. "Though they won't match the rest of my nails . . ."

"Who says they all need to match?" he says. "I'll do one of each."

I laugh, torn between my perfectionism and the voice in my head telling me I should try to let loose a little. That *is* essentially the point of why I'm here, right? To do things I wouldn't usually do—and to be okay when my circumstances aren't exactly what I envisioned.

He takes my hand in his, holds it up close to his face. I move the lamp closer so he can see what he's doing. By the tentative way he holds the polish brush, I can tell he doesn't have any sisters and never spent time in an emo/punk band—but his hand is surprisingly steady as he paints, slowly adding a few careful layers of the light pink Strawberry Scone before switching over to Lavender Stems for my pinky.

The sight of him etches itself into my memory: the way his brow furrows in concentration; the focus he's putting into it so he can get everything just right.

"You're actually pretty good at this," I say when he's done, admiring his work. "Might need to have you redo all the rest of them while you're at it!"

"Whoa, whoa, whoa," he says, grinning as he holds up his hands. "Let's not get carried away."

I listen to the rain, still going strong, as he tucks the bottles away so my nails can dry. The colors actually look pretty cute together. More than that, from now on, the two shades he painted will be linked with the image of *him* painting them.

Maybe it's not so bad to go with the flow sometimes.

Maybe it's not so bad to spill your entire bottle of nail polish if it means the hot hiking guide can make something even more beautiful than what you'd originally planned.

Abby would be so proud that I'm not only *tolerating* my mismatched nails, but . . . actually . . . really liking them?

Or maybe I just really like *him*.

I didn't come out here looking for a guy, or even a hookup. Being out here is changing me on a molecular level, though, I can feel it: this place, this experience, is carving its mark on me—and Thorn is bearing witness to it.

I think, again, of *Survivor.* I've never understood how the contestants could form such tight bonds over such a short period of time, but now I see that the experiences they go through—being far from their comfort zones, out in nature, with almost no contact with the outside world—all combine to function as a pressure cooker. When you're at a pivotal moment in your life and stripped down to your core, it's only natural that the people you share those experiences with become deeply bonded with the experience itself.

Maybe that's what's happening here. I feel like I've known Thorn for four *weeks*, not four days—

And everything in me wants to know *more.*

It's a tight fit with both of us in my tent, especially with Thorn's height. He's examining my sleeping bag at the moment (the soaking-wet end, not the covered-in-nail-polish end).

"How does it feel on the inside?" he asks.

The sleeping bags are supposed to be water-resistant to some extent, so maybe it's just the outer layer that's still cold and wet.

I slip inside, stretch my legs all the way out. There's so little space in the tent that we'd be touching if not for the thick layer of sleeping bag fabric between us.

"Not too bad, actually," I report. "It's like I can tell it's wet, but can't actually *feel* it—it's just a little heavier there than it would be without the extra weight the water adds."

"I'd offer mine," Thorn says, right as another boom of thunder drowns out his voice. "But . . . yeah."

His sleeping bag has got to be a hopeless bundle of rain and mud at this point.

He sits up on his knees, assessing our situation. I have to tear my eyes away from his black boxer briefs, and the carved stretch of his stomach that isn't covered by my hoodie that he's still wearing.

But the alternative is his face, and *ugh*—it's *such* a good face.

He's hot when he's smiling, and he's hot when he's perplexed. Right now, with his five o'clock shadow and the way he's biting his full lower lip, he's kind of off the hotness charts entirely.

"You'll be warm," he finally says after a long moment of silence, as if the conversation that led him to this conclusion wasn't just in his own head. "That's all that matters."

"And what about you?" I ask.

"You'll sleep in the sleeping bag, and I'll sleep next to you. Not in the sleeping bag."

"But you're . . ." My eyes drift to his bare legs, veritable tree trunks that support his over-six-foot frame.

The corner of his mouth quirks up. "I'm what?"

I pretend to ignore the way he's caught me staring. "Won't you be cold?"

The night air turned chilly hours before the storm rolled in, but there's even more of a bite to it now.

He shrugs. "I might be."

This sleeping bag is mummy-shaped, barely enough room for one person, let alone two—especially when we're talking about trying to squeeze an entire Thorn-sized human inside.

Still, I'm tempted to try.

"Okay, this is going to sound like the dumbest idea," I say as I unzip the sleeping bag and climb back out. "But what if we, like . . . spread some clothes underneath us for cushioning and then share the sleeping bag as a blanket?"

He considers it, eyeing my short sleeves and even shorter shorts, then shakes his head. "I'm afraid *you'll* be too cold that way."

"Easy," I say. "Just sleep close enough to keep me warm."

His eyebrows raise, and I slap a hand over my mouth. I didn't mean to say that *out loud*—

But—

Maybe it's good that I did.

Maybe it's good that I was honest.

"Sure, why not," he says after a beat, grinning. "Let's try it."

And that's how I end up spooning with Thorn in the middle of a thunderstorm: every inch of him pressed up against every inch of me, his left arm wrapped around me and pulling me in tight, the sleeping bag in no way big enough to share.

He generates more than enough warmth, though—so much that, an hour later, when we're both clearly still wide awake, he whispers something in the dark, his breath hot in my hair.

"Mind if I take the hoodie off?"

I will not sleep a wink if he takes the hoodie off.

Sadie of Tomorrow might regret it—but right now, all I care about is Sadie of Tonight.

"I don't mind," I reply.

A moment later, it's clear *why* he wanted to take it off: the heat of his bare chest radiates through my silk pajamas. He's a furnace.

Neither of us pulls away. If anything, we get closer: he's so tall it's like I'm totally enveloped by him, his lips pressed into the top of my head and my toes curled against his ankles. His hand slides down the length of my arm and settles at my hip.

"Okay like this?" he murmurs.

I smile to myself, eyes wide open in the darkness.

"Yeah," I say, barely more than a breath.

I'm aware of every inch of him, truly not sure how I'll make it through this situation without taking it further—

But we just stay like this, together, and it's perfectly enough.

I count a thousand raindrops before I finally fall asleep.

For once, none of my dreams live up to reality.

DAY FIVE

Mackenzie Lake to Swallowtail Pass to Thimbleberry Grove

The view from Swallowtail Pass is magnificent: each turn of the switchback takes you higher into the heavens—be sure to stop at the scenic overlook once you get to the top. In addition to Helen Theresa Peak in the southwest, the overlook gives a stunning glimpse of the Three Daughters off to the east. Hikers of all levels should take precautions on these narrow trails, as they are rockier and steeper than the terrain covered previously along the Mackenzie Lake Loop.

—Henry Herrington, *Backpacking the Sierras: A Beginner's Handbook* (Fourth Edition)

17

THORN

We wake up face-to-face, Sadie's knee hiked over my hip—and my hand holding her leg there, right on top of the place where her silk shorts end and her soft skin begins. She must have turned over sometime in the middle of the night while we were asleep.

I can't believe I slept at all. Today is going to be hell.

Her eyes flutter open.

"Hey," she says sleepily.

I swallow. "Hey."

Her eyes grow wide when she realizes how tangled we are—but she doesn't move, not even a little.

I grin, tightening my grip on her thigh. "Worried I needed a little extra warmth last night?"

"Must've been," she says.

Her voice is raspy with sleep, too, and—*sweet* miserable goodness—the things it's doing to me are impossible to ignore.

Probably for both of us.

Her gaze flickers down to my lips, then back up again. Instinctively,

I do the same, which is a mistake, because now all I can think about is what it would feel like to kiss her.

My job, I remind myself. *The rules.*

Danica would understand why I slept in here, given the circumstances; the rules are black and white, but she's usually fine with shades of gray if they make sense. She'd give me hell if I'd slept out in that thunderstorm while this tent was an option.

That said, now that I'm here, the boundaries aren't merely blurred—they're obliterated. I'm tangled up with a beautiful girl, and it's been years since I've felt anything close to a spark with someone like I do with Sadie.

Maybe Danica would understand this, too. What if I were to push Sadie away for the sake of abiding by the rules only for Danica to tell me I should have gone with my gut? It's not like I'm a chronic rule-bender. This isn't the norm for me, not by a long shot.

Sadie's arm is draped over me, just like her leg. Until now, it's been loose, relaxed—but I feel her hand curl around the back of my head, her fingers raking up through my hair, a signal that she'd maybe be okay with getting even closer.

It's still raining outside. I have no idea how early it is . . . but instinct tells me we have a little time before the others are up.

I make the first move, leaning in, a clear invitation—

And she meets me halfway.

The kiss is sleepy and slow and tender, something I could sink into for hours if we had time. Her fingers tighten in my hair as I trace the line where her shorts meet skin, then rub away the goosebumps I've caused. She shifts under my touch, hiking her knee up even higher, and we fuse even closer together.

Her mouth is so soft against mine, the lingering taste of whatever lip balm she last used sweet under my tongue—coconut, I think, and a hint of lime—and her skin smells like flowers. She's a tropical paradise caught in a California monsoon.

I settle my hand onto her hip, dig in just a little, not so hard as to hurt. She makes a sound, the slightest sigh that will play on a loop in my head for days, and it's all I can do to just stay in this moment instead of wishing for a million more.

She shifts again, her toes curling into the back of my leg, but it gives me a surprising jolt: she's cold as ice.

I break away on instinct. "Holy— You're *freezing*!"

We lost our sleeping bag cover sometime in the middle of the night, not that it was all that effective in the first place.

Sadie gives a little shrug. "Only my toes. The rest of me is fine, thanks to you." She burrows in even closer, tucking her head against my chest. It's impossible to go back to our kiss in this position, but it's good even so.

As if reading my thoughts, she shifts, turning her face back up toward mine. "You're a good kisser, Thorn." Her eyes are shining even in the dim light. "We should do that again sometime."

I'm stuck on the way she's said my name, soft and round and delicate—but then the rest of it registers.

"Like now?" I say, both of us still grinning even as we fall back into another kiss, this one hungrier, more electric than the first.

Her knee digs into my hip, my fingers grip the back of her thigh. There's not much fabric between us—only her silk pajamas and my boxer briefs—and as soon as I wrap my mind around that, I can't think of anything else. I resist the urge to push the limits of where my hand could go, keeping it firmly in we-only-just-met-this-week territory, but it's not easy. Not easy at all.

The rain picks up, heavier than it's been for the last twenty minutes. It's cozy—peaceful, even—the two of us safe and dry in our tent as nature rages all around us. My hand is dangerously close to exploring uncharted territory, teasing the hem of her shorts, when a peal of thunder rips our quiet morning in two, startling us apart.

If anyone was still asleep, they'll be awake now.

I run a hand over my jaw, my days-old stubble rough to the touch.

She sighs. "Guess you should probably go check on the others now?"

"I don't want to go *anywhere*," I say, with one last kiss because I can't help it. "But yeah. Probably. And I should touch base with Matteo."

Only now does it occur to me that I'm not the only one who was set up outside last night—what on earth did Matteo do once the storm hit?

"Are we still planning to leave for the next campsite today?" she asks, leaning up on one elbow.

"We hike in all weather as long as it's not dangerous," I tell her, reaching over to grab the pocket-sized AM/FM radio I use when I don't have easy access to my phone. "I'll see what the weather guys have to say, and also check the radar—my guess is that it'll be fine after another hour or so."

"Wait, how are you going to check the radar?" she asks. "I thought we didn't get a signal down here?"

I bite my lip, regretting that I'm going to have to tell her this, especially when she's done such a good job with limited access to the real world.

"I've got a satellite phone plan," I say, "so we always have a lifeline in case of emergencies."

Her eyes grow wide. "So, theoretically, I could upload some vlog footage or check my socials if I really needed to?"

And *this* is why I don't make a habit of telling anyone about it: it's hard enough to get people to forget about their phones and just embrace the experience of being out here, but once they realize they could stay connected—as long as there's a signal—it becomes a distraction again.

"I mean, you could . . ." I say, choosing my words carefully. "But it didn't look like your phone made you any happier yesterday, right?"

It's the first time either of us has acknowledged what happened up on the cliff. How her tears wouldn't stop; how I pretended not to notice when all I wanted to do was wipe them away.

She meets my eyes.

"No, yeah, you're right," she says. "I liked being able to text Abby. But not the rest of it."

I want to ask what happened, what made her so upset, but I don't want to push. She'll tell me when she's ready, *if* she wants to.

"I know what you're thinking," she says after a long moment. "If I'd just stayed off my phone in the first place, I could have avoided all that drama."

"That does sound like me," I say, grinning.

"Please resist the urge to say 'I told you so,'" she goes on, "but honestly? I actually kind of like not being attached at the hip to the internet. I thought it would be harder not to check it, but it's like being in another world out here."

"I know exactly what you mean." It's why I forget I even *have* sat-phone access most of the time. "I like seeing the world with my own eyes, not just through a camera lens or through someone else's pictures."

"I never thought about it that way," she says, brows pinching together—very adorably, I can't help but notice—as she considers it. "I like that, thank you."

Her eyes meet mine, and it's all I can do not to kiss her again.

If I kiss her again, we will never make it out of this tent.

"My absolute pleasure," I manage. "I'm glad you're here."

I swallow, finally look away.

My clothes from last night are still damp in the corner of the tent; I tug them on and head out to find Matteo. I stop by my pack first, dig around until I find my charger and my phone, then tuck both in my pockets along with the radio.

I do a double take once I'm out of our clearing: there's Zoe, all alone, doing yoga on the big rock by the lake despite the lingering rain.

How she's keeping her balance, I have no clue—I can only hope she won't slip and hurt herself.

It takes longer than it should to find Matteo. He's not in the clearing he originally shared with Zoe and Joshua, though I do see the tarp I lent him stretched out over his pack. Eventually, I find him over with the tennis girls—chatting, specifically, with Brittany as he gnaws on a protein bar. She's laughing at something he said, and he's grinning, no obvious trace of his heartbreak from yesterday. He actually looks well rested, even.

But I know better.

I know his tells: that smile that doesn't reach his eyes, the way he avoids talking about himself and masks it by asking a thousand questions to whoever he's with at the time.

You'd never notice he was hurting if you didn't know what to look for.

"Sleep okay, man?" I ask when there's a break in the conversation.

He and Brittany look up. She bites back a smile, her eyes cutting to Matteo, though he pretends not to notice.

Ah. No wonder he seems well rested—I probably have the same look about me this morning, a take-refuge-with-gorgeous-girl aura that's distinctly different from the wet-dog-left-out-in-a-thunderstorm situation I was expecting.

"Yeah," he says, shaking the hair out of his eyes. "Not bad."

Like he can hide it . . . Brittany's face gives everything away.

Not that I have room to talk.

"Good," I reply.

"You?" he asks.

I shrug. "Fine."

Brittany glances between us uncomfortably, clearly picking up on our monosyllabic awkwardness.

"Head out in an hour unless conditions look too bad?" I ask.

He nods. "Sounds good."

"Okay."

"Okay."

I can't get out of this clearing fast enough. There's no coffee this morning—it's too wet for a fire—and the coffee bros all share the same heavy scowl. Emma and Parker aren't exactly smiling, either, chatting quietly off to the side.

Today's going to be a blast.

"All right, everyone," I say once we're packed up and ready to go. The deluge has fizzled out into a light mist, and the worst of the storm has already passed over the area we'll be covering. "Today's hike is a bit more challenging than the terrain we've covered so far—we'll pace ourselves this morning to conserve energy for the more difficult stretch this afternoon. Any of you ever done switchbacks before?"

Trey raises his hand.

For everyone else, I give a brief overview. "Switchbacks are a type of path that gains elevation up the side of a cliff—it's an upward incline to the end, then a sharp pivot to the opposite direction, over and over until we get to the top. The one we'll be trekking this afternoon is called Swallowtail Pass, named for the butterfly. You're going to *wish* you were butterflies about halfway up. It's *very important* for you to step carefully, okay? We'll take some time up at the top—there's a great scenic overlook—and then continue on to our campsite at Thimbleberry Grove. Any questions?"

Ten minutes later, we're off. I'm in the lead again today; the trail is a gloppy, slippery mess, and we'll be on it for a long while before we get to Swallowtail Pass.

"I don't think these will ever be white again," Sadie says, looking mournfully at her shoes, which have progressed from merely dirty to being absolutely covered in mud.

"How're your feet holding up?" I ask.

She tightens her ponytail under her ball cap. “Oh, they’re fantastic,” she replies. “Never been better.”

It’s sweet how she thinks I’ll believe that for a second.

“That’s good to hear,” I say. “In my experience, wet socks and muddy shoes are kind of miserable on blisters.”

She grins, an admirable effort at hiding the grimace just beneath. “Good thing I don’t have blisters, then,” she says.

“Yes, good thing.”

Two hours later, still on the mild part of today’s trek, she can’t hide the pain in her left foot. Not from me, anyway—I know a subtle limp when I see one, the shift in gait when someone’s trying not to put pressure on a certain part of the body—but that doesn’t mean she isn’t still *trying* to hide it.

I call for a break, to no complaints. Everyone seems over the dreary weather, the caffeine headaches, the mud, the mosquitos. It’s the best place to stop before we start the switchbacks; hopefully this break will revive our collective energy levels—we’re going to need it. We bust out the trail mix and protein bars and settle down near a small stream lined with moss-covered boulders.

Sadie, of course, has some sort of gourmet trail mix, a spicy-sweet combination of peppery pistachios and dried cherries.

She sees me eyeing it and holds out the package. “Want some?”

“I’m okay, thanks.” I shove a handful of raw walnuts in my mouth, but they’re so dry I have to wash them down with a swig of water.

“Those aren’t too bitter on their own?”

They are, but I don’t want to admit her fancy trail mix looks more appealing than mine. I’m an outdoorsman—it’s not practical to make a habit of doing gourmet *anything*.

“They’re fine,” I say.

“Thorn. Please. Walnuts were put on this earth to make life miserable for anyone who can’t be bothered to find a better nut.”

"'A better nut'?" I laugh. "Should've known you'd be a nut snob."

She shrugs. "Coffee snob, nut snob—I know what I like, is all."

Her eyes meet mine, and instantly, I forget everything that was on the tip of my tongue.

I've never met anyone quite like Sadie.

I never thought I could *like* anyone like Sadie, but I do. I like her a lot. All of her particular preferences, the way she knows exactly what she wants and won't waste her time on anything less—

The way she seems to want *me*.

Which means, I think, I've passed some sort of test to live up to her high standards.

I hold my hand out. "Fine. I'll try your fancy nuts."

"Warning," she says as she pours out a larger handful than I deserve, "once you try them, you'll never go back."

That's what I'm afraid of, I want to say but don't, because it's not just about the trail mix—it's about Sadie herself. Her strong opinions, her sense of humor, her stubborn bravery in the face of all her fears, her eyes and her smile and her long hair and long legs and—just—

Everything.

I got a taste of her this morning, and I'm afraid I'm already in over my head.

I pop the trail mix in my mouth—because she likes it, because she wants to share it with *me*—and it's good. Really good. Somehow I knew it would be.

"Terrible," I tell her. "Just completely awful."

But she already knows me well enough to see right through me, and she grins. "You can keep the rest. I've got eight more of these in my pack."

I shake my head, laughing. "Of course you do."

18

SADIE

It's rainy and muddy and there are mosquitos everywhere—but somehow, none of it has managed to ruin my day.

In fact, it's been a pretty *good* day, all credit to Thorn.

I can't stop thinking about this morning.

His lips. His hands.

His hands on *me.*

It's been a long time since I've kissed anyone—and a *really* long time since I've kissed anyone other than Caden. I've also never kissed anyone so quickly after meeting them. But then again, this week has been full of things I've never done.

I'm actually . . . having *fun* out here.

That said, I'm a little nervous for what lies ahead. The terrain has taken a turn for the dramatic: it's wide and open, rocks and mud everywhere, the path we're on headed straight toward the cliff full of switchbacks Thorn mentioned this morning.

The closer we get, the worse it looks.

"You really undersold how *big* it is, man," Trey says, awed.

Zoe crosses her arms, coming to a stop. "You expect *us*," she says, "to get to the top of *that*?"

Even from here, it's obvious the switchbacks are going to be a challenge. They're significantly steeper than any trail we've been on thus far, and there are five of them cutting across the face of the cliff.

"Try not to sell yourself short before you even start," Thorn says. "Just put one foot in front of the other, over and over, until it's done." He glances from face to face, his gaze lingering on Zoe's before ultimately landing on mine. "If I had reservations about any of you being able to do this, I'd say so. But I don't."

I swallow. Thorn doesn't have my terrible shoes, or the pain I feel in at *least* five places, or my heavy pack that's definitely about to make this ten times harder than it would be if I were a minimalist. Maybe *I* have reservations about my own ability to do this—maybe I should say so before I crumple into a pile of backpack and bones halfway up the cliffside.

I'm too stubborn for that, though. I can put one blistered foot in front of the other, over and over, just like he said. It might be horrible—but the idea of making it to the top, especially when it seems so impossible, feels strangely exhilarating.

We're barely up the first incline when Zoe's voice echoes from down below. "I never signed up for this!" she calls out, trailing at the back of the pack with only Matteo behind her. "Did I *ever* express *any* interest in doing *anything* like this, Joshua?"

He keeps his mouth shut. Mercifully for us all, she doesn't push it.

I, on the other hand, *did* sign up for this—and by the third switchback I'm seriously starting to wonder why. Would it really have been so bad for me to just lounge by the pool with Abby for all of June? That would have been the far more rational choice. I want to cry, thinking of how incredible it would feel to be there right now instead of here, where

I feel increasingly like I'm losing a war with gravity. My pack is a million pounds heavier than it was when we started, even though there's less in it thanks to my diminished snack reserves; my leg muscles have simultaneously turned to both lead and jelly.

I grit my teeth and keep going.

After the next turn, we're dizzyingly high up. We've come so far, and we're almost there—only one more turn after this stretch of the path—but there is a very real possibility that I might pass out before we get there.

"You're doing a good job, Sadie," Thorn says a few minutes later, when my progress grinds to a halt and I can't help but take a break, slumped against the solid cliff wall just to give my back a little relief. "We're almost there. You're doing great, okay?"

I nod, but I'm too winded to talk back. It's been pretty quiet for the last two stretches, most of us similarly struggling—even the tennis girls, whose staminas have bordered on inhuman until now—so I doubt anyone minds a couple of extra minutes to catch their breath.

Thorn's eyes search mine. "How can I help?"

"Carrying my pack for me isn't an option?" I ask, even though I already know the answer. "Or throwing it off the side of the cliff, maybe?"

The corner of his mouth quirks up. "I strongly suspect you'd regret that later. And even though I *could* carry your pack, I think you'd regret that, too, yeah?"

He's right. Unfortunately. If I'm going to do this, *I* am going to do this—not in a half-assed way, but with every bit of strength I can muster.

"Distract me instead, then?" I suggest. "Keep my mind off how hard it is until we get to the top?"

"*That* I can do." He grins.

"So," I start, once we're finally moving again. "How'd you decide you wanted to do this for a living?"

He gestures out at the expansive view. "I mean, look at it!"

I squint, try to figure out exactly what I'm supposed to be appreciating—from this height, we can see for miles. "At what?"

He scoffs. "At *everything*."

"I see rocks. And mud. And lots and lots of trees."

He bites down on a smile. "You're thinking too small, focusing too much on the details," he says. "Think of it like one of those Magic Eye puzzles—look at all of it together. What stands out? What does it make you *feel*?"

I inhale the damp afternoon air, trying to look at the world through his eyes. When I look beyond the rocks and the mud and the trees—at the cut of the landscape, the far-off mountains carving a jagged line into the distant sky; at the butterfly that flutters past, and the hawk that swoops low across the horizon—I think, maybe, I see it.

"It makes me feel woefully powerless and small," I finally say.

His eyes light up. "Yes! Yes. That's *exactly* it."

I laugh. "You do this for a living because it makes you feel powerless and small?"

He laughs now, too. "Okay, well, no. But also kind of yes? It makes me feel powerless in a *good* way—it's freeing to think about how big the world is and how small I am. That no matter how big my problems feel, I'm just a tiny speck in the universe."

I consider it. I think I know what he means, at least on some level—it's a distraction from the real world, if nothing else. But also, I feel calmer than I've felt in months. Maybe it's the fresh air? Maybe it's the fact that I've done something that scares me, something so far outside of my comfort zone that I almost don't recognize myself, all bug-bitten and sweaty and muddy-shoed. I didn't even put mascara on this morning, I realize.

For all the ways I've been miserable out in the wilderness, it's been at least a little bit healing, too.

"So you feel, I guess . . . peace out here?" I ask. "Or maybe just simplicity?"

I try to imagine what it would be like to be someone like Thorn, whose entire home is probably less full than my backpack. For all the crap he gave me about *Wild* and *Eat Pray Love*, it seems like Thorn lives his own version of nature-heals-the-soul on a daily basis.

"Always have," he says. "My dad used to take me on hikes when I was young—it was our thing. Orienteering, camping, everything. When Matteo moved in, he picked it up, too."

"I bet your dad loves that you turned your adventures together into a career."

He gives a sad smile. "He does, yeah. He misses being able to do it himself."

"Wait, why can't he do it himself anymore?" I ask, then immediately regret it—what if this is the sort of thing Thorn only talks about with people he's known for *more* than one week?

But he doesn't close himself off, doesn't act like I've crossed some sort of personal boundary.

"Lots of reasons," he says. "The biggest is his lung disease—he just can't physically be out here like he used to, and it's frustrating for him. And because of the lung stuff, he had to take an office job in downtown San Francisco instead of all the welding and woodworking he used to do, so he's also not nearby like he was before."

"Wow . . . that sounds like a lot of change." Thorn seems to take after his dad, and I can't imagine him being cooped up in an office. "Is he doing okay?"

Thorn shrugs. "*Okay* is a good word for it," he says. "He's learned how to manage. He likes the job itself even if he's never loved living in the city."

I watch as Thorn navigates a patch of mud in the path, his steps so quick and natural: the landscape isn't an obstacle for him like it is for me—for all of us amateurs.

It's familiar. It's home.

"I think he feels like he's only *half* living sometimes, though, not being able to do all the things he loves," Thorn goes on, stepping over a thick, gnarled root. "This was his favorite place in the world."

I carefully step over the same root. We're so close to the top, only one more turn to go—and I'm so, so ready. I'm keenly aware of the dizzying elevation we've covered, and of how narrow this path is, only eight feet between the cliff wall to our right and the steep drop-off of switchbacks at our left. I'm ready for the relative safety of the scenic overlook, ready for a break.

I'm just past the thick root when the world turns to slow motion: there's a strong tug at my pack, someone trying to steady themselves by using me as their anchor—and then the world goes sideways, and suddenly I'm face-to-face with the rough cliff wall.

I'm okay, I tell myself, breathing hard from the surprise of it, and from the relief that I've fallen *away* from the steep drop-off and not toward it.

But then I register Brittany, who was right behind me, now dangerously close to the edge as she struggles to regain her balance. She must have tripped on that thick root—and tried, unsuccessfully, to stabilize by grabbing onto my pack.

Her shoes are covered in mud—she's sliding—

And I'm too slow, too stunned, to help.

Silas, who's closest, springs into action, grasping the handle of Brittany's backpack—but the straps start to slide off her shoulders, and she's still flailing, seconds away from a treacherous plummet. Thorn is at her side a split second later, curling one strong arm around her waist to pull her back from the edge.

The rest of us look on, speechless.

Brittany, shaking, lets out a wail that echoes far below. Parker and Emma rush to her; Silas stands as a strong barrier so they don't come anywhere close to the edge.

"Are you okay?" Emma asks, while Parker's face says everything we're all thinking: Brittany could have *died* just now. We're high enough up, and the terrain is rocky enough below, that the fall wouldn't just have been painful—it would have been devastating.

I blink, my cheeks hot with tears as that reality sinks in.

That could have been any of us. That could have been *me*.

"My ankle!" is all Brittany, breathless, can manage.

I can see the swelling even from here. What will she do? It's not like we have crutches just lying around, and we still have a long way to go before the end of the trek.

Also, I cannot reiterate this enough: Brittany almost died.

My mouth has gone dry at the mere thought of it. It's *terrifying*.

Life—the gift of *being alive*—suddenly feels much more fragile than it did just a few minutes ago.

"Can you put any weight on it at all?" Thorn asks.

His deep voice is calm, controlled. The only hint of stress I see on him is the crease between his eyebrows—well, that and the veins popping on his lean forearms, adrenaline still going strong.

Brittany winces as she tests it out, shakes her head. She's clearly in a lot of pain.

It's slow going after that. Brittany wraps her arms around Silas and Hunter, who support her as she hops on her good foot; they're both tall and sturdy, while she's petite but athletic. When we all finally make it up to the top, the guys settle Brittany onto a bench at the scenic overlook while the rest of us take in the view.

"Hey, Danica," I overhear Thorn saying ten minutes in to our extended break. He left a voicemail for her immediately after the incident, but she only just called him back.

"Yeah," he says. "Yeah. No, I think she's done—yeah." His voice sounds more exhausted than I expected, given how rare it is for him to ever seem anything but perfectly composed, perfectly capable. "Can we push the supply drop up by a day, do it tonight instead? If we skip Thimbleberry, we can be at Wild Gate by six, if that works for you."

When he's off the phone a few minutes later, my curiosity gets the better of me.

"What's Wild Gate?" I ask.

"It's a campsite," he replies. "A little less remote than the other places we've spent the night—running water, toilets, the works. We always do supply drops there since it's somewhat accessible by car, but Danica will still have to hike about a quarter mile in order to get to us. It's the closest spot for a pickup if Brittany can't finish out the trek."

I take it in: Brittany will most likely be leaving us tonight.

I'm not particularly close with Brittany, but it will be weird to not have her here. She's got good energy and she's always sharing her snacks.

The rest of the afternoon passes in a blur. Thorn and Trey and Matteo take turns carrying Brittany's pack in addition to their own gear, trading off every fifteen minutes or so. And the rest of us? We just keep our heads down and try not to cause any more scares. I feel shaken by today's events—I think we all do. It was a close call, like the day I almost slipped at the waterfall. I definitely didn't realize just how exposed we'd all be when I signed up for this. Having Thorn and Matteo to guide us has always felt like a safety net—

But we've had two near-disasters *despite* that.

The stakes out here are more than just bug bites and sweat and rain and the utter absence of all but my most portable comforts; more than the massive headache I feel from today's lack of coffee, and the way all of my muscles and blisters are screaming for rest. *Everything* hurts.

At the same time, things could be so much worse right now. For Brittany—or me, or any of us if we'd stepped the wrong way.

The shock of it all lingers even after we get to Wild Gate.

5:45 P.M. • WILD GATE • SADIE'S JOURNAL

What did I expect from the wilderness? Wild comes with the territory. I shouldn't be surprised that it isn't a walk in the park . . . and yet.

I guess there's a difference between knowing something and experiencing it: you don't know what it feels like to be on a mountain just from looking at a postcard, in other words.

My body, right now, is screaming for the things it knows.

A soft bed. A gigantic bowl of mac and cheese with a side of mashed potatoes. Air conditioning. Abby sprawled out on my floor, painting her nails and telling me all about her date with Jonathan as the latest Gracie Abrams album plays in the background.

When I look down at my own mismatched nails, something in me settles. It's the memory of Thorn's hands on mine, the way he was so careful and focused . . . but it's also the way I'm surprised to find I actually *like* the randomness of the colors. It's so unlike me, honestly. I like neatness and order—and, yes, classic manicures—so it's comforting to realize I can be okay without things being exactly as I planned. I like to be in control: to be prepared for every single situation that could possibly come up so I can conquer it with ease . . . or so I can know how to avoid anything too risky in the first place.

I guess what I'm trying to say is that, out here? You just can't know every single thing that will come up. Sometimes it's as small and inconsequential as a nail polish crisis, and sometimes it's a girl nearly falling over the edge of a cliff.

I'm really glad Brittany is okay.

19

THORN

I can't get today out of my head.

I keep seeing what could have happened had Silas and I not gotten to Brittany in time—keep kicking myself for the fact that we had an incident at all. I saw that thick root, stepped carefully so my own shoes wouldn't get caught.

Why didn't I warn anyone? Isn't that my job, to keep an eye out for the things that could trip people up? These are amateurs. They're trusting me. And I let them down.

You didn't let anyone *down*, Danica's voice echoes in my head. *Your quick reaction time* saved *her.*

We had a long talk earlier; she was waiting at Wild Gate when we got there, a pair of crutches for Brittany in tow along with a couple of pepperoni pizzas for everyone to share. I couldn't stomach any of it, and Danica had already eaten, so we headed over to the old wrought iron gazebo that probably looked really nice before the rust set in. The wood benches need maintenance—termites, from what I can tell—so we sat on the steps that lead out to the gravel walking path.

I'm still there now, even though Danica drove Brittany out of here a while ago. Matteo's getting the others settled for camp tonight, their tents popping up one by one amid the sea of wildflowers.

"Knock, knock?"

I turn and see Sadie leaning against the gazebo, her long hair loose after being tied up all day. She gives a little wave.

"You okay?" she asks, then quickly adds, once she sees my face, "I can leave if you want to be alone."

It's only now that I realize I'm scowling. I try to relax a little, let the tension melt out of me.

"You can stay," I say, shifting on the steps so she'll have room to sit down.

When she does, something about her being this close—her body pressed right up next to mine, her soft curves and warm skin—finally puts me at ease. Her leggings are splattered with mud all the way up to her knees, with a few tiny holes in the fabric from the brush we hiked through today. There's even a little mud on her cheek, I notice when I take in her face, and a splash of freckles she usually covers up with makeup. The hint of dark circles under her eyes, too.

"How are *you*?" I ask, all too aware that I still haven't answered her question—but I'm tired of thinking about me right now. I want to know about her.

"Other than the massive caffeine headache and how everything hurts and how I need a massage so badly I could cry?" she says, laughing, even though I sense it's more a defense mechanism than anything. "Pretty good, actually. The pizza helped."

My stomach growls at the mere mention of food, loudly enough that Sadie hears it, too.

"Guess my appetite is back," I say, trying to crack a joke, but she just studies me.

"Why didn't you eat?"

I let out a long exhale. "Today freaked me out," I admit.

Maybe I *shouldn't* be telling her this—but it's the most honest thing I have right now. My instinct says Sadie is a safe place, despite the fact that she's one of the inexperienced people out here who I feel like I let down today. It could have been *her* who tripped and almost fell over the edge.

Maybe that's what's freaking me out, if I'm even more honest with myself. It could have been Sadie, and it could have been worse. And it could have been my fault.

The fact that it terrifies me to think about Sadie falling over, specifically—that she's *different* somehow, despite how I always try to be neutral and professional when it comes to the trekkers—only amplifies the fear that's haunted me all day: that I'm failing at my job.

She's quiet. I follow her gaze to a pair of butterflies out in the field.

"Yeah," Sadie eventually says. "Me too." She bites her lip, turning her hand over to examine her mismatched nail polish. "You know, I really thought I knew what to expect, coming out here. I did so much research—but some things just don't translate well over the internet. All those pictures of nature, not one mention that it'll be trying to kill you the whole time you're out in it."

I have to laugh. "Pretty sure that was in the fine print."

Sadie grins. "Today wasn't all bad, though," she says, cutting a glance at me from under her long lashes. "Can we just rewind to this morning, back in the tent?"

I swallow. We're already sitting closer than we really need to be, her legs angled and resting against mine—

I wish we were back in the tent, too. I wish we were someplace private.

"You're welcome in my tent anytime, for the record," she goes on.

My mind flashes immediately to the memory of being tangled with her this morning, and as much as this is new—dangerous—territory for me, I can't deny it: I want to do it again.

"Even if it's not raining?" I ask.

"*Especially* if it's not raining," she says, and I laugh. "My stuff is probably still drenched from your wet clothes."

"Your stuff is probably still drenched from the *rain* we hiked through all morning," I reply. "Not my fault at all."

"Details, details."

I reach out and run my fingers lightly over the splattered mud on her leggings. "They've got actual showers at this campsite, you know—if you haven't seen them yet."

"Are you implying I need one?" she says flirtatiously, her eyes flickering down to my hand before meeting mine again.

"Not implying," I reply. "Flat-out suggesting."

She swats my shoulder playfully. "You really know how to make a girl feel attractive."

"Glad you got the message," I say with a shrug. "You *are* attractive."

Sadie tenses beside me, the smallest, subtlest movement—she might not even be aware of it.

"My hair is full of dry shampoo," she argues, "and the closest I've come to a shower is the lake yesterday."

"And?" I reply.

"And I suspect I look like I've just been on *Naked and Afraid* and, like, totally disheveled. I promise I look better in my real life than I do out here."

"Impossible," I tell her. "And for the record, you don't look naked *or* afraid right now."

She laughs. "I hide my fear well."

"Really, though, Sadie." I wait until she looks me straight in the eye before continuing. "You're beautiful, even without all the makeup or whatever you're used to. I'm sure you look amazing in your everyday life, too . . . but I need you to know that you look pretty damn attractive just as you are."

She takes in what I've said, and I can tell by her expression—how her eyes linger on mine, vulnerable and unfiltered—that my words mean a lot. The next thing I know, her hand has found its way to mine where it still rests on her leg.

"So," she says with a dramatic pause, "you *don't* think I need a shower?"

I burst out laughing, and she cracks up, too. It's the last thing I expected her to say.

"You *absolutely* need a shower, Sadie Whitlock. I'll walk you over myself."

"Don't get your hopes up," I tell her. "This isn't the Four Seasons."

She comes to a stop beside me and stares at the lackluster concrete building. It's in worse shape than I remembered, paint peeling from the sides and a cluster of dead beetles resting in the corner with some empty glass bottles and a tipped-over In-N-Out bag.

"You are suggesting I go get clean . . . in there?" she says skeptically, arms crossed over her chest, hugging her pajamas and the monogrammed toiletry bag we made a special detour for before heading this way.

"The pipes are fine," I assure her.

The vibes: not so much.

Even I'm a little wary about what she might find inside—there could be anything from used needles to an actual heroin junkie in the flesh, judging by the detritus. It's quiet, though, no other signs that anyone else is around for miles. I'm 99 percent sure it'll be fine.

"Want me to go in with you to check it out first?" I offer.

"Um, yes," she says. "Yes, *please*."

I pull open the worn wooden door, and the motion-activated light illuminates everything in a dim fluorescent glow. Sadie gasps, looping her arm through mine so hard it almost hurts.

"What?" I ask, looking around. "What happened?"

"This place," she says with a sour look. "It's just . . . horrifying."

I laugh. "It's actually better than I expected."

There are two small stalls with toilets in them, and one larger area with a flimsy shower curtain—no obvious mildew or mold, so that's a plus right off the bat. The tile isn't too grimy, the trash has been emptied relatively recently, there aren't any obscene odors, and—most importantly—we're alone in here. It's pretty great by campsite standards, honestly.

Sadie takes it all in, still clinging to my arm like her life depends on it.

Not that I mind.

"Where am I supposed to put my stuff while I shower?" she asks.

Huh. I guess there aren't any benches or shelves or anything like that—I never thought to look.

"Maybe those hooks over there?"

She loosens her grip and heads over to inspect them, adorably scrunching her nose. "They're a little rusty . . ."

Emphasis on *a little*—even up close, I can hardly see it.

"I can hold everything for you, if you want?" I offer, and her eyes light up—

Which is how, five minutes later, I find myself standing two feet away from Sadie, only a flimsy shower curtain between us, as she reaches out to hand me a bundle of clothes.

The clothes she was *just* wearing.

Her strappy neon-pink sports bra peeks out from within the otherwise black fabric. I bite the inside of my cheek as hard as I can to counteract the things I'm feeling—the idea of her, not even a bikini on her body, is almost more than I can stand.

"Do you want me to wait outside?" I ask.

"I think I'd be too creeped out by this place to stay in here alone," she says. "I feel better knowing you're right there. Is that weird?"

"It's not weird," I reply, my heartbeat picking up at this show of trust: that she feels safer *with* me than without me.

I swallow. It's torture, being this close, especially after waking up tangled with her this morning—and knowing she's open to doing that again. *You're welcome in my tent anytime.*

I count the tiles on the floor, navy blue and white and egg-yolk yellow, while she turns on the water. I try not to count the spiderwebs, or the spiders themselves. I dutifully hand over small silicone bottles of body wash and shampoo and conditioner, trying to focus on how matching and organized her toiletry bag is and not, say, the water dripping from her bare skin whenever she stretches her arm out for whatever she needs from me next.

"Are you taking a shower in lava or what?" I ask a few minutes later when the steam is so thick I've started to sweat.

"Nothing is hot enough to wash off the ick of this bathroom," she replies, her voice echoing off the tile.

I run my thumb over the soft lavender leather of her toiletry bag, the gold zipper keeping it all together. The bag itself, and everything inside, tells the story of someone who enjoys beauty and order . . . the precise opposite of this run-down bathroom.

"I'm really proud of you for taking a shower in here at all," I tell her. "I know this is new territory for you."

"Thank you, Thorn," she says. "That means a—*aaauuuuuuggghhhhhh!*"

Sadie's piercing shriek is still bouncing off the walls when she scrambles out of the stall, dripping wet, clutching the shower curtain to cover as much of herself as she can. The curtain rod falls to the ground with a resounding clank.

"What *happened*?" I ask, looking around wildly for an explanation.

I don't have to look for long: a vibrant green lizard races out of the shower, running across Sadie's foot in the process before disappearing into a crack over near the sink.

"Ew, ew, *ew*," she says, with quick little steps as if to shake off the memory of the lizard's touch—but in the process, her foot slips in the puddle of water she brought out of the shower with her, and she's losing her balance—right into *me*.

I brace myself as Sadie falls, instinct taking over as I wrap my arms around her, pulling her in close until we're both steady. All the stuff she trusted me to hold drops to my feet, right into a puddle, but I can't say I'm sorry: she was one slick step away from seriously injuring herself.

Her eyes meet mine as I hold her, my hands slippery on her bare back and the shower curtain crumpled between us. She's shaking, shivering despite the steam, her hair long and dark and wet, and she smells like a flower shop.

"You're okay," I say as she tucks her head against my chest. "You're good."

I feel her breathing start to settle. The longer we stay like this, the more aware I am of how close we are—how she's still extremely naked under the shower curtain—but I am committed to being the safe place she needs right now.

"Have I mentioned I'm terrified of lizards?" she mumbles into my shirt.

I laugh. "I got that impression, yeah."

When she pulls back, her gaze flickers down to my lips.

It's all I can do to keep myself from kissing her right now.

"Hate to break it to you," I say instead, "but I kind of dropped all your stuff."

The corner of her mouth turns up. "You had *one* job," she says with a playful pout. "I guess I'll forgive you, though, since the alternative was me cracking my head open."

She bends down to pluck her soaked pajamas from the pool of water at our feet, keeping herself carefully covered by the shower curtain.

"One second," I say, peeling out of the hoodie I've been wearing ever since we got to camp this evening. It's wet, but the shirt I have on underneath is perfectly dry—I unbutton it and hold it out for her. "Take this?"

The way her eyes linger on my bare chest makes me really glad I've been consistent with my push-up regimen this year—I'm stronger than ever, even though no one usually sees what's under my shirt. That's never been the point, but at the moment, it definitely doesn't hurt.

"You sure?" she asks.

I grin. "I mean, unless you'd rather wear soaking-wet clothes that have gotten up close and personal with this bathroom floor?"

"You make a good point," she says with an exaggerated shudder as she accepts my shirt offering. I turn around, giving her the privacy she needs to change, zipping back into my own hoodie while I wait.

"All clear," she says.

I'm not prepared for how beautiful she looks when I turn back around: with her wet hair clinging to her shoulders and the way my shirt looks more like a minidress—its sleeves too long and half the buttons undone and the bottom hem grazing the tops of her thighs, covering just enough for her to not show *everything*.

"Thorn?" she says, a smile creeping over her face as she tucks a section of loose hair behind one ear.

I snap back to reality.

We head back to camp, the smell of campfire smoke and s'mores swirling on the night air, mixing with the wildflowers in the field and the scent of Sadie's shampoo. In the darkness, she darts to her pack for a change of clothes before anyone else sees she's come back wearing nothing but my shirt.

When she rejoins the group, wearing a fresh pair of pajamas that haven't spent quality time with the bathroom tile, no one but me knows where we've been.

It didn't start as a secret, but it sure feels like one now.

"S'more?" I say, handing her a perfectly charred marshmallow with a special square of melted dark chocolate I picked out just for her, the kind with raspberries I told her about on one of our first nights. I know she'll love it.

She grins and takes it, stars and firelight dancing in her eyes.

I am so far in over my head.

VIDEOS > FAVORITES > VLOG FOOTAGE

In the glow of the campfire, two silhouettes sit in shadow, the beam of a flashlight illuminating the trees overhead and not much else.

SADIE: Emma, can you adjust the flashlight—*there*, okay, yes. Better.

The camera flips around and Sadie's face, dim but visible, fills the screen.

SADIE: Hi, everyone. Today was pretty intense, but we made it. Well, most of us did—

ZOE [offscreen]: When you say it like that, it sounds like someone *died*.

SADIE: No one died. But yeah, like I said, it was pretty intense.

EMMA [offscreen]: Can we record a message for Brittany?

SADIE: Oh, yeah, of course! Hang on . . .

The flashlight beam overwhelms the screen when Sadie flips the camera around to face it, but only for a split second before Emma trains it on herself. Parker leans in to catch some of the light, too.

EMMA: Brittany, we miss you so much already! It's not the same without you!

PARKER: Rest up so you can *kill* it next season, okay? Our team needs you!

EMMA: You'll probably still be the fastest person on court even after an ankle injury, honestly.

ZOE [offscreen]: Is that shampoo I smell, Sadie? Did you wash your hair? Is there an *actual shower here*?

The video abruptly cuts off.

DAY SIX

Wild Gate Campsite to Moonbow Falls at Alexandria Flat

Seasoned hikers will want to pay attention to the lunar phases when timing a visit to Moonbow Falls. A full moon is best for optimal moonbow visibility—the more light refracting from the mist of the falls, the stronger the phenomenon will be. For hikers visiting during a new moon, however, the stargazing at Alexandria Flat is second to none. Time your visit accordingly, but rest assured: you cannot go wrong with either option.

—Henry Herrington, *Backpacking the Sierras: A Beginner's Handbook* (Fourth Edition)

20

SADIE

I wake with a pounding headache, intensified by the bright morning light. I really wish I'd remembered to wear my sleep mask.

Thorn never made it to my tent last night. Matteo pulled him aside after s'mores, and I waited as long as I could without it being totally obvious that I was waiting *for him*. But then everyone eventually split off for bed, and they were still out talking somewhere, so I headed to bed, too.

I thought for sure Thorn would make his way back to me at some point, especially after I explicitly told him he was welcome—and after the shower incident, which I still can't get out of my head. I replayed it over and over again before falling asleep: the lizard, the terror, the slick floor, the shower curtain.

Thorn's big hands on the bare skin of my back, steadying me.

The look on his face, slack-jawed and vulnerable and smitten, that made me want to kiss him right then and there.

How it felt like it was just the two of us in a dream world when we joined the group back at the campfire—how disorienting it was to be around the others after having such an intimate moment on our own.

It's back to business as usual today, though.

I make a pour-over while Silas and Hunter drink their coffee in silence—Silas is probably already on his second cup, while Hunter prefers to sip his so slowly it gets cold. Zoe's over in the wildflower field leading Emma, Trey, and Parker in a sunrise yoga session. Joshua's sulking, as he has been ever since the epic meltdown he and Zoe had a couple of nights ago, gnawing on one of the bison-bacon-cranberry protein bars he loves so much. Do they make him feel like more of a man in the wake of his relationship crisis? I have to assume so, since they sound utterly disgusting.

I don't see Thorn anywhere.

Matteo's here, though. He looks exhausted, no trace of his easy smile or the buoyant energy I've come to associate with him.

"Can I sit?" I ask, gesturing down at the blanket he's spread out.

He nods, then takes a bite out of a protein bar with the same logo as Joshua's.

I sip my coffee, follow his silent gaze.

I have no idea what he's looking at.

There are so many things I want to ask: Where is Thorn? What did they talk about for so long last night? Why does it look like Matteo just crawled out of a grave?

In the end, I settle on something neutral and practical: "Are we still heading out by nine?"

"That's the plan," he says between bites.

By the time I'm packed and ready to go, Thorn still hasn't come back to camp. I've been hyperaware of his absence for the last half hour, ever since I realized he was a no-show for breakfast. I hope he's okay.

My pack feels unbearably heavy today—those switchbacks really did a number on me. The thought of carrying it on my aching shoulders for even five minutes makes me want to cry: I wish I could go back to Past Sadie and tell her she should really think twice about packing all the things.

But it's not like I've *regretted* the stuff I've packed.

I've been glad to have spades of clean underwear, breathable pajamas, my touch lamp, and all the snacks that keep me from fainting after hours of being out on the trails. My Neosporin and Band-Aid stash has come in handy for my blisters, my sleep mask has helped me get some decent sleep, my face wash and dry shampoo and wax strips and nail polish have all helped me combat the ick I feel when sweat and dirt start to cling too much to my skin.

I could go on.

That said: I have a choice to make.

We're only halfway through the trip, and I think my body might just go on strike if it has to carry this much weight for the rest of our time out here.

I sigh, knowing what I have to do.

There's a Little Free Library over near the gazebo; it caught my eye last night on my way over to talk with Thorn, a number of colorful spines just begging me to take them.

But alas, I don't think I'll be *taking* anything today.

The little glass-paned door creaks on its hinges when I open it.

Wild and *Eat Pray Love* are the first to go. I slide them onto the top shelf—right next to three other copies of *Wild*. I'm sorely tempted to take two romance novels I recognize from Instagram to replace them, but both are hardcover Book of the Month editions, even thicker and heavier than the paperbacks I just put on the shelf.

I take a long look at my pack, mentally going over the inventory of its contents. The problem with being a chronic overpacker is that everything feels necessary: I chose each item for a reason, and have made use of almost everything.

If I'm honest, though? Not all of it is *actually* necessary.

Caden once made a comment that stuck with me: "What's going through your head when you stuff your bags with all of this shit?"

It felt like a barb then, and it still feels like one now.

My answer to that question has always been that I like to be prepared for everything that might come up. Cold at night? That's okay, here's a thick hoodie and pajama pants and cashmere socks. Picky coffee drinker? Not an issue—here's how I make it on the road. Not sure what I'll want to wear ten days from now? Pack everything I own!

Yesterday, though, after seeing Brittany almost fall over the edge, I spent the rest of the hike thinking about how you simply *can't* prepare for everything—some things just happen.

It terrified me. And it made me think, maybe at the root of my desire to be prepared . . . it's *fear* driving me.

Fear of not having everything I need to be comfortable.

Fear of not having everything I need to *survive.*

Fear of being in a situation where something comes up that desperately needs a solution—and me not being able to fix it.

So many what-ifs.

I thought I was challenging myself by coming out here, leaving behind the things that make me feel safe and happy and whole. And it *has* been a challenge, don't get me wrong. In a lot of ways, though, I think I've insulated myself from having to deal with the things I fear most. Doesn't it just prove Caden's point—that I'm too high-maintenance, too extra, too much in general—if I'm only able to survive out here if I have a backpack full of emotional support items?

Screw it. It's time.

I keep one pair of pajamas and leave the rest in a neat stack at the base of the Little Free Library. I leave my fuzzy slippers, my wax strips, the remnants of my nail polish. I weed out more than half of my clothes;

someone is about to hit the lululemon jackpot, and it makes me want to cry thinking about how much money I spent on all of that just to leave it behind.

It only gets harder from there.

I leave my Viktor & Rolf Flowerbomb perfume behind, along with my entire stash of makeup except for a tin of coconut-lime lip balm.

Finally, I unload every last bit of coffee, my pour-over setup, and my one-of-a-kind ceramic mug that miraculously hasn't been crushed yet—the artist who created it always sells out within minutes, and I was over the moon to finally snag it during his most recent drop.

My pack is a sad, deflated carcass just begging to be fed. I'm tempted to stuff everything right back inside—but then I see the journal Thorn gave me, peeking out from underneath *A Hiker Girl's Guide to Bugs & Berries*, the pocket-sized nature handbook Abby gifted me before I left for the airport. It feels important to keep both.

I've kept up writing in the journal twice a day, even if it's just a single line. (See: the entry from yesterday morning, right after Thorn left my tent, that simply reads *Thorn is a good kisser, and I want to do it again.*) Every time I open it, my memory flashes back to what he said when he gave the journal to me: *People like you tend to get a lot out of journaling. I think you'd be surprised to read back over it after the trip ends.*

I haven't read back over anything I've written, not yet, but I already know he'll be right.

"What happened here?" a deep voice says behind me, one I'd recognize while half asleep, or probably even after being shot with a tranquilizer dart.

I turn and see Thorn, dripping with sweat, his expression stormy.

"I could ask the same," I say, gesturing to his soaked shirt. There isn't a cloud in the sky. "Did another lizard try to attack you in the bathroom?"

He laughs, though the crease between his eyebrows doesn't totally disappear. "Needed to let off some steam. Ran three miles."

"You ran three miles . . . even though we're about to hike all day?"

"Maybe not the smartest thing I've ever done," he replies. His eyes drift down to the pile of clothes at my feet, then back up to my face. "And . . . this?"

"My shoulders are killing me," I say with a shrug.

He softens when he notices all of my coffee stuff. He picks up the beautiful mug, turns it over to examine the happy-face sunrise that peeks out from under the cheery little rainbow, the puffy white clouds, all of it painted by hand.

"You're leaving this behind?" he asks. "All of it?"

I really don't want to, I think but don't say. *But I think I should.*

"Yeah," I tell him. "I am."

He's scanning the shelves of the Little Free Library itself now, pausing to take in the stash of makeup and perfume I stuck in there, when—out of nowhere—he bursts out laughing.

"Wait, wait, wait," he says. "You had *four* copies of *Wild* with you?"

"What? No!" I protest. "I only had one. The others were already in there, I promise!" The fact that I'm not the first one to bring a copy with me only to leave it behind halfway through a hike suddenly strikes me as hilarious, and now I'm laughing, too.

"And the *Eat Pray Love*?"

"I think you already know the answer to that," I say, conceding my defeat.

His smile lights up his entire face. "I *knew* you had both books with you!"

"And I have had the most painful blisters for days now, and I should absolutely have invested in some hiking boots like you said,"

I go on, because why not. "You were right about everything. Literally everything."

He bites back a smile, and probably an *I told you so*, too.

"I would remind you to make good on the bet we made," he says, gesturing to my sad pile of coffee gear, "but it looks like you did that on your own."

I'm sure he knows it isn't *that* much of a sacrifice to leave my coffee beans behind, since the coffee bros have been more than generous with theirs—but I don't feel the need to bring it up, especially since I went back and forth for a good five minutes about whether I should put it back in my pack after all.

"I feel like we need a moment of silence for all this stuff," I say with a sigh. "A funeral of sorts."

Thorn holds a finger up as if to say *be right back*—and when he returns, he has a fistful of wildflowers.

"Don't tell anyone about these," he says conspiratorially. "It's illegal to pick them out here."

I laugh. "Thank you for risking your reputation."

He grins, then tucks the makeshift bouquet into the cone-shaped coffee dripper I use for my pour-overs as if it's a vase. At the last second, he plucks a single flower out of the bunch—a lovely shade of blue with white at its center—and tucks it behind my ear. His skin brushes mine, and my cheeks grow hot.

"Won't this be a dead giveaway that you deserve prison?" I tease.

His eyes are playful, flirty, intense.

"I can take it back if you—"

"No." I bat his hand away. "I'm attached, it's too late. And I've already said goodbye to too much today."

He glances down at my stuff, then back up to me, probably wondering how on earth the Sadie standing before him is the same Sadie who arrived in California nearly a week ago. *That* Sadie would never have even considered leaving more than half her pack behind at a campsite, let alone actually followed through with it.

Honestly, I'm as surprised as anyone.

"Maybe I should put some things back in?" I say, wistfully eyeing my perfume. It's such a small tube, I'd barely notice it. Why did I take it out in the first place, again?

Thorn puts his arm around my shoulder and sighs.

"Sorry, Sadie," he says with mock solemnity. "I try not to make a habit out of digging up what's been laid to rest."

I snort. "Fine. But when I smell like nature and everything in it within a few days, just remember things could have been different."

His gaze locks with mine. "You're perfect just the way you are," he says.

I wait for the punch line—*nature smell and all*, I expect him to add—but it never comes.

21

THORN

Tonight, we get to stay in one of my favorite places in the entire trail network: Alexandria Flat, an expansive, rocky clearing where we'll sleep under the stars. The night sky is always unbelievable there, a billion pinpricks of light amid surprising shades of dark teal and lavender, the Milky Way on full display. A sheer cliff juts high into the horizon at the far end of the flats, a massive waterfall spilling down its center; we'll rappel down the cliffs tomorrow. There's also a cave behind the waterfall—I can't wait to show it to Sadie.

The *group*, I mean. I can't wait to show it to the group.

Today has been exhausting.

Not on the hiking front—it's my *mind* that's been a battleground. I've been hypervigilant, on high alert for anything that might prove tricky or dangerous.

In good news, no one has come anywhere close to having another accident.

In not-so-good news, things that usually come so easily have been a lot harder today.

Most days, I never have to remind myself to engage with the others about landmarks and wildlife we pass along the way, and all of my familiar catchphrases—*step here, watch out for that branch, remember your sunscreen and bug spray, don't forget to hydrate*—come out on instinct.

Today has been a struggle.

The harder I try to stay hypervigilant, the more my thoughts wander to the two dueling forces vying for my attention: Sadie and Matteo.

Matteo pulled me aside last night after s'mores.

"We need to talk," he said, unsmiling.

Naïvely, I assumed we were on the verge of some sort of heart-to-heart—a follow-up from our conversation by the stream earlier this week, or maybe him breaking down about his breakup with Blair. I pictured him groveling for my support since Blair ditched both of us in the exact same way.

What he *actually* said caught me off guard.

"What's going on with you and Sadie?" he asked instead, before proceeding to make all sorts of accusations: that my head had been in the clouds all day—that if I hadn't been so absorbed in chatting with Sadie, I would have warned Brittany to watch her step, and she wouldn't have almost fallen over the edge.

Basically, he jabbed his finger right into the open wound of the insecurities that had already been plaguing me ever since the incident.

"Nothing," I told him, as if I could hide the feelings that have started working their way into my heart like stubborn weeds.

"*Right*," he scoffed. For a moment, I thought he might have seen even more than how Sadie and I had been chatting each other up on the trail—had he seen us at the gazebo? Or, worse, coming back from the shower?

If he did, he didn't call me on it.

"Well, you need to get it together, man," is all he said.

Never, for as long as we've known each other, has Matteo initiated a conversation with me—with *anyone*—that was anywhere close to confrontational. The fact that it happened at all feels as unsettling as his actual words. It's not like him.

Also: Does he think I'm not already feeling terrible about what happened with Brittany? Shouldn't he know me well enough to know I've had a guilt trip going through my head ever since the incident, telling me I should have been more vigilant about keeping everyone safe—and that I'm already paranoid about how distracted I've been?

I think he knows all of this and decided to give me shit about it anyway.

The worst part is, he has a point.

There was no way I could take Sadie up on her offer after that—especially since Matteo was watching me like a hawk. I couldn't let him see me climbing into her tent, as much as I wanted to.

So I slept outside.

Woke before dawn.

Ran three miles, even though we had a long hike ahead of us today.

And then, just as soon as I thought my head had cleared enough for me to step up like the leader I'm supposed to be, I ran into Sadie at the Little Free Library—and all the feelings I'd tried to snuff out with logic and discipline came blazing back as soon as I saw her standing there, looking down at the pile of her stuff.

If you'd asked me on Day One what I thought Sadie Whitlock would get out of this experience, I would have confidently told you she was destined for confirmation that she is not cut out for the outdoors.

No one is as surprised as I am to see how wrong I was.

I've been thinking about it all day. About *her.*

About her stash of coffee stuff, about the ceramic mug she drinks out of every morning—she told me once, adorably, that the little happy-face sun made her feel a little less afraid of being out here in nature.

I couldn't just let her leave it all behind.

It's been burning a hole in my pack all day. I circled back at the last second before we left camp, tucked the mug and her coffee stuff inside when I was sure she wasn't looking.

Ever since, it's been a constant battle to rein in my thoughts; whenever they drift to Sadie, Matteo's words drag me right back down to earth. Over and over, all day long—

You need to get it together, man.

When we finally make it to our campsite, it will be sweet relief.

Alexandria Flat is one of my favorite places for a reason.

There's just something so breathtaking about these cliffs, their faces imposing and severe, and the roaring waterfall that divides them almost perfectly in half—the view is even more majestic than the lake where we camped for the kayaking segment of the trip. Especially now, at sunset, with the way the brilliant orange light glints off the surface of the water, it feels like the last moments before a movie starts, when the lights dim to prepare you for the real show.

Out here, the entire night sky *is* the theater.

"We have a special stargazing opportunity tonight for anyone who wants to sleep out in the open," I tell the group when we've all reconvened after dinner and downtime. Even at a bit of a distance, I have to speak up over the crash of Moonbow Falls at my back. "Once the sun goes down, it usually gets a little chilly—we've got hot cocoa packets and extra handwarmers if you need one. You're welcome to set your tents up, but I'd like to personally challenge you to spend the night out here in the open—you can thank me in the morning!"

I go over a few details about how rappelling will work tomorrow: Matteo and I are both certified (as is Trey, apparently), no one is obligated to participate, we'll start midmorning for anyone who's interested.

A few people opt to set up their tents when we disperse—Sadie included.

Only now do I realize my vision for tonight involved her sleeping bag right next to mine, both of us sipping on hot cocoa, maybe even sharing a blanket before we tuck in to sleep . . . if we can get away with any of that without calling too much attention to ourselves.

I've only ever seen one guide get fired for getting involved with a guest—Brad, a year ago—and he's the reason the rule exists at all. Brad had a pattern of hooking up with people at the expense of doing his job well. Three groups in a row, the post-hike surveys were full of comments saying he was distractible and downright irresponsible at times.

Even if people were to make similar comments about me, I'm the most reliable guide Danica's got, and she knows it. Not that I ever want to abuse that—I'm just saying, she'd probably be more curious than angry if she found out I'd developed feelings for someone.

I make my way over to Sadie, feeling Matteo's eyes on me as I pass—he's helping Zoe with her tent, and I'd hoped he'd be too busy with her to notice me.

Apparently not.

"You're not sleeping outside?" I ask Sadie quietly, hoping I don't sound as disappointed as I feel.

She pokes her head out of her tent, smiles. "Oh, no—I am."

"Why'd you set up, then?" I ask.

"Promise not to make fun of me?"

"I'm not sure that's a promise I can make," I reply, crouching down so we're face-to-face. "Tell me, Sadie—why would I make fun of you?"

"Number one, I don't want to change into my pajamas in front of the whole world. And number two . . . I guess . . . it just feels weird *not* to? Like it's just part of the routine we've had every night, setting up the tent. Having a place that's only mine makes me feel a little more settled out here. And maybe I'm low-key afraid that it'll start pouring on us and we'll need a place to take shelter?"

There's not a cloud in the sky, but I decide against pointing that out.

"Why would I have made fun of you for that?" I ask instead.

Her cheeks turn pink in the glow of her touch lamp. "I'm a creature of habit, I guess? I take comfort in routine, even if it doesn't totally make sense—I like knowing I'm prepared for anything." She glances down at her mismatched nails, then back up at me with a look so vulnerable I can't tear my eyes away. "Some people would tell me it's dumb or unnecessary."

Sadie's words hang between us. The way she's phrased it makes me think someone *specific* made her feel bad about that in the past.

Again, I feel the unfamiliar urge to throw a punch. What a jackass.

"You need what you need," I tell her now. "That's all there is to it."

Personally, I think she needs the comfort of familiarity far less than she realizes . . . but I suspect that's something she'll have to figure out for herself.

"Want me to take your sleeping bag?" I offer. "Save you a spot?"

"Only if you're sure you don't want to spend the night *in* the tent," Sadie says, flipping seamlessly from unguarded to flirtatious.

"As tempting as that sounds," I tell her, matching her tone, so close my lips brush against her ear, "I cannot be held responsible for you missing tonight's sky."

"We can still do tent things under the stars, if you want?" she says, then presses a kiss so quick and light onto my collarbone that I very truly may have hallucinated it.

I'm tempted to take it all back: forget the stars, and the sky, and everyone who might possibly care.

It'll be a miracle if I last an hour without giving in.

Maybe that wouldn't be so bad. Maybe I'm overthinking all of this, maybe it would actually be *good* for me—it's been so long since I've had a connection of any sort out here, let alone one like *this*, that I forgot what it felt like for my cracked heart to be anything but still as stone.

Sadie makes me feel *alive*.

"Give me ten minutes," she says, her breath hot on my skin. "I'll meet you there."

22

SADIE

I stumble in near-darkness, a pair of hot cocoas in hand, until I find Thorn and our sleeping bags.

Even though there's plenty of room to spread out, we're all still relatively close together, six or eight feet between the various clusters of friend groups. Thorn's at the far end, integrated enough that it won't be too obvious that the two of us are attempting to carve out some alone time.

He takes one of the cups as I sit down beside him.

"You weren't kidding about the view," I say.

He grins. "Just wait till the fire's all the way out. It'll blow your mind."

I don't know how it can get any better than this, honestly: the sky is bursting with light, pinpricks of white splashed all over the dark, velvety canvas. The twin cliffs cut into the horizon, their white rock faces dim in the shadow of night. We're not terribly close to the waterfall, or the creek that carves into the basin just below it, but its soundtrack is a constant crashing that makes this place feel alive, magical.

I sip my hot cocoa, taking in two gooey marshmallows in the process.

"So," I say a moment later. "When was the first time you discovered this place?"

Thorn squints, like he's trying to see far back into the past.

"First time I *remember* was when I was around eight years old," he says. "Hiked the Mackenzie Lake Loop with my dad one time, probably came back here every couple of months after that. He always tells people I've been hiking since I was a baby, though—he and my mom used to come on weekend trips, and they'd take turns wearing me in one of those little carriers."

"Does your mom still hike?"

"Hell if I know," he says, then takes a long pull on his hot cocoa.

"Did she break his heart?" I ask, tentatively stepping through what I *think* is an open door. "Or was it the other way around?"

He gives a little half laugh. "Dad couldn't break a heart if he tried." As quickly as his mood darkened at the mention of his mom, it shifts lighter now—the smallest hint of a smile plays at his lips. "He *did* try to break a heart one time, actually. This woman he dated while I was in college, his first relationship after the divorce, it just wasn't working out. She still came for Thanksgiving that year because she didn't want Dad to have to prepare a feast for Matteo and me all on his own."

"Your dad sounds like a nice guy," I say.

"Yeah," he says. "He really is."

I hug my knees tight to my chest. At first, the hot cocoa was like a little furnace, warming me from the inside—it was nice while it lasted. Now that it's gone, the chill in the air is hard to ignore.

"Cold?" Thorn asks, taking immediate notice of the goosebumps all over my arms and legs.

He pulls a thin flannel blanket from his pack and wraps it around my shoulders, tucking me in close to him in the process. The blanket helps, but the heat radiating from his body is even better. I breathe in the smell of him, outdoorsy with a hint of spice.

"Want to know a secret?" he says quietly, his lips brushing against my temple. "There's a little cave behind the waterfall that isn't part of the tour, just big enough where you can sit and watch the sunrise. The light looks incredible from behind the water . . . I can show you tomorrow, if you want?"

The idea of going on my own little private excursion with Thorn is too tempting to resist.

"Yeah?" I reply. "Won't the others feel like they missed out, though?"

"Not if they don't know what they're missing." He pulls back just enough, and I turn so we're face-to-face. "And besides, it's not like it's off-limits—it's just not advertised. They can go on their own if they want."

I hear his words, but they hardly register. We're so close right now, all it would take is the slightest tilt of my head—or his—for us to kiss.

And now kissing him is all I can think about.

My eyes flicker from his eyes down to his lips, then back up again. We're already this close, and the moment feels like magic.

"I really, really want to kiss you right now," I confess, barely a whisper.

He smiles. "I really, really want to kiss you right now, too."

"Is it too risky out here?"

It's extremely dark now that the fire's out, and it's quiet—most people, I think, are either watching the sky or have already fallen asleep. Without the tent for privacy, though, we're just so . . . exposed.

I feel his chest rise and fall as he considers it, probably thinking the exact same thing I am: that as close as we are, we *already* look like a couple.

We can explain it away—it's cold out, he's helping me warm up. It would be harder to explain the other things we both clearly want to do.

"Tomorrow," he says like a promise. "At the waterfall."

It would be so easy to steal a kiss right now.

He still wants to, too, I can tell—he hasn't budged at all, and I can see the restraint it's taking written all over his face even in almost pitch darkness.

"Tomorrow," I agree.

We slip into our sleeping bags, mere inches away from each other. I miss his arm around me already, and I'm shivering within minutes.

"Here's a trick I learned a long time ago for when it's cold out," Thorn says. "It's going to sound weird—you're going to have to trust me on this."

"Let me guess," I say, intrigued. "We both cram into a single sleeping bag and get so distracted by how cramped it is that we forget about being cold?"

He stifles a laugh, careful not to wake anyone up. "Not exactly. Okay. So it's going to sound counterintuitive, but if you strip down to just your underwear, you can stuff your clothes at the bottom of your sleeping bag, by your feet—that will help block cold air from getting in, and your body heat will circulate better as a result."

"Strip down *to my underwear*?" I whisper-hiss. "What is this, some sort of prank? Is a camera crew about to jump out from behind the waterfall?"

"I'm not pranking you, I swear—so that's a no on the camera crew," he says, laughing. "But I did warn you that it'd sound counterintuitive."

I do as he says and shimmy out of my pajamas—discreetly, not because I'm ashamed for him to see anything (*if* he could even see anything in this darkness) but because I don't want anyone else to get the wrong idea—then kick them into place at the bottom of my sleeping bag.

Thorn is making a huge effort to not look too interested, but the fact that he's being so deliberate and obvious about it tells me he's very, very aware of how little I'm wearing right now. I'm thankful I wore a sports bra—I'm not sure he and I could make it through an entire night of keeping our hands off each other with me being *that* naked right next to him. It's hard enough already.

"I hope this works," I say, my teeth chattering.

"It'll work," he replies, eyes trained on the stars.

I look to the sky, too.

It's a much-needed distraction—from the cold, from the sleeping bag fabric rubbing up against my skin, from Thorn himself. In my wildest imagination, I never guessed it could look *this* beautiful. I count one tiny cluster of stars until my eyes cross, losing count somewhere around fifty. I take in the depths of the Milky Way, its explosive streak like a gash across the night sky.

I'm all too aware of Thorn, stretched out in his sleeping bag beside me, and I'm almost certain he's not asleep.

"Thorn," I whisper a while later, when I'm still wide awake and the constellations have shifted in the sky. "At what point should I start feeling warmer?"

But his breathing has finally evened out, and he doesn't reply.

Eventually, I fall asleep too.

I wake up gasping and shivering.

It's still dark out—dark and extremely cold. It is the absolute *worst* time for a steamy dream in more ways than one: not only am I *not* drenched in sweat from Thorn's body being pressed up against mine, as I was just a split second ago in whatever subconscious haven my mind spun up while deeply asleep, but I am fully regretting my choices. What was I *thinking*, putting my clothes at the bottom of the sleeping bag?

"What happened?" Thorn says beside me, instantly awake—and instantly panicked. "Sadie? Are you okay?"

This can only mean one thing: I was loud enough to wake him up somehow. The fact that he's asking if I'm okay is my only reassurance; I *probably* didn't moan anything X-rated before my rude awakening.

"S-so c-cold," I manage. "The t-trick didn't w-work."

His eyes go wide, landing on where the sleeping bag is draped over my collarbones.

"I, um. I might have forgotten to mention one crucial detail."

"What, that clothes might actually be helpful with *not* freezing my ass off?"

He tugs at a little bungee cord that hangs limply from the top edge of the sleeping bag. "The trick only works if you pull this as tight as it will go so your body heat stays inside—and so no cold air can get *in*."

"Seriously?!" My eyebrows shoot as high as they'll go. "That would have been a fantastic detail to know about!"

Thorn bites back a laugh.

"It's *not* funny!" I protest, but I'm teetering on the edge of a giggle fit myself despite it all, made funnier by how we're both trying to be quiet—and coming dangerously close to waking up the entire camp.

"Here," he says, his voice gravelly with sleep as he stretches an arm across me, pulling tight. "I'll warm you up."

A couple of inches is all it takes, and then we're pressed together as tightly as two people can get with a pair of sleeping bags between them. I'm the little spoon, and I feel every inch of him pressing up against the back of me. It's nothing like the dream I just woke up from—he's not on top of me, we're not in a sailboat off the coast of Italy, and we're very much not alone.

Still, though: this reality feels almost steamier. It's not just my imagination fulfilling whatever subconscious hopes spring up in the dead of night—Thorn is here, *right* here, flesh and bone and heart and hands making sure I don't turn to ice before the sun comes up. I'm all too aware of his arm around me, strong but gentle, his fingers splayed over my bare skin just below my shoulder. Nothing risqué there, but it's close enough, especially given that my clothes are still stuffed at the bottom of my sleeping bag.

It doesn't take long to warm up. He's his own heating system, generating more than enough warmth for us both, his breath hot on the back of my neck even through the curtain of my hair.

The longest night ever suddenly can't last long enough.

I don't care that I woke up shivering. I don't care that I woke up at all, or that I'm going to have the hardest time trying to fall back asleep—or that I'll be miserably exhausted tomorrow if I don't get at least a little bit more rest.

I want to feel every second.

DAY SEVEN

Day at Moonbow Falls and Alexandria Flat

Swimming in the wild can be one of nature's purest joys—but only if the proper precautions are taken. Where waterfalls are concerned, it's wise to stay alert and aware of your surroundings: not every waterfall is equally swimmable, and even from day to day, conditions could be more or less favorable depending on the weather. Exercise particular caution after a strong rain, intense meltoff from alpine snow, or if the telltale froth of whitewater is present.

—Henry Herrington, *Backpacking the Sierras: A Beginner's Handbook* (Fourth Edition)

23

SADIE

"*Sadie?*"

Thorn's quiet voice cuts through the predawn half-light and the dark, dreamless sleep I must have eventually settled into.

I shift under his arm, which is still draped over me, and turn to face him. I feel instantly compelled to touch the scruff of his jaw, to plant a trail of kisses down his neck and see how the contrast of skin and stubble feels under my mouth.

"Yeah?" I reply instead, just as quietly.

"Still want to go see the sunrise through the waterfall?" he asks. "No worries if you need more sleep."

I do need more sleep.

I doubt I'd be *able* to sleep again, though. And I really, really want to see Thorn's secret cave.

"Let's do it," I say.

I use my toes to fish my pajamas out from the bottom of my sleeping bag and shimmy into them without so much as a nip slip. Thorn and I make our way over to the waterfall pool—

And realize the flaw in our plan at the exact same moment.

"How are we supposed to *get* to the cave?" I ask, eyeing the pool of water and the cascading falls at its far side.

Clearly, the answer is that we'll need to swim across fully clothed.

It's already warming up, thankfully, but I don't exactly care to know what the breeze feels like while soaking wet.

Thorn's gaze shifts across the landscape. The waterfall pool spills out into a winding creek—while there's dry ground on the other side of it, I don't see any way to get there without getting wet.

"It's not terribly deep, I don't think," Thorn finally says. "Maybe waist-high? It's calm today, at least, pretty good conditions. There's a crossing farther down the creek, but if we backtrack, we'll miss the sunrise."

He glances at the horizon behind us—the sunrise is imminent, from what I can tell—and then back to me.

I must have a strong *please don't subject me to an ice bath* vibe at the moment, because his features shift from perplexed to determined as he makes a snap decision.

"Okay," he says, kneeling down. "How about this?"

"You're going to pray for a Red Sea situation?" I ask, imagining the waters parting down the middle, because the only other thing I can think of that he'd be doing in that position is proposing—and it's *definitely* not that.

"Or," he replies, grinning, "you could get on my shoulders?"

Oh. Right.

He's so tall, and I'm so not, that he has to crouch over just a little more so I can climb on. I settle onto his shoulders and tuck my feet behind his lower back to make sure I'm locked in; he wraps his arms around my legs to help me feel extra secure.

Thorn's skin prickles with goosebumps as soon as we're in the water.

As soon as *he's* in the water, anyway. It comes up to his hips, a fraction of an inch below my toes. He takes steady, confident steps; I feel his core stabilizing as we make our way across.

"A little looser?" he grits out.

Only now do I realize my thighs are clamping his neck like a vise.

I ease up, but my butt shifts in the process—and for a single, slow-motion moment I fear I've altered his center of gravity in a way that's going to leave us both submerged right here in the middle of the pool.

With one quick flex of his shoulders, though, we're back on track. He edges us just to the side of the waterfall—it's *so* loud, this close—and bends down so I can step off him and onto the rocky ledge.

It's a clumsy dismount in which he gets a face full of my pajama shorts, possibly even a glimpse at the strawberry-print underwear I have on just underneath. My cheeks are on fire, as is the rest of me.

"I—um. Sorry about that," I manage.

His hair is disheveled, entirely my fault, and there's something new in his eyes: a hunger I haven't seen in him before.

He hoists himself onto the ledge and then holds out his hand for me.

I take it, winding my fingers with his, and follow his lead.

His shoes leave wet footprints all along the rock as we slip behind the waterfall. Sure enough, as promised, there's a small cave, a semicircle no more than six feet deep. The waterfall crashes, its cascade like warped glass separating us from the outside world.

We don't waste a single second.

Thorn's hands are in my hair in a heartbeat, his mouth on mine, making up for everything we couldn't do last night now that we're tucked away in private. His kiss is hot and hungry, an electric surge lighting me up all over; his touch is a fire that I can't get enough of.

His hands make their way down to my hips, and in one effortless motion he's lifting me, my legs curling around him. I pull him in as close as we can get, only my pajamas and his wet clothes between us. It's that day in the lake all over again, except now he backs me up against the smooth rock of the cave wall—

And I can't get enough: of him, of his body against mine.

His mouth moves from my lips down to the curve of my neck. I bury my hands in his hair, watch as the first rays of morning sunlight turn the cascading waterfall into the most incredible kaleidoscope of sunbeams dancing all over the cave floor.

It's so beautiful, everything about this moment.

It feels like waking up after sleepwalking for months.

It feels like stumbling out of darkness into a cathedral made entirely of stained glass.

I must gasp, or sigh, or something—Thorn pulls away, looks right at me. "Everything okay?"

"More than okay," I tell him. I can still feel him on my skin, his soft lips and rough stubble. I nod to the light; it feels like something I shouldn't keep to myself. "Look how pretty it is."

When he turns, his whole face is bathed in sunshine.

But then he looks back at me, gaze skimming from my lashes to my lips and back up again, and says, "*Very* pretty."

My cheeks heat up. I'm just about to lean in for another kiss—but the sound of voices, so close they could be just outside the cave, brings both of us back to reality in an instant.

"We should probably—" I say at the same time he says, "Is that Zoe?"

I uncurl from around him, set my feet back on solid ground. If anyone were to walk in on us right now, they'd know *immediately* what we were just doing—it's written all over our faces.

Now the question is, how do we get out of the cave without advertising to everyone that we were in here, just the two of us, alone together?

"I didn't think anyone would be over here this early," Thorn says quietly.

Something snags my memory. "Did Zoe say she wanted to do sunrise yoga?"

Even if she didn't mention it, she's been incredibly dedicated to her daily practice.

"Guess we're going to yoga," Thorn says with a grimace. "And if anyone asks . . . we just wanted to do a little 'exploring' this morning?"

I slip out of the cave first, and sure enough, Zoe and Trey and Emma are all present. Trey and Emma are distracted with each other, splashing around near the waterfall—flirtatiously, I might add—and Zoe is preoccupied with how they're delaying what she clearly thought would be a punctual start time.

Watching them, it occurs to me that I'm still suspiciously dry—and not only that, but I'm not going to be able to ride on Thorn's shoulders to get back across.

I dip a toe in the water.

It's definitely on the cooler end, so I ease myself in only as far as I have to. Emma and Trey are so wrapped up in each other they don't even glance my way.

Zoe notices, though. I can see her trying to work it out—where I came from, how I managed to slip past her—when her gaze darts to a spot behind me.

I turn to look, and there's Thorn, standing directly under the waterfall, arms skyward and eyes closed as it cascades over and around him. A moment later, he steps out from underneath it, running one hand through his hair to shake off the excess water.

In my very objective opinion, he's never looked hotter. I can't stop staring.

"Anyone else see the cave back there?" he says. "It's pretty cool if you want to take a look."

This, finally, snaps Emma and Trey out of their little flirt bubble. I can read their heart eyes from here: they seem intrigued, probably for the exact same reasons Thorn and I made a point to "explore" it.

"*Later*, people!" Zoe calls out, arms crossed. "Yoga first—caves some other time." She trains a pointed look on me, then Thorn. "Sadie? Thorn? You're here for yoga, too?"

Oh, Thorn is going to *love* this.

And I am genuinely going to love watching him go through it for the second time.

"Of course," Thorn says, doing an impressive job at sounding at least a little enthusiastic. "Why else would we be here?"

He meets my eye the second Zoe's back is turned, and I bite down on a laugh. Whatever torture she's about to put us through—and I suspect said torture will be significant—this morning was entirely worth it.

24

THORN

It's a clear, sunny, 75-degree day: perfect rappelling weather.

It would be even better if Matteo weren't hovering like my own personal storm cloud—especially since it's up to us to inspect all the equipment and make sure the anchors at the top of the cliff are properly secured before our people get anywhere close to it.

All of which requires focus.

"Just say it, man," he grunts out as I check all the knots, hitches, and carabiners.

"Say what?"

"Say *anything*," he replies. "The silent treatment is killing me."

"I'm not being silent on purpose," I say, which is mostly true. "I'm making sure everything's ready to go."

I move on to the ropes, check for any sign of fraying. They all look good.

"If you're mad about the other night," Matteo goes on, "just say so."

The other night, when he not-so-subtly told me to *get it together*.

My jaw twitches. "Okay," I reply. "What if I am?"

I feel his eyes on me.

"Be mad if you want," he says tauntingly. "But if you're mad at anyone, it should be yourself, not me—you know I made a good point. You've been distracted out here. Don't give me the silent treatment just because I called you out on it."

I swallow down everything I want to say: how I'm only human, how I'm doing my best to keep everyone safe, how it's unfair to expect me to not have feelings of my own, or know how to navigate them perfectly—how my anger with him runs so much deeper than just the accusations he threw at me two nights ago.

The bitterness clings to my mouth.

"If you really cared about me being distracted," I grit out, "you wouldn't be trying to start a fight right now. Everyone down there at camp is depending on *us* to make sure they don't die today."

This shuts him up, at least temporarily.

We work together in silence, triple-checking every last piece of equipment until we're both satisfied. We've almost made our way back down to the bottom—there's a series of wide rock ledges about fifty feet away from the waterfall that serve as a natural staircase to the top of the cliff—when he ruins it.

"You have more tunnel vision than you think," he says almost under his breath. "Maybe if you'd paid better attention you wouldn't have been so blindsided by what happened with Blair."

This stops me dead in my tracks.

"*That's* your take?" I'm genuinely perplexed. "Please enlighten me—what, exactly, would have changed if I'd been paying more attention? Are you saying you *wouldn't* have stolen my girlfriend and run off with her to a whole other continent if I'd just . . . noticed it was happening before it got to that point? That makes zero sense, Matty. Zero."

"I'm saying that maybe you would have noticed our friendship had started deteriorating a *long* time before that. You were never around to hang out. You treat your phone like an afterthought." The look in his eyes levels me, unsettles me. "We weren't as close then as you make it sound."

This: *this* is a blindside.

I didn't think he could hurt me in a new way, not after all we've been through. I absolutely considered him my best friend. And the fact that his words still have the power to cut this deeply . . . his friendship matters more to me, even now, than I want to admit.

Until Peru, he always acted like the feeling was mutual. There was never even a hint of tension from him, let alone anything on the level of frustration he's projecting now.

"What are you talking about?" I ask. "You were my best friend since *high school*—since the day you moved in. Even when Blair came along, you were still my closest friend."

"We hardly ever hung out, Thorn. We rarely *talked*. You were always out here, or you were with Blair. And when we did talk, you were always so guarded, like you were afraid to let anyone in."

I'm genuinely at a loss for words; it's not at all how I remember it. He's playing the victim, making it sound like *I* am the one who drove the wedge between us—and if that were true, I'd apologize in a heartbeat. But it's just not how it happened. The last time we hung out, Matteo was as chill as ever, scarfing pepperoni-pineapple pizza and crashing at my apartment after a marathon night of *Mario Kart*. We talked and laughed until three in the morning.

Two days later, he and Blair took off for Peru.

"I don't know what to tell you," I say, trying my best to envision our history from his perspective. "I remember working more than usual that year, saving up for—"

I cut myself off before I say the words *down payment*, because even in this moment, I am not cruel enough to kick Matteo where it hurts when his own Blair wounds are this fresh.

"And my phone," I go on, "you know how it is out here. You were the only person I ever texted, or hung out with when I wasn't on a trek, other than Blair."

My words hang between us.

They echo in my head, stark and lonely.

I think of Matteo's giant smile—the one he wears around everyone else these days, the one that's always drawn huge circles of friends to his side, effortlessly.

My own circle, by contrast, has never been large. I'm a quality-over-quantity guy, and would rather go deep with just one or two people than have countless people who don't know me at all. Maybe all this time I've been treating "only" and "best" as the same thing, never realizing that I didn't rank as highly on Matteo's hierarchy of friends.

He was *my* best friend. But that doesn't mean I was still his . . . or that I ever was in the first place.

Everything's unraveling. I've lost the thread of how we got here. I try to follow it back, but I'm hung up on the knot of *We weren't as close then as you make it sound.*

But we were. I know we were.

I've never been a high-maintenance friend, and neither has he. Sure, maybe I was gone more than usual in that last year, but we always picked up right where we left off—our talks might have been infrequent, but they were still deep, and the furthest thing from guarded.

We talked about his family in Italy.

We talked about his dreams for the future.

We talked about the things we both loved and despised and craved.

He's one of the few people I've ever cried in front of—the night my parents announced their divorce. He cried, too. He was that much a part of our family.

Never, not once, did he give any indication that he was unsatisfied with how much I was bringing to the friendship. I'll be the first to admit I treat my phone like an afterthought, but I've always been like that, and last I checked, it works both ways—it's not like he was blowing up my texts, and it's not like I was blowing him off. I always wrote back even if it wasn't immediately.

It's unsettling to think I could have read things *this* wrong. Do we just have different ideas of what being a friend *is*—or has the gigantic rift between us blurred his memories of how tight we actually were?

Maybe he remembers *too* well. Maybe the truth simply hurts.

The clarity hits so suddenly it's almost physical: I'm pretty sure this is textbook gaslighting. And I suspect it isn't just meant to make me feel worse—he's trying to make himself feel *better*, to ease his conscience.

How many days did he spend repeating it in his head before *we weren't close* became reality for him, rewritten?

If he convinces himself we weren't best friends, that means he's off the hook for *betraying* his best friend. From that warped lens, what he did becomes less *running off to Peru with his best friend's girlfriend* and more *running off to Peru with a girl who just got out of a relationship.*

I swallow, meet his eye. "The others are waiting," I say evenly. "We should go."

There's so much more I could say.

I could call him on his bullshit. I could twist the knife Blair put in his back. I could tell him that as much as it all hurts—as much as he doesn't deserve it—every road I see us on eventually ends in forgiveness, because he's like a brother to me, and I care more about healing the rift between us than punishing him for it indefinitely.

But it does still hurt, and I'm not ready to forgive just yet.

So I keep it all to myself for now, make my way down the cliff.

He doesn't say another word.

"It didn't look this high from the ground," Sadie says, half an hour later, when we're back at the top of the cliff with everyone for the group's rappelling session.

"You make that sound like a bad thing," Trey replies.

"It's *terrifying*," Zoe chimes in. "And we're about to be dangling from this cliff on a rope? No thank you."

This morning's yoga session did nothing to improve her mood—if anything, it's only gotten worse.

"No one says you have to participate," Joshua tells her. "You can go right back down the rocks the same way you got up here."

The last day or two have been blessedly free of bickering from Joshua and Zoe, as they've been giving each other the silent treatment—some new development must have happened overnight, though, because they've been back at each other's throats today.

Zoe reaches out for Matteo, her hand landing light as a bird on his bicep. "Help me get my harness on?" she asks him, the look in her eye dangerously flirty for everyone involved.

It's clearly a show meant for Joshua—and I can only pray Joshua won't push them both off the cliff before we're done here.

"Okay, people!" I call out, eager to get everyone to the bottom *safely*. "If anyone truly does want to change their mind, there's no shame in that—just be careful not to slip as you make your way back down the rocks."

I glance around the group, expecting at least one of them to be on the fence about trying it, but for now, everyone seems committed.

"This is a beginner-friendly activity, but it still involves descending a cliff while dangling from a rope, so there's always a bit of risk involved," I go on. I know from the pre-tour paperwork that most of them have never tried this before.

I scan the group, avoid lingering too long when I meet Sadie's eyes. My memory flashes instantly back to this morning in the cave, where I'd much rather be right now—her lips on mine, her legs wrapped around me, the two of us alone together in secret.

Matteo clears his throat.

I swallow, pry my attention back to the group of people depending on my focus.

"You're in good hands with Matteo and me," I go on. "We've both had over a decade of outdoor adventure experience, and we're both up to date with our certifications in climbing and rope rescue. Trey is actually certified, too, so you've got lots of reasons to feel safe and confident."

All eyes drift to Trey, and he gives a small nod.

"Now," I say, "Matteo will demonstrate everything you need to know about getting to the bottom. Please pay close attention—if you have any questions, one of us will be happy to answer before you try it."

"We've already done the hardest part for you," Matteo begins, showing them where we've knotted the climbing rope around a nearby tree and piled some heavy rocks on top for extra security. "Your job is to stay calm and trust the process as you make your way down to the bottom."

He uses Zoe as a model to demonstrate how to get into the harness—not the wisest choice, considering Joshua's increasingly dark expression—and then puts his own harness on, too.

Zoe does a double take as Matteo tightens the harness onto his pelvis; the straps combined with his pants create an impressive bulge, and I want to roll my eyes at his desperation—and even more so when I see how many people are staring.

Now it's *my* turn to clear my throat.

Matteo gets the message and starts his actual demonstration. He runs over all the safety features—the auto-lock carabiners, the Prusik knot at the top of the cord, the figure-eight knot at the bottom—and reiterates that our climbing ropes are dynamic and can withstand more than seven thousand pounds.

"The first step over the edge is the hardest part for most people," he says. "Once you're there, though, the goal is to stay perpendicular to the rock, like this, with your feet planted"—his climbing form is casual but precise—"and if you need more stability at any point, you can spread your legs out a bit wider. After that, you'll want to just let the rope out a little at a time, stepping backward until you get to the bottom."

It doesn't take him long to make the full descent, and as soon as he's clipped out and I've pulled the rope back up, it's time for everyone else to try.

"Ladies first," Hunter says, nodding specifically to Parker and Emma—the tennis girls and coffee bros have been spending more and more time together lately.

Parker, definitely the more adventurous of the two, is eager to give it a go. You'd never know she was a novice by the way she steps confidently over the edge.

"She makes it look so easy," Sadie says, coming to stand beside me.

"She really does." I'm watching Parker closely in case she needs help, but so far, she's a natural. "How are you feeling?"

Sadie wipes her palms on her tennis skirt. "Well," she says. "The YouTube videos I watched before the trip did *not* do a good job preparing me for how it would actually feel to be up here. I'm, like, two parts dizzy and one part nauseated?"

"Nauseated from the dizziness?" I ask.

"Nauseated from the anxiety of knowing there's a risk, however small, that I could end up just . . . like . . . *splat* . . . at the bottom."

She says it with a smile, but I can see the nerves just underneath and the tension in her features.

There's a distant cheer—Parker's made it all the way down—and I turn to Sadie now that I can afford to give her my full attention.

The look in her eyes disarms me. She's *terrified*, way more than I realized.

"Listen to me, Sadie." It takes all of my professional discipline to not wrap her in the world's biggest bear hug right now. "Try to focus on what you know is true, okay? Matteo and Trey and I have done this a thousand times, and none of us have . . . splatted. There are multiple fail-safe security measures in place. I would absolutely *not* send you over the edge of that cliff if I thought it would end badly."

She blinks rapidly, fighting tears.

"You don't have to go just yet," I tell her. "You really don't have to go at *all*."

Her expression shifts, as if my words have just unlocked something for her.

"I do, though," she says, with sudden determination that reminds me of Zoe earlier, clearly trying to prove a point to Joshua—only with Sadie, I get the sense that she isn't trying to prove a single thing to me or anyone else.

She needs to do this for herself.

25

SADIE

Focus on what you know is true.

Knowing too much can be a curse: knowing how gravity works, and exactly how far of a fall it would be, and that common sense and self-preservation instincts all scream *people don't make a habit out of walking off the edge of a cliff for a reason*—

All of it feels true to me.

But I get what Thorn means, I think: he wants me to focus on what's most likely to happen, based on fact and not fear.

"Ready to do this?" Thorn asks when it's finally my turn.

I've watched Parker, and Zoe, and now Silas, all get to the bottom without issue; Emma's having the same second thoughts that are plaguing me and has decided to wait a bit longer.

I take a deep breath. *No, no, no,* fear screams in my head.

"Yeah," I tell him. "I'm good."

Not *ready,* necessarily. But good enough.

"You've got this," he says, his lips barely moving, as he double-checks my harness and the rope and clips me in. "You can *do* this, Sadie. You can."

I nod. Swallow. My heart is in my throat.

I was feeling so, so good after this morning. Kissing Thorn in the cave, the way it felt like magic to see that kaleidoscope of sunlight distorted and dancing through the waterfall, even Angry Yoga 2.0—all of it left me feeling calm and centered and confident.

Reality hit the second we got to the top of this cliff. The vertigo was unexpected, and so was my near–panic attack. After all I've experienced so far on this trek, I figured I'd desensitized myself to discomfort and this would just be one more challenge—

But my body says otherwise.

My heart is racing, my mouth is dry. My mind keeps spiraling toward fear, not fact. I keep steering it back.

I want to do this, though. I *need* to do it. I've come so far and done so much—surely I can do this, too.

Thorn holds out his hand.

I take it, and he gives the smallest squeeze.

You can do *this, Sadie. You can.*

My nerves settle a little, calmed by the belief he has in me, that in just a few minutes I will get to the bottom in one whole, uninjured piece.

I grasp the climbing rope with both hands. What did Matteo say earlier—that taking that first step over the edge is the hardest part?

I can now confirm: it's true.

Be brave, I tell myself. *You* are *brave.*

I step out over the edge, fumble with the toe of my shoe until it feels steady against the rock. I let out just enough slack on the rope to get me fully over the edge—and before I know it, I'm leaning all the way back, standing on the side of the cliff and facing the intense blue sky.

I haven't fallen. I'm not a splat . . . not yet.

Have fun and don't die! Caden's voice echoes in my head, and I grit my teeth.

"You don't have to grip it quite that tightly," I hear Thorn say, but it doesn't register that he's talking to *me* until he says my name. "Sadie? Take a deep breath, okay?"

I find his eyes, do what he says.

The deep breath helps. I take another.

The sooner I get moving, the sooner this will be over. *The worst part is over*, I remind myself, and it actually helps—I did the hard part. I took the step of faith. Now I just have to finish.

I step backward, one small movement at a time, focusing on only the things I can control: how I handle the rope, how I handle my fear.

It's all good until about halfway down, when the rope suddenly gives a small but sudden downward jerk.

My pulse picks up; my hands cling so tightly they might just go numb soon. I look around wildly for Thorn, see his face peering over from the top.

"What was *that*?!" I try to call out—but the words get stuck, and I can't swallow them down because my throat suddenly feels too dry and too tight, and I can't get a deep breath, and it's all starting to spiral.

Stepping over the edge was *not* the hardest part. Not by far. Panic attack halfway down the side of a cliff while your life feels like it's hanging on by a climbing rope–sized thread? This is way, way worse.

I might throw up.

"You're fine, Sadie, everything's fine!" Thorn is yelling from far above me. "Hunter tripped over the cord, but it's still totally stable. You're good. Take a deep breath and keep going, okay?"

I practice my panic-attack breathing: slow inhale through the nose, long exhale back out again. I try to ground myself in the moment, thinking of things I can see—blue sky, stupid flimsy rope, the face of a guy I'd really love to kiss again if I make it to the bottom in one piece.

When I make it to the bottom, I correct myself.

Little by little, the tension evaporates, enough that I feel brave enough to get moving again. A moment later, though, a bit of the cliff crumbles under my foot—it's just dirt and rock, I think, sediment knocked loose. The surprise of it catches me off guard, wrecking my balance—I'm flailing—

I reach out a hand, try to stabilize, but my palm finds something sharp. A rock, or maybe a branch? It hurts like *fire*—and I'm pretty sure I'm bleeding.

Deep breaths, deep breaths.

I can't believe people do this sort of thing for fun.

"You're almost here," Matteo calls out from down below. "You never have to do this again—but you're doing great, okay?"

Matteo has hardly said a thing to me in the last few days—awkwardness by association, I guess. Still, his encouragement is just what I need to kick it into high gear and finally get to the bottom. Descending with only one good hand is uncomfortable, but at least it's a distraction to keep my mind from spiraling.

I rip the harness off as soon as my feet are back on solid ground.

"You did it!" Matteo says, reaching up for a high five, his smile so contagious I almost forget the gash in my hand, and the blood, and the way I truly feel like all the coffee and lunch I had earlier might be on the verge of coming back up.

I'm still reeling from the adrenaline when Thorn appears at my side.

"Are you okay?" he says, breathless from sprinting down the cliff's rocky staircase.

I hold up my hand and watch as his eyes go wide at the sight of all the blood.

He mutters a curse under his breath. "That looks like hell," he says, brow furrowed and intense. "I'll get you cleaned up, okay? Wait here."

A few minutes later, Thorn finds his way back to me.

"Matty, you got this?" he says. "Trey's going to help out from the top while I take care of Sadie back at the campsite."

"Yeah, man," Matteo replies. "Whatever."

His mood has done a total reversal from the guy who high-fived me at the bottom of my descent, and the same is true of Thorn. The tension between them is especially high today.

"What was *that* all about?" I ask when we're out of earshot.

Thorn shakes his head. "We had another talk this morning."

"Didn't go too well, I guess?"

"To say the least."

He's quiet after that. It's only a short walk back over to my tent—we stowed both of our packs inside it this morning after yoga.

"I brought a first-aid kit," I offer.

He grins. "Of course you did."

It turns out his first-aid kit is more than sufficiently stocked, though. He's got iodine tablets and antiseptic—liquid *and* wipes—and all sorts of ointments and gauze and bandages.

Once we're settled inside my tent, Thorn takes my hand in both of his, gently, and inspects it with a grimace.

"I'm sorry for this," he says as he reaches into his kit, then holds up a small pair of tweezers. "It will probably hurt a lot worse before it feels better."

"Your bedside manner could use some work, Thorn."

"Hey, I'm a hiking guide, not a surgeon."

"And that inspires *so* much confidence," I say, laughing.

My laughter turns into a gasp of pain as his tweezers find the first splinter. It feels like a fireplace poker, searing and sudden, like fire straight down to my bones.

"It's okay," Thorn says, his voice soft and soothing as he plucks another splinter out. "You're okay. You're doing great."

"That"—I gasp—"was better bedside manner."

He runs his thumb over the back of my hand. Focusing on how good that feels helps to distract from how terrible the rest of it is.

I've engineered my life to feel as little pain as possible. Who doesn't? I don't usually *do* things that could result in splinters and open wounds. I do things that involve tasty beverages and comfortable seating locations and pleasant aromas—things that make my senses tingle in a good way.

My senses, right now, are screaming.

"Done with splinters," he tells me. "There were only a couple."

I'm just about to say how relieved I am to be past the worst part when—*aaaugghhhhh*—a white-hot flood of pain eclipses the previous sting, knocking the wind out of me.

"That was the antiseptic," I hear him say. "It'll get better from here, I promise."

He spreads a layer of ointment on. Next comes the gauze, wrapped just tightly enough to protect my hand while it heals.

"I feel like a mummy," I say when he's done, admiring his neat work.

"Hottest mummy I've ever seen," he replies, grinning. "You've got something—there—"

I glance down at my lavender tank top, which is now marred with a small but noticeable splatter of blood.

"I should probably—" I start, at the same time he says, "I can close my eyes while you change, if you want?"

"Or," I say, suddenly all too aware of how intimate this moment feels, just the two of us in here while everyone else is out climbing near the waterfall, "you could leave them open?"

He bites his lip, and now that's all I can see. "If that's what you want," he says slowly, "who am I to say no?"

It is what I want. It's what I've wanted since the very first morning we found ourselves tangled together after he took refuge from the rain.

Using my good hand—my dominant hand, thankfully—I try to peel my shirt off. It's a struggle. I never realized how much I took for granted having *both* hands to do this sort of thing.

Thorn notices, his gaze flicking down to the bare strip of skin where my tank top is partially hiked up.

"Need help?" he asks.

"I don't know," I say playfully. "Last time you helped, it involved tweezers and antiseptic and almost made me black out."

He laughs. "My surgeon days are over," he says as his fingers find the hem, leaving a trail of chills behind as they graze my abdomen.

"It's a good thing," I tease.

"I take a lot of pride in my work," he says, glancing down to my mummy hand. "You're welcome, by the way."

His fingertips slide up under my shirt—the anticipation is killer. I can't get this tank top off fast enough.

"Thank you," I say, my words lost in lavender fabric as he helps me slip the shirt over my head. "For everything."

His eyes dart downward—this sports bra does *great* things for me—then back up to my lips.

"We probably only have a few minutes . . ." His voice is raspy and quiet; his hands linger at the crisscrossing straps between my shoulder blades before skimming down to my lower back.

I grin, inching closer. "Then we should probably take advantage while we can, yeah?"

Never in my life have I fallen for someone so fast, but then again, I've never met anyone like Thorn. He makes it easy to be vulnerable: to let him see my entire self, my fears and my tears and the stubble that's growing in on my legs, without worrying that I'm *too much*.

He's never made me feel like too much. Never made me feel out of place here, even though I've possibly had the hardest time adjusting out of everyone.

He swallows, palms flexing over my bare back to pull me toward him. I ease my way onto his lap, wrap my legs around his hips. We pick up right where we left off this morning, minus the cave and the waterfall, but still very much in secret, his kiss so warm and soft and tender it almost makes me forget my pain.

I taste chocolate and coffee on his tongue, bittersweet. He's days past a five o'clock shadow, and it'll probably leave me red and raw after this, but right now I don't care—I want it all.

His fingers press tighter as he works his way up my rib cage, then teases the band of my bra. He plants a hungry kiss on the tender part of my neck, just beneath the curve of my jaw. My pulse picks up, so strong I'm aware of every racing heartbeat.

My good hand finds its way to his hair, tightening too hard on instinct, and he makes a little noise.

"Sorry," I whisper. "Did that hurt?"

He smirks. "Yeah," he says. "In a good way."

He leans in for another kiss—but the sound of footsteps on the rocky ground outside makes us both freeze.

"Thorn?" a voice calls out. "Sadie—are you in there?"

Parker, Thorn mouths, eyes wide.

I back off him, accidentally knocking into the flimsy tent wall in the process. I need a shirt. I need a shirt *now*.

"Yeah!" Thorn replies, his voice cracked with thirst. He clears his throat. "Almost done in here."

Now that my pack doesn't have as much in it, it's easy to find the fresh tank top I'm looking for. I whip it over my head as fast as I can, even though my left hand *hurts*.

I wish I had a mirror, maybe also some concealer—that make-out session is most definitely written all over my face, and I have no way to hide it.

Thorn unzips the tent and climbs out.

Why did we zip it in the first place? That's not suspicious *at all*.

"What's going on?" I hear Thorn ask.

I tighten my ponytail and straighten my shirt, making doubly sure it isn't inside out, and then I follow his lead.

Parker looks panicked, frantic.

"Um . . . we've got a problem?"

26

THORN

It's whiplash, going from Sadie to . . . this.

Parker's all over the place. I can hardly keep up.

"Emma finally got brave enough to try rappelling, but only after I went back up to give her a pep talk," she's saying, full of nervous energy. She keeps glancing over her shoulder, back toward the climbing site. "By the time she started going, none of us realized Matteo wasn't down there anymore, and something happened about halfway down, and now Emma's stuck—Trey says the rope is twisted, or caught on a branch or something, and—and—"

Her words get caught in her throat.

"Is she okay?" Sadie asks.

It's a good thing she's here, because *of course* that should have been the first question on my mind, too. Not *Where the hell is Matteo?*

"I mean . . . define *okay*?" Parker says. "She's hanging in there. Literally. But, like, freaking out?"

I leave for twenty minutes and all chaos breaks lose.

And seriously—where the hell is Matteo?

"Let's go." My words sound like I'm spitting fire.

Trey has the climbing situation under control by the time we get back—he knew exactly how to fix whatever snag caught Emma up on her way down, and must have done a good job keeping her calm enough to finish her descent.

He shouldn't have had to. That's not *his* job.

"Thanks, man," I tell him. "You shouldn't have had to take over like that."

He waves it off. "I don't mind. I'm just glad I knew how to help. How's Sadie?"

It takes me a minute to realize he's asking about her hand. Every thought of Sadie, right now, involves the things we were doing when we were interrupted.

"Better," I say. "Got her all fixed up."

Got her all fixed up, and then—and then—

I swallow down my desire, my guilt. As much as I enjoyed it, and as much as I wish Parker had never cut into our time together, I never should have let myself get sidetracked like that.

And I never should have trusted Matteo.

His words haunt me, even if he's lost all right to have any say whatsoever about being responsible: *You need to get it together, man. You've been distracted out here.*

I thought I could do both. As much as I hate to admit it . . . I accept that, maybe, he had a point.

"What happened with Matteo?" I ask.

"Your guess is as good as mine," Trey says. "None of us noticed he was gone until Emma was stuck and he wasn't around to help."

I scan the group. Matteo's not the only one missing, I realize: Zoe and Joshua aren't here, either.

"And the others?" I ask.

Trey looks perplexed for a moment, but then realization sinks in. "No idea."

This particular area isn't densely wooded like so many of the other campsites we've stopped at—there are only so many places they could be.

The first, the top of the cliff, is easy to rule out. That's where everyone was when all the drama started, and Zoe had already rappelled down before Sadie even took her turn.

Second: the flat, rocky expanse where we slept last night—Sadie's not the only one who set her tent up, so it's possible they might be inside another one. But all three of them? To each their own, but I'm gonna go out on a limb and guess that's not happening.

The only other place that's out of sight is the cave behind the waterfall.

I can think of just one good reason for any of them to be in there together—that Joshua and Zoe are finally working things out in private—but then a movement near the tents catches my eye.

"There's Joshua," Trey says.

He'd be hard to miss on a normal day, but today his shirt is electric pink, bright against the pale landscape.

It only takes a moment to realize Zoe's not with him—and neither is Matteo.

Ohhhh no. No, no, no.

"Thorn!" Sadie calls as I rush past. "Where are you going? What's wrong?"

I can't tell her what I'm thinking without telling everyone. Maybe my instincts are off—I *hope* my instincts are off. But Zoe's performative flirting has been in full force this afternoon, and I've seen Matteo rebound twice in the past with people he hardly knew, forgettable girls who helped him forget his own pain. Hell, even on *this* trip, he spent the night in Brittany's tent after Blair broke up with him.

I have a strong suspicion about what I'll find behind that waterfall, and the flash of anger I feel at the pit of my stomach burns. Not just for the hypocrisy of it all—Matteo has no right to accuse me of being distracted ever again—but also for Joshua.

I'm vaguely aware of the others trailing behind me as I retrace the path Matteo and Zoe must have taken when they slipped out of sight. It's only a short walk from our climbing site to the cave, and on this side of the creek, it doesn't even require a swim.

Despite the waterfall, it feels too still, too silent.

I'm the first to crash the party.

Sure enough, there's Matteo—a very shirtless Matteo—and, by process of elimination, Zoe. She's practically eclipsed by him; from all the clothes littering the cave floor, that's probably for the best.

I clear my throat.

It echoes, bouncing from the rock walls, refracted back on itself over and over. I don't have to say a word: they break apart—as if I haven't already seen everything. At least she's wearing underwear, and a bra.

Matteo keeps a neutral expression. No acknowledgment that he left the rappelling group without a leader by ditching his post, and definitely no acknowledgment that he's just been caught rebounding in the world's sexiest cave with the fiancée of one of our trekkers.

I have no words.

"Please don't tell Joshua," Zoe says, too busy rushing to gather her clothes that she doesn't notice him slip into the cave right behind me.

"Don't tell Joshua what?"

His voice is a live wire, steady but lethal.

The cave suddenly feels suffocatingly small.

I have my own issues with Matteo, but now Joshua does, too—with Matteo *and* Zoe.

"What were you thinking?" I explode at Matteo, who's casually shrugging back into his T-shirt as if two of the three people in this cave aren't staring daggers at him. "This is completely inappropriate in so many ways, Matty."

The smirk he gives me is absolutely infuriating.

"I don't see how it's any different than what you've been doing," he says. "Everyone knows you've been hooking up with Sadie."

"You can't be serious," I shoot back. It takes effort to not go for his bait—to not get sidetracked by him bringing Sadie into this. "It's different in *every* way. I left you in charge back there, but you ditched the group and put them in a dangerous spot. Trey didn't sign up to colead this trip, *you* did. It's a good thing he was there—Emma got stuck and he had to handle it on his own."

"How long does it take to bandage up a hand?" Matteo retorts. "You were off with Sadie for a while, so I could say the same about you."

Do not. Take. The bait.

"So you thought you'd sneak off with my fiancée to, what—prove some sort of point?" Joshua cuts in. "Or are you just a clueless jackass?"

"*Ex*-fiancée," Zoe corrects. "Or did you think I wasn't serious last night when I told you I wanted to call it off? Excuse me for finally having some *fun* out here."

Joshua bristles. "How was I supposed to know you were serious this time, Zo? You always say you want to break up when things don't go your way, but you never really mean it. I figured you were just in one of your moods, like you have been for the *entire trip*."

"You never should have brought me out here!" she says, her passion melting into fury. "You should have known the wilderness isn't my thing, and that springing this sort of trip on me would only make me miserable. You thought our summer trips could fix us, Joshua, but honestly? All yours does is prove how wrong we are for each other. I'm sorry, but it's the truth."

"How wrong we are—" he sputters. "You can't be serious—you didn't even return the ring!"

"Oh, I'm very serious," Zoe says. "We're *done*. Really, really done. And I didn't injure my hand like I told you." She rips her bandages off her left hand and holds it up for him to see. "I lost my ring in the lake. *Days* ago."

Joshua's eyebrows shoot as far up as they'll go. "What do you mean, you *lost* it?"

Matteo seems more than happy to let the focus stay off of himself, but I see him all too clearly: he could have been kissing anyone out here in the cave. Anyone at all, so long as they take his mind off Blair.

"Third day of the trip," Zoe says. "Good luck finding it again."

When her words finish bouncing from the walls, the cave falls into a silent stillness that reminds me of disaster movies: the instant before a bomb goes off—one wrong move, then everything explodes.

Joshua, frozen in fight-or-flight, studies Zoe—

And then he takes off, a man on a mission.

"*Shit*," I mutter, then follow him out.

Sadie and the others are waiting just outside the cave—they probably overheard every single word.

I try to catch up to Joshua, but he's too fast, too determined. He's sprinting down to the place where the creek is shallow enough to cross without getting too wet.

I'm fast, but he's faster.

Finally, I catch up to him at his tent, where he's furiously stuffing his belongings into his pack.

"You're not seriously thinking about going to try to find the ring?" I ask, my breath ragged from the effort.

"I'm not *thinking* about it," he replies shortly. "I'm doing it."

"You have no idea where you're going," I protest. "You shouldn't go off on your own, man. It's too dangerous, and there's a very good chance you'd never find it again anyway." I swallow, searching for just the right words to talk him out of it. "It's completely understandable that you wouldn't want to be around the group after what just happened. Let me call my boss, arrange for her to pick you up—"

"I'm not interested in anyone picking me up," he cuts me off. "I want *my ring*."

I take a deep breath. "Okay," I say, scrambling for something, anything. "One of us can take you back to the lake after the trek ends, if you want. We'll get a metal detector—we can help you look."

But it's no use. Joshua isn't thinking rationally, probably isn't thinking about anything other than Zoe's multifaceted bomb.

"I've got GPS on my phone," he says as he slings his pack over his shoulders, tightens the straps, and turns his back to me. "I'll figure it out."

In all my years as a hiking guide, I've never had anyone desert the group before a trek is over. It's a first I would rather not experience, but it appears he's hell-bent on getting out of here and not interested in being convinced otherwise.

"Please reconsider?" I call out. "It's not worth it—it's not safe to go out by yourself. You're not even taking your tent?"

But he doesn't answer, only picks up the pace.

He's halfway across the rocky flat when I hear a long exhale from behind me. I turn and see Matteo, arms crossed.

"You need to go after him," I say.

"That's the last thing *either* of us needs," Matteo says. "Dude wants to throw me off a cliff."

At least he's seeing things clearly.

"You made this mess, Matty. You need to fix it. He'll try to take the loop all the way back around, and he'll never make it on his own—if you go with him, you can show him the shortcuts."

His brow furrows. "Cloverleaf Creek? And . . . what else?"

I nod. "Cloverleaf Creek all the way back up to Mackenzie Lake, then you can take Hedge Key Pass over to catch back up with us at Sparrow Valley. Shouldn't take more than a day, two at most. You probably won't find the ring, but hopefully he'll drop it if you at least help him look."

I don't know why Matteo doesn't fight me on it—maybe because he's aware enough to realize this situation is very, very bad, both for us as leaders and especially for Joshua.

"I'll go," he says carefully. "But this isn't all on me, man."

All his accusations from in the cave, and earlier, slither like vipers back into my head: his insinuation that I, too, irresponsibly ditched my post at the rappelling site—that maybe if I hadn't been so distracted with Sadie, we wouldn't have ended up here.

"I wasn't the one making out with one of our trekkers' exes," I say through gritted teeth. "That was *you*. No matter what led to it."

This is a disaster.

I honestly think *no* coleader would be better than this—which is fortunate, I realize, since that's exactly what this situation is boiling down to.

Matteo doesn't say another word.

Ten minutes later, he's gone, following at a distance after Joshua, armed with a tent and a tarp and enough food to get them both through the next day or two before we all meet up again.

Until then, it's all on me to get everyone else through this trek in one piece. More than ever, I can't afford any distractions—not from Matteo, not from Sadie.

Not from anyone.

27

THORN

I need to call Danica. The sooner, the better—I should have called already, honestly—but my trust is so frayed right now that I'm struggling to step away from the group, even for a few minutes.

The other thing holding me back: I'm still working up the nerve.

How do I explain what just happened without also confessing that I was off with Sadie when all the chaos went down? It scares me to think of how easily I lost track of time today. I let my guard down, forgot myself and everyone else for just long enough that it turned into a big problem.

Not to mention I'm down a coleader.

Deep down, I think there's a part of me that thinks if I just do a good enough job on my own—get us through the next few days without any more injuries or incidents—Danica will never have to know the extent of what went down until we're all back in one piece.

But I'm not sure my conscience could live with that.

I find a quiet spot at the far end of Alexandria Flat, the only place around here where I can get some privacy while still keeping an eye on camp.

"Come on, Danica," I mutter under my breath as it rings. "Pick up."

"Thorn?" she says, her voice crackling; one of us has a sketchy connection. "Everything okay?"

It's not, and the fact that I'm calling at all from out here means she already knows it.

"Things took a bit of a turn today," I tell her.

I give her the bullet-point version: Joshua and Zoe's epic breakup, Matteo's bombshell of a make-out session, Joshua going rogue despite me trying my damndest to talk him out of it—with emphasis on how my hands were tied when Joshua made it crystal clear he had no intention of staying at camp *or* being picked up early—and that the best we could do was for Matteo to go with him so he wouldn't be out on the trails alone.

I leave out the part about Matteo ditching everyone at the climbing site—since that would implicate me, too—and, for now, focus mostly on the relational drama of it all.

When I finish, it's so silent on the other end I have to double-check that my phone still has a connection. Danica doesn't get angry often . . . she's one of the most levelheaded, even-keeled people I've ever met. So when a full minute passes without her saying a word, I know it's bad.

"Okay, so, there's not a lot I can do from here at this point," she starts. "We don't have anyone else I could send to fill in for Matteo—and I'm actually relieved to hear Joshua declined a pickup, because I would've had a hard time getting out there this evening. Charlotte's down with a stomach bug."

Charlotte is Danica's six-year-old daughter.

"Sorry to hear that," I offer. "Hope she feels better soon."

"Thanks," she says. "It's been a *day*. As far as the trek goes, it sounds like you did the best you could in light of the circumstances. Tell me their planned route so I can have a record in case of emergency?"

I run through the shortcuts I suggested to Matteo—Alexandria

Flat up to Mackenzie Lake via Cloverleaf Creek, then a different trail back down to Sparrow Valley.

I hear her take notes, the scratch of pencil on paper loud in my ear. "Good instincts," she remarks. "Those are efficient shortcuts without holding the group up for two extra days."

"You're okay with us going on to Sparrow Valley, then?" I ask. "Even though I don't have a coleader?"

I wondered, after Matteo and Joshua were already gone, if I should have told them to just meet us back here.

"It's obviously not ideal," she says after a long moment, "but given the unusual circumstances, I'm fine with you leading solo until they meet up with you again. Just use your best judgment to get everyone back in one piece, okay?"

She means it as a weight off, I'm sure—but all I feel is pressure.

"Did I lose you?" she says a moment later, when I still haven't replied.

"I'm here," I finally say. "Thanks, Dani."

"How's morale?" she asks.

"Exhausted, for the most part."

"And how have things been with Matteo otherwise?"

I fixate on a distant hawk as it swoops low over the horizon, resisting the urge to divulge every single detail—specifically, Matteo's accusations about how I've been distracted out here. I don't want to give Danica any reason to worry or doubt my ability to take care of the group, especially when she's already told me there's nothing she can do at the moment to help.

"Pretty uncomfortable," I admit. "Blair broke up with him over text a few days ago, so things have been a little rough since then."

"What a mess," Danica says. "I'm so sorry, Thorn." She sighs. "And you said he was off with . . . Zoe?"

"Zoe, yeah."

There's another long pause, but this time I can tell we're still connected.

"Well," she says, "I hate to make things even more uncomfortable, but whenever the guys get back, please remind Matteo what a terrible idea it is to get involved with the trekkers—even the ones who *aren't* there with their ex-fiancés. We've got rules about that stuff for a reason."

That conversation will go over well. This is not good, not good at all.

"Between you and me, Thorn, can I just say what a relief it is to have someone like you in a situation like this?" Danica continues. "I'd be nervous if it were anyone else leading solo, but I'd trust you with just about anything—and you're the *one* guide I've never had to worry about when it comes to catching feelings."

I know she means all of this as a compliment, but it feels more like a punch to the gut: that I've let this job define my life to such an extent that she can't even fathom me falling for someone out here. There's no way Matteo will accept the sort of feedback she's asking me to give—he'll never take me seriously, not with how close I've gotten with Sadie, even if I'm somehow able to put an end to those feelings and cut things off for good.

But I definitely can't tell Danica the depths of my concerns now.

My only way forward is to do everything I can to be the strong, focused leader she believes I am—the one I've always been, and am still capable of being.

"You've got this, Thorn," she says, her voice cutting in and out. "It's only two days on your own—I'm not worried. Just trust your gut and it'll all be fine."

This time, the call really does drop.

I'm so screwed.

28

SADIE

I didn't hear everything that went down in the cave, but I heard more than enough. *Everyone* heard.

Thorn hasn't been the same since.

All afternoon, he's been brooding and distant. He's had a couple of chats with Trey off to the side, and spent a bit of time on the phone—with his boss, he told us before he stepped away—but has otherwise kept to himself.

His mood has been pervasive throughout camp; all of us seem a little shell-shocked by what happened. Usually at this time of day, as the sun dips low on the horizon, the air is thick with laughter and the sounds of lively conversation around the campfire.

Today, it's nothing but whispers. If that.

Emma is still a bit on edge after her rappelling experience, and who can blame her? I had a panic attack even with a smooth, untangled rope—I can't imagine how much harder it was for her. Fear has a way of clinging to your bones even after you're safely through whatever sparked it—it's the what-if that shakes you up the most.

My life motto has always been that it's easiest to just avoid risk altogether.

Which is why I'm so proud of what I accomplished today. I was as terrified as Emma—but I trusted Thorn, trusted the process. It was scary, but I did it.

Tonight, that sense of accomplishment has been muted by the dramatic turn of events with Matteo and Zoe and Joshua.

"I never meant for him to do something so stupid," Zoe confesses to me now, the two of us roasting a pair of lonely marshmallows over the fire.

"Who, Joshua?" I ask.

She gapes at me. "Yes, Joshua."

I didn't think the answer was *that* obvious—he and Matteo both did stupid things today—but apparently only one of them is living rent-free in her head.

"I don't regret it," she goes on.

Regret . . . what? I wait for her to clarify, because it feels as ambiguous as her last comment, but she just turns her marshmallow over, letting it burn. Does she realize she's talking *to me* and not just having this conversation in her head?

"Kissing Matteo?" I venture.

"What?" she says, gaze drifting to meet mine. "Oh, right. No, I don't regret that, either. I was still talking about Joshua—I don't regret breaking up with him." She tilts her head thoughtfully. "Though maybe I should have thought twice before trying to make him jealous. I didn't expect it to turn out like *this*."

I'm not sure she thought at *all* about the potential fallout from her actions, but I don't say so.

Zoe and Joshua are like a cautionary tale of everything I could have been going through if Caden had actually come on this trip. Doing this experience together wouldn't have brought us back together—it most definitely would have driven us apart.

I turn my marshmallow over in the fire, try to imagine him here.

Caden likes to think of himself as chill and unbothered, but I think he would have hated the bugs and the fact that he couldn't wash off the sweat and the dirt in a hot shower at the end of every day. He would have been good at the rappelling, though. Probably the kayaking, too. But the two of us out here together—yikes. I shudder to think about how he might have treated me. I'm pretty sure I would have suffered a crisis of confidence by this point, at best, barely holding myself together under his myriad little jabs about my heavy backpack, my shoes, how not-cut-out-for-any-of-this I am.

Without him here, I've been able to stretch my wings instead of having them pinned down at every turn.

The breeze picks up, and all of a sudden Zoe's fiery marshmallow blooms into a small inferno at the end of her stick.

"Zoe!" I exclaim. "Your marshmallow!"

She shrieks, panicked, and attempts to shake the flames out. It only makes things worse—she comes dangerously close to setting Thorn's shirt on fire when he rushes over to help.

Swiftly, he swipes Zoe's stick from her hands, then dumps out a generous pour from his canteen. The flames sizzle out, leaving only a soggy, charred marshmallow corpse.

"You, uh . . . might want to start a new one," Thorn says, handing the sad stick back to Zoe.

I bite back a laugh. His comedic timing hits just right even when it's unintentional—and I know it's unintentional now because his expression is every bit as sober and unsmiling as it's been all afternoon.

Thorn's eyes lock with mine.

Can we talk? I mouth behind Zoe's back.

He glances over at the rest of the group, Parker and Emma and the coffee bros, all having a picnic dinner together a bit farther away from the fire.

Where? he mouths back.

It would probably be a bit too obvious for us to sneak off right now, especially after what Matteo said in the cave: *Everyone knows you've been hooking up with Sadie.*

If they didn't know before, they know now.

Later, I tell him. *My tent?*

He seems to be on the fence about the idea of alone time with me—and I get it, I do.

Just to talk, I add, even though I would do much more if given the chance.

He nods, and that's that.

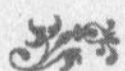

It's a full three hours later when he finally stops by. I'm in pajamas and a hoodie.

"Knock, knock," Thorn says quietly.

I unzip the door to my tent, let him in.

"Maybe I should turn my lamp off?" I whisper. "So it's harder to tell we're both in here together?"

Also because if I look at his face for a second longer—that stubbled jaw, those perfect lips—it's going to be really, really tough to stick to the whole let's-just-talk plan.

The touch lamp's metal sensor is cool under my fingertips; an instant later, the world is jet-black. I know my eyes will adjust eventually, but for now it's just Thorn and me and my oh-so-helpful imagination reminding me of all the things we could do together in the dark.

"How are you?" I ask instead.

He's quiet for so long the silence starts to bend in on itself, thick and heavy.

I wait.

"I shouldn't be here," he finally says, his voice low and gravelly. "We shouldn't be doing this."

"We're not *doing* anything," I reply. "We're just talking."

And we're barely even doing that.

"I just—" He cuts himself off, lets out a long exhale. "Today was partly my fault. We shouldn't have stayed out here so long after I fixed up your hand."

It's the last thing I expect him to say.

"Is this because of what Matteo said?" I ask, thinking back to all I overheard at the cave. "Don't let him get into your head, Thorn. He has no right to tell you how to lead, especially after what he did."

"That's just it, though," Thorn says, more urgently. "He did some stupid stuff, but he still had a point when he said I've been too distracted out here."

That's outrageous—Matteo's in the worst position to be slinging accusations, not to mention Thorn is the most responsible, reliable human on the face of the planet. It doesn't sit well with me at all that Matteo has caused Thorn to doubt himself like this.

"Um, have you *met* you?" I ask. "You're the most incredible wilderness guide I've ever known."

"Correct me if I'm wrong," he says, "but am I not the *only* wilderness guide you've ever known, other than Matteo?"

"Details." I grin—a joke is good progress right now.

He gives a little half laugh, shakes his head.

"As I was saying," I go on, "in my *very extensive experience* with all the wilderness guides I've encountered while on planet Earth, you are not only the most attractive, but also the most attentive. You always know exactly where everyone is at every single hour of the day—you anticipate when we'll need rest breaks, and snacks, and water, and sunscreen, and bug spray, before we even realize those things ourselves. You don't need the internet to tell you about the landmarks out here, or the terrifying night beasts—"

"The *night beasts*?!" Thorn interrupts, laughing despite himself.

"Yes, Thorn. The night beasts." I'm laughing, too, but not too loudly—I can tell he feels like all eyes are on us right now and wants to keep whatever this is between us chill and out of sight. "You know about the night beasts, and even the day beasts, and you know about stargazing and waterfalls and how to do surgery on scraped-up hands without making your patient pass out from the pain."

It's possible I'm performing, just a little: that my instinct, when things get hard, is to try to make them fun instead—to make him forget whatever guilt trip he's putting himself through right now.

Hopefully it's working.

"What I'm saying is," I go on, "even if you *have* been a little more distracted than you're used to, you are still incredibly attentive. Emma's rope could have gotten tangled even if you'd been there, right? Trey handled it, and Emma's fine. *Matteo* is the one who dropped the ball, not you. It bothers me that he's trying to make you feel guilty when he knows it isn't your fault."

I'm breathless when I finish.

And Thorn . . . is speechless.

My eyes have finally adjusted enough to see the outline of his profile, the dip of his lashes as he stares into the darkness.

"You give one hell of a pep talk, Sadie," he finally says.

His fingers brush against mine. It's the lightest touch, but I feel like we've just bridged a canyon-sized gap, finding our way back to each other after the afternoon forced us apart.

"I'll be here all night!" I reply, like I'm some sort of stand-up comic.

It's part defense mechanism, part invitation; it's code for *I want to touch so much more than your hands right now.*

As if he can hear every word, he runs his palm up my arm, all the way up until his fingers graze my neck, then find their way into my hair. I inch closer, feel him do the same—but I can still sense him holding back, pulling away.

Maybe I was too quick to hope we could just move on. Today must have shaken him up even more than I realized.

"Get some good sleep, okay?" he says, his breath hot against my skin.

He plants one soft kiss on the curve of my jaw, slow and purposeful, lingering just long enough that I think he *wants* to keep going, but can't trust the voices in his head—*Matteo's* voice in his head—telling him we've done too much already.

"See you in the morning," I say as he slips out into the night, without me.

9:27 P.M. • DAY 7 • SADIE'S JOURNAL

Today was full of extremes: highs and lows, pleasure and pain, ice and fire (okay, not *literal* ice and fire, but Abby always says I love a poetic metaphor).

Highs/lows:

- **I rappelled down the side of a (literally quite high) cliff!!**
- **Hit an emotional low while dangling from said cliff**
- **Fought through it, finished rappelling, not sure I've ever been so proud of myself**

Pleasure/pain:

- **This morning in the waterfall cave with Thorn was one of the most romantic things I've ever experienced in my ENTIRE LIFE**
- **Tearing a gash through my hand while descending the cliff was one of the most *painful* things I've ever experienced (but the pain of Thorn doctoring me up afterward was even worse)**

Ice/fire:

- **Woke up absolutely freezing in my sleeping bag after Thorn's hot tip**
- **WATERFALL KISS = FIRE**
- **File "searing-hot pain of tending my wound" under fire, too, but not in a good way**
- **Thorn had a rough day, and for a while he was icing everyone out . . . I feel a bit better now that we've talked, but not entirely. Hopefully he'll continue to thaw out tomorrow because I much prefer the aforementioned fire (of the waterfall kiss variety).**

DAY EIGHT

Moonbow Falls at Alexandria Flat to Sparrow Valley

The foothill paths along the southeastern stretch of the Mackenzie Lake Loop offer some of the most spectacular views in the entire park. After a day at arid Alexandria Flat, the sprawling vista of trees is quite the wonder to behold—just be mindful of the steady incline in the first half of the trek, which can be troublesome for the unprepared. Hikers will rejoice at what awaits on the other side, though: Sparrow Valley—along with the majestic Sparrow Valley Falls—is the perfect landing place for anyone planning a day trip to summit Mount Valerie, offering no shortage of beautiful scenery and a respite from the arduous trails. Spend two nights, if you can, to take in the sights.

—Henry Herrington, *Backpacking the Sierras: A Beginner's Handbook* (Fourth Edition)

CAPTAIN'S LOG // AUGUST THORN

Day 8 • 6:34 a.m. • 68°F • Partly cloudy

TREK NOTES

I'm up early, down at the waterfall, trying to get my head on straight before I have to be around humans again. Yesterday was the messiest day I've ever had out here.

Matteo's a problem. Coleaders are meant to help, not make things worse. And am I really at the point where I'm nostalgic for the days where Joshua and Zoe were making out all the time instead of the catastrophic implosion they've become?

FOR DAD

Saw a white-headed woodpecker on one of the sugar pines lining the cliff. Dad would have loved it—they're one of his favorites. I've never related to a bird more than I do right now . . . kind of feel like bashing my head against a tree and hoping I feel satisfied afterward. Unfortunately, that would probably just make my headache worse.

29

THORN

No one got a good night's sleep, from what I can tell—which is *great*, since we have another long day of hiking ahead of us.

I'm not satisfied with how this stop on our itinerary has gone, to say the least. Alexandria Flats is always meant to be inspiring and motivating: *Look how big the night sky is*, I like to tell our groups before stargazing. *And even though this cliff is high and goes straight down, with enough ingenuity and bravery and confidence—and the right knots—you can conquer it.*

I'm gonna go out on a limb and say *inspired* and *motivated* is very much not the mood today.

"I told you we shouldn't have shared so much," I overhear Hunter saying to Silas when they don't realize I'm listening.

There's no coffee this morning; apparently, they ran out.

I feel a little guilty having Sadie's entire coffee stash tucked away in my pack, but I feel like it would raise more questions than anything—from her and everyone else—if I were to whip it all out right now.

When everyone's packed up and ready to go, I give the rundown for today's trek. The group feels so intimate compared to the first day: now it's just Hunter and Silas and Trey, Parker and Emma, Zoe and her yoga—and Sadie. And me.

"We've got a full day ahead," I announce to the seven exhausted faces staring back at me. "Matteo and Joshua should be able to meet back up with us at our next campsite, so for now, we're going to continue as planned."

Sadie's words from last night echo in my mind as I go on in more detail about our itinerary—the foothill path along the southern rim of the Mackenzie Lake Loop—and the reminders I give every single morning: bug spray, sunscreen, don't forget to hydrate, and on and on.

I am *attentive*, I think to myself. *I am responsible*.

But as we set off, the doubts creep in. I can't shake my conversation with Danica, the confidence she has in me: *Can I just say what a relief it is to have someone like you in a situation like this?*

I want those words to be true.

I *need* those words to be true.

But do I really have the focus, the *willpower*, to be the leader she's relying on me to be?

Last night was good progress. It took incredible restraint to leave Sadie's tent when I did; I slept out under the stars again, but it was even lonelier than I expected without her by my side. I couldn't stop thinking about our waterfall kiss—how the day started so perfectly, the two of us together in our own little world, but went steeply downhill from there. Dueling shades of guilt battled it out in my head all night long: that I let my guard down in the first place—and that I would do it all over again in a heartbeat.

Which is why I can hardly look at her today.

It's not that I don't want to—

It's that I want her too much.

We trek single file along the foothill path, following the shape of the landscape, each view more incredible than the last as the path winds higher and higher. There aren't any designated rest stops like on other trails in the park—just a few areas where the path widens a bit more than it does elsewhere. Despite the scenery, it's one of our more arduous hikes.

"Wow, it's really pretty up here," Sadie says quietly, pulling me out of my head. It's the first time we've spoken all day—I'm painfully aware of how little I've said to her since last night.

"Yeah," I reply. "It really is."

A flash of blue catches my eye in the treetops below. My tradition along this stretch of the trail is to count all the mountain bluebirds—whenever Dad or I spotted one flitting between tree branches for the first time each trip, he'd whistle the melody of their birdsong. One time, a bird sang back. We used to wear matching ball caps in the exact shade of their feathers, but mine eventually faded so much it was practically white—a reminder that everything changes in time, like it or not.

We pause for a snack break in midafternoon. With no benches or boulders to sit on, most of the group sits down on the trodden dirt path—even Sadie, who most certainly would have scoffed at the idea on her first few days out here.

Zoe is the only one who insists on standing.

"I've got a tarp if you want it?" I offer, but she declines.

I settle down between Sadie and Trey, then rummage around in my pack for a protein bar. There's a vibration from one of the interior pockets—my phone. Maybe it's Matteo, finally checking in to let me know how his progress with Joshua is going?

When I pull it out, though, it's not a text notification on the screen, and it's not from Matteo at all—it's an email from Sky Ranger.

I swipe it open.

To: august.thorn@summitwildernessexpeditions.com
From: skyranger@skytoursandoutdoors.com
Subject: Update on the Job Opening

Hello again, Thorn,

Hope all is well. Brief update here: I've got someone with serious interest in my Lead Hiking Guide position, but since I offered to you first, I thought it was only right to circle back to you before moving forward. This isn't to pressure you unduly, but if you do think you might be interested in making the move—especially to my Arizona or Texas locations, where I have the most need at the moment—I'll give you priority if you want the job. I know there are a number of factors to consider, so I truly don't mean to pressure you—but if you are interested, the sooner you can let me know, the better. I can hold it for a day, maybe two.

Talk soon,
Sky Ranger

"Thorn?" Sadie says. "You good?"

Only now do I realize I'm not looking *at* my phone so much as fixated on its screen like I'm trying to decipher an alien language.

"Oh, yeah, it's just an email," I tell her, though the words feel inadequate as they roll off my tongue.

It's hard to describe the feelings that hit while reading Sky's email: an immediate gut reaction of *I could never leave* followed by the smallest whisper of *But what if I did . . . ?* It's been months since he first brought it up, but now that I have to make an actual choice—and soon—it feels real.

I can measure my life in experiences I've had on the trails of Valerie Forest National Park: first with my dad, later with Matteo *and* Dad, and for the last six years, with the tour company and the thousands of trekkers I've guided along the way. I've got roots deep as any trees out here—it's hard to imagine ever leaving, both on the personal and professional fronts.

That said, I can't help but wonder what life would look like if I were to move somewhere else. I don't know anyone in Arizona or Texas—

Except, actually, I do. *Sadie* lives in Texas.

I tuck my phone back inside my pack, resisting the urge to check just how far the drive would be between Sky's tour headquarters—somewhere in the Hill Country—and Austin, where Sadie lives.

I shake the thought out of my head, try to put it completely out of my mind.

The very last thing I need right now is to think about spending *more* time with Sadie.

We make it without issue to our campsite: one day (mostly) down without a coleader, and one more to go.

Tomorrow is the traditional day of solitude and silence that we work into every itinerary prior to summitting Mount Valerie, and Sparrow Valley is the perfect place for it: between the peaceful meadow, the nature trail, the stream lined with flowers and boulders and trees, and one of the park's more majestic waterfalls just down the waterbed, there are a multitude of places we can all spread out without being too far from each other.

If I'm honest, our day of solitude and silence can't come soon enough. I've fallen hard for Sadie Whitlock, despite my best efforts to resist her, and I need to get my head on straight. The trek is on my shoulders alone right now—I can't afford any distractions if I'm going to be the leader Danica's trusting me to be, the leader the group deserves. I *have* to be able to trust myself.

The only way to do that, as much as I wish otherwise, means putting some distance between myself and Sadie. It's the last thing I want—but it's for her own good. It's up to me to keep her safe.

If her safety means sacrificing my own comfort, well, that's what I have to do.

To: skyranger@skytoursandoutdoors.com

From: august.thorn@summitwildernessexpeditions.com

Subject: RE: Update on the Job Opening

Good evening, Mr. Ranger, and thank you so much for checking in.

There are a lot of factors to weigh, you're right—and unfortunately, I'm out on a trek right now and not in a position to make such a big decision on short notice. If you have to move forward with the other candidate in the meantime, I'll understand.

Thank you again,

August Thorn

To: august.thorn@summitwildernessexpeditions.com
From: skyranger@skytoursandoutdoors.com
Subject: RE: RE: Update on the Job Opening

Thanks for your quick reply, Thorn, even if it's not the answer I hoped for. I'll move forward with the other candidate and will reach out in the future if we're ever in the position to offer competitive pay for an additional Lead Hiking Guide.

Best,
Sky Ranger

30

SADIE

I have been a ray of sunshine all day long.

I made it a point to stay chipper: to not complain, even though I had the worst caffeine headache *ever*, and to be a bubbly fount of optimism since our collective well has run somewhat dry.

I swatted away mosquitos.

I made peace with the sweat.

I didn't run screaming when I saw a snake on the trail—Thorn reassured us it was harmless, and I chose to believe him, despite my self-preservation instincts kicking into high gear.

And I didn't cry when said snake made the phrase *day beasts* pop into my head, reminding me of how easy it's been to laugh with Thorn about anything and everything—how easy it *was*, anyway, before he started avoiding me.

All day long, I was determined to be sunshine, overcompensating for the persistent thundercloud hanging over Thorn and, by extension, the whole group. I was determined to not let his sudden coolness toward me get under my skin.

Honestly? I did pretty well, all things considered.

The thing that makes my sunny bubble burst, though, comes out of nowhere: I catch Thorn watching me from across the campfire, the most unguarded look on his face . . . until our eyes meet, and his shield goes right back up.

Was it something I said?

Was it something I did?

After he slipped out of my tent last night, I replayed his kiss on a loop: nothing about it felt like a *final* kiss. If anything, it felt like an *I so wish we could do more but am restraining myself* kiss. I figured he'd be back to himself after a good night of sleep.

This morning was awkward, too, though—something has definitely shifted. I told myself he was just tormenting himself with an unnecessary guilt trip, that it had nothing to do with me . . . but the longer it's gone on, the more it feels like it has *everything* to do with me.

I could sit around and worry about it all night, or I could go do something about it.

Most people don't even realize they're making you feel unseen or unheard, in my experience—especially not nice guys who'd never try to hurt someone on purpose. How is Thorn supposed to know he's making me feel like this unless I *tell* him?

This is the pep talk I give myself as I make my way across camp, later, when the tennis girls and coffee bros are telling ghost stories around the fire. Zoe retreated to her tent as soon as dinner ended, and Thorn has mostly kept to himself, too.

I find him down by the stream, sitting on a boulder.

My shoes might as well be an alarm with how they crunch in the gravel.

He turns, giving me what he clearly thinks passes for a smile—but I see through it. At least it's not an outright rejection.

"Mind if I sit?" I ask, climbing up on the boulder with him, because I can already tell he won't tell me no.

"Go ahead," he says, scooting over so I have a little more space.

"Little dark to be fishing, yeah?" It's as good a start as any, never mind that he obviously doesn't have any fishing gear with him.

"Little bit," he says, not meeting my eyes.

I lean back, taking in the view. The night sky is much more obstructed by trees than it was at our stargazing site, but there's still a sliver of Milky Way peeking out above us.

My gaze flicks over to his profile, lit by the faint glow of the campfire behind us.

"So," I finally begin. "What's going on with you today?"

The corner of his mouth quirks up, like he's fighting a smile. "Something's going on with me?"

"You tell me," I say. "I mean, unless kissing a girl and then avoiding her the whole next day is how you usually roll?"

He bites his lip. "Point taken."

I give him space, wait for him to find words for whatever's weighing him down.

"There is no *usually* when it comes to this," Thorn finally says. "I've never gotten involved with anyone while on a trek—you're the first. I thought I could handle myself, you know? I thought I could stay focused *and* have a little fun for once."

Thorn is so attractive, so capable, so kind: I'm kind of shocked to hear I'm the first—the only!—person he's gotten close with like this while out on a trek.

"So, what, you never bring your girlfriends along?"

Surely there have been others besides the ex he told me about, the one who ran off to Peru with Matteo.

"Haven't had a girlfriend in years," he says. "I'm out here working pretty much all the time."

"That sounds lonely," I say, trying to imagine what it's like for him.

"It is," he replies. "I mean, there are always people around—but I'm the one responsible for them. They're here, and then they leave, and then the cycle starts over."

His words hang in the air.

It sounds even lonelier than I imagined—especially when factoring in that he's on the clock the whole time, with the group but not really part of it. It hadn't occurred to me that life for him might feel like a big revolving door, new people who are just passing through, none of them staying long enough to ever go deep with.

Does he see me, too, as someone who will inevitably leave? He'd have to, right? It's not like I'm signed up for another hike after this. I've managed okay out here, far better than I expected, but the thought of not going back to air conditioning and my own bed at the end of all this feels like staring down a deep, dark hole.

I push those thoughts aside, try to focus on what he's actually said and not just the things I sense simmering underneath.

"You've got friends outside of work, though, right?" I ask, meaning it to be encouraging.

As soon as I say it, I can see I've struck a nerve: Matteo *was* his friend outside of work.

"Matteo was my best friend," he says after a long pause. "Like a brother." He swallows, picks at his thumbnail.

"I take it he hasn't apologized yet, then?" I ask. "For . . . Peru?"

Thorn laughs—a genuine, huge, unexpected thing that probably puts a few owls on high alert.

"Yeah, no," he says. "If anything, he did the opposite. Told me it was partly my fault, said we were never that close in the first place, said I spent all my time out here and neglected both him and Blair. That if I'd just 'paid better attention,' maybe I would have seen it coming."

No wonder things are still so intense between them—and no wonder he's having a hard time shaking things off. Matteo's words have clearly gotten under his skin.

"To be fair," Thorn goes on, "he's kind of reeling. He found out a few days ago that Blair's dumping him in the same way she dumped me."

"The *layers*!" I say, eyes wide. "You guys have more drama than *The Real Housewives*."

"The real who?" he asks—and he's serious.

He really must spend all his time out here, looking at the world with his own eyes and not through various screens.

"Never mind," I tell him. "But wow, yeah, Matteo sounds messy." And like not a very good friend *or* a helpful coleader.

Thorn sighs. "It's a lot of pressure, making sure everyone gets the experience they signed up for—making sure they don't get injured or lost, making sure they feel *safe*. It's all on me right now."

"You're used to it, though, right?" I say. "You're *good* at it. You must enjoy it on some level . . . ?"

"It isn't that I don't enjoy it," he says. "I love it out here. It feels more like home than my actual apartment—and it reminds me of my dad. He'd give anything to be out on these trails again, camping under the stars. And I love seeing people push themselves, discover they're so much more capable than they thought."

For the first time since we started talking, his gaze meets mine.

People like you, he doesn't say, but I hear it anyway.

"Well," I say. "If there's anything I can do, let me know—I know I'm new at this, but maybe there's something I can help with?"

My words hang in the air between us, like a trail of bubbles drifting into the sky.

He turns away now, and the silence is overwhelming.

For the first time since we met, I feel completely self-conscious, like maybe I said something offensive or wrong. All I offered was help, though.

Is it laughable that I offered?

Maybe it is. What could I—an amateur who couldn't be bothered to bring the right shoes—possibly bring to the table?

"What?" I say a moment later, when he still hasn't answered.

"I really appreciate the offer," he finally says. "I do."

He still won't look at me.

"But?"

"But the most helpful thing right now would probably be for us to stop spending so much time together," he says. "The group's depending on my focus, and I can't afford to be distracted."

It hits like a cascade of embers: just a little sting, at first . . . and then it *burns*.

"I— Wow," I say. "Okay." Out of nowhere, a pair of hot tears streak down my cheeks. I'm thankful for the darkness. "I thought maybe it would help for you to talk through your feelings, Thorn, but I can stop *distracting* you now, if that's really what you want."

I'm already scrambling down from the boulder, too embarrassed to stay. He's been avoiding me all day—why couldn't I just take the hint?

"Sadie . . . please don't take it like that."

His voice is earnest, already full of regret.

"How am I supposed to take it?" My voice cracks, the traitor. "I just offered to help, and you told me it would be most helpful for me to go away."

I've listened to him.

Cried in front of him.

Laughed with him, so many times.

Escaped a lizard attack while half naked with him.

Woken up tangled with him.

Shivered under the stars with him.

Kissed him during a thunderstorm, and behind a waterfall, and inside my tent.

He's seen me at my most vulnerable—I've shown him parts of myself I've never even shown Abby, even though I've only known him for such a short time.

But it's too much of a distraction, apparently. *I'm* too much.

My whole life, I've always been too much for most people—

I really thought it might be different with Thorn.

31

THORN

Well, that was the cherry on top of the shit sundae the last couple of days has been. And unlike so much of the rest that's gone wrong, this particular mess is entirely my fault.

Sadie has been the best part of this trek by *far*—I never meant to hurt her.

If I could, I'd spend the rest of our time together out here with just her: exploring the wilderness by day, exploring each other by night. And I don't just mean physically, though of course there's that—I want to know everything about her, what she loves and what she wants, what scars she's endured and overcome, what made her cry that day on the cliff, what compelled her to leave so many of her comfort items behind out of nowhere.

All of this is why I had to say what I did.

All of it.

I don't know how to do my job *and* spend time with Sadie, it's as plain as that. Being with her is disarming—not in the bad way she assumes, but because she makes me feel like a different person altogether. A person who was put on this planet for *more* than the job that requires so much focus; a person who was put on this planet to *actually live*, not just help others along on their own journeys.

If I think about that too much, it makes me not want to do my job at all. Which is obviously not an option right now, seeing as seven people—Sadie included—are dependent on me to get them through the rest of the trip.

The way I see it, my job isn't just to know how to *fix* problems—it's to keep them from happening in the first place.

I didn't see the warning signs with Dad until it was too late: his labored breathing the last time we came out here, how we had to cut our trip short and head out from Wild Gate, straight to the ER.

I didn't see the warning signs with my parents, either, in the months leading up to their divorce. The signs were there—but I assumed they'd fade in time.

I didn't see *anything* coming when it came to Blair, or Matteo, or Peru.

Maybe Matteo was right, back at the cliff—maybe, if I'd just paid better attention, I could have saved myself a lot of pain.

Well, I'm paying attention now.

If I'm vigilant, no one will get hurt.

I make my way back to the campfire, scan to see who's missing. Everyone's here but Zoe.

"Did Zoe go to bed already?" I ask.

"She's in her tent," Parker says. "Went there a while ago."

"I can go check on her, if you want?" Emma offers.

"That would be great, thanks," I say. "Just need to give everyone the rundown for tomorrow."

The fire crackles and pops, loud against the otherwise silent night. Emma is always able to draw out the talkative sides of Hunter and Silas and Parker, but once she's gone, they revert to their usual introverted ways. Trey can also usually be counted on to fill the silence, but he's preoccupied with getting a splinter out of his thumb at the moment.

Sadie's extra quiet tonight, too. I hate seeing her like this—defeated, frustrated, upset—and I especially hate knowing *I* am the reason for it.

Emma returns, Zoe in tow. The circles under Zoe's eyes look almost like bruises in this low lighting, shadows and firelight flickering across her face.

"Hey, everyone," I say. "I'll make this quick—I know you're eager to get some rest. But tomorrow is our traditional day of solitude, so I just want to go over what that will look like since it starts at sunrise."

All eyes are on me except Sadie's.

I swallow, trying to shake off the way it snags my attention, the way I wish I'd worded things better when we talked—the way it would be so much easier if someone else were in charge and I were just another hiker.

But that's not my reality right now, so I've got to find a way to put my feelings aside. To put *myself* aside.

"The traditional day of solitude," I go on, "is built into every itinerary as a day of rest before we summit Mount Valerie together. From sunrise to sunset, we'll spend the entire day in silence—no talking to each other, except in cases of emergency."

"A whole day of silence?" Zoe says, arms crossed and clearly ready to get back to her tent. "What are we supposed to *do*? That sounds super boring."

"We like to build in time for reflection," I reply. "Is this trek everything you expected it to be, or totally different? Is there anything that surprised you along the way? Have you experienced any big shifts in perspective? Things like that."

Parker and Silas and Hunter look eager, while Trey and Emma seem less convinced—and Zoe is just impatient.

When my eyes land on Sadie, she finally looks up.

Her intensity is magnetic. I can't turn away.

She breaks first, though, so that's that.

I clear my throat, trying to remember what I was going to say next.

"I have a couple of extra pens and can tear out some journal pages if anyone wants to write out their thoughts," I go on. "There's also a nature trail if you want to take a walk—it's a pretty short loop, and all I ask is that you don't stray from the path. We've got plenty of space to spread out, so you'll *feel* alone throughout the day even if you're not totally by yourself. Don't go so far away that you're off my radar—and this waterfall pool isn't one you want to swim in, by the way. The last thing we need is for someone to get lost or hurt. Any questions?"

I glance around, leave space for the others to speak up.

No one does.

I'm just about to wish them good night and good luck when Sadie catches my eye.

"So, just to be clear, when can we talk again?" she asks.

Something about her question sends my mind straight back to an hour ago—the way I told her it would be most helpful for the two of us to not talk anymore, even though that's the last thing I actually *want*—and it throws me for a loop, making me forget the context entirely.

When can we talk again?

I force my attention back to what she's actually asking: after our collective day of solitude and silence, when can the *group* feel free to talk again?

"Sunset tomorrow," I say. "Silence is a discipline, so just do your best. If you forget, it's okay to reset and start fresh."

When we're done, Zoe heads back to her tent without another word. Everyone else seems eager to talk as much as possible while they can. They start with Two Truths and a Lie—with a dash of Truth or Dare—that culminates in Emma launching into a very loud, very off-key song.

I don't realize I'm watching for Sadie's reaction until her eyes flick toward mine. This would most definitely spark some sort of flirty banter between us on any other night—but tonight, again, she just looks away.

They move on to more ghost stories, and Parker tells everyone about the house where her grandmother lives, which definitely sounds haunted.

"Could you keep it down?" Zoe interrupts a while later, not even bothering to poke her head outside her tent. "*Some* of us are trying to sleep!"

Emma and Trey exchange an eye roll, though everyone lowers the volume a few notches without Zoe having to ask twice.

As loud as the others have been, Sadie's hardly said a word, a shell of her usual self. If anyone's noticed, they haven't shown it.

"I think I'm going to try to sleep, too," she says a few minutes later, out of nowhere. "Y'all have a good night, okay?"

It takes everything in me to not follow Sadie to her tent—to not take back every word I said earlier—but she's been front and center in my thoughts all night as it is. If I'm this distracted *not* talking to her, how much worse would it be if I were to give in?

I can't stand the thought of her thinking I don't *want* to talk to her, though. That I don't want her around.

There has to be some way I can show her how I feel without risking the steep slide of accidentally falling into her tent for the rest of the night.

I help Silas and Hunter and Trey clean up around the campfire before heading to bed—and that's when it hits me, courtesy of the speckled blue camp cup Hunter uses every day.

When everything is still and quiet, I slip over in secret to Sadie's tent. I'm thankful for the crescent moon, which gives off just enough of a glow that I won't have to turn on a light of my own.

I hold my breath, careful not to crunch too loudly as I step through gravel and fallen branches to get there. Just outside the door to her tent, I set everything up where there's no chance she'll miss it: both boxes of coffee, the various pieces of her pour-over equipment, and her favorite mug—all of it acting as a paperweight on top of my note, scribbled hastily on a page torn from my journal.

Sadie's so close right now, and the temptation is real; I hurry back to my tent before I break down and ask if I can climb into hers instead.

Make it through the rest of this trek, I tell myself. *If she's still on your mind after that, you can . . .*

I pause, unsure how to even finish that sentence.

Can *what*?

Can tell her how much I've enjoyed getting to spend time with her, knowing she's just going to fly back to Texas while I'm ushering in a brand-new wave of hikers for the next adventure?

It suddenly seems like a never-ending cycle: I'm a pony at a state fair, walking the same circles over and over. And while the rider dismounts after a little while, I never leave. The track just gets deeper and deeper the longer I'm on it, a trench that's simultaneously comforting—it's what I know, what I'm good at, and in a lot of ways, a home I love—and stifling. At what point does the trench become a trap that I'm unable to climb out of?

Maybe I should have thought twice before writing back to Sky Ranger, maybe I shouldn't have been so quick to say no.

But what other option did I have? Now more than ever, Danica needs me. It's not like she has a stable full of reliable guides just waiting for their turn in the ring—she's got Jess, who didn't plan well enough to be here and got stuck in Hawaii. She's got Matteo. She's got a few others, too, but they've made it clear they're not here for the long haul. What would happen to the tour company if I left?

More than that, I simply love being out here. I always have.

Right?

Sure, it's the same thing over and over, but the people make it different every time—it's never the exact same adventure, and it always brings new challenges. It's never bothered me to this extent before.

Tonight, I can't seem to let it go.

For the first time in as long as I've been a hiking guide, I'm starting to wonder if I'm less of a risk-taker than I've always believed. If I truly want to be brave and stretch myself, maybe I should consider stepping out of the rhythms I've built here and try something new—

With someone new.

But the idea of leaving the pony circle of these trails feels overwhelming, if I'm honest.

What is my life outside of this place?

DAY NINE

Day of Solitude at Sparrow Valley Falls

With the base of Mount Valerie a mere half mile's walk down the trail, it can be tempting for visitors to forge ahead to conquer its heights without pausing to take in the beauty of Sparrow Valley. I would caution against this. Summitting Mount Valerie is a feat, to be sure—but there is also value to be found in stillness, in purposefully carving out a time of rest and reflection. The discipline to embrace this period of stillness can have a profound impact and, for that reason, has become tradition among those who frequent Valerie Forest National Park.

—Henry Herrington, *Backpacking the Sierras: A Beginner's Handbook* (Fourth Edition)

ABBY ❁ BLACKBURN

5:12 a.m.
Sadie

5:12 a.m.
SADIE

5:12 a.m.
Ohmygosh I'm SO SORRY, just remembered the time difference between here and California

5:13 a.m.
Maybe that's for the best though

5:13 a.m.
Whatever you do, don't open instagram. Just trust me. Don't do it.

7:23 a.m.
(But I'm here for you if you can't resist and open it anyway.) (Don't say I didn't warn you . . .)

32

SADIE

I wake to birdsong and warm sunlight streaming in through my tent walls. Combined with the babbling brook outside, I feel like I'm in a fairy tale—

Until I remember my conversation with Thorn, and register the raging caffeine headache from yesterday that's still going strong this morning.

This day of silence and solitude came at a great time: it's the perfect excuse to keep to myself and work through all the *feelings*.

From somewhere deep in my backpack, my phone vibrates, a sound I'm not used to at all after so many days out here. I honestly can't believe I've managed to forget about my phone for this long—the only reason I even charged it last night is so I can film more vlog footage at some point. I rummage around until I find it, then discover I've missed a series of texts from Abby, the most recent from just a minute ago.

Dread pools in my stomach as soon as I scan through them.

How am I supposed to *not* look at Instagram after seeing her texts? My phone is a grenade, a ticking time bomb. I want it as far away from me as possible—in another solar system, perhaps, or at the bottom of an active volcano.

Whatever it is, it's probably better to just *know* than to put it off—I'm only going to wonder until I check. It'll be like a bikini wax, I tell myself: even if it turns out to be a searing flash of pain, at least it'll be over soon.

I take a deep breath and open the app.

Caden's photo is at the very top of my feed.

Actually—to be more specific—the *collab post* between Caden and Gabriella is at the very top of my feed.

Glittering Italian water. Glittering diamond ring.

Smiles, sunlight, sparkling champagne in sparkling glasses, glaring and blindingly bright, every bit of it filtered and airbrushed to cover up the inevitable imperfections that might have marred their moment.

They're *engaged.*

He *proposed.*

I don't even want to do the math on that timeline. It's either too fast or too insultingly, infuriatingly, overlappingly slow.

Even if I'm over him—which I absolutely am (this is all the more confirmation that we would *never* have worked out in the long run)—the sting of being rejected, not good enough, pushed aside and moved on from at lightning speed is a jagged pill to swallow—

Especially right after Thorn pushed me away, too.

Tears streak hot and fast down my cheeks.

Suddenly, the birds are too chipper, the morning too bright, the ground beneath me too rocky and uneven and hard.

What I could really use right now is a spa day.

I close my eyes, try to imagine I'm anywhere else but here, all alone in my tent in the middle of nowhere: I'd start with a long, hot shower. My hair would be clean, and I'd get a blowout in the salon—yes, even before my two-hour massage and the facial that would wreck it to pieces.

The massage would come with eucalyptus essential oil and hot stones and a soundtrack that would *almost* put me to sleep, but not totally, because why sleep through something that hurts so good?

The facial, too, would be relaxing in its own way. And when I emerged from all this pampering, I would take a paperback into the sauna, read until I couldn't stand the heat anymore, take yet *another* shower (followed by another fabulous blowout), and then read for a few more hours by the pool.

All of this would need to happen in, say . . . March? *Late* March, or maybe even early November. Any other month in Texas, I'd just get sweaty again by the pool, or it would be too chilly to be enjoyable.

So in this fantasy, we'll just say the weather is perfect.

My daydream includes a fruity beverage, complete with an umbrella and a tray of chocolate bonbons.

Also, crucially, it is all free.

To my left, Abby and Jonathan would be on lounge chairs, too. She would be reading a magazine, while he would be . . . hmm. I bet he's the sort of guy who reads really twisty sci-fi novels, so maybe one of those?

To my right, there's—

Thorn.

My eyes fly open. The sudden brightness only intensifies my headache, so I fling my arm across them to block the sun, but in such an uncoordinated way that I accidentally hit the bridge of my nose with my wristbone.

Welcome back to reality, Sadie.

Sweaty, rocky, achy, miserable reality.

I have a choice to make, I decide an hour later, after I've (unsuccessfully) tried my best to just go back to sleep and forget.

I could either continue to wallow—about Thorn, about the engagement grenade, about how I'm stuck out here for another few days—or I could try to look for silver linings somehow.

Wallowing has its appeals.

But I've been *so* good this whole trip, not spiraling into a boneless heap of self-pity—and I kind of feel like the smoke from my bonfire of self-destruction would somehow find its way out of this forest and into the internet and across the ocean, all the way to Caden and Gabriella in Italy, and they'd just look at each other and laugh.

Did Sadie seriously think she could make it through a twelve-day wilderness excursion without *completely falling apart?* they'd say to each other. *I bet she's been miserable this entire time! At least she didn't die.*

Well, screw that.

I'll be going the silver-linings route after all, I guess.

Step One in the playbook: if I can't pamper myself with a spa day, I can at least put on my freshest set of clothes. I've only worn my light green tank top twice, and my flouncy sky-blue lululemon skirt (skort, technically) has spent most of the trek at the bottom of my pack.

Step Two: my hair.

My dry shampoo is on its last legs, so I've been going extra days between applications. Now seems like a good time to use it—and a few minutes later, after I've distributed it throughout and run a brush all over, I can say it was definitely worth it for the smell alone.

People have given me a hard time, on occasion, for getting all dressed up even when I'm not planning to go anywhere. To which I've always replied: never underestimate the power of feeling cute. *Everything* is easier when you feel put together, I don't care if it's the dishes or the laundry or being in survival mode out in the middle of the wilderness.

I'm testing my own theory today—fake it till you make it, as they say—hoping that everything underneath my skin will start to feel as fresh as I look on the surface.

As soon as I unzip my tent door, I freeze: it's like I've seen a ghost—and the ghost in question is all of my coffee stuff, complete with my beautiful ceramic mug.

I know who it's from before I even notice the note tucked beneath it all. Only one person even knew I left it behind, and only one person would rescue it, and carry it in his pack, and then leave it for me when I need it most.

Unfortunately, that person is one and the same as the guy who essentially told me to go away last night. So rather than being purely thrilled to see it all again . . . I'm feeling mostly confused.

It doesn't get better when I read the note.

Sadie, it reads, *Heard the guys ran out of coffee. Saved this for you—you've come a long way out here, and I thought now might be a good time for you to have it back. I did not, unfortunately, rescue your copies of WILD and EAT PRAY LOVE. ;) xo, Thorn*

The more I read it, the angrier I get.

He says I'm a distraction, and he expects me to keep my distance—but he leaves the most thoughtful gift ever, all while calling back to one of our first conversations and making a joke?

And what is with the winky face?

And the "xo, Thorn"—???

It is the most jumbled of mixed signals. Does he want me to leave him alone, or does he want me to fall head over heels in love with him? Because this note—this gift!—does not communicate *go away*. Not at all.

If he'd wanted to talk to me, though, he would have just *given* it to me. He would've wanted to see the look on my face and reap the rewards; I can think of a number of ways I would've liked to say thank you.

I have no idea what to make of this.

Silver linings, I coach myself.

I won't have to have the caffeine headache from hell today. Neither will Hunter and Silas and Trey—after all the coffee they've shared with me, I'm happy to return the favor.

I rip out a page from my journal and scrawl out a little note. Before I left home, Abby helped me portion my coffee grounds into their own little Ziploc bags so it would be easy to know how much I needed without having my coffee scale with me; I pull out six of them, enough for the coffee bros to have two servings each. There's plenty left over for me.

The guys aren't around when I finally emerge to go drop off their surprise, but I arrange everything in a neat pile outside of Hunter's tent like Thorn did at mine.

At least I can feel good about that one thing today.

Twenty minutes later, I've successfully brewed my own cup.

Thorn was right, I admit, despite myself: today really is a good day to have this small luxury back. The guys' coffee was delicious, but mine feels like *home*. So does my beautiful mug, the weight of it just right in my hand—and the artwork, its cheery little sun-and-rainbow scene, feels like a pep talk from Past Sadie, who paid an eyebrow-raising amount of money for this little ceramic vessel simply because it sparked joy.

I meander down by the brook, looking for a good place to set up for a while. Some of the others had a similar idea—Parker is reading in the meadow, and Trey's made his way to a little hill full of wildflowers. Zoe's much farther down, set up with a good view of the waterfall, sunbathing in her stylish one-shouldered swimsuit.

For the first time today, I spot Thorn: he's about halfway down the brook, a central location between here and the waterfall where he can keep an eye on as many of us as possible. Probably best to keep my distance.

I climb up onto a boulder and get as comfortable as I can; it's rough against my bare legs. I only brought a few things with me: My coffee, of course. My journal. Trail mix. The only physical book I have left in my possession—*A Hiker Girl's Guide to Bugs & Berries*, from Abby. And my disposable camera, just in case I encounter something I need to remember forever.

Okay, so in typical Sadie fashion, that's more than a few things. But it's not my entire tent, so I consider it a win.

I pull out my journal.

The blank page feels more overwhelming than ever—there's too much swirling in my mind, and I don't even know where to start. Thorn said the purpose of our solitude day was for us to reflect on our own personal adventures, so maybe I should start with that?

Every memory I have out here eventually leads back to him, though. Even the memories before we ever officially left: how he was the first person I met; how I caught him changing his shirt in that hollow tree display; how I left so many of my comfort items behind in his mop closet of an office.

Thinking back to that, I'm *so* glad I took his advice—I had no idea just how hard it would be to carry everything, how painful.

And have I missed that stuff at all?

Not one single bit.

I guess I really have come a long way since then. I've missed a lot of other stuff, yeah . . . but I've survived. I've been determined. I've done better than I ever expected to in this environment.

Out of nowhere, a memory comes rushing back in screaming clarity, Zoe yelling at Joshua the day they officially broke up: *You never should have brought me out here! You should have known the wilderness isn't my thing.*

Her words seared into my subconscious without me even realizing it.

I pick up my pen, write in neat letters: *Why is *that* what stuck with me? Why did Zoe's words hit a nerve?*

The rest of the page stays blank for a long time. I mull it over while taking in my surroundings, only realizing I'm tapping my pen against the page when Parker looks up at me from her book.

Oops.

I watch the puffy white clouds, then a pair of bluebirds as they flit over to a nearby tree. It's peaceful out here—I can see why Thorn likes it.

I close my eyes, try to shake the memory of him out of my head. I came on this trip to stretch myself, not to meet a guy, so why am I so preoccupied with whether he wants to talk to me or not? I had every chance to back out after Caden flaked—but I chose to be here.

That's it, I suddenly realize: the reason Zoe's words stuck with me so much.

You never should have brought me out here! You should have known the wilderness isn't my thing.

The wilderness is very much not my thing, either. That's what I would have said before this trip, anyway—but all these days in, I'm low-key incredulous with the way I've managed to adapt, especially given that I'm a particular person and a creature of habit.

Zoe, by contrast, only came out here for a guy. She didn't know this wilderness adventure was in the cards for her until Joshua's unwelcome surprise—hence, Zoe has had a harder time adapting. Her attitude is very *I can't* and *I don't want to* and *This is terrible and uncomfortable and I want to go home.* Which . . . is relatable.

But.

I've felt every single one of those things. Difference is, I've chosen to not let them define my time out here.

Some might say my willingness to adapt is simply a manifestation of my desire to be comfortable at all times—if the choices are *Do this difficult thing* or *Do this difficult thing with a bad attitude*, I'm going to choose to do it the more fun way.

Does it really matter, though? Whatever it is that's helped me not end up hating every step like Zoe, I can say with absolute certainty that I've changed out here.

I've been away from my routines.

I've been away from my comforts.

I've done things that scared me: nearly slipped off those slick rock stairs on our first day, slept out in the wilderness despite my fear of every wild animal, made it out alive after kayaking in snake-infested waters (I presume), conquered a panic attack while dangling off the side of a cliff.

I've been prepared for a lot—but not everything.

I've made peace with the fact that I *can't* prepare for everything.

And maybe I've had more fun thanks to Thorn being around, and laughed more than I have in ages, but it's not like he's the *reason* I've been able to thrive.

He didn't climb inside my head and give me the determination to have a good attitude. He didn't give me the strength to keep walking, without complaint, when my blisters burned like fire. He didn't make me leave half my pack behind at the Little Free Library—though I admit his advice planted the seed in my head.

He is, however, the one who saw me clearly enough to know how much it meant for me to leave everything behind.

He rescued things that mattered to me *because* they mattered to me. He carried them for days, then left them for me when I needed them most.

Even though I didn't come out here to find a guy, and I'm no longer trying to prove anything to anyone but myself, I admit I miss him. It would be so much easier to move on if he were, like, Matteo levels of thoughtless and selfish—

But Thorn is extremely thought*ful*.

And the fact that he clearly still cares about me, but is determined to push me away, proves he's selfless.

I can tell myself all day long that I don't *need* him.

That doesn't change the fact that I want him.

Seven feverishly scribbled pages later, I look up in a daze. My hand is cramping, my coffee's long gone, and my left foot has started to fall asleep.

Time for a walk.

I scoot off the boulder, not at all gracefully, and tuck everything into the tote bag I brought along.

The nature path is beautiful and serene, following the curve of the brook all the way down to Sparrow Valley Falls, the crash of the waterfall louder by the minute. All sorts of vibrant things poke out amid the green: brightly colored mushrooms, wildflowers, berries, and birds.

Before coming on this trip, I assumed all places in nature looked more or less the same. Now, though, it's easier to spot the differences: all the variations of plants and rocks and trees, the way some spots are more rugged than others, how the sunlight bends throughout the day, how the stars and the moon make their way across the night sky.

At the moment, I'm fascinated by the berries; I pull out *A Hiker Girl's Guide to Bugs & Berries* to see if I can find a match for the ones right in front of me. As I crack the book open, something small and rectangular flutters down to the ground, the distinct size and shape of a mini Polaroid picture.

Sure enough, when I inspect it, that's exactly what it is: a candid of Abby making a heart with her hands.

I flip it over and find a note scrawled in thin silver Sharpie ink.

*So, so proud of you, Sadie! You're doing this! YOU ARE A HIKER GIRL!! Hope this little book comes in handy . . . I *cannot* have you eating any poisonous berries out there, okay? We can get raspberry crème brûlées once you're back! ❤ —Abby*

I love Abby for this thoughtful gift, and it's good to see her face. This must be what it feels like to get a letter from home on *Survivor* after being out in the wild for so long: a much-needed boost of encouragement, a re-kindling of energy. I miss her so much—and crème brûlée, too—but I'm on the home stretch out here. I've made it this far, and I can make it to the end.

I fish around in my tote for my disposable camera. Abby will get a kick out of me taking a picture of her Polaroid and the book next to some actual berries.

I snap the photo and move on; I'd really like to get a nice shot of the waterfall while I'm down this way. Even from here, it's surprisingly loud.

When I emerge from the nature path, the waterfall comes into full, majestic view: it's bigger in every way than the first two we encountered on this trip—higher, wider, faster, fuller, the pool at the bottom frothing with whitewater.

I've just framed the perfect shot through my disposable camera's viewfinder when I notice Zoe in the lower-left corner. She's no longer merely lounging *near* the waterfall—she's climbed up on a wide, flat rock right at the edge of the pool, doing yoga like always.

She's perfectly balanced, holding one of the warrior positions she taught us before shifting out of it again. A bird swoops low into the frame, the perfect shot—

I click the shutter at the exact moment Zoe jumps in.

33

SADIE

“Zoe!” I call out, but of course I’m too far away to cut through the crash of the waterfall.

This is not good, not good at all.

This is not a waterfall any of us should be swimming in: not only did Thorn specifically warn us about it, but there was a whole section about dangerous water in the Henry Herrington handbook I studied before coming on this trip—from the frothing whitewater alone, it’s obvious this falls into that category.

“*Thorn!*” I shout, hoping he’s within earshot as I rush over to help—we can’t afford silence *or* solitude right now. “Zoe, get out of there!”

But she still doesn’t hear me over the waterfall.

I’m at the edge of the plunge pool in no time. Zoe waves, smiling and oblivious, completely unaware of everything that could go wrong. It would only take a heartbeat for her to be swept up in the turbulent water and pinned into the narrow gap between boulders.

I don’t even want to think about how bad that could be. She could get stuck from the suction—

She could *drown*.

"You have to get out of the water!" I shout again.

This time, she hears me.

Her smile disappears as she registers my panic. She attempts to swim closer to the bank so I can reach out and help from where I am, but the water is unpredictable, pulling her farther away instead—into rougher water, straight toward the boulders.

"Sadie!" she cries, flailing, barely keeping her head above the frothy bubbles.

"Try to stay calm, okay?" I call out as I follow the bank, trying to get closer. "Swim toward my hand if you can!"

If she can break away from the current at an angle, I might just be able to reach her—but there's no way I'm strong enough to pull her out on my own.

She's fighting, trying her best to swim in my direction.

The water is a force. Every time I think she's getting closer, it tugs her back again, countering her every move.

I inch closer, as close as I can without losing my footing—the last thing either of us needs is for me to fall in, too. I reach out, trying not to think too much about what could happen if she gets pinned up against the boulders just ten feet behind her. I might have to jump in at that point, since they're not accessible from dry land. I'm not sure that would be the *wisest* choice—

But I think it might be my only choice, if it comes down to it.

"Fight, Zoe! Is there anything you can push off from?"

She grits her teeth, still treading water—and then, in a sudden forward surge, finally breaks out of the current.

I reach out, try to grab her hand before she's sucked right back in.

Our fingertips brush, so close.

"Sadie!" she cries, flailing toward me, trying again.

This time, my fingers find hers, enough to grab onto—but I'm not a strong enough match for the water, and her hand is slick, sliding out of mine.

I'm just about to try again when a pair of strong arms wrap tightly around my waist—Thorn, *thank goodness.*

"I've got you, Sadie!" he says, slightly winded. "Reach out until you've got her! I won't let go."

I do as he says, trying to trust his words, his strength.

I lean out as far as I possibly can, stretching both of my arms toward Zoe, who's still fighting the water. The extra inches make all the difference; her hands grasp mine so hard it hurts, especially in light of the tender spot that's still healing after my rappelling injury.

I grit my teeth and hold on tight as Thorn anchors us, leaning back to help bring Zoe closer to the edge.

"Stay steady," he instructs me. "I'm going to take over so I can pull her out, okay? Do whatever it takes to stay out of the water!"

I nod, still focusing all my energy on Zoe: her hands are so slippery, and my bandaged palm is hurting like hell—but I refuse to let go until Thorn's got everything under control.

"Three . . . two . . . *one*!" Thorn counts down.

We switch places like we've done it a million times. The sudden absence of his grounding weight is jarring—but I manage to stay on land as I stumble backward.

Thorn pulls Zoe the rest of the way out of the water. Her knuckles are white from holding on to him so tightly, and he doesn't let go until she's steady on her feet.

"Zoe!" I cry, pointing down at her shin, where red rivulets drip down to her ankle.

She's dripping, shaking, bleeding—and a bruise is already blooming on her upper thigh. Emma appears from somewhere behind me, handing Zoe a long-sleeved shirt so she can dry off and, hopefully, stop shivering. Only now do I notice we have an audience: my voice is raw from how loudly I screamed for Thorn—I guess it makes sense that everyone else came running, too.

"I'll get my first-aid kit," I announce, adrenaline kicking in. I have to move, have to help. That gash on her leg looks like an infection waiting to happen.

Thorn doesn't protest. He's got his hands full with Zoe, who looks even more pale and panicked than when she was *in* the water.

I run as fast as I can and return with supplies in no time.

Zoe's huddled with Parker and Emma when I get back, wearing the shirt Emma brought over. I don't have to ask Thorn what to do—I go through all the same steps he used on me for my hand. I can feel him hovering, just in case I need backup.

When I finish, Zoe just looks numb.

"Thank you," she says, glancing from Thorn to me. "I'm . . . I'm so sorry."

"I'm just relieved we got you out of there in time," Thorn replies.

He doesn't make a point to remind her that he warned everyone against swimming in this waterfall, even though he could. He never seems to need other people to feel worse at the expense of him being *right*—he's so kind it hurts—

Especially because my first instinct is the exact opposite.

I want to yell at Zoe for making us all worry, for putting us in the position of having to save her. What if we hadn't been able to? What if I hadn't spotted her when I did, what if Thorn hadn't been able to get there in time? It felt eternal in the moment, but couldn't have been more than a minute or two before he arrived to help.

I also feel an urge bubbling up to point out how much worse this might have turned out if Thorn and I hadn't worked *together*: that despite him telling me the most helpful thing would be for us to keep our distance, today proves we make a pretty great team.

But I keep my mouth shut, because we're all just a bit shaken up right now, and I already *know* I'm right.

I just wish he could see that, too.

34

THORN

The silence is so thick between us while Sadie and I walk back to camp that I wonder if we've both simply reverted to the rules of the day—but then, just before we get to our tents, she breaks it.

"Thanks for the coffee this morning," Sadie says quietly, head down, focused on the path in front of her. "And my mug. That meant a lot."

I stop walking.

I want to see her face—need to see it. I can't tell from her voice what she's feeling.

A moment later, she stops, too.

When she looks at me, it's like an arrow to my chest, seeing her expression so careful, so guarded.

I made those walls go up. I'm the reason she's not smiling right now.

"Sadie, listen," I start to say. "I just— I want—"

My words break off.

I want to kiss her. I want to time travel back to before I ever told her it would be most helpful for her to go away, and tell her what I truly meant was the exact opposite: that she's the first person in years who's made me feel *alive*. I want to spend the rest of this day having a picnic with her in the wildflowers, talking each other's ears off, counting butterflies and dreaming about clouds and, later, searching for constellations. And then, under the moon, I want to stop talking entirely, to see how quiet we can be and how close we can get.

Touching her back there at the waterfall—I almost didn't want to let go.

Also, I owe her an apology.

"What do you want, Thorn?" she asks.

I swallow.

A loud buzzing in my back pocket slices clean through this moment and everything I was about to confess.

I pull out my phone.

"It's Matteo," I say, showing her the screen, as if she needs proof—proof that I'm not just looking for another excuse to push her away.

"You should probably answer it, then."

I pick up the call a second too late.

A moment later, it starts vibrating again.

This time, I answer on the first ring. "Matty? What's going on—are you okay?"

His voice, patchy and broken, barely pierces through the static.

"I can't hear anything you're saying," I say, even though he's still talking away on the other end. "I'll call you right back, okay?"

When I hang up, I turn to tell Sadie I'm off to find higher ground, see if the connection is any better up there—

But she's already gone.

"Pick up, Matteo," I mutter under my breath ten minutes later, when I've managed to find a slim two bars of signal on the high hill across the stream. I can see our entire camp from here, but it's far enough away that no one will be able to listen in. "Pick *up*."

I've tried calling twice now. Twice, it's gone straight to voicemail.

Third try's the charm, hopefully.

"Thorn?" Matteo says when we finally connect. "You there?"

The signal is a thousand times clearer here than it was down on the nature trail.

"I'm here," I say. "Is everything okay?"

"We're, uh . . . how do I put this?" Matteo says, a panicked edge to his voice. "We're extremely lost."

"Define *extremely*," I reply, as calmly as I can manage. "Also please define *lost*."

There's a long pause, but I hear his ragged breaths on the other end. He's either been running or hyperventilating—from the sound of it, my guess is the latter.

"I think we've been going in circles," he says. "Or maybe we took a wrong turn? Or maybe both."

I pinch the bridge of my nose, trying to mentally calculate how far they would've been if they'd managed to stay on track.

"Did Joshua find the engagement ring, at least? Did you even make it back to the lake?"

Matteo heaves a sigh so loud and crackly I have to pull the phone away from my ear.

"I don't think we're anywhere near the lake," he admits. "I tried to tell him he should just forget it . . ."

"But?"

"But he's not really the forgetting type, as it turns out."

I take in all of this, not sure what to make of that statement—and not sure what Matteo's asking me to *do* about it.

"So, what do you need from me?" I ask. "You've still got your phone, obviously—so you *should* be able to get back on track with GPS, right?"

Though maybe I shouldn't make any assumptions, considering they're this lost already and the park itself is huge.

"That's the other thing," he says. "I can't find my charger, and my phone is at two percent."

I mutter a curse.

If they got this lost *with* GPS, there's zero chance they'll get back on track without it.

The only way Matteo and Joshua are getting un-lost is if I go and find them, then lead them back to camp myself.

"Send me your coordinates before your phone dies," I say, suddenly all out of patience. "Stay *exactly* where you are, Matteo, do you hear me? I'll be there as fast as I can."

We end the call, and he texts their coordinates a minute later.

I do a double take when I see where they ended up—it's not anywhere near where they were trying to go, but on the bright side, it's not terribly far from here. I won't have to leave camp for too long . . . but I will have to leave.

A wave of realization comes over me: if Matteo's gone, and I'm gone, that means the seven hikers who've entrusted themselves to our care are going to be out here alone.

It goes against everything I know, all my training—all my *instincts*—to do what I've just promised Matteo. The rest of the group shouldn't have to suffer because of his myriad mistakes.

At the same time, though, if I'm fast, I can make it to where he and Joshua are an hour or two before midnight. It's only late afternoon right now; we could easily be back before morning.

The rest of the group knows how to make a fire, how to watch over it, how to put it out before bed. Trey's got climbing experience and safety certifications; he's already shown natural instincts we look for in hiking guides. Sadie was impressive today, too—she spotted Zoe a split second before I did, accurately identified the treacherous aspects of the water, and gave the exact same advice I would have when she beat me there to help. They'd do okay for one night, I think.

Still: I'm not used to relying on anyone but myself. The thought of leaving—even if it's a search-and-rescue for two other people who are technically still my responsibility—just doesn't sit well with me. *Especially* when the people I'm rescuing are the reason we're in this mess in the first place.

I need to call Danica, give her a chance to weigh in—but it rings and rings.

I try again. No answer.

I can't wait much longer. If I'm going to go, I need to leave soon.

The third time it kicks over to voicemail, I leave a message.

"Hey, Danica," I say. "Just got a call from Matty saying he and Joshua are lost and need help. They're not too far from the rest of us here in Sparrow Valley, so"—I let out a long exhale, glance down at my watch—"unless I hear back from you saying otherwise, I'm planning to head out within the next half hour to go get them. I'll touch base when I meet up with them."

I run a hand over my jaw, then slip my phone into my pocket and head back to camp. This is an unprecedented situation. If this happened on a normal trek, protocol would be for one guide to stay with the group while the other went off on the rescue mission—but on a normal trek, no one would need rescuing in the first place. *Especially* not a guide who's supposed to be partly in charge.

This entire trek, Matteo has been more of a hindrance than a help.

All this time, he's given me such a hard time about Sadie being a distraction . . . but in reality, *he* is the one who's caused unnecessary problems on this trek. Matteo wasn't even here to witness the water rescue today—and if he'd called ten minutes earlier, he would've interfered with it.

Parker and Emma glance up as I pass them, not even trying to hide the fact that they've given up on all things solitude and silence.

"Have you seen Trey?" I ask.

"I'm here," a muffled voice calls from one of the tents at the far perimeter. A moment later, Trey sticks his head out, runs a hand through his hair. "What's up?"

I tell him to sit tight—I want to make sure Sadie's in the loop, too.

"Sadie?" I say quietly when I'm right outside her tent. "You in there?"

She doesn't answer.

I wait for a bit, and *think* I hear a rustle from inside, but it doesn't amount to anything else.

"Sadie?" I try again, a little louder this time. "Can we talk?"

Okay, that—that was definitely a rustle.

She zips open her tent door. I catch a whiff of something fresh; her hair has looked really incredible all day.

Focus, Thorn.

"Can you come with me for a minute?" I ask.

She scrunches her nose. "We can't talk here?"

"Oh, um. We need to talk"—*not about us*, my mind fills in—"with Trey. You and me and Trey."

Now she's really confused.

I don't blame her. I realize, now, that it must have sounded like I wanted to apologize, or at least explain myself better. And of *course* I do—just not right this second. I don't want to rush it, not when I need to make sure camp is settled before I head off.

"Sure, I guess," she says.

She follows me, and soon it's just the three of us in a semiprivate spot where I can lay everything out for them.

"Matteo and Joshua are lost," I say, getting right to it. "They have also, somehow, misplaced their phone chargers—which means they have no GPS to help them get back here."

It takes effort to sound neutral about the whole thing, and not a panicked mess who wants to have a quick off-the-record rant about how ridiculous it is that my coleader has completely wrecked this entire trip in a thousand different ways—

But that would be unprofessional.

Mark this down as one more way I stifle myself, who I really am, for the sake of my job.

"So," I go on, "I really don't want to do this, and this shouldn't be on either of you—I hate to put you in this position, but—"

Trey laughs. "If you're trying to ask for help, you can chill out a little."

Sadie cuts her eyes at me, clearly sensing my trust issues. "He doesn't *want* help," she tells Trey. "But I think he's trying to say he needs it?"

Busted.

"I should only be gone for the night," I say. "Matteo sent me their location before his phone died, and they're actually not too far—I can be there and back by morning, we'll climb Mount Valerie tomorrow as planned, and ideally you'll never even feel like I was gone. But that means you're all without a guide overnight, until I get back."

"It's just eating and sleeping and hanging out, man," Trey says. "No need to stress."

When I take a step back, look at it from his perspective, it sounds so simple: eating, sleeping, hanging out. They're not navigating any trails, they're not attempting any risky excursions. They're all extremely aware of the waterfall risks after today—I expect they'll be hypercautious now, considering what happened with Zoe.

So *why* is it still so hard for me to step away and trust someone else to take over, even just for a single night?

"You put too much pressure on yourself, Thorn," Sadie says, her voice softer toward me than it's been all day. "It's going to be okay. *We* will be okay. Okay?"

"We're all adults," Trey adds. "And you're a hiking guide, not a babysitter. We're not hiking tonight, so if we're being technical, a 'guide' isn't strictly necessary. If something happens, we can handle it."

When he puts it like that, it makes a lot of sense. Maybe I'm overthinking this.

"I'm more worried about *you* being off on your own, honestly," Sadie says. "I really do think we'll be fine, Thorn."

I meet her eyes. She does still care, even though I clearly hurt her by pushing her away—and she's done a damn fine job all day of not letting it show. She cares a lot.

A spark of hope flickers amid my racing heartbeat.

Maybe—

Maybe, after all of this is over—

Maybe I should focus on rescuing Matteo and Joshua first, and then I can think about *after*.

"Just kiss her already," Trey says, oblivious to the fact that we've had some drama of our own. "It's obvious you want to."

Sadie's gaze flits down to my lips.

I want to. I really, really do.

But I don't want to if she's not comfortable.

She reaches for my hand instead, and I take that for the answer it is. "Don't get lost out there yourself," she says. "If you don't come back, we'll really be screwed."

Everything in my chest tightens: from the rejection, from the fresh wave of panic at how it feels to let go of the reins and trust someone else for once—and how, underneath the surface, there's a part of me that thinks Matteo deserves to stay lost a little while longer, seeing how this is entirely his fault.

"That was a joke," Sadie says, squeezing my hand. "We'll see you tomorrow, okay?"

I feel her touch for hours, long after the sun has gone down and I'm in the middle of the dark woods, alone.

35

SADIE

Maybe I should have kissed him.

We need to talk first, though—he's been sending me mixed signals ever since our last conversation, and while I *think* he regrets pushing me away, I can't be totally sure about what he wants until he tells me.

Besides: Trey was *right there*, which would have been weird.

But.

What if that was my last chance? What if something happens to him out there while he's all alone on the trails tonight? Yeah, he's a pro. Yeah, he knows these trails like the back of his hand.

That doesn't mean he has a lot of experience hiking at night, or hiking all by himself. Won't he be exhausted by the end of his journey there and back? What if he has to take an unplanned break to sleep for a while, but isn't able to tell us for some reason, and then doesn't make it back by sunrise and we all start freaking out wondering if he's fallen into a bottomless pit?

Did he take enough food?

Did he take enough water?

Will he be warm enough?

These thoughts and more spiral in on themselves all evening. I can't stop worrying—not about us, we'll be fine.

About *him*.

About things I couldn't control even if I wanted to. About how I won't feel settled until he comes back safely to us tomorrow.

All my worst instincts flare to life in his absence: my tendency to worry that things will go horribly wrong until proven otherwise; my active imagination, dreaming up a thousand scenarios in which Thorn ends up in distress; the way I can't set my fears aside and just *enjoy* this otherwise-pleasant evening with the people who are still here.

"Sadie," Hunter says.

It sounds like it isn't the first time he's said my name.

My eyes focus just in time to see my marshmallow turn into a blazing torch—but from the way Hunter's looking at me, I don't think that's why he was trying to get my attention.

The way *everyone* is looking at me, I realize.

"He's going to be okay," Hunter goes on. "He knows what he's doing."

"Who—Thorn?" I do my best to keep my voice light and casual, as if it hadn't occurred to me that he might *not* be okay.

I blow the fire out, examining my marshmallow.

"Of *course* he means Thorn," Emma says. "You're obviously worried."

So much for trying to act chill.

"I'm more worried about Matteo sitting still, honestly," Trey adds. "Imagine Thorn making it all the way there, only to find they got bored and went somewhere else . . ."

Parker swats him on the arm. "*Not* helpful. Sadie's already freaking out as it is!"

"I'm not freaking out!" I protest.

"Show of hands," Trey says. "Who here thinks Sadie is freaking out?"

One by one, all the hands go up . . . except for Zoe's.

She's been in her own world, in her own head, ever since the waterfall. At the moment, she looks extra checked out.

"Zoe?" I say, and not only because I desperately want the spotlight off myself. "Are you feeling okay?"

"I'm— I just—" she starts. "Today was a lot. I think I'm still a little shaken up?"

Not to mention she must be hurting from the scrapes on her legs and the purple bruise on her upper thigh.

"Have you been drinking enough water?" Trey chimes in. "When's the last time you ate?"

"Um," she says. "Yesterday, I think? Maybe at lunch?"

Zoe hasn't eaten since *yesterday*? No wonder she seems checked out.

"Here," Trey says, offering his canteen. "Drink this."

She takes a tentative sip.

"You need some food, too," I say, "as long as you're not nauseated. Are you nauseated?"

Zoe shakes her head and takes another sip from the canteen. Silas offers her some berries he foraged today—thimbleberries, non-poisonous—and Parker manages to get her to eat a protein bar. She perks up considerably after that.

An hour later, once the guys have moved Zoe's tent right next to mine so I can keep an eye on her overnight and give a fresh dose of ibuprofen if she needs it, my thoughts shift back to Thorn.

Has he made it to Matteo and Joshua yet? For the first time, it occurs to me how hard it must have been for him to head out today. Not just because he was afraid to leave us alone—but because he and Matteo weren't on good terms *before* all the drama that went down.

Matteo is lucky to have a friend like Thorn . . . if *friend* is even still the right word.

I really hope Thorn is okay.

Zoe shifts in her tent, turning to face me. The guys positioned us so we could leave our doors unzipped and see straight into each other's tents; she's lying on her side, tucked into her sleeping bag, one arm curled up underneath her like a pillow.

"You're so good at this," she says sleepily.

My eyebrows raise. "Good . . . at what?"

Sitting in a tent, writing in my journal until she falls asleep? Being a silent neighbor so I don't disturb her?

"*This*," she says. "Camping. Hiking. Knowing what to do to help people. All of it."

I'm so stunned I can't quite process her words.

Not even Abby would say I'm good at camping and hiking with a straight face, and she knows me better than anyone else on the planet—though it occurs to me that Abby hasn't lived this experience with me like Zoe has.

Still, my instinct is to deflect.

"I don't know about that," I say. "I've never done this before—and I've missed my bed and the air conditioning and, like, *so* many other things, from the moment we left."

"Really?" she says. "I never would have guessed you hadn't done this before."

I'm speechless.

My clothes are all wrong. My shoes are all wrong. I had a panic attack on the side of a cliff.

But I guess I must have done something right if she had no idea how uncomfortable and out of my element I've felt at so many points along the way.

"Yeah, no," I say. "I got broken up with for being 'too high-maintenance'"—I exaggerate my air quotes—"so I signed up for this to prove a point. My ex told me to my face that he thought I'd *die*. That I should vlog about it for 'great entertainment' because it's such a joke that someone like me would sign up for something like this." I glance down at my hands, at my mismatched nails that remind me of Thorn. "I thought if I just did a lot of research, I'd be good to go, but it's been *so* much harder than I thought."

"You never complain, though," she says.

I consider it. "Not out loud, maybe?"

She laughs, but then her smile fades. "Sorry about your ex, Sadie. Sounds like you're better off without him."

"Thanks," I say. "I definitely am—but sometimes his words still get under my skin." I swallow. "He made it sound like some sort of personality flaw for me to be . . . the way I am. Overprepared, particular. All of that."

Zoe scoffs. "People can find flaws in *anything*. That doesn't mean there isn't good there, too."

It's a surprisingly insightful thing to hear from Zoe, of all people. She's got a wistful look in her eye that makes me think we're not just talking about my issues now—that maybe she's been thinking about this for a while.

"I hope Joshua's okay," she goes on, in a small voice. "I still don't regret breaking up with him, and there's a *lot* about him—about how he was with me—that makes me want to scream. We're so wrong for each other, and I think I knew it a long time ago . . . but . . . yeah. This trip just made that crystal clear in so many ways."

I hug my knees to my chest, give Zoe the space she needs to work through things.

"He's out there because of me, though," she continues. "He's angry—

and I get it—but I should have known he'd do something rash when he found out about the ring. And, um. What I did with Matteo." She tilts her head down to the arm she's using as a pillow and wipes her eyes. "He does stupid things when he's angry. I don't want—I don't want him to— What if—"

She takes a deep breath and tries again. "What if he gets hurt or something and it's all my fault?"

"I think Matteo would have told Thorn if something had happened to Joshua," I say. "Try not to worry about that, okay?"

Even as I say it, her fears blend with mine: my mind drifts, again, to the many terrible things that could have happened to Thorn.

I try to redirect my thoughts, focus on Zoe instead.

"Is that why you haven't been eating?" I ask. "You're worried sick?"

She bites her lip, lowers her eyelashes.

"I feel like that's the answer I *should* give?" she says hesitantly.

"But?" I ask.

"But it's more selfish than that. I'm worried sick about *me*." There's an intensity in her eyes that I haven't seen for days. "We were together for years, then engaged, then drowning in wedding plans. I wasn't satisfied, or happy, but I guess it felt easier to stick with what I knew after sinking so much time and money into everything."

Her tears are falling fast now, streaking down her cheeks.

"I just couldn't take it anymore, you know?" she goes on. "It terrified me to think of spending the rest of my life with someone who didn't really love the real me—someone who tried to *change* me into someone he thought I should be, over and over."

For the first time, it hits me how *grateful* I should be to Caden: that he broke up with me when he did instead of trying to change me into someone else altogether.

If Caden had come on this trip, I might be trying to change *myself.*

Instead, our breakup became the freedom I needed to find out who I am at my core, when all of my comforts are stripped away, and to discover parts of myself I never knew existed. Even if I don't agree with why he did it—and even if he is a total hypocrite for getting *engaged* to someone even more high-maintenance than I am—there's integrity in being honest, with himself and with me, about how wrong we were for each other.

"It's terrifying to have no clue what comes next," Zoe says, pulling me back to this moment. "For better or worse, my life has been tangled with Joshua's for a really long time. I have no idea what mine looks like on its own."

As someone who loves to be prepared for everything, it's overwhelming to think about facing a completely blank page. How do you prepare for *anything* when you have absolutely no clue what comes next?

A mix of instinct and confidence, I guess—and the willingness to embrace whatever the future holds with an open mind. Choosing to believe it will be *good.*

"You don't have to have it all figured out," I tell Zoe now. "Just take the next step, and then another one after that. You're going to be okay."

A breeze meanders through the gap between our tents, carries my words back around to me: *You're going to be okay.*

Logically, I know it's true, for myself as much as for Zoe.

Still, I feel an undercurrent of fear.

What if all I ever have with Thorn, after this, is the memory of how brightly we burned in each other's lives for only a short time? Like shooting stars, there and then gone, the briefest flash of beauty.

Clarity—knowing exactly who you are, exactly what you want—is such a great thing until it's not.

Sometimes you simply can't *have* what you want.

36

THORN

This might just be the darkest night of my life.

Underneath the canopy of this densely wooded area, the glow of the moon barely breaks through; I've been at the mercy of my headlamp for the past couple of hours, only able to see what's immediately ahead of me.

On the bright side, I can now be confident that what I've always claimed is actually true: I know these trails inside and out and could navigate them with my eyes closed. I've covered so much ground tonight that I'm practically sleepwalking right now, coasting on pure adrenaline to keep me moving and alert.

Finally, just down the trail, I see a small campfire.

And, in the firelight, a shadowy figure.

It's too dark to see much at this distance, and he doesn't see me yet—he's facing the fire. I'm fairly certain it's Matteo, given the build, but it's hard to tell for sure.

The closer I get, though, the more it looks like whoever's sitting there is all alone. I squint, trying to make out whether the hulking black blot on the other side of the fire is another person . . . or just a tree.

"Matty?" I call out. "Is that you?"

It *is* him—a few more steps and it all comes into focus, Matteo and the fire and the tree I thought might be Joshua—but he doesn't answer, doesn't even turn to look at me.

My teeth clench on instinct.

I traipse *three hours* in the forest, at night, alone, and he can't even be bothered to say hello?

I join him in the clearing, drop my pack. It lands with a thud, nearly crushing a grasshopper in the process.

Finally, Matteo looks up.

The sight of him is a force: he looks absolutely, utterly spent.

"Where's Joshua?" I ask.

Clearly, he's not *here*.

"Thanks for coming, man," Matteo says, stoking the fire with a stick, back to avoiding eye contact.

"Where," I repeat through gritted teeth, "is Joshua?"

I count embers—ten, nine, eight, seven, six—before he finally answers.

"If I said I had no idea, what would you do?"

I can't tell if he's taunting me or serious or what. His tone is completely unreadable. Is he sleep-deprived? Delirious? Just an asshole?

"I think I might be more than a little pissed off," I reply, an understatement.

"Well, then," he says. "Prepare to be more than a little pissed off."

A shiver of dread makes my skin tingle.

"I'm listening," I say, keeping my voice as even as I can.

He makes me wait for what feels like an eternity.

When he finally looks up, I know that whatever's about to come out of his mouth is the dead-honest truth.

"He went rogue," Matteo says. "Haven't seen him since yesterday, and I have no clue where he is now."

I'm filled with a white-hot flash of rage.

This is so much more than just a little pissed off—this is Matteo losing an entire person.

"You had *one job*, Matty. What do you mean he 'went rogue'?"

"Oh, I'm sorry," he says, voice dripping with sarcasm. "Do people usually leave little notes of explanation behind before they ditch people in the middle of the night? Because I sure as hell didn't get one. I have no idea. He was there when I fell asleep, and when I woke up, he and his stuff were just *gone*."

It wouldn't be fair of me to throw an *if you'd just paid better attention* accusation in his face, because it could have happened to anyone—but I'm sorely tempted.

If Joshua's been gone since this morning, though, why am I only finding out *now*? I'm sure he's miles away, long gone in who knows which direction. Where would we even begin to start looking for him?

CALL ME ASAP! I text Danica, even though she still hasn't replied to any of my messages from earlier. **Joshua's unaccounted for. I thought he was with Matteo.**

"You didn't think that might have been a relevant detail to mention when you called me?" I say as soon as I'm done. "I left everyone back at camp without a guide so I could come help you *and Joshua*. You led treks in the Andes, Matty—you shouldn't need me to come rescue you!"

"He took our only phone charger," Matteo says bitterly. "And most of the snacks."

"Again—relevant details."

"We both know you wouldn't have come tonight if it was just *me* out here," he protests.

He's right about that much.

"You dug this hole for yourself," I say. Maybe it's going a little too far, but it's the truth. "You were all over Zoe—I'm not surprised he didn't want to stick around! Just because you're hurting from Blair doesn't mean you get to hurt everyone around you, too."

My words land like the sharpest little blades.

I never meant to say them out loud. I never meant to cut this deep.

Despite everything, all the distance and damage we've sustained these last few years—these last few *days*—he's still like a brother to me.

Deep down, I think he knows it. Matteo has pressed right up against the limit of what a friendship can come back from, crossed into betrayal territory, doubled down and blamed *me* for said betrayal, and then went on an emotional bender as soon as Blair broke up with him—

But at the end of the day, I think he knows he's not beyond forgiveness. He's *right there* on the edge . . . but it all comes down to this, right now. He needs to own up to what he's done before we can ever begin to mend the canyon-sized rift between us.

He doesn't speak for a long time.

I take a seat on the ground, wait him out. Grab a handful of trail mix from my pack and make it look like I could do this for as long as it takes even though I'm anxious that Danica hasn't replied yet, anxious about Joshua.

"I—" Matteo eventually starts, but cuts himself off.

He takes a deep breath. Swallows.

"I should never have said yes to coming out here," he finally says, staring into the fire like it's a window to the past, until his eyes suddenly flick up to meet mine. "There are a lot of things I should never have said yes to."

It's not an apology, but it's a start.

After all his avoidance, this direct eye contact feels a bit on the intense side. I don't break, though: I look and I listen, trying to see inside him so I can finally *understand*.

"I told myself Blair would be worth it," he goes on. "She made me feel like my life could be so much *more*, you know? Like I wasn't truly living until I took some sort of huge, unexpected leap of faith."

His gaze shifts back to the fire, back to his memories.

"I didn't realize how stagnant I'd been feeling," he says, tucking his hair behind one ear. "Blair told me her secret one night—a secret she said not even you knew—that she'd bought a one-way ticket to Peru. She painted the idea of this huge adventure, the thrill of never knowing what comes next, just taking it day by day."

He swallows, brows pinching together as he looks down at his hands.

"I've never met anyone who lives in the present like Blair," he continues. "She doesn't have regrets about her past, she doesn't worry about her future—she just lives in the moment. So when she asked if I wanted to start over with her in Peru, it sounded pretty magical."

It's the most perfect description of Blair, and exactly why I came to the conclusion a long time ago that it would never have worked out between us no matter what—if she hadn't run off with Matteo, it would have been someone else.

"It's a lot less magical when you're the one getting left in the dust," I say, unable to keep the bitterness from creeping into my voice.

Blair's flightiness in the name of adventure has always struck me as extremely self-centered. It never mattered who she was leaving behind so long as she kept moving forward—and the farther the better, because that way, she couldn't even see her old life in the rearview. Out of sight, out of mind.

It's tough to see how Matteo has changed after spending the last two years with her. He used to be one of the most thoughtful people in my life.

"Yeah," he says after a moment. "I see that now."

He pokes at the fire with his stick, setting off a spray of embers that flicker and then disappear. His face, usually so happy-go-lucky—even this week, with everyone but me—is a shadow of itself right now, sullen and unsmiling.

"If I'm honest," he says, still poking at embers, "I think I always knew how wrong it was, what I did to you."

He throws the stick into the fire, finally meets my eyes.

"I felt these little stabs of guilt for so long—they started in the airport, before Blair and I ever left, but there were a lot of other times, too." He shifts his weight, pulls one knee up to his chest. "I told myself Blair would be worth it, though . . . that the adventure would be worth it. That it was time to choose something for *me* instead of just tagging along with the career *you* had chosen here in Cali."

I take it all in. I'm not sure if it makes me feel better or worse to know he's felt guilty off and on over the years.

It's good to know his conscience is still intact, even if he tried to bury it, but the fact that he still got on a plane and went into full-throttle YOLO mode at the first sign of those feelings is disappointing, to say the least.

"Even though I *know* how she is, I thought I could be the one to keep her—the exception," Matteo goes on. "I thought we'd go on adventures together for the rest of our lives, so her breakup texts were a real blindside. And it's been *miserable*, man. How could I have been so stupid? How could I have thought I was special? I stole my best friend's girlfriend and then fully believed she wouldn't leave me in the exact same way. I'm an idiot."

It feels like a rush of lava, the way everything he's been holding in is pouring out now, hot and fiery and bright.

"Seeing your face, the day I got her text—I couldn't handle it, man. I was barely holding it together, trying to process what she'd written, and then there you were, a reminder of all the things I screwed up because I thought Blair would be worth it."

He blinks rapidly, clearing away the glassiness in his eyes.

"All I could think about was how miserable I felt." He swallows, hard. "And how miserable *you* must have felt back then, how much worse it must have been for you when I was the person who'd blindsided you with Blair. I couldn't handle it, Thorn. I've been such a disaster out here. And I'm—I'm really, really sorry, man. For everything. I don't blame you for never wanting to speak to me again."

My eyebrows raise. "I never said that."

He's quiet, all out of words.

"Matty." I wait to go on until he looks up. "Just because what you did made me miserable, it doesn't mean I enjoy seeing *you* miserable." The words feel weighty on my tongue—weighty and true. "You've changed since we were close, yeah. Had different priorities that led you to some things I think you probably regret. You weren't always like that, though, so I'm choosing to take that as proof that you can change back." I pause, then add, "If you want to."

The fire crackles and sparks.

As the silence expands between us, I realize I haven't acknowledged the fact that he finally owned up to his betrayal.

"Thanks for your apology," I say.

I knew I needed to hear it in order to close the door on our painful past, but I didn't realize how much lighter I would feel. It doesn't excuse his behavior, everything he told me, but at least I understand it a little better now.

One comment he made stuck out in the moment: *It was time to choose something for* me *instead of just tagging along with the career* you *had chosen here in Cali.*

I'm honestly not sure I chose this career so much as I fell into it. My dad took me out here so often as a kid, and then as a teen, that when someone offered to start paying me for it—part-time at first, and later, full-time—it just made sense.

I was good at it, a natural.

I loved being out in the wild; I loved seeing people expand their worldview.

It made me feel close to my dad to hike the trails he adored but could no longer experience himself—like I was hanging on to part of him, maybe even doing it *for* him.

This trek has been different.

I didn't realize how much I could relate to Matteo's desire for adventure . . . that just as his was born out of an aversion to stagnancy, mine might be, too. Not once did I expect that this active job—where I'm always moving, rarely sleeping in the same place two nights in a row—might start to feel like I'm stuck, moving in circles but ultimately going nowhere.

I always considered myself such a risk-taker, purely because it comes with the territory: there's nothing inherently safe about sleeping under the stars, or navigating tricky terrain and surprise downpours, or rappelling off the side of a cliff.

Those things, for me, though?

They feel like home.

They're *my* comfort zone.

And maybe they've been holding me back.

A series of vibrations hits my phone: texts from Danica, hours' worth of messages only just now finding enough of a signal to get through.

Got your voicemail, sorry I couldn't pick up. Stay safe out there.

Have you found Matteo yet?

Please have him call me as soon as possible.

I clear my throat, and Matteo looks up.

"You need to call Danica," I say.

He nods, no fight left in him. "Can I use your phone?" he asks. "Mine's still dead."

I hand it over.

But before he gets the chance to call, it starts ringing. Danica—finally.

I nod for him to pick up.

"Thorn?" she says, her voice loud on the other end. "Sorry, Charlotte's still sick, and I've also been having issues with my phone today—I only just got your last text—"

"No," Matteo cuts her off. "It's me."

He doesn't have to elaborate—she'd know his voice anywhere, that light Italian accent that still clings after all these years.

"What *happened*, Matteo? Joshua called a little while ago for an emergency pickup; he's at the hotel now. He said you'd left him on his own—care to explain?"

"That's a load of shit," Matteo says. "*He* left *me*."

"You do realize that's not much better, right?" she says. "Care to tell me why he felt so desperate to get away from you, and apparently throw you under the bus to your boss?"

Matteo fumbles his words, but finds his way to a full confession after some meandering: how he ditched his post at the rappelling site, how he kissed Zoe behind the waterfall, how he followed Joshua into the woods only for Joshua to leave him behind. He tells her how Joshua stole his phone charger and snacks—and left some seriously filthy laundry behind in its place, which is news to me.

I overhear enough to gather that Matteo's out of a job.

And when she says, "Let me speak to Thorn," I start to worry that maybe I am, too, even though I'm not the one who lost an entire person out here.

He passes the phone to me.

"Hey, Danica—I'm so sorry about Joshua, I had no idea—Matty told me they were lost, and his phone had died, and I didn't want them stranded without GPS, so I weighed my options and decided it made the most sense for me to come help, and—"

"Thorn. Stop," she interrupts. "You're not in trouble—you were in an impossible spot. You don't have to defend yourself for things you had no control over."

Her tone catches me off guard. It's night and day from the clipped voice she just used with Matteo, and I don't know what to say. It's not at all what I expected—and it's slow to sink in: *You don't have to defend yourself for things you had no control over.*

I most definitely always feel responsible for everything that goes down while I'm in charge, whether they're within my control or not.

"You're not in trouble," she reiterates, "but, given the circumstances, I do think it would be in everyone's best interests—yours included—to cut the rest of this particular hike short."

I need a break.

I do.

But I can't help feeling like I've failed: that the rest of the group won't get to finish out the final stretch of our hike as planned.

That I won't get much of a chance—if I get *any* chance at all—to smooth things over with Sadie.

"We're so close, Dani," I tell her. "Just Mount Valerie, and then Lavender Fields. The group has come so far—I think we owe it to them to finish strong."

She's quiet on the other end, for so long I fear we really will have to cut the trek short. Instead of being at the top of a mountain tomorrow, everyone will disperse to go home.

Sadie will head back to Texas.

And I will return to my empty apartment, where I'll try to work up the energy to do all of this over again when the next trek begins.

I'm exhausted just thinking about it, and I don't think it's only because *today* has been exhausting.

"You can finish out the trek," she finally says, "but I want you and Matteo in my office the second you get back to the museum, okay?"

"Sounds good, yeah," I reply. "We can do that."

I slip my phone into my pack when we're done.

Under normal circumstances, I would probably opt for a decent break before heading out again—it's late, I've barely eaten, and the idea of hiking for several more hours tonight feels excruciating, especially considering we'll be getting up with the sun to summit a mountain tomorrow morning.

Sadie is on the other side of that hike, though. And she deserves the chance to climb that mountain—I want to see her face when she's on top of the world, looking out over all the ground we've covered together. It might be brutal for me, but it will be worth it for her.

"Ready to go?" I ask. "We should put the fire out and head back."

"I've been sitting here for most of today," Matteo says, rising from the boulder he's been using as a chair. "Let's move."

DAY TEN

• **Sparrow Valley Falls to Mount Valerie to Lavender Fields**

Mount Valerie—while not the tallest peak in the Sierras, measuring just shy of ten thousand feet, about two-thirds the height of Mount Whitney—is the perfect way to finish off a trek around the Mackenzie Lake Loop. Bring significant sun protection and a way to filter water fresh from the crystal-clear alpine lakes you'll encounter along the way, and make sure you have the correct permits on hand to present to the attending park ranger. Look out for the lockbox at the base of the mountain, where you can store nonessential personal items and pick up a set of hiking poles—just remember to trade everything back at the end. If you experience symptoms of altitude sickness, retreat to lower elevation as soon as possible. Mount Valerie is a challenge, but it's well worth it. Enjoy the stunning view when you get to the top!

—Henry Herrington, *Backpacking the Sierras: A Beginner's Handbook* (Fourth Edition)

37

SADIE

I wake before the sun, in the half-light of dawn, after a night of fitful sleep.

For once, I didn't dream at all: nothing steamy to make me miss Thorn even more, and no nightmares to amplify my concern for his safety—just fragments of awareness interspersed between shallow sleep.

I give up trying, rummage around for my coffee gear.

As soon as I unzip my tent, I'm met with a surprise: a very Thorn-shaped surprise, stretched out and sleeping in the narrow gap that separates my tent from Zoe's, not even a sleeping bag beneath him. He's out cold like he's never met a more comfortable bed in his life.

Maybe I should make sure he's breathing, now that I think about it.

I'm pretty sure he is, though he's lying at an angle that makes it hard to tell. I lean down until we're face-to-face, hoping for clear proof that he's not just a corpse on my doorstep.

His eyes fly open, two inches from mine, and it's all I can do to stifle my shriek of surprise before I accidentally wake the entire camp.

It takes him a minute to process the fact that it's me right here in his face, especially since I must look like a freshly minted ghost after that jumpscare—but when it registers, he dissolves into a fit of silent laughter.

"What are you doing here?" I whisper, still trying to catch my breath.

"I *was* sleeping," he whispers back.

"Well, I did gather that much," I reply. "What time did you get back? Aren't you exhausted?"

"Hence," he says, "the sleeping." He gives a sleepy grin. "Sometime around two in the morning."

It's the sort of easy banter we had before everything went sideways between us, surprisingly effortless after all that's happened.

"Danica wanted to end the trek early," he mumbles, eyes back to half closed. "Today."

"What do you mean *today*?" I ask. "We're not climbing the mountain?" After it sinks in for a beat, I also add, "Why?"

"No, we're still going up, I talked her out of that." His eyes flutter open again as he runs a hand over his jaw; his stubble has turned darker and thicker over the last day. "Everything's a disaster—Matty, Joshua, everything. But we're so close to the end, and she agreed you all deserve the chance to finish strong. The only thing I could think about, the entire way back, was how much I wanted you to experience the view from the top—and how much I owe you an apology."

He looks like a wreck.

He pushed himself harder than he probably should have, just so he'd get a chance to talk to me as soon as he possibly could.

I can hardly handle it, so I try to make a joke instead. "You're welcome for the distraction," I say, emphasis on the *distraction* part, just to call back to the reason he pushed me away. "I'm glad it was the good sort this time!"

He doesn't laugh, though—and on second thought, I realize it wasn't very funny at all.

"Sadie," he says earnestly, propping himself up on his elbow, "meeting you has tipped my world on its side. I can't get you out of my head—even when we weren't talking, and even when I was alone in the woods, you were right there with me. I don't think there are any circumstances in which you *won't* be in my head, ever."

He's fully awake now, fully aware.

"What I realized last night is that I *like* it that way. I'm so, so sorry I told you it would be most helpful for you to go away. I've never been in this situation, and I see now that I handled it in the worst way possible. I said what I did because I liked you so much I couldn't see straight, or think straight—not because I didn't want you around. I wanted you *too* much, Sadie. And I guess I just worried that it would be all too easy for me to lose myself in you, and that scared the hell out of me, because it's my *job* to care about other people out here. All I wanted was to just be selfish for once, to spend time with you, but I didn't know how to do that *and* stay focused enough to do right by the group. It's a me problem, and very much not anything wrong with you." His brows pinch together. "I'm so, so sorry if I hurt you in the process. I can tell I hurt you, right?"

I consider it, everything he's telling me.

I know it's all true because it's completely in line with what I already suspected—it makes so much sense. I think I just needed to hear him say it.

"It did hurt," I say. "It hurt to know you were pushing me away just because you thought you had to—especially because I could tell, underneath, that was the last thing you actually wanted."

"You're right," he says. "I didn't want that at all. You're the best thing that's happened to me in a really long time, Sadie."

"You too," I tell him, and it's the honest truth. "You've made it so easy to just be myself out here. Everyone I've ever dated has made me feel like I need to tone things down somehow, or pretend to be chill or flexible or whatever else, even when I'm not—but with you, I can just be *real*. I can show you all the ways I feel anxious or afraid or particular, and instead of making me feel like those are flaws that need fixing, you make me feel stronger and more capable."

I hadn't realized until now just how *safe* Thorn makes me feel—and not only the being-in-the-wilderness-together aspect of things. He makes me feel comfortable in my own skin, exactly as it is, whenever I'm with him.

"So, yeah." I swallow. "I've *loved* getting to know you out here—but I do understand why you were trying to push me away. Our lives are so different. When this trek is over, I just . . . I can't . . ."

My thoughts flutter around in my head, butterflies on a breeze, impossible to pin down.

"When this trek is over," I start again, "I'll go home, but you'll still be here. Doing your job. So even though it hurt when you pushed me away, I understood. You have to be in hiking-guide mode out here, and not just because someone's paying you to do it—it's more than that, isn't it? You care about every single person. You're committed to keeping everyone safe. You're the most selfless person I've ever met, Thorn . . . you're just an incredibly *good* guy."

My gaze flicks down to his lips, and that stubble I wish I could feel, rough against my skin.

"I wish there was some way for our worlds to be more compatible," I say sadly. "Because you make mine infinitely better."

He's quiet, taking in everything I've said.

"I feel the same way," he finally replies. "About all of it."

Birdsong fills the early morning silence, a pair of chickadees calling out for each other from somewhere in the woods.

"At least we have today together," I say. "Want to go climb a mountain?"

Thorn smiles, the biggest one I've seen from him in days. "Absolutely, yes."

Not everyone *wants* to finish strong.

Zoe's still exhausted after yesterday and has been extra quiet ever since Thorn told us Joshua wouldn't be joining us again. As for Emma, she has no desire to experience another heights-induced panic attack, this time on top of a mountain—rappelling was more than enough for her.

Matteo agrees to stay behind with them; there's a little rest stop with picnic tables and a (currently closed) building called the Valerie Portal Store where they'll hang out in the meantime. It apparently has incredible cheeseburgers and fries we can look forward to after we get back approximately seven hours from now.

Which leaves only six of us braving Mount Valerie's 9,872 feet of steep, rocky trails: Silas, Hunter, Trey, Parker, Thorn, and me.

We pare down our packs to only the essentials. And I mean the *bare* essentials—I empty mine of everything but my water supplies, snacks, a lightweight long-sleeved shirt, sunscreen, and my disposable camera.

"You're leaving your phone?" Zoe asks, watching as I transfer it into the tote bag of deadweight that'll hang back with them here at the picnic tables. "Don't you want to get vlog footage from the top?"

I feel Thorn's gaze land on me as I answer, but I hold mine steady on Zoe.

"That's what this is for," I say, holding up my disposable camera. "I just, you know . . . thought it might be better to see it through my own eyes. Not a screen."

It's more than just that, though I keep this part to myself: the whole reason I started filming vlog footage in the first place was so I could show Caden how wrong he was to underestimate me, and that I not only didn't die, but passed the wilderness test with flying colors.

Now that the only person I'm trying to prove something to is myself, the entire vlog just feels . . . pointless. I might still post everything someday since I have so much footage, but it'll be more travel documentary than anything else, and for better reasons.

When I finally glance Thorn's way, I can see it written all over his face: he's proud of me.

"Hey, Sadie," Emma says, just before the six of us head up. "Maybe you should take these? I definitely won't be needing them while you're gone."

She's pointing down to her hiking boots.

My poor, battered Ultraboosts have carried me this far—barely—but I'd be foolish to reject her offer.

"What size are you?" I ask, already pretty confident they'll fit just from looking at them.

"Seven and a half," she says.

We trade shoes as Thorn passes out hiking poles, and as suspected, they're a perfect fit. A little stiff compared to what I'm used to, but what they lack in comfort, they make up for in support and traction.

"Everybody good?" Thorn asks, looking from the coffee bros to Parker to me, and then over to the group that'll be staying behind. "Matty? You good?"

Matteo nods. "Milkshakes on me for the three of us whenever they open," he says, tilting his head toward the shop. And probably because he can hear everything Thorn isn't saying—*Can I trust you to stay put? Can I trust you at all?*—he adds, "We're good. We'll be right here when you get back."

Seven hours is a long time to stay put, I can't help but think.

Seven hours is also a long time to hike.

"Let's go, then," Thorn says, and he leads the way.

We follow, ducklings in a row, with Trey bringing up the rear. It isn't too steep—not at first. We'll be covering roughly two miles every hour, Thorn tells us, and it's around seven miles to the top.

It starts feeling like a mountain around mile two.

The incline grows gradually steeper with every step, and I'm thankful for so many things: Emma's hiking boots (there's a ton of loose gravel, *way* more than any trails we've hiked so far), the hiking poles (for balance), sunscreen (the sun feels extra potent up here), and the long-sleeved shirt I packed (it's June, but it's already a little chilly, and I see snow higher up on the mountain).

We take our first break at an alpine lake about three miles up. The water is so glassy and clear you can easily see every tiny pebble at the bottom.

"*Wow*," I breathe, taking in the scenery. "This is *incredible*."

But Thorn's not looking at the lake or the huge jagged rocks at its edges—he's looking at *me*.

"This is only the beginning," he says, eyes sparkling. "Just wait."

We press on.

I have nothing good to say about miles four and five. Nothing good at all, except that Thorn was right, and the view from the lake was only just the beginning. From this vantage point—past the mountain's halfway point, and not a moment too soon!—I can see forever, far out over all the land we've covered these last ten days.

It's a little dizzying, honestly.

I do my best to not look down—to not look *up*, either, for that matter—and just focus on taking the next step, and the next after that. My legs burn from the incline.

"I'm glad Emma decided not to come," I tell Thorn, slightly breathless from the effort, the two of us at the front of the pack. And then, a confession: "It's messing with me a little, too. Being this high up."

Thorn glances over his shoulder just in time to see me lose my footing, the tiniest little slip, not enough to be dangerous.

"You okay?" Thorn asks.

"These boots are gold," I tell him. "Someone really should have added them to the suggested packing list."

He laughs, so fully it echoes off the rock wall to our left, his eyes crinkling at the corners.

I make a mental note to buy Emma a second milkshake when we get back down to the bottom, or fries. Or a cheeseburger. Or anything, really. Maybe she'd like a spa gift card?

"The dizziness, though?" he goes on. "Are you feeling nauseated? Lightheaded? Headache or anything else?"

I recognize the symptoms of altitude sickness, but thankfully, I'm pretty sure that's not what this is.

"None of that," I say. "Just . . . height anxiety? Is that a thing?"

He laughs again. "I think that's got to be the official term, yeah."

It's only going to get worse the closer we get to the top. I can do this, though: mind over matter. Faith over fear and all that.

Fear leapfrogs ahead at the beginning of mile six.

I should find it comforting that, suddenly, there are cables to hold—a zigzagging line of them held up by steel poles, as if we're in line at a theme park and just can't see the roller coaster anywhere up ahead—

It's not comforting. Not at all.

The only thing it puts in my head is that there's a good reason for the cable railings from here on up: that it's so steep, so dangerous, that we're most definitely going to need to hold on to them.

All I can think of is Brittany, twisting her ankle and nearly falling over the edge of the switchbacks that day.

My mouth goes dry, and I'm suddenly having trouble swallowing.

I still have a decent amount of water left; I take a sip and hope it helps.

It does—but only a little.

"You've got this, Sadie," Trey says, the back of the group catching up to us where I've paused. "You can do this."

Hunter takes advantage of our brief break, seeming completely at ease up here as he whips his camera out to snap a shot of the expansive view.

"Can I borrow some of your fearlessness?" I ask him, only mostly joking.

Right now, I can't fathom feeling anything but a burning desire for this to be over.

"Sadie?" Thorn says, looking down on me with concern from his slightly elevated position. "You good?"

He offers me his hand—a warm alternative to the cold, metallic cable that I will have to hold on to eventually—as in *immediately*—and it's just the right thing to get me moving again.

As soon as my hand closes around the metal cable, I feel better.

Safer.

I'm not going to fall. Scratch that—I *refuse* to fall.

I have two jobs: to hold on, and to keep going.

Which I do, to surprising success—

Until we get to the switchbacks.

There are *twenty-six* of them, Thorn tells us.

They're not all that long—the total length adds up to just under a mile—and when we finish, we'll be at the top.

I cannot overstate just how different it is to *be* here, starting the seventh and final mile of climbing this mountain, versus merely reading about it in Henry Herrington's guidebook. His pictures and bullet lists and hot tips didn't do justice to any of how it actually *feels* to experience this place.

We haven't even reached the summit, and I'm suddenly overcome with a wave of emotion.

My relationship with Caden ended because he thought I was too *much*—but it also ended because he thought I was too *little.* He had zero faith that I could do any of this.

Caden laughed at me, treated me like a joke.

Abby tried to talk me out of it.

And deep down, I'm not sure *I* truly thought I had it in me.

But I'm here. I'm terrified, but I'm doing it.

I've *been* doing it.

Now I just have to finish.

Spoiler alert: switchbacks don't get any easier just because you've conquered five, then ten, then enough to lose count.

They also don't get easier just because you're more determined than before.

We've come *so* far—we're close enough to see the top, and I'm finally brave enough to look out into the distance beyond it—but it's challenging in every sense of the word just to keep going, one step at a time, until it's done.

The instant I set foot at the top, my eyes fill with tears.

I'm laughing, I'm crying—I'm *elated*, so light on my feet and surrounded by such a surreal, foreign view that I suddenly feel like I'm on another planet altogether, one with a strange sense of gravity.

But no: this is *our* world.

This is every forest and meadow and lake and waterfall and boulder we've met along the way, so far beneath us it's hard to believe they're really down there.

I'm still looking, *marveling*, when I feel his fingers intertwine with mine.

I turn, and there's Thorn, eyes as ice-blue as any alpine lake. I could look at them forever—

But then his mouth is on mine, and we're kissing on top of a mountain, on top of the *world*, and I take it back: *this* is what I could do forever. He's a furnace, warming me up against the chilly breeze; he's a soft place to land, a *safe* place to land.

I kiss him like we're running out of time.

Hot tears streak down my cheeks, and I'm certain he can taste them at this point, but neither of us pulls away.

If this is all the time we ever have together—if we never even see each other again, a thought I do my best to shove down—he's changed my life just by seeing me so clearly at the exact moment I most needed to be seen.

"Thank you," I say when we finally pull away. It comes out as a whisper.

He brushes my tears away, grins.

"That was all you, Sadie Whitlock. You *did* this." His grin becomes a full-blown smile, beautifully bright.

"How are you still standing right now after hiking until two in the morning and only getting four hours of sleep?" I ask, laughing.

"This is my whole life," he says with a shrug. "I'm used to it."

"Hey, lovebirds!" Trey calls out from beside a tiny hut built of bricks and beams, a shelter of some sort—for people who want or need to spend the night up here, maybe? "Come sign the wall!"

The building looks bigger on the inside, but not by much.

Nearly every inch of it is covered in black Sharpie.

Silas hands me the marker when he's done. It takes a minute to find the perfect spot, but I know it as soon as I see it: a blank spot just beneath a little window that peeks out over the sprawling view.

Halfway through signing my last name, I feel Thorn behind me, the heat radiating from his body welcome to say the least.

I offer him the Sharpie, but he waves it away.

"Great minds think alike," he says, then points to a signature about two inches to the right.

AUGUST THORN, it reads in uneven capital letters, the sort that look nothing like the practiced handwriting from the journal he gave me. It's dated nineteen years ago: he wasn't even a teenager yet.

On instinct, my gaze lands on the name just below Thorn's, in a neat architectural slant: DAYTON THORN.

"Your dad?" I ask, knowing the answer before the question is even past my lips.

"My dad," he echoes, shoving his hands in his pockets. "He loved it up here."

His words hang between us, suspended in the air.

When I finally say something—"I bet he loved it so much because he got to do it *with you*"—Thorn's face changes into an expression I've never seen on him.

"Yeah," he says, brows knitting tightly together in a way that looks like he's trying to keep himself from breaking.

He swallows, takes a deep breath, and his shadows change into something more like peace.

"Yeah," he says again. "I think you might be right."

38

THORN

The trip down the mountain is almost always just as hard, if not harder, than the climb.

The top is only halfway! a sign boasts at the summit, as if it can help prepare the inexperienced hiker for what comes next, all while neglecting to mention that at that point—if you haven't paced yourself already—it's too late. Your legs will be toast, and your next week will be misery.

Fortunately, the people in my care have a guide who's done this climb hundreds of times, if not more than a thousand.

Today is the lightest I've felt in years.

Sadie's words at the top unlocked something for me: something I hadn't realized I needed to hear until the precise moment she said it.

It isn't just this *place* that was special for Dad.

It was being here *with me*.

With that revelation, it hit me that it doesn't matter where I choose to spend my time—my memories of us together won't fade just because I'm not here in this specific location, hiking in circles until the day I start to haunt them as a ghost.

I only wish I hadn't said no to Sky Ranger.

That's not something I need to think about right now, though. Right now is for cheeseburgers and milkshakes and fries, and trying not to look as surprised or relieved as I feel that Matteo did, in fact, keep Zoe and Emma safely in one place.

"This is the *best* cheeseburger I have *ever* eaten in my *entire life*," Trey says around a mouthful of meat.

"This coffee is the worst, though." Silas makes a face, and everyone laughs.

"I'm shocked you were brave enough to try it," Sadie says. "I'd rather have no coffee than bad coffee."

"Thanks for sharing your stash, by the way," Hunter says, and Sadie raises her vanilla milkshake to his chocolate one in cheers.

It's news to me that she shared her stash, but it makes perfect sense: Sadie doesn't gatekeep the things she loves—she wants everyone to experience them, like how I am whenever a brand-new hiker sets foot in the park.

It's hard to believe Sadie was brand-new at the start of this trek. She's come so far, overcome so much. I've met a lot of different people out here, but I've never met anyone like her: someone so completely out of their element that, somewhere along the way, she *made* it her element.

She still stands out, don't get me wrong, thanks to her loose interpretation of the packing list: her long, beautiful hair under that cute black ball cap; her yoga-studio clothes that haven't faded under nine days of sunshine and one of rain; her shoes and her pack and her eye mask and her pajamas and that bikini at Mackenzie Lake that left an indelible mark on my memory.

But despite all that—or maybe *because* of it—she seems more at home out here than I ever expected based on my first impressions.

I'm really going to miss her on the next trek.

"Can we move out to Lavender Fields pretty soon?" Matteo says, dipping a fry into what's left of his milkshake. He's been pretty quiet ever since we got back. "We've been here so long this bench has fused to my ass."

Lavender Fields—aptly named for its meadow full of purple flowers, a scene that's particularly beautiful during golden hour—is only a ten-minute hike away. As soon as we get there, my adrenaline wears off and a deep exhaustion sets in. I want to make the most of the time I have left with Sadie, but for once, I think I truly overdid it. The only thing that will help is sleep.

"Go rest," she tells me. "We'll all be right behind you, honestly. Even my sleeping bag sounds good at this point."

She looks completely spent, too, now that we've set up camp and daylight is quickly running out; her hair falls over one eye, casting a shadow.

"Tomorrow," I say as I reach up to tuck her hair behind her ear, "we won't be staying long before we head out, but we'll at least be here for one last sunrise. Want to watch it with me?"

Her eyes are pale green pools in the sunlight. I never want this day to end—but it's fading fast, and so am I.

I'm already dreaming when her voice cuts through the haze: "Wouldn't miss it."

DAY ELEVEN

Lavender Fields to Mackenzie Lake Loop Trailhead

There's an inscription carved into the wooden sign at the Mackenzie Lake Loop Trailhead that reads: THOUGH THE MOUNTAINS NEVER CHANGE, THE MOUNTAINS CHANGE YOU. If you look closely at its post, you'll notice it is covered in scratches—rest assured that these were not made by any wild animal, but by every hiker who came before you. Tradition holds that each hiker, upon completing the loop, reserves the right to carve a small tally line into the post. Use a pocketknife or a humble house key to make your mark.

—Henry Herrington, *Backpacking the Sierras: A Beginner's Handbook* (Fourth Edition)

39

SADIE

We're perched on a huge granite rock, rewriting our memories of the last boulder we sat on together: instead of him telling me how much easier it would be if I were farther away, he wraps his arm around me, pulling me in close. I tip my head to his shoulder.

It all just feels so perfectly *right*.

I didn't bother making coffee—today's coffee can wait.

The sunrise, on the other hand, will happen whether we're ready or not.

When the first rays peek out over the horizon, the view nearly takes my breath away. It is utterly unadorned: no clouds for as far as I can see, just a brilliant ball of fire making its way into the sky.

"It never gets old," Thorn says. "I've seen a thousand sunrises—thousands, maybe. They're never the same."

I could tell him so many things right now: I could tell him how it took hours for me to fall asleep the night he was gone because I was worried he might not make it to Matteo, or back to us. I could thank him for helping me realize I'm the sort of person who enjoys a good sunrise every bit as much as I enjoy my silk eye masks. I could tell him that for all the ways this trip has been uncomfortable and challenging and terrifying, I'd do it all over again—especially if it meant I'd get to do it with him.

I could tell him all of this and more.

But our time is limited, and with every inch the sun climbs higher above the horizon, I'm reminded of the hardest thing I'll *have* to tell him, only two hours from now: goodbye.

We sit together, soaking it all in for as long as we can.

And then it's time to go.

40

SADIE

Everything happens in a whirlwind: one minute we're packing up camp, and the next, I'm back in an airport shuttle, on my way to catch a flight. The seats feel strange after spending so much time sitting on rocks and logs and my sleeping bag.

It's also weird to hear music again. I can't hear a single buzzing insect, or any babbling brooks, or the crunch of hiking boots (and one extremely soiled pair of Adidas Ultraboosts) on gravel.

I never thought I'd miss the soundtrack of these last two weeks. And for how out of place I felt when I first arrived in the wilderness, it's surprisingly jarring to be back in the real world—like a severe case of whiplash.

The airport feels too bright, too busy, too loud.

It's weird that I can just walk up and buy myself a slice of pepperoni pizza, or a latte, or a family-sized bag of Cheez-Its. (I definitely buy all of these things.)

It's weird to use an actual toilet again. This one is *good* weird—going to the bathroom in the woods is one of the primary reasons I won't be making a career out of this like Thorn has.

Thorn.

I miss him so much already. Danica pulled him away for a long talk as soon as we got back to the museum. We found out on the way over that she had arranged for an airport shuttle for those of us with early departures—the tour group handles all return flights since weather and injuries like Brittany's can cause changes to the original itinerary—and I was whisked away, along with Trey and Hunter and Silas, not fifteen minutes later.

Like I said: whiplash.

I didn't think eleven days would throw me so thoroughly out of sorts, but wow, everything feels foreign and sterile and digitized. Did I really wake up in a tent this morning? Did I really watch the world transform under the sunrise—lavenders into oranges into the full spectrum of daylight?

We kissed, one last time, while we still could.

It wasn't long or steamy, like in my spiciest dreams—

But it was everything I needed, and the perfect way to remember him.

The only problem was that it had to end.

"*Whoa,*" Abby says when she flings open her front door five hours later. I came straight here from the airport—she was thrilled when I texted her from California, and insisted we have a girls' night. "Who are you, and what have you done with my best friend?"

I don't have to ask what she means: when I first saw myself in the airport bathroom mirror, I almost didn't recognize myself.

"You smell like campfire," she adds, laughing as she pulls me in for a huge hug. "I already booked us an actual spa day for next Saturday, but in the meantime, I stocked up on some stuff to make you feel like you're at the Four Seasons! Go pamper yourself, Wilderness Queen!"

I almost burst into tears right then and there. For all the ways the real world feels jarring, Abby feels like home.

She wasn't kidding about stocking up on stuff—she must have bought one of everything from our local spa's line of products. There are more bottles than I know what to do with, and a trio of candles, and some fluffy white towels I'm almost certain she must have acquired today.

I shower first, washing the campfire off my skin and out of my hair, and then I soak in the tub, and then I shower again.

Even after I've scrubbed the wilderness off, I'm left with a lingering sense that it's fused to my bones. There's still something different when I study myself in the mirror—something in my eyes, I think. Maybe my cheekbones, too.

Or maybe it's just that it's been a while since I've seen my own bare face and *not* felt the pressing urge to cover it up with foundation and concealer and mascara.

I think that's what it is.

Maybe I've always looked like this, and what's changed is much deeper: for the first time in years, I'm truly seeing myself—flaws and all—and instead of wishing them away, I see someone beautiful and strong staring back.

I swallow hard, blinking until my eyes clear.

My phone buzzes on the counter, lighting up with a notification: the name *August Thorn* on the text gives me a hit of dopamine.

Hi :) Miss you already, and I hope you made it back okay. Wanted to let you know I found all the stuff you stashed in my office before we left—did you leave it behind intentionally? If you still want it, I can get it to you.

He's sent a picture, and I almost laugh out loud . . . why did I ever pack all of those things in the first place? I want to give Past Sadie a hug, bless her sweet little overprepared heart.

Totally forgot to grab all of that, I write back. **If it's not too much trouble, I wouldn't mind having it back, but please don't go out of your way.**

I hit send and then type out one more message on a line of its own: **I miss you, too.**

Over dinner—a gigantic spread of sushi, courtesy of Jonathan, who made a brief appearance to drop it off before going to a movie with friends—I fill Abby in on everything.

She hangs on my every word.

She can't believe I went kayaking, and rappelling, and that I actually came to enjoy all the hiking and being out in nature. She can't believe I summitted a *mountain*.

I tell her I still hate mosquitos, and snakes, and sweating, and the feeling of needing a shower but not having anything but a lake to wash off in. I tell her how much I missed real shampoo and conditioner—but how, actually, I feel like I could throw my phone off a cliff now that I'm not used to checking it compulsively out of habit.

Except, I add, for one thing.

One *person*.

"Tell me about him," Abby says.

So I do.

A little over a week later, Jonathan and Abby and I are hanging out at the JW Marriott, like we did every day at the beginning of the summer. Jonathan's just starting his shift at the poolside bar, so Abby and I are perched on a pair of stools while he works, enjoying some on-the-house appetizers.

"Let's see," Abby says, holding a french fry in midair. "I despise this idea with every fiber of my being because I would die without you here—but—worst-case scenario—you could move out there, maybe work at the tree museum you told me about?"

Thorn and I have been texting every day since I got home. It's great, but it's also not. I miss laughing with him in person, face-to-face. I miss his arm around me—I miss kissing him. We've tried phone calls and FaceTime, but his connection is so sketchy most of the time; it's easier and less frustrating to stick to texts.

"*Or*," Jonathan says as he shakes a cocktail, "you could go be a hiking guide, too."

Abby and I both burst out laughing.

"What?" he says.

"It's sweet that you think I'm cut out for that," I say. "But I know my limits."

Abby and I are still brainstorming two days later when we finally go for our epic spa day. We're in the sauna, post-massage and pre-facial, soaking up every minute of relaxation together.

"I'd miss you if you moved," she says, "but I would totally understand."

Our latest great idea involves a cabin she found for sale that might actually be doable on my income—it's adorable, and has a gorgeous view, and I've even put feelers out at work to see if they'd have any issues with me working remotely from the West Coast.

My boss told me *he* would move into that adorable cabin in a heartbeat if he could, and would I be willing to host any work retreats?

So that was an easy yes.

Still, I'm reluctant to upend *everything*—maybe the wilderness loosened me up in some ways, but I'm still an overthinker and a planner at heart. I like where I live. I love being close to Abby. I don't know anyone but Thorn out in California, and I've always been of the *don't move somewhere just to be with a guy* mentality, so it's hard to fully commit to that leap, especially this soon.

That said, I have not yet ruled it out.

All day at the spa, I think it over.

It's fascinating how different it feels being here now; even though I've been home for a week and a half, I'm still seeing the world through a new filter.

The spa's chilled cucumber water, for example, feels unnaturally cold now, and the ambiance—especially the nature soundtrack they're pumping through the speakers on a loop and the "rainforest room" full of themed showers—feels extra artificial compared to the real thing.

It's still the most relaxing day ever.

I'm so blissed out by the end of it that I'm tempted to take a rain check on dinner and head straight home to binge an entire season of *The Great British Baking Show.*

When I float that idea, phrasing it as a joke, Abby hesitates.

"Jonathan pulled some strings to get us a reservation tonight," she says. "They were totally booked."

We're going to Uchi, one of our favorite spots in town, where it's nearly impossible to snag a table at all, let alone on the day of. It's fancy, and expensive, and delicious—it really does sound amazing, but if I'm being honest? The idea of going just with Jonathan and Abby makes me feel like I'd be imposing on a date, not to mention how extra aware I'll be that my own personal date of choice lives two time zones away.

"You're sure I won't be a third wheel?" I ask as I check out my freshly blow-dried hair in the spa's locker room, then adjust the little black dress Abby told me to bring.

"Sadie," she says, meeting eyes with me in the mirror. "This is a celebration *for you*. It's our treat. We're so, so proud of you—Jonathan and I talked about you every single day, wondering what you were up to. He's as invested in your badassness as I am." She grins. "You deserve this. Let us celebrate with you?"

It honestly doesn't take that much to twist my arm when a fancy dinner is involved, especially when said fancy dinner is a) free to me, and b) at Uchi.

"Okay," I give in. "Let's do it."

Uchi looks completely unassuming from the outside: at a glance, it's just a renovated old house with bright red paint and a rock garden off to the side. The rock garden is simply decorated with black patio furniture, the occasional green plant, and twinkling globe lights strung overhead—the perfect place to sip sake and nosh on edamame while waiting for a table.

We don't have to wait tonight, though; whatever strings Jonathan managed to pull get us seated right away.

It's much fancier on the inside than you might expect, but cozy, too, with its warm wooden tables and rich red floral wallpaper. The atmosphere is lively, typical for a Saturday night in Austin, not an empty table in sight.

"Right this way!" the host says, and the three of us follow like ducks in a row.

I reach out ahead of me, tap Jonathan lightly on the sleeve of his jacket.

"Thank you so much for making this happen," I tell him.

I can't believe I ever considered being a blob on the couch tonight.

As the host leads us to our table, I see countless dishes I'd love to try. Uchi is one of those places where you give the server your budget and say *Surprise me!* at the start of the meal, then share course after course of nontraditional Japanese cuisine—revelatory things you never knew you needed in your life. I was completely overwhelmed the first time I came here, but quickly learned to trust the server, and it's worked out every time.

When the server stops at our table, I'm—

Confused.

Someone is already sitting there, sipping from a glass of water. Is *this* how Jonathan snagged a reservation at the last minute—by convincing some random stranger to share his booth with us? Because that wouldn't be awkward at all.

Jonathan slides in on the opposite side, completely unfazed. Abby too. She tilts her head, a suspiciously large smile on her face—

And that's when I realize the man in the navy-blue suit isn't a random stranger at all.

My heartbeat picks up.

"Thorn?" I say, in disbelief.

He turns, beaming, and the sight of him takes my breath away: *this* is why it took a moment to place him—not only was I under the impression that he was out on a hike right now, but he cleans up really, really well. It's hard to reconcile the rugged man I met out in California with the person in front of me, who looks like he was born to wear this suit.

"I thought you were on a trek this week?" I say as he unfolds himself from the booth to give me a proper greeting.

Thorn pulls me into a tight embrace, one hand between my shoulder blades and the other at my lower back. "Surprise," he says into my hair.

My face already hurts from smiling.

This has been the very best day—and I have Abby to thank for this little plot twist, I assume. Her impish grin says I'm right.

"I can't believe you sat on this secret all day!" I say.

"Jonathan and I both knew," she confesses. "Thorn actually got in touch with Jonathan first—he called the JW Marriott since you'd told him how we were practically living there this summer."

"Happy to be of service," Jonathan says.

It's great to see him out from behind the poolside bar for once; he cleans up pretty well, too, the perfect match for Abby.

We eat the best meal of my life—a far cry from protein bars and trail mix around the campfire—that culminates in the most perfectly fitting dessert: an elevated, deconstructed take on s'mores. It's a whole presentation, one that involves a scoop of hazelnut gelato perched atop a perfectly circular bed of superfine graham cracker crumbs, salted fudge sauce drizzled artfully over the top, and finally, the pièce de résistance: a gigantic homemade marshmallow toasted by our server right there at the table.

At the end of the night—after Abby and Jonathan have made a flimsy excuse to slip off together, clearly for *our* benefit even more than theirs—Thorn and I find ourselves alone in the rock garden.

It's dark out now, a hot summer night, the globe lights casting a warm glow on everything. We're standing in the back corner at a high table, sipping on chilled white wine, an excuse to linger just a little longer.

I have no idea how long he's staying.

I think both of us have been reluctant to acknowledge the reality that, after this fancy evening in our fancy clothes is over, we'll have to go back to our regular lives.

"I can't believe you're actually here," I say quietly, once I'm down to my last two sips of sauvignon blanc.

I've been avoiding the last two sips for ten minutes now, because once my wine is gone, this magical night will be that much closer to being over.

"I know," he says with a shy smile. "Neither can I."

He sets his wineglass down, and just like that, his smile fades.

This is it, I think. *This is the part where we acknowledge reality.*

"So," he says slowly, "I've been thinking."

"Me too," I interject, afraid of facing what will inevitably come next. "I've been thinking *a lot*."

Before he tells me how impossible it is for us to be together, even though we've been living in wishful-thinking land ever since I flew home from California, I just want him to know I've been trying to come up with ways we could make it work.

"I found a cabin," I say in a rush. "Out in California, close enough that we could see each other whenever you're not at work—I would really miss Abby and Jonathan, but I can already do my job remotely, so at least that would be taken care of, and—"

"Sadie."

All the words on the tip of my tongue evaporate at the sound of his voice, so gentle but firm.

"What if," he says slowly, reaching into his jacket pocket, eyes intensely on mine, "I stayed here instead?"

He opens his palm, revealing a key.

My mouth falls open. I blink, surprised by the tears that have instantly sprung up—

Surprised by *him*.

"I got a new job with a tour company that does hikes out in the Hill Country," he says. "Got a place of my own here in town, too."

He tells me how the job offer was on the table for months, but then they found someone else—which fell through when the guy decided not to move after all. Thorn said yes in a heartbeat when they reached back out, even though he was afraid of breaking the news to his current boss. She was surprisingly supportive, and insisted they'll find a way to make things work without him.

I take in everything he *isn't* saying: his role at the tour company in California was so much more than just a job for him—it was his entire life. It was home.

"You're sure you want to do this?" I ask, afraid that if I breathe too hard, this sparkling glimpse of hope will turn to ash.

He grins. "Already done," he says.

"Isn't it hard to leave someplace behind when it means so much to you?" I've been struggling with the same questions, and Austin doesn't mean nearly as much to me as the Sierras mean to Thorn.

"I've spent my entire life there," he says. "It's hard in some ways, but at the end of the day, it was surprisingly simple." He grins again, then stashes the key back in his pocket. "It's time for a new adventure. A new adventure *with you*, if you're up for it."

I throw my arms around him, wishing more than anything we were inside a waterfall cave right now, tucked away in secret where I could kiss him for as long and as hard as I want to.

There will be time for that, I realize: there will be time for *everything*. Fancy dinners, campfires under the stars, whatever we decide, wherever we end up. For once, I don't have to know all the details to know it's exactly what I want.

I'd follow this man on an adventure anywhere.

I'd trust him with my life.

"I'm incredibly up for it," I tell him.

Thorn's fingers land lightly on the curve of my neck, and he pulls me in close, until his lips find mine and there's no space between us at all. I let myself get lost—this moment could last forever and still not be long enough.

He kisses me like we have all the time in the world, like we're the only two people on the planet. It feels like a dream, the best dream yet. It hasn't sunk in yet that this is real life . . . that it's *my* life.

When we break away, his eyes are sparkling under the globe lights.

It's beautiful when I think about it: this moment may be over, but it isn't the end. There will be more, many more, because the road ahead of us is long—and we get to explore it together.

"I was hoping you'd say that," he says, his smile bright as he leans in for another kiss.

Every single step that brought us to this point—every difficult, miserable, uncomfortable turn along the way—has been more than worth it, because all of it led me straight to him.

Wherever the road takes us from here, I'm ready.

ONE YEAR LATER

Ennetbürgen, Switzerland

Elegant and inviting, Hotel Villa Honegg is the perfect destination for adventurous couples who love a touch of luxury—prepare to rest, relax, and enjoy the view at this five-star boutique hotel in the heart of Switzerland.

—Henry Herrington, *Switzerland: A Travel Guide* (Second Edition)

Epilogue

SADIE

I'm a bird in the clouds, on top of the world.

This terrace has to be the most serene place on the planet: it's the crown jewel of our boutique hotel, nestled high in the Swiss Alps, overlooking Lake Lucerne and the entire rim of the surrounding mountains.

The view is breathtaking.

Across the lake, the first rays of sunlight have just started peeking out above the horizon, piercing through the hazy morning sky to cast the world in a pink-orange glow. I'm stretched out on a lounger, sipping coffee from delicate china, enjoying some much-needed relaxation after the last six months—planning a wedding is no joke!—and especially after the last few days, which culminated in a night so glittering and magical it will be seared into my memory forever.

Abby was the most wonderful maid of honor, balancing out my extravagant wedding-planning instincts with practical wisdom—and Thorn's father, who also served as his best man, made everyone cry with his speech. Matteo flew in from Portland and seems to be in a much better place these days: he's in culinary school and hopes to open his own restaurant someday, but took a job working for the coffee bros in the meantime. He and Thorn talk every week—and while they're still rebuilding after the rift between them, they're in a better place, too.

We said our vows in Texas under rows of twinkle lights, danced under the stars, and feasted on hors d'oeuvres and cake and champagne. Thorn's new boss, Sky Ranger, gave us a substantial deal on the venue—a vineyard he owns in the Hill Country—and I finally met Thorn's old boss, Danica, too. She and Thorn might technically be colleagues again soon, even though they're now based in different states: there's been talk of a merger between the two tour companies, with Sky Ranger acquiring Danica's business in a generous deal.

All of that feels so far away, though, like it's in an entirely different world—it's utterly silent up here, entirely still.

It's the perfect place to kick off our honeymoon.

Thorn planned every detail of our itinerary. I told him I trusted him to surprise me—a huge symbol of progress for me and my chronic overplanning ways, if I'm being perfectly honest—and I waited patiently for *months*, not having a clue where we'd be going until we arrived at our airport gate.

He more than delivered.

Not only did he make arrangements for all of our stops, he put together an actual itinerary for me to flip through on the plane: where we'd be staying, what we'd be doing, why he picked each specific place.

Every single choice blends natural beauty with a sense of adventure, dotted with luxurious touches all along the way—scenic waterfront promenades in Zürich, a helicopter tour and hiking in Zermatt, paragliding in Interlaken, a luxury resort in St. Moritz, and more.

It's the perfect trip for the two of us, a lovely echo for the way our lives have blended together in the year since that first epic hike we experienced together out in California.

"Sadie," Thorn says, waving me over. "You've gotta try this!"

He's lounging in the heated infinity pool, taking in the view from one of its built-in bench seats. I set my coffee down on a nearby table, head over to join him.

I strip out of my robe, down to my blazing red bikini. It's chilly, even for late June, so I'm eager to get in. The water feels practically steamy compared to the crisp morning air.

We're alone out here, and for a moment it's easy to pretend we're the only ones at this entire hotel—maybe in all of Switzerland.

I slip deeper into the water, settle in beside him on the bench. He's so strong, so handsome, so kind. We've laughed together every single day since he moved to Austin—we've cried, too, but thankfully *not* every single day.

My life is so much richer with him in it.

More unpredictable, too.

We have so much adventure ahead of us. Not just the next ten days here in Switzerland—but forever.

I'm eager to get to it: eager to experience everything with him by my side, eager to see more and more of the world through his eyes, eager to see what tomorrow holds.

For now, though, I'm exactly where I need to be.

I lean in close, and he wraps his arm around my shoulders, pulling me in tight.

We watch the day break, together, and it's beautiful.

ACKNOWLEDGMENTS

Turning the tiniest spark of an idea into an entire book takes a village every time—and this one is no exception! Thank you, as always, to my brilliant agents at Root Literary, Holly Root and Taylor Haggerty (with special thanks to Holly for doing a lightning-fast read of this book when I needed to bounce some thoughts!), and to Kat Miller, who does so much work behind the scenes. Holly and Taylor, I've loved having you in my corner for more than ten years now: Thank you for everything.

I'm so grateful to have gotten the opportunity to team up with my editor, Kaitlin Olson, for this third KOlson^2 romance together—and so grateful to the entire team at Atria for all the heart and attention they put toward my books and the others on their list for any given season. Megan Rudloff, thank you for your efforts on the publicity front (and for inspiring Abby's love of corn!); Heaven Jenkins, thank you for all you do on the marketing front. Thank you to everyone else at Atria who's played a part in making this book happen: Libby McGuire (senior vice president, publisher of Atria Publishing Group), Ifeoma Anyoku (editorial assistant), Morgan Hart (production editor), Linda Sawicki (copyeditor), Andrea Monagle (proofreader), Sam Hoback (cold reader), Vanessa Silverio (production manager), Paige Lytle (managing editor), Shelby Pumphrey (managing editorial assistant), Sofia Echeverry (managing editorial assistant), Abby Borchers (managing editorial assistant), Jill Putorti (designer), William Ruoto (interior designer), Kelli McAdams (cover designer), and Bee Johnson (cover art).

I want to give a special shout-out to Brandon L'Heureux, my tennis coach, whose offhand comment one night during a tennis lesson sparked the idea for this book. Like Sadie, I'm a chronic overpacker, so I arrived to the courts with my tennis backpack and my work tote—and, knowing me, probably also a duffel bag with a change of clothes, a snack bag, and two water bottles. Brandon took one look at me and said, "I'd love to see you go on a camping trip where you can only bring *one* backpack and have zero control over what you eat along the way." I recoiled at the idea and told him, "That sounds like my absolute nightmare . . . and I think I need to write a book about it!" So thank you, Brandon! I hope you enjoy having a waterfall named after you in this book!

I'm thankful to have such a sprawling village of cheerleaders, both online and in person, and wish I could thank every single person by name! For the sake of not making the acknowledgments longer than the book itself, I want to thank a few specific people who helped me bounce ideas and gave encouragement along the way—

Emily Bain Murphy, I'm so glad we found each other when we were both just embarking on our publication journeys—and I'm so glad we continue to get to do this author thing together! I've loved pivoting from YA to adult alongside you, and am also excited for your MG debut. You are a light in my life, and I can't say thank you enough for all the ways you've supported, loved, and encouraged me.

Bre Smith, thank you for being my "self-appointed hype woman" and for being such a wonderful friend. You are so much fun, and I love that we've found each other through books! You played a huge role in making my launch events for *The Lodge* feel so special, and you've been such an encouragement throughout my writing and revision process on *The Great Outdoors*, too. I'm thankful for your friendship!

Sarah Damoff, I've loved watching the world fall in love with your debut novel (*The Bright Years*), and I'm thankful to have such a thoughtful, kindhearted author friend living right down the road. Thank you for all the phone calls and brunch/coffee dates where we've had so many great conversations, and thank you for weighing in whenever I needed another trusted opinion in the mix as specifically relates to this book.

Thank you to my family (Hahns, Holubecs, and Olsons) for all the love and support, to my tennis community for being a fun place to unwind after long days at my desk, and to all the booksellers who have championed my books and introduced them to new readers (with a special shout-out to Joe, Diane, Charlie, and Stephanie at Patchouli Joe's in Denton, Texas).

To my wonderful husband and son, Andrew and James, thank you so much for your love and support and patience as I've worked on this book—there were challenging times (as with every book) and you helped make them feel easier at every turn. You are both bright spots in my world, always, and I love sharing life with you.

As is my tradition, thank you to Jesus Christ for being my peace and my hope throughout every season, the good days and the hard days and all the other days in between—I keep coming back to Philippians 4:4–9 and Matthew 6:25–34, not only because they've been meaningful in my own life, but because they're in keeping with some of the themes in this book (specifically, learning to trust and have faith when things are out of your control and you don't know what comes next).

And finally, to all of my incredible readers: Thank you for spending time with Sadie and Thorn as they trek through the wilderness (and beyond)! Please book yourselves a spa day and/or treat yourself to your favorite drink or dessert—and here's your reminder to try something new, too, because you just might surprise yourself and love it . . . or, at the very least, have an entertaining story to tell someday!

ABOUT THE AUTHOR

Kayla Olson is the author of *The Reunion* and *The Lodge*, as well as two books for young adults, *The Sandcastle Empire* and *This Splintered Silence*. Whether writing at her desk or curled up with a good book, she can most often be found with a fresh cup of coffee and at least one cat. Visit her at KaylaOlson.com or at @authorkaylaolson on Instagram and TikTok.

Discover the rest of KAYLA OLSON's swoony romances!

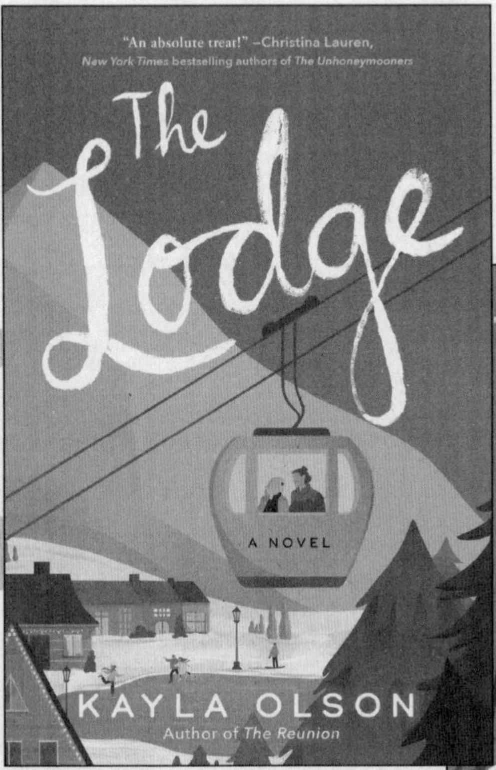

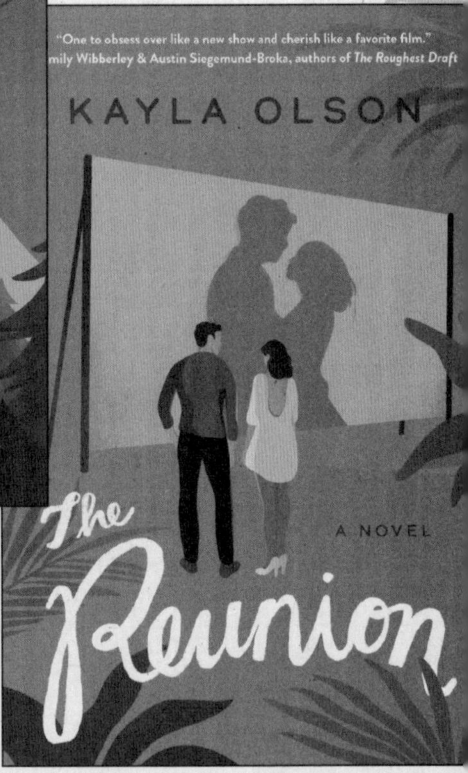

Available wherever books are sold.

99652

ATRIA BOOKS